C0053 45588

KT-162-542

Suzie Wilde left full-time English teaching to go sailing. She has an MA with Distinction in Creative Writing from the University of Sussex. In 2014, she was selected as one of the first six playwrights to take part in a series of workshops at the Criterion Theatre with professional actors. She occasionally teaches creative writing in all genres.

"Mind, maidens, we spare not
One life in the fray!
We corse-choosing sisters
Have charge of the slain."

Darraðarljoð ('Battle Song of the Valkyries'), *Njál's Saga*

With Special Thanks to Hotel Rangá
www.hotelranga.is

THE BOOK OF BERA

(PART ONE: SEA PATHS)

SUZIE WILDE

unbound

This edition first published in 2017

Unbound
6th Floor Mutual House 70 Conduit Street London W1S 2GF

www.unbound.com

Text Design by PDQ

Art direction by Mark Ecob

A CIP record for this book is available from the British Library

ISBN 978-1-78352-277-4 (trade hbk)
ISBN 978-1-78352-279-8 (ebook)
ISBN 978-1-78352-278-1 (limited edition)

Printed in Great Britain by Clays Ltd, St Ives Plc

1 2 3 4 5 6 7 8 9

In memory of my mother, Dorothea Davies,
who made me what I am.

Dear Reader,

The book you are holding [illegible] to most others. It was [illegible] website: Unbound. Unbound [illegible] started the company because [illegible] had the bankwriters and a [illegible] shared the ideas for the [illegible] readers. If enough of you [illegible] advance, we produce a beautiful [illegible] and distribute a [illegible]

[illegible]

The new way of publishing [illegible] publisher funded his [illegible] in his [illegible] after a [illegible] book, you'll find the names [illegible]

Publishing in this way [illegible] consumers of the books [illegible] books they really want. [illegible] nurture these books [illegible] everyone.

If you're not yet a subscriber [illegible] publishing revolution and [illegible] in the future. To get [illegible] pledge. Just visit unbound [illegible] in the promo code box when you [illegible]

Thank you for your sup[illegible]

[illegible]

Dan, Justin and John
Founders, Unbound

Dear Reader,

The book you are holding came about in a rather different way to most others. It was funded directly by readers through a new website: Unbound. Unbound is the creation of three writers. We started the company because we believed there had to be a better deal for both writers and readers. On the Unbound website, authors share the ideas for the books they want to write directly with readers. If enough of you support the book by pledging for it in advance, we produce a beautifully bound special subscribers' edition and distribute a regular edition and e-book wherever books are sold, in shops and online.

This new way of publishing is actually a very old idea (Samuel Johnson funded his dictionary this way). We're just using the internet to build each writer a network of patrons. Here, at the back of this book, you'll find the names of all the people who made it happen.

Publishing in this way means readers are no longer just passive consumers of the books they buy, and authors are free to write the books they really want. They get a much fairer return too – half the profits their books generate, rather than a tiny percentage of the cover price.

If you're not yet a subscriber, we hope that you'll want to join our publishing revolution and have your name listed in one of our books in the future. To get you started, here is a £5 discount on your first pledge. Just visit unbound.com, make your pledge and type **BERA** in the promo code box when you check out.

Thank you for your support,

Dan, Justin and John
Founders, Unbound

PROLOGUE

The longhouse slumbered in its winter-bound dusk. The woman listened for voices but there was only the crackle of the fire. All gone. Shadows thickened the cobwebbed corners but she knew her skern was there, waiting for her to die, so that they could start their last journey together as they had the first.

She needed to get her daughter here. She struggled to prop herself against the rough wooden frame to begin the words of command but the tearing sensation deep inside frightened her into stillness.

The fire bowed as a draught swept in with the chilling dark.

'Mama?'

'Bera? Come to me, I need you.'

The latch clacked and the gloaming settled once more. Smoke hazed the spaces of her narrowing sight. Her breath was shallow, raspy.

'Don't be afraid, Bera. I have to give you something.'

The child made no move.

She reached out. 'Don't be frightened of your mother.'

Footsteps rustled the new firs Sigrid had put down after the birth. Their sharp smell rallied her enough to make out the small, pale face hovering in the gloom. Her child looked too serious, too young.

'Good. Now you have to help me.'

'How?'

She clutched her hand. 'I can't do it myself, Bera. You must.'

'You're hurting me, Mama.'

'Take off my necklace.' She bent her head.

It was some time before she felt icy fingers fumble at her neck, a rough smock brushing her face. The bead necklace slithered down her neck and fell onto the floor with a clatter. She gasped, her throat exposed to danger. It had not been off her neck since her own mother had died.

At last, the scratch of the beads being gathered.

'Keep it safe, Bera. You're so young and I didn't... Listen. It's our lifeline. You are a Valla. The black bead…' The pain returned, stealing breath and reason.

Her only son had gone full term. If only her death could have given him life. Her skern swept round her like a cloak and the gnawing need to slip away was taking over.

'Bera?'

The child put a small, cold hand against her cheek and the touch freed her. Her breath left her like the tide, leaving only the beads hanging between them like a cord.

1

Bera reached the waymark and took the path towards the Ice-Rimmed Sea. Marsh reeds and grasses whispered, husky in the frosted air. It was dawn, at the tipping point of the year; when long, barren months gave way to fishing and trading. Until winternights, those left alive were too busy to visit the sacred sites.

Only someone who needed to.

Her mother's rune stone sat on top of a hillock at the edge of their inlet, the place she had chosen at the height of her power. Bera paused while she was still quite far away and gazed at the grey sentinel in the bleached landscape. Beyond it, a skein of whale paths stretched to the flat sea-rim, with furrows and cat's paws where the wind whispered on the water. She sensed the distant swell of long waves, their slow tumble in the deep. The edge of the known world.

The rune stone was close enough to be reached from the village where her father had brought her and her mother, leaving behind the rest of their folk to die from the red-spot sickness. Closer to the Seabost raiders, too, who needed his boats and would trade. Folk resented Seabost arrogance and feared their battle scars but they needed meat, so deals were struck.

This was the seventh time Bera had come here on the day of her mother's death. Sigrid always said the baby had killed her by being born with a monster face that couldn't suckle. Bera had been too young to remember much, except the fire of the skin at her mother's neck. She quickened her pace.

At the rune stone Bera opened her bag and took out a shallow dish. She had no idea how to scry and Sigrid was useless. She may have been her mother's best friend but Sigrid was frightened of 'Valla stuff' and had no knowledge to pass on to Bera. It made it even harder to live up to folks' expectations – and now they needed her more than ever.

It's never going to work without water, dear.

Her skern was leaning against the rune stone, studying his nails.

'If you know that much, why don't you tell me how to scry?'

I can tell you how but you either have the knack or you don't. Seems you don't.

'You're supposed to predict for me. So tell me where to find water.'

I'm not here to replace your eyes, ducky, so open them. There's a spring over there, look.

Not for the first time, Bera wondered if her skern was unusually exasperating. A Valla like her always kept her twin spirit close, supposedly to receive support and guidance. Normal folk were born with their skerns, then lost them until the point of death. Bera often had cause to envy this, given her skern's nature. She stomped over to collect some clear water in the bowl and carefully took it back to rest on flattened earth, near the rune stone. The water stilled and Bera stared at the dark surface.

Her skern smirked back.

'Stop leaning over me.'

He flumped down beside her in a sulk.

'I need you, Mama.'

The bowl reflected nothing but Bera felt close to her mother here and some signs might one day come.

'It's the time of Drorghers, Mama. But worse than that, I think the red-spot has started here.'

It has.

'I'm talking to my mother.'

I don't hear her saying much. Go on, ask me what to do.

'You never give a straight answer.'

I'm getting the hang of it. So listen up. I happen to know that a fabulous creature, other than me, has wandered far off its normal track.

'What has that got to do with the sickness?'

Always so impatient!

'So is death.'

He held up a hand. *Its tusk will protect from red-spot. Or any evil.*

Bera pictured herself being held high on shoulders, a hero. 'How do I get it?'

That's up to you. Look into the dish.

The wet back of a huge beast surged out of a frozen sea. Old battle scars marked runes in its mottled white hide. Bera tried to read them but its head surfaced, pointing a spiralled spear at the sky.

'That's the tusk!'

An overgrown tooth, actually. Now study the land behind it.

'Cleft, shingle beach, gnarled tree.' She shivered. 'What beast is it?'

Narwhale. There are always... conditions attached to using its tusk.

'I'm getting better at healing, even Sigrid says so. I'll work out how to use it.' Bera leapt up. 'I've always wanted to see a narwhale!'

The runes on its back are signs.

'I'll get Bjorn and the others.' She was already on her way.

Killing the creature was the price of their safety.

The six families had moved into the mead hall for the dark days, to keep safe and eke out the food until late spring. It had been a hard winter and scant food remained. There had been one time of starving, after they had failed to pay Seabost, and Bera vowed she would never let them be that hungry again. But now there was the outbreak of sickness and, for the first time, she knew how to help. She glanced up at the ribbed cross of timbers, ruddy in the fire's glow. It was like being inside a whale.

Seabost was best passed in darkness but it was too late for that now. There had been too much drinking and her father would probably refuse to give her a crew. Still, Bera took a ladle of water from the bucket, poured it down her throat and then banged it on the cooking pots.

'Come on! Wake up! We need to get going!'

The hall was full of folk bundled in furs, the air sour with ale-sodden snores and old smoke. There were moans and shuffles as they stirred. Her father pushed off his bedroll and stood up. He coughed, hawked and spat. The gobbet sizzled in the fire. He banged his chest with a massive fist.

'You're not going anywhere.'

'I'm going to the Skerries so I need your crew.'

'We've got boats to re-rig ready to go out.'

'You don't need to rush if I bring back food.'

He gave a warning growl, like an old bear. It would have stopped her but she was determined to start being a proper Valla.

'I'll go alone,' she said. 'Who needs your scabby crew anyway?'

'You do. So you're staying put and we'll have less lip.'

Bera got close. 'It's red-spot. Do you want us all dead?'

A square bundle of clothes pushed forward, with only a nose and mouth visible. Sigrid minded the cold.

'It's too dangerous.' Sigrid shoved her shawl back with mittened hands. 'You'll be too close to Seabost and they won't have it.'

Her father pulled on his boots. For some reason he looked smug, like when he had a big boat order. 'It's not Seabost she needs to fear.'

'I don't fear anything,' Bera lied, and crossed her fingers.

'Tend the sick, then. Brew some herbs.'

'She doesn't know the best ones, Ottar.' Sigrid scratched. 'Her mother never had time to show her.' She burrowed under her furs and triumphantly crushed a flea.

'So try helping me, Sigrid.'

'Your mother would—'

'Enough gossip.' Ottar strapped on his tool belt. 'I'm off to get the kitting-out started.'

He kicked his lad awake and headed for the double doors. Big Falki stopped him but Bera didn't wait. She needed Bjorn.

Her friend was Sigrid's son but everyone said he was more like his father, Bjarni, who drowned soon after he was born. Bjorn had come into the longhouse to live with them afterwards as Ottar's foster-son, which surprised folk considering how Ottar used to call both parents useless.

Bjorn was slightly younger than Bera. He was sleeping like a toddler; blond hair tangled over his creased face. There was darker fuzz on his upper lip. When had that appeared? Bera didn't want him to become a man and go off and drown like his father. She kicked him crossly, as if he had willed himself to grow up.

'That hurt!' He rubbed his thigh.

Bera snarled like a bear and flung herself at him. Bjorn rolled on top of her and tickled her until she wept and they laughed so much they were crying.

Bjorn said, 'Do you know how to get a man off you? I mean, if it was real.'

'How would you know?'

'Big Falki told me. You have to go all limp, don't fight. Let him think he's got you, then twist …'

'I can guess what,' she said. 'Come on, we're taking a boat out. The others won't come so it's just you and me.'

Bjorn grinned. 'As ever. What are we after?'

'Something to cure the red-spot,' she whispered. 'My skern told me about it.'

Bjorn slept fully dressed and only had to pull on his sea boots.

'No wonder you stink,' Bera said.

He also believed in her skills, though, so Bjorn hurried off to fetch their fishing gear. Bera was grateful.

She went to say goodbye to his mother, who would be working hard and complaining about it. Sure enough, she was at the back of the hall, tidying away the bedding.

Sigrid didn't look up. 'You're leaving me with all this, then?'

'Come with us, Sigrid.'

'Never! I'm not drowning, even for you. When have I ever got on a boat?' She stopped. 'Teasing me again. But listen, I feel a bit mizzy-mazey today. Don't go.'

Perhaps she should stay. Or did some growing Valla instinct want Sigrid aboard? Either way, Bera batted away the thought of danger.

'I have to find a narwhale.'

'They don't come down this far.'

'The Skerries?'

'Bjarni went up past Seal Island, only time he ever saw one. How do you know where to look?'

Bera wanted support, not doubt. 'I'll take Blind Agnar.'

Sigrid bridled. 'That old fool.'

'It was a whale that blinded him, so now he senses them.'

Sigrid sniffed and rubbed her nose on her sleeve.

'Chop some more wood when it's full daylight,' Bera said. 'One of the fires was nearly out when I got up.'

Sigrid made the hammer sign at her throat. 'Were there Drorghers?'

'Not yet.'

Ottar arrived. 'Take the fast boat. Big Falki will row.'

Bera was surprised. 'What changed your mind?'

'You need more than Bjorn.' Her father glanced at Sigrid. 'Falki's wife died in the night and both his sons are sick.'

'I will stop the red-spot!' Bera braced herself for their scorn but none came. It felt good.

Bjorn beckoned to her.

Ottar went instead and spoke into his foster-son's ears. Then he shouted back to Bera. 'Tell me if the Seabost traders are heading out yet.'

Was her father letting her go because he always gave in to Bjorn?

Sigrid caught Bera's arm. 'I don't like this. My friend's just died. It's a sign. It's the wrong time, the wrong place, I don't want Bjorn going.'

Bera's scalp prickled, which was a sign of danger, or sometimes anger. 'Why do you and Ottar spoil everything? It's my one chance to prove I'm as good a Valla as my mother and you ruin it. Bjorn trusts me, why can't you?'

Sigrid made the hammer sign. 'Then look after Bjorn for me, Bera. If anything should happen … Look after my boy.'

Bera clenched her teeth. There was to be an end of doubting herself. She would find the narwhale and come home in glory.

Ottar's boat was tied up at the jetty, butting against the posts as if urging her on. Big Falki and his oarsman were throwing the kit aboard. Beyond it, at the far end of the jetty, Blind Agnar was sitting, as he did every day. He was shamefully old. His equally ancient dog was curled at his feet. Both turned to face the sound of her approach with opaque blue eyes, like sea-milled glass.

'That you, Bera?'

'It is.'

'I'm smelling a storm coming.'

'There's a mackerel sky, but I don't think the bad weather will come till this evening.'

'Could be so. Where you off to?'

'I'll get out there, then see. I want you to come.'

His face lit up. 'Out on the sea paths?'

'I have to find a narwhale.'

He turned away. 'Then bring me and the dog back some fish, for you won't find no narwhale.'

'I will.'

Her new confidence must have shown in her voice, for he allowed her to help him and his dog aboard the boat, even when Falki moaned about the extra weight.

'He can row,' said Bera. 'And if the wind stays light, you'll be glad of it.'

Bera watched her village grow smaller. It clung to a ribbon of land where they scratched a living in the far north of the Ice-Rimmed Sea. Gales came early and midwinter lasted an age. She hated the grinding weight of snow and ice that trapped them ashore. In winter, all the quick and lively fish followed the whale roads, taking birds with them to battle in the pounding surge, or glide on sleepless wings over ocean rollers. Only blind monsters remained in the frigid darkness, slowly crawling after smaller ugliness with gaping mouths like sacks full of teeth. White mountains teetered over their home and the long forests were silent; suffocated and shapeless in vast drifts of snow. Whenever a wind blew, it was funnelled into a drilling blast that went either straight up or down the fjord. It was an endless night that swallowed the stars. It was the time of Drorghers.

Bera shook herself. Brighter days were coming but for now she was shrammed with cold, as though the walking dead were upon her. She wished it could always be summer, when waters chopped and boiled with sparkling silver shoals and the killers who surged in to eat them. Then there was a whirling soup of fins and teeth, spumes and spouts and crashing waves. Bera was always out fishing. It was more than getting food, for her; it was her joy.

'What are you smiling about?' Bjorn patted his rowing bench. 'Thinking of me?'

His silly, lovesick face made Bera want to slap him. She lifted her face to feel the sun and breathe the soothing sea air – but the wind made her eyes stream. She pulled her hood round her face in case anyone thought she was weeping and then gave in and sat next to Bjorn.

Their boat butted through sluggish water whose chill seeped through the wooden hull and froze the bones.

'Why did Ottar let Falki and his mate come?' Bjorn asked.

'I thought he told you. Falki's wife died in the night.'

Bjorn made a face. 'Less mouths to feed.'

'Stop sounding like Ottar! Big Falki wants to save his sons. And we will.'

They hit rougher water and Bera was briefly thrown against him. Above them the striped sail creaked. It was old and patched but had been woven by Bera's mother and folk believed it gave them the best luck.

'Do you think Alfdis is watching over us?'

'My mother is always with me.' Bera crossed her fingers. She was as unsure of this as she was about her skern. 'The sail won't fill until we're past the headland,' she added, making sure they all heard.

The men bent to their oars and Agnar's old dog settled against the stops. They were speeding towards the prospect of a narwhale she claimed was waiting for them. But where? Bera wished her skern would point the way but she was yet to find any appeal or sign that would make him appear. It was up to her to raise everyone's spirits, including her own. She started Bjorn's favourite song, with its rumbustious tune:

'In the bones, in the bones
Feel the east wind in the rigging
And the boat-song in your bones.'

Bjorn took over, grinning at her.

'In the blood, in the blood
Feel the rumble and the tumble
And the boat-song in your blood.'

Then they all finished together, lustily.

'In the heart, in the heart
Feel the pulsing of the whale road
And the boat-song in your heart.'

They were a boat crew, joined in the love of the sea and a childhood song.

Bjorn mistook the feeling and tried to take her hand. Bera snatched it away. She needed him as a friend and hoped he would fix on some other girl soon. Or a widow.

'Show me your necklace.'

'No.'

'I want to see the bead with my rune on it.'

'The B is not your rune. It's mine. Or possibly my grandmother's.'

His lower lip jutted. 'It's the same rune, anyway.'

'Stop sulking and help me raise the sail.'

The wind stayed fair and Bera felt confident that all would be well.

Until Seabost came into view, a filthy smudge on the steerboard side. To make themselves less visible to any Seabost lookouts, they got the yardarm down onto the deck and rowed. Bera took the end of Bjorn's oar to help in the roiling sea. Their splashing oars sounded loud enough to wake the dead. She could smell tension, which was strongest near Bjorn.

'Is your skern with you?' he asked.

'Some trading boats are in, look. How did Ottar know they were coming?'

'They'll see us!'

'They'll all be drunk.'

'You hope.'

Blind Agnar spat. 'Seabost, it smells like dead flesh.'

The hairs on Bera's arms rose with fear.

'Is my skern here?' Bjorn asked her.

'Stop asking about skerns! You'll bring yours if you keep talking about it. You're years away from dying.'

'Am I?'

'You're still a baby.'

'I'm not!'

'Well, I'm glad Sigrid let you come.'

'I don't need a mother's say-so. I'm old enough to do as I please.'

Bera smiled. Teasing Bjorn always made him forget his fear.

'Keep your voices down, young 'uns,' said Falki.

Their little fishing boat seemed to stand still in the water in plain view. If a lookout did see them the reprisal would be swift and brutal. Bera dreaded seeing warships setting off from the jetties. Her nerves snagged her breath and she felt sick. Any moment now she would surely hear the rattle of lines and rigging as the Seabost fleet launched and she would be tested.

'Not many boats,' Falki said softly.

'Perhaps they're off on raids.'

Bjorn pushed up his sleeve and scratched at the scar on his arm, made by a Seabost fisherman's boathook. They had come poaching one season and Bjorn's temper had got him into an uneven fight.

'Those raiding boats won't come back today, will they?' he asked.

No one answered.

Very, very slowly, Seabost was passing and no alarm sounded. Bera kept scanning all the time, still fearing an attack, but nothing stirred. Then, at last, she saw some dark shapes. Fishermen had described them to her but not done them justice. Each had sheer cliffs that jutted out of the troubled sea at impossible angles.

'The Skerries!'

'Them islands are pips spat out by troles,' said Agnar.

Bera laughed at him. But she felt uneasy as they closed the islands. The whole group looked like a mouth of jagged teeth that they were about to enter. Would it snap shut and swallow them?

Bera pushed away her fear. 'The narwhale's here somewhere,' she declared. 'And I will find it.'

Now they were out in clear water, it was Agnar's turn to steer. He turned his cheek to the wind but Bera sat on a barrel beside him in case he went off course and gently pulled at his hound's ears. She was sure Agnar brought her luck.

'That old dog's got no answers.' Agnar knew her too well. 'Tell me what you see.'

'We're passing the waterfall where the bears go to die. There was a mist earlier but it's clearing and a rainbow is touching the water. Way above its arch is a sea eagle, gliding inland to the mountains. The peaks are snowy but there are white streaks where every stream is flowing.' Saying it aloud made Bera feel its beauty. The last word came out in a sob, as if she would never see such a sight again.

'See an island with three horns?'

'Only one with a sort of nose sticking out.'

'That's the Trole. The horned one's behind it.' Agnar sniffed deeply for its trace. 'All kinds of whale beach themselves there, oftentimes.'

'I can't see any horns,' said Bera.

'That's where the whales go.' Agnar's voice was small. 'Leastways, they used to.'

Some burrs and thorns were caught in the dog's rough fur and Bera teased them out, trying to think what to say to the others. They were in enemy waters. She wanted a quick raid, not a dangerous search – and she daren't let them see her uncertainty.

Falki rested his oar. 'Where's this narwhale then, girl? That's the last island before open sea. You taking us over the Ice Rim? Because I don't think you've got the guts.'

He spoke to her without respect. Bera feared she wasn't worth any.

'Got to have faith in this world, Falki,' said Blind Agnar.

'You should be dead, you and that hound both.'

Bera's flash of anger made her feel better. 'Ottar pays you to row.'

'Breaking my back for nothing,' he grunted, but took up the stroke.

His mate was strong and they bent to it, driving the hull through the waves and butting out into the longer swell. As they got closer to the land it became clear that what had seemed to be all one island was in fact two. The second had horns.

Bera pictured a cleft between the cliffs, and then a shingle beach, a gnarled tree. The truth of her skern's vision made her scalp tingle. Or perhaps it was the dangerous opening.

Bera took the helm. 'You need to row again, Agnar.'

'It's a tricky entrance, mind.'

Tiny scraps of white, like specks of ash, spiralled in the breeze. They were countless sea birds, soaring up or swooping down onto shoals that seethed in the iron-grey waves. Bera steered for the cleft, where water restlessly churned.

Bjorn's oar jerked skywards. 'These breakers'll have us over!'

'Not when I'm steering, so row properly!'

Bjorn's fright made his skern flicker around him like an early dusk.

Furious with him, Bera boldly brought them into the lee of the island. Several long dark tusks emerged out of the calm water.

'I'm right! Narwhales!' Bera punched the air, grinning, then gathered her dignity and solemnly added, 'There are many.'

Bera reckoned there were more than twelve in the pod, including females. Some were young and only slightly mottled; last year's calves, perhaps. The oldest male was livid white with dark scars. Runes? He was the one.

'Corpse whales,' said Bjorn. 'They say they're the bodies of drowned sailors.'

'Rare as hen's teeth,' said Agnar. 'See their tusks, boy? Magic, they are.'

'I'll take one spear,' said Bera, forcing herself to do the thing she most dreaded. Her scalp prickled painfully. 'Who'll take the other?'

Bjorn snatched it.

Falki gave a low growl. 'Them'll dive deeper than any other beast and not come up for days.'

'I know,' said Bjorn. 'My father missed killing one off Seal Island once. He nearly froze waiting and gave up.'

Bera could sense that Falki didn't seem happy about leaving their prize to two youngsters but, as Ottar always said, money talks. Besides, much of the skill was manoeuvring the boat so that the strike could be made. He gave the stroke and the men set to rowing.

Bjorn made sure the rope was lashed tight to their spears.

'Are the creatures drowned men?'

'I don't know,' said Bera. 'Remember that story about a young Valla who was thrown into the sea for loving the wrong man? She came back from the depths as a narwhale.'

'Don't you go and fall in.'

Bera refused to look at him, hoping he would soon stop this new doting.

The narwhales were gently rubbing each other's tusks, then pointing them up to the sky.

'What do they do that for?' Bjorn asked.

'Perhaps it's a dance.'

'A mating dance.'

Now she felt even worse about killing the narwhale. She called on her skern but he did not reply. Bera pictured the sick folk at home that the tusk could heal. It was the balance of nature that Vallas respected. She was there to keep folk safe, as she had promised Sigrid to protect Bjorn.

But her scalp warned of something, and besides, she just couldn't kill it. She would not show weakness, though.

'I'm better at helming. Falki, take the spear.'

He was quickly in place. Bera saw an opening and drove the boat through the middle of the pod to separate the large male from the others. She ran the boat beside him and when they were sure of the target Falki and Bjorn let fly with their spears. The beast roared and tried to dive but was held by the ropes, fastened at one end to the boat, which tipped and rocked. The men tried to keep it balanced while Bera went with it. Falki took the killing spear, steadied, then drove it cleanly through the narwhale's eye. Wild beasts had no skerns but as it died Bera caught a glimpse of something coiling like smoke around its tusk, which shocked her.

'What have you seen?' Bjorn's face was so white she could see the blue veins at his temple.

'Stop staring at me like a boggelman! Let's take this tusk and get going.'

They towed the beast to shore. Its females followed, slowly. Bera could not bear the sound of their keening.

As soon as the boat was beached Bjorn went to study the twisted tusk. 'I wonder what it's for?'

'Always asking what things are for! I'll tell you. It's for protecting us from any bad thing. Remember that.'

'It's you that should remember it!' Bjorn stomped back to the boat.

He was right – and she would say so later. It was just that this first killing filled her with strange dread. Scavenging a dead whale was different; it was making use of what Fate gave them, but this... No wonder her scalp flared. And waste made it all worse. Could any good come from killing the whole beast just to get its tusk?

The whorled spear was almost twice as long as her. She went to touch it but then snatched her hand away when she felt its power. There was something questing about it, as though the beast used its tusk like she used her skern. Or would, if he was ever reliable.

'I'm sorry, Old One,' she whispered. 'I promise to use it wisely.'

Bera pictured their triumphant passage home in the dark with stars like buttermilk. They would sing in the joy of seafaring and she would be proud of healing the sick.

Agnar's dog charged at the body and then shied away, as if stung. It brought Bera back to the present. The men returned with saws and axes.

'Can't we take all of it?' Bera asked. 'The body looks as good as a right whale.'

'Slow us down, towing it,' said Falki, who got to work.

'What's Bjorn doing?' Bera asked.

'Sulking.'

They decided it was easiest to chop off the whole head. Bera looked away, to where the narwhales were heading out to sea, their tusks raised in a final salute. It made her think of Sigrid. Falki's wife and Sigrid gutted fish together. What if she'd given Sigrid the sickness? Perhaps that's why her scalp was prickling, because Sigrid was in danger! The narwhale had to die to save Sigrid.

'The tide's turning,' she said. 'You carry this to the boat while I say some words of thanks.'

There was a sudden clatter of shingle and there was Bjorn, fallen face down on the beach. Bera laughed and then froze. A longboat with Seabost sails had entered the channel.

'Too late,' she said. 'They've seen us.'

Bjorn scrambled up beside the others. Each man put a hand on his knife-sheath. Here she was, full of doubts on a beach where a noble beast had been killed. Had she been wrong to do it? Was a blood debt to be paid? She grasped her necklace, given to her by her mother, passed on by her mother before her, but had no sense that they were with her. She willed her skern to do something, anything, but there was no help. The men were watching her, so she tried to sound like a Valla.

'We own this tusk by right,' she said.

'Seabost don't ever see it like that.' Agnar drew his dog to him and kept a hand on its neck.

'Are we going to die?' Bjorn's voice was high.

'She didn't see this coming,' sneered Falki. 'No good asking her.'

The men spat on their hands, made the hammer sign from head to belly, shoulder to shoulder, then planted their feet steady. Bera turned her thoughts inward, trying to find some Valla strength of her own, but there was only chattering panic.

The enemy's hull rattled the stones, three men leapt ashore and pulled the boat up the beach with practised speed. The ones who followed carried swords. All wore the blue cloaks of Seabost, crusted with dried blood.

'Them's bad men, girl. What'd you bring us to?'

Falki and his mate had knives and nets in their hands, ready for a fishermen's fight. It was all they knew.

The enemy advanced slowly. Their faces were grimed and savage. Two weren't much older than Bera, but were taller and as hardened as their elders, one of whom had a badly broken nose, flat against his face. The last man off the boat was the worst. He had a recent scar that ran right down one side of his face, pulling his top lip upwards in a sneer. The slashing violence was visible.

He unsheathed his sword with the easy movement of a killer.

Bera's mouth was glued with terror but she had to try and speak. Ottar had raised her to face fear. She wanted to run so made herself step towards them instead.

'We are from the small village further up the fjord.' Her voice betrayed her.

'Crapsby,' said Flat-Nose, making the others laugh.

'Home,' said Falki.

Bera tried to drag her eyes away from the swordsman's vivid scar. 'My skern, my... spirit guide, told me the narwhale was here to stop the sickness in our village. It is not theft. He foretold it and we took it with our own skill.'

Flat-Nose spoke again. 'This island belongs to Seabost, and so does everything on it. You get back to Crapsby now, or die.'

'It's not Crapsby!' cried Bjorn. His voice warbled. 'Why call it Crapsby?'

'Because it's crap,' Scarface said flatly.

Bera was frightened by his coolness. 'There are more narwhales out there. Hunt them.'

'Oh, we shall, little girl,' Flat-Nose said. 'But we'll have that horn, too.'

Scarface slapped his short, wide sword against his palm. 'Move away,' he said. His puckered smile was at odds with his menace.

Bera fumbled under her cloak until she could hold on to the string of beads and then will her Valla ancestors to bring some scraps of courage. She took up the same posture she used to face Drorghers, her arms wide. But she was used to the walking dead; these men were the first living enemy she had ever challenged.

She began haltingly. 'The narwhale is a free sea beast. It belongs to no one until it is killed. I brought us here. I am Bera, a Valla. Do not blame these men. No blood will be spilled on this shore. My skern has just told me so.' Two lies.

There was a sudden squabble of gulls, then deeper silence. They were still, in a swelter of hot blood. Nothing moved. Slowly Bera began to believe her spirit and words were winning the day.

The sun came out from behind a cloud and Bjorn charged, crouched low, his head aiming for Scarface's stomach. He never reached it. With careless skill the man caught him with a swift punch that made him straighten, then swept upwards with the blade-tip, slicing him from groin to rib cage. Bjorn crumpled to the ground, clutching his belly.

Bera saw the Seabost men through a red veil of fury. 'You coward! You have killed a boy. Perhaps you will kill this blind old man next? Or how about me? Or would you gutless pigs baulk at killing a young girl?' She liked how anger took fear away. 'How about the rest of you? Too scared? I'd love you to try; then my Valla ancestors can punish you for all eternity.'

The men opposite her looked dazed. Bera seized the advantage.

'Take our boy back to the boat. You Seabost brutes can keep the narwhale tusk in return for our safe passage. Do not strike us as we go or follow us.'

The men went to Bjorn's sprawled body and lifted it. Bjorn gave a terrible cry. He was alive! They carried him off at speed to the boat. Bera slowly turned her back on the killers and her spine grew icy, dreading a cleaving blow.

None came.

Falki held the boat steady in the shallows. Bera waded out and he helped her step up into it, then pushed off into deeper water, swung himself aboard and took his oars. He did not meet her eyes.

Bera looked back. Men were carrying the tusk to the Seabost boat. Alone on the beach, the swordsman watched them go. He raised his sword to the sky, then lowered it to point straight at her. And then he was hidden as the boat passed through the cleft to open water.

Whether Bjorn lived or died, one day that monster would suffer. Ottar would claim the blood debt but she would cause pain. One day, when she was in her full power, like her mother.

2

Bera used her thick underskirt to bind Bjorn's wound but it was red in an instant. She sat back against the gunnel and took her friend's head in her lap. He held her eyes a long time then licked his dry lips before he could speak.

'Pocket.'

She felt inside the blood-soaked cloth and drew out a piece of linen, folded tightly many times and bound with waxed string.

'Keep it safe.' His chest rattled. 'Am I dying?'

'No,' she lied, looking at his skern.

It settled round Bjorn as closely as they had once been in the womb. Birth, death, the same progression. Except this was the last time Bera would see her childhood friend on this earth.

'Remember how you used to love to play hide-and-seek? I always found you, Bjorn, didn't I?'

There was no reply in his empty eyes.

Bera stayed fixed on the soft down on his face, too numb to cry. How would she ever be able to tell Sigrid that her only child was dead?

The men's faces were like stone. Was even Agnar against her? Bera was guilty and the pressure of their silence, to make her feel it, flared as anger.

'Shout at me or do something!'

Falki began counting the strokes out loud.

'That man with the scar was battle-hardened. He could have killed us all, single-handed, but I stopped him.'

'You gave the tusk away,' growled Falki. 'My sons'll be the first to die back home and then how many more?'

'I blame myself, for all it was fated.'

Falki stood up, making Bera stagger as the boat tipped. 'Fated? You never know what's fated, do you? Your precious skern's nothing but hogswill. You didn't see the lad's death, nor my wife's. Did you?'

'I saw the narwhales.'

'But we're going home with nothing but a dead boy.'

His mate pulled him back down and he grabbed his oar. There was a crack of colliding wood, cursing, and then they took up the stroke. Bera went back to where Bjorn's body lay beneath her mother's sail. The one person who ever stood up for her was dead and she hoped the woven words would protect him till they got him safely home. And then at last she felt the welcome warmth of her skern around her and she let the tears fall, chilling her face and splashing onto the mound that was Bjorn's head. How small it seemed. Why had she been so hard with him?

Falki was right. She had no command over her skern and was too stupid to know if he was present or understand what he showed her.

'Damn you, skern!'

He was insulted and unclasped from her so sharply that her ribs ached. Bera refused to let him see her surprise and hurt and did not rub the place.

'You closed the boy's eyes?' Agnar asked.

Falki's voice was dark. 'Is he going in the sea?'

'Bjorn's not becoming a corpse whale! He'll have proper rites, like his father.'

The men rowed hard for home. Bera thought she might die of grief and shame before they got there and hoped she would.

The jetty was golden in the setting sun. As soon as they tied up, folk gathered round to get a first glimpse of the tusk. There was a moan of dismay when they saw only Bjorn's stiff body. Word of his death spread and a hubbub of excitement began. Life could be dull.

Bera avoided everyone and headed for the boatyard to tell Ottar what had happened. She was numb with despair, sleepwalking. When she met her father it was like starting awake.

'Look at you, covered in whale blood,' Ottar said. 'Go home, girl, and get yourself decent.'

'It's Bjorn's blood. He's dead.'

'Tell me later.'

'Didn't you hear me? Bjorn's dead.' Her teeth were chattering.

'Go and wash. I'm ashamed to own you for my daughter.' He beckoned to someone behind the workboat. 'This man's come all the way from Seabost.'

A man stepped out wearing a vile blue cloak. Bera wanted to tear his head off to pay the blood debt but all she managed to do was spit at him. She set off before Ottar could hit her.

She ran through the boatyard, ignoring her father's shouts. It was all out of control. And unless her skern started giving proper advice she would be punished. She started down the slipway. Ottar's yard lad tried to trip her but she jinked, ran down to the water and plunged in. She thought she would feel nothing ever again but the water was freezing, like an ice shark's clamping jaws. She hoped it killed her. She tried to stay under and drown but a panic reflex forced her upwards.

Someone was speaking. She tilted her head, gathered her wet hair and wrung it. Years of hunching work had bent Ottar's old boathand so his face was level with hers.

'I was down at the jetty,' he said. 'I'm saying they've laid Bjorn out in the boat proper, like.'

'Not to be burned!' Boats were too precious to waste these days.

'So he'll look right for Sigrid.' The man picked up his bag of nails and clenching hammer. 'So someone ought to go and tell her.'

'Someone will.' But please not her. Bera dreaded Sigrid's desperate hurt and dawning blame when she realised Bera's total failure to keep her word.

'Folk are saying it would have been your mother doing the telling.'

'I have to take off these wet clothes.'

'Him being Ottar's foster-son and that.'

'Then let my father do it!'

The man went off to his work. They both knew she would do it. A Valla presided at birth and death – and Bera owed it to Bjorn.

Sigrid was neither in the hall, the longhouse, nor the byre. Bera bundled her wet clothes in a corner, threw on an old shift and went up to the goats. Not there either. She gave her favourite a quick scratch behind the ears, longing for it to be the simple day it had been when she last did it, then headed back to the jetty. Perhaps Sigrid was already there; perhaps someone had told her by now. Would Sigrid ever speak to her again? She was doomed whatever happened.

The wooden boards of the walkway bounced as someone hurried towards her. Rounding a corner at speed came one of the fishwives. Her cheeks were flushed and her eyes lit up when she saw Bera.

'Terrible news. Have you told poor Sigrid?'

'Where is she?'

'I'll come with you.'

Bera hated the woman's pleasure in causing Sigrid pain.

'No. I will do it alone, as a Valla.'

'You're not that good yet and we were girls together, your poor mother, Sigrid and me.'

'Just tell me where she is.' Bera was determined to prove this woman wrong.

The drying racks, in plenty, made a ᚢ rune of stiff grey stockfish, right down to the ground. Bera ignored the empty rows and went on to sparse racks of older stockfish to find Sigrid. Her back was to Bera; sturdy legs wide, braced against whatever life threw at her. Today she had lost her son, except she didn't yet know it.

Bera tried to call out but shame gripped her throat. She was close before Sigrid noticed her.

'You gave me a turn! How did you get on? Wasn't it there?'

'What?'

'The narwhale, of course.'

'Oh, yes, but—'

'Help me move this basket, will you? I'm aching all over.'

They each took a handle and carried it to the edge of the racks. Bera wondered how to begin.

Sigrid burrowed under her clothes and scratched. 'I'm that itchy and my back's playing up. I shouldn't be carrying this lot.'

Bera watched the night clouds turn golden. She always thought of her mother when the setting sun made a blaze of branching beams over the whole sky. Two sea eagles flew in, their bodies black runes. Probably her mother telling her to do her duty.

'Look at that sunset.' Sigrid smiled. 'It was like that the night your mother died.'

'I know. Listen, Sigrid—'

'We'll have a lucky year, Bera, I feel it. After the bad. We can trade those tusks.'

'One tusk. But then—'

'Only one, eh? Well, it'll do. Stop the red-spot and folk might start trusting you. I would help you, Bera, only your mother'd start that scrying and I'd be off. Scared to death of it all, I was. And I don't ever want to see a skern.'

'I saw one today.'

'Maybe the gift's stronger, then. Mind, Alfdis was a full Valla and a mother herself when she wasn't much older than you. Though it has a price.'

'Listen...'

'Shame about all her babies and the poor little boy. I was the other way, couldn't fall with a child all the years I was with Bjarni. Well, I got one, one way or another. Hark at me blathering when we should be getting back before it's full dark. Glad you're here for once to help lug this lot.'

The reminder that Bjorn was Sigrid's one blessing made it impossible to speak. Bera hoped she might manage it on the way home, when she wouldn't have to meet Sigrid's eyes, but she had still not told her by the time they reached the longhouse. In the food store the fishwife was waiting, her eyes glittering in the taper's guttering light.

'Sigrid, my dear, I am sorry for your loss.'

Sigrid lifted her chin, as though to meet a real punch.

Bera's duty. She took Sigrid by the shoulders and looked her in the eye. 'It's the worst. Bjorn.'

His mother rocked, like a sturdy tree in a gale, but did not fall. 'At sea?'

'No, we brought him home. He didn't drown.'

'How?'

'He charged at a Seabost man who cut him. He stood no chance.'

Sigrid clenched her jaw so hard Bera heard the crack.

'Ottar will make him pay the blood debt,' Bera said.

The fishwife made a move towards Sigrid.

'You – get out!' Bera's anger made the woman leave quickly.

Sigrid's mouth was a line of pain. 'Take me to him.'

'I'm so, so sorry, Sigrid, I was afraid to tell you.'

'Where is my son?'

The sun, beneath the sea rim, burnished the waters. The small group of villagers parted when they saw Sigrid approach. She paused at the boat and then stepped aboard, making it rock and bump against the jetty. A brown bear fur, his namesake, covered the boy's body. The crewman on vigil drew it back from his face before leaving. Sigrid sat, pulled her son to her and rocked him like a baby.

'His skern joined him,' Bera reassured her.

Sigrid was humming the song she used to sing to both of them when they were small and the sound was like a stick beating Bera for failing her friend. She vowed to make sure the burning was done properly, so he would not become a Drorgher. It was all she could do for him now.

Bera stood guard. Sigrid fell silent, her face stony with grief. As time passed, Bera's determination grew. Paying Ottar any amount as a blood debt would not be enough. It had to be death. She was the one who had let Bjorn be killed after Sigrid had told her to look after him. So Bera would make the scarred man pay for it with his life, however long it took her to reach him.

Flame ribboned up to the hall. It was the line of torches that would keep Drorghers away.

Then Ottar arrived with Falki and two of his boatmen, who lifted

Bjorn onto a bier. Ottar bent to kiss the boy's cheek. It shocked Bera. He had never shown tenderness like this to her. Her dart of jealousy disgusted her and she dug her nails into her palms. She wished she had died, not Bjorn. Then her father would be happy. He only ever wanted a son.

'Let's take him home,' Ottar said.

The two women stayed with Bjorn's body. Sigrid tenderly pushed back inside what should not be outside and stitched the long wound with her best walrus tusk needle. Bera washed his boyish body from head to toe. He would never become a man. A flicker of relief startled her, which she quickly thrust away.

They took turns to kiss his forehead, chin, cheeks, and then Sigrid began her vigil. Bera kept company for a while but the smell of death brought back the loss of her mother. The slip of beads sliding through her grasp. Guilt weighed heavily – as did other emotions. She dared not break down in front of her brave friend, or face the rest of the folk in the hall with their accusing eyes, so she took herself off to the byre, wanting its sweet scent to soothe her.

She checked it for any lurking dangers, then sank down in an empty stall and ran her fingers through the scratch of straw, wanting the tears to come now they could. She ached for her skern to join her. There was only the cow, who stamped and nudged the wood, expecting Bera's usual treat.

No Bjorn. No true friend. Although Ottar had taken Sigrid and Bjorn into his care after Bjarni drowned, Sigrid had been her mother's friend and wasn't like kin. Bjorn was. Always so curious, he kept trying to get her to scry and tell him their future. Now he had none. She remembered the small packet he had made her take. She took a taper to the dark corner, found her smock and took it out of the pocket. She dithered and then kissed it.

The hairs on her nape prickled and there was her skern. He began an expansive gesture but Bera picked up a large soapstone jug and hurled it at him. It shattered.

That won't change your feelings.

Unfolded, it was a love poem. Bjorn should never have written it.

It was dishonourable and brought into the open feelings Bera had not shared. It was childish, too, but that made her sadder, especially the last two lines.

> My love will last until I'm old
> And even dead it won't grow cold.

Hot tears melted the words into the linen cloth. Bera screwed up the poem and then smoothed it out again. Her nose ran and through snotty lips she vowed again to make Scarface pay.

'I don't know when but I will do it, Bjorn. I'll be strong.'

Bera was not strong now, and weaker without Bjorn. She had teased and snapped at him in life and taken him to his death. She was a useless Valla, not the daughter her mother would have wanted. She lashed herself with every failing she could think of, then every regret, and fell to the ground, sobbing.

There was a heavy blow on the byre door. Bera waited for another, holding her breath. The dead knock only once.

No other came.

This was her duty, the only thing she could do well; other folk couldn't even stand the howling out in the open. The Drorgher had come to take Bjorn and steal his skern. Only Bera stood in its way. She scrambled upright, still hoping for more knocks, but nothing living was outside that door. She touched the black bead to her lips, opened the door a crack, slipped through and shut herself off from safety.

The one who had knocked was the boldest Drorgher, as he had been in life before the snow took him last winternights. His eyes, unblinking circles of impenetrable black, drew Bera like lodestones. She must not get close.

The nearest torch was nearly out. Sigrid must have forgotten to build it up as Bera had asked. Beyond the low flames the other Drorghers waited for the glow of ash to dull; shadowy corpses in a moonless night. The last ember fell with a grey sigh. Their heads swivelled to the place and they softly shuffled forward, all the unburned dead, wanting to join their leader and then pour like snowmelt into the byre and on into the hall.

Bera took up her stance. 'You shall not have Bjorn.'

That told them. Her skern made his knees knock.

'Stop it!' she hissed. 'I'm doing my best.'

There was a snort of derision from her skern. No wonder her confidence was low.

But then he presented the sky like it was his special gift. It shivered. A curtain of lights, greens and blues, moved in waves above the mountains. The North Lights always kept them at bay. It was late for the display and this was especially strong; the sky crackled with energy and burned with colour. The Drorghers shrank back from the flickering blaze. Swirls of pink and yellow forked down at them and voices whispered in some ancient tongue:

'Twisting together sighing we hear our mother's blood, our blood, calling to us...'

'Are they warning me?'

It's a lament.

'... and we are in space and time, scorched by the flash of dying stars until at last we gasp and breathe.'

'Are they my Valla ancestors? What are they saying?'

Shh. It's about us.

'We two, an entire world, pushing against unbroken velvet walls. Until we are ripped apart.'

The Drorghers shambled off, keening, with vivid green flames licking their heels. A shooting star streaked across the brightening sky: it was nearly dawn.

Now I'd get back inside, dear, and hear the news.

'Why don't you tell me it?'

There was a carefree humming.

Bera dashed inside, spitefully hoping to shut him out. But after she slid the bar across the door he tapped her on the shoulder.

Want to know why Drorghers knock?

'No.'

They want to trap you at a threshold, a liminal place. So that, my dear, is where you might get to speak to your poor dead mother.

'Why tell me this now?'

It's by way of being a peace offering.

'I meant, why haven't you told me before?'

Even a true Valla can't always hear her skern.

'This is the worst day of my life and you always —'

She spoke to empty air. Bera flexed her fingers and stamped her feet to get the blood flowing. Her fur boots were thinning round the heels. She was hardly old enough to marry but she felt like an old woman after everything that had happened. If only she could just be a girl on a boat. She took some comfort from the dim shapes around her in the grey light, recognising every box, tool, halter and harness.

Apart from a new sharp-edged squareness in one of the stalls.

It was a chest. Bera ran her hand over the wood. A rune was carved on the top and she traced its shape with a finger: B, her rune. And Bjorn's. Ottar must have made it at the yard, for her coming of age. It wasn't for a while but perhaps the poem was going to be Bjorn's gift. She flushed at the trouble it would have caused. But when she touched the chest again, the love for her father was a meltwater torrent. It was crafted like the small boat he made her just before her mother died; the last time he made her anything. But now she was his little Bera again!

Don't get your hopes up.

Bera jumped. 'Stop sneaking up on me! First you won't come and now you're never gone!'

Moan, moan. We shared a womb, as you've just been reminded. We were that close. Her skern crossed his first two fingers to demonstrate.

'The ancestors made no sense. Anyway, I thought you didn't deal in history.'

I only look forward but our past is who we are. Why don't you like boys?

'I do! Don't I?'

You blame them. Learn to love the male of the species, dear one.

It was a parting riddle because her father burst in, carrying a rushlight.

'Where in Hel's name have you got to? You should be inside offering hospitality.' He caught hold of her arm. 'And you look a shambles. Get your things ready to pack. What will he think?'

'Who?'

'I'll bring the chest.' His rough hands cudgelled her through the low doorway into the hall.

The fire was low but even in the gloom she knew the stranger was there, with his foreign smell. Bera was filled with icy dread.

The brute came and prodded her ribs. 'She's like a shrimp,' he grunted, returning to the fire.

Ottar followed him. 'Don't you try and back out...'

'We're leaving now.'

At last Bera found her voice. 'I'm not going to Seabost or anywhere with you!'

'I've come to take you home.'

This was her home.

Bera was given no time to think or prepare. The Seabost animal told her the box was her wedding chest. Ottar couldn't get rid of her fast enough. He gave her no time to say farewell to Sigrid before he marched her down to the boatyard and lifted her onto the boat. And although there never was a parting kiss, this time it was an agony.

'Is it because I let Bjorn die?' she asked.

His eyes were stones. 'The blood debt is paid. So do your duty, as I've done mine.' He cast off the lines and left.

Her skern enfolded her as the boat left the empty jetty. The world was grey. Bera clung onto her necklace like a drowning sailor to a piece of flotsam. A sea mist hid the sun, confusing time and thought.

Watch. Her skern tenderly placed his finger on her forehead and she saw...

... a torchman knocking on the hall's double doors, three slow blows. The funeral pyre was ready. Ottar reopened the gap in the wall he had made for Bera's mother. Although ashes could not become a Drorgher, it was still the custom to use a corpse door. No one took chances. Bjorn's fishing mates carried the body out feet first, so that it would not be able to see the path they took to the pyre and return that way to take its living kin. Ottar nailed it shut behind them. Every precaution.

It was a beautiful day, at home. Everything had a crisp edge against a clear sky. The small procession wound up the path towards the pyre, built on a hill to get the tallest flames. Bjorn's body, guarded by fishermen, was rested at the foot.

'Is Falki's wife to be burned, too?'

The torchmen are waiting with her, on top.

Bera was glad Bjorn would not be alone. The fishermen passed up Bjorn's net and knife to the torchmen, who set them on the high plinth. Then Sigrid gave food and Ottar coins. The corpse was slowly lifted three times before being laid amongst his few possessions. The men climbed down then set their torches to the kindling at the base of the pyre. They were skilled at their craft and the flames quickly took hold.

'He'll be with his father soon.'

The air was hazy and shimmered with heat. Motes of ash flew and Bera screwed up her eyes...

... and then her skern took his finger away and Bera was back, on her way to Hel. She would have burned Bjorn's blotched verse with him, so she dropped it over the side, where a darting fish swiftly took it.

'Look at me.' The Seabost brute pulled her head round.

Bera jerked free. The thought of him getting close made her retch.

'You're a spirited bint,' he said. 'I'll give you that. I reckon you'll be more trouble than the deal's worth, though. And you're a scrutty waif, more like a boy.'

She spat, aiming for his eyes, but splattered her own shoulder. She had even forgotten her wind-sense. He went off, laughing, and she hated him more. He had ripped her away from everything safe and loved and stopped her parting properly from Bjorn.

When Bera looked back, all she called home was hidden behind the jutting headland on the Seabost side of the fjord. What was before her was marriage – and she had no real idea what that meant. They all joked about the nightly grunts and moans, but what was happening? How could she suddenly be a woman? She was a sailor, with all the freedom of the sea paths, not some shrivelled old hag with children tugging at her skirts. She had no father to protect her and no mother to explain. No Sigrid, no kinsfolk, none of the animals she loved.

Bera pulled her sea cloak round her and sobbed.

3

Bera felt like the walking dead, trudging numbly after the man she was to marry, who carried her wedding chest.

There were more jetties, walkways and twittens than at home but no one was about. The huts were grey and deserted, or studded with black spars, and the air was sharp, like wet smoke.

Out of the corner of her eye Bera became aware of dead things everywhere: whale ribs crossed to form doorways; shark jaws as window frames; stomachs for fishing floats; and skins stretched tight on walls. It was like walking on the bottom of the sea where the giant beasts sink. It was like the end.

Though no one was visible, Bera felt observed by hostile eyes. She kept her head high. It took all her strength.

They stopped before a longhouse, its high timbers blanched by salt-laden storm-force winds. A colossal whale jaw at its entrance marked the importance of the family who lived there. She shivered as she was led underneath the arch of bones. It could have been Norgrind, the corpse gate to Hel.

'Smile. You're home.'

Could this pig really live here, with his caffled hair and clothes that were stained and smelly? There were snarling dragonheads at each end of the towering lintel. The doors beneath stood wide and she passed through a narrow stone passage towards a closed inner door. She was trapped at a threshold; pressed on by the family's ancestral spirits that whispered secret scourges.

Then a small person smelling of tallow pushed past, opened the door and stood back to let her step inside.

It was bigger even than the mead hall at home, with a high roof.

Her steps echoed as she went further in over clean spruce boughs. She let her eyes accustom to the haze-blue light. There was a sweet note in the smoke that was pleasant but made her feel foreign. She sensed watchers in the shadows and the sleeping platforms were too far away to be seen. There was a large central hearth and, at the far end, a bright cooking fire with shelves of pots and pans on the walls around it and hams being smoked high up in the rafters above. A woman was stirring a stewpot and, in a moment of giddy joy, Bera thought it was Sigrid. A man was standing near the long trestle table but she did not want to turn her head to look at him. She was overwhelmed and scared.

'Come inside.' The man's voice was friendly.

She dared to look. He was smiling and held out his hand.

'My name is Hefnir. Come further in. There's nothing to fear. You're going to be my wife.'

Relief made her sway. At least she was not to marry the brute, who went off with her wedding chest to wherever she would sleep with this other man. Fear returned in a flush of shyness and she did not resist when the small person who had opened the door took her cloak. His head was shaven and knobbly. Slant-eyed women who did not raise their gaze led her to the table. They filled her beaker with mild ale. Men with cropped hair did all the mealtime chores. One of them gestured to her to sit – in a chair – and then, before she broke bread, he brought her a bowl of water and a towel to dry her hands. It was completely strange.

'Who are those folk?'

'Thralls.'

'Is that where they come from?'

He laughed. 'Slaves, you'd call them.'

She choked on a piece of bread. What did you do with slaves? Their snooty silence made her feel as if she should be serving them. So she sat, twisting the beads of her necklace; not belonging, not wanting to; wanting to go home.

'Is the bread not to your taste?'

'What?'

'The bread.'

'It's different. Thank you, er...'

'Hefnir.' He smiled and pushed the thin horn beaker towards her. 'Drink. It will help you swallow.'

The brute returned, said something about red-haired twins and left, smirking. Other men came with storm-worn faces. They had reports of tool sharpening and jewellery making; of hunting trades and numbers of skins.

Bera's anxiety made her alert to every name and piece of business. One day it might help her. They all spoke respectfully about someone called Thorvald.

'This business bores you,' Hefnir said. 'Why not visit the bath hut? One of the women will help you.'

In other words, she stank.

At home they washed in the river. When it froze, a cauldron of water was heated and they scrubbed themselves with rags. Ottar always went first. Bera liked this more. She sat in a wooden tub and someone – a thrall – poured blood-hot water over her head and shoulders. The warmth soaked into her bones and there was even soap. Bera wanted to stay there, safe from wifely duties (whatever they were) but an unsmiling woman got her out, rubbed her with coarse cloths and then dressed her. The garments were soft linen and fine wool, not like her own scratchy clothes. There were two silver brooches, both of twining serpents.

'Whose things are these?'

The woman's eyes slid away. She held out a thick, blue cloak.

It would make Bera belong to the old enemy that had killed Bjorn. Anger scorched through her. She threw the cloak to the floor and trampled it, furious with everything, even her ancestors, who had conspired with Fate to get her here.

The woman was sneering at her. Bera looked round for her own cloak but it had been spirited away, leaving her dressed like an imposter. She picked up the blue cloak and shrugged it round her, as though she didn't care. She knew how to live amongst others – but not slaves. Did it matter that they saw her true feelings?

Some men watched her on her walk back to the longhouse. None looked welcoming. Bera was glad it was a short twitten and she ran into the passageway to escape. The ancestors shrieked the scourge words as she rushed through.

'Perfidy! Violation!'

Whatever it meant, it was nasty. She searched for the latch, scrabbled to open it and then burst into the hall.

'I'm glad to find you so eager,' said Hefnir.

'I'm not.'

'Don't be scared. Come.'

He took her arm, led her to his billet and gestured at something lying on top of the wedding chest.

'A gift of courtship,' he said. 'You fix it to your brooch.'

He picked up a thin silver chain, with an ear-spoon and nail cleaner attached.

'I – um – I haven't fixed my brooches on.' Bera held them out and blushed when Hefnir raised his eyebrows at her red hands. She hid them behind her back while he fixed it all in place.

'It's no crime to have the calloused palms and broken nails of a worker but it is a shame. That life is past. No sailing.'

So this was the first wound inflicted by marriage. Some part of her had known it but hearing it filled her with despair.

Hefnir went on. 'You have a new role to fulfil.'

The second wound. Fear clenched her guts at what that might entail: things no woman had told her. And from the way he was looking at her, it would be soonest. She had seen it in the mead hall, when drunken women lifted their skirts. Then what? If she disappointed him, would she become a thrall, not a wife? How could she bear being less than she was at this moment?

Bera wanted to escape but fear kept her rooted. All the spit in her mouth dried and she stared at him, like a rabbit gazing at an eagle.

There were voices from the hall and then a man appeared, smelling of the sea, and saved her.

'Dragonboats. Off the Skerries.'

'Coming here?'

'Heading west, but—'

'The watchers are in place?'

'That's why I'm here.'

'Get Thorvald back. I need him by me.'

Hefnir went through with the man. Bera wanted to put as much distance from his bed as possible, so she followed. They were already at the door.

'And ask the other if this is a new threat,' Hefnir muttered.

The man gave him a look Bera couldn't read, and left.

'Who is Thorvald?' she asked.

'My second.'

Hefnir came and gazed at the fire. He was not wearing a sword-belt. Surely he was supposed to protect his household, which now included her.

'Will you not go yourself, to fight with him?' she asked.

Hefnir looked surprised. 'I doubt they'll come. Besides, I make plans, hunt and trade. I pay my second to fight.'

'Why is he not here, then?'

'Thorvald? I sent him off at first light... on business.' He looked thoughtful again. 'Though perhaps I feared the wrong thing.'

Bera wondered what she had come to. Being close to the sea roads brought wealth but also danger.

'Are they raiders?'

'Could be sea-riders. We've had trouble here but their dragonboats attack at sea, too.'

Old enmity made her glad Seabost had suffered – but she hoped they would not return. She hoped her face wasn't showing all her thoughts, though Bjorn said it usually did. Or perhaps only he knew her so well. Homesickness squeezed her heart.

Hefnir made a decision. 'I shall go and make sure the danger is past. You can start your duties as my wife. Your keys are on the long trestle table in the hall. The thralls can understand if you speak clearly.' He turned at the door. 'Tonight is our wedding feast.'

Saliva flooded her mouth. 'Do you mean a feast? With proper food? Meat?'

He laughed. 'That's the first time you've looked alive. Yes, proper food. There's a place where they can grow food all year round. And they are anxious to... please us. Even after the pirate raid, we have enough.'

Then he was gone and Bera was left alone to run a household with expectant thralls and a bunch of unknown keys.

It was worse at the mead hall later. Strange folk came and pinched and prodded her as if she were a traded sow. Boys with wild, sea-tangled hair and no shoes rushed about.

'Those bairns will have someone over,' said an old woman.

A new word, bairns. She gestured at the boys and Bera understood.

Hefnir came to her side and the jabbing stopped. Bera was grudgingly grateful to this polite man with his neatly trimmed beard. Seabost men had different styles. At home, beards grew until they got in the way and then they were cut. These men had braids and plaits; spade-shaped or cut to the chin.

'Why do you not have a longer beard?' she asked Hefnir.

The man next to him said something and Hefnir laughed.

'Tell me!' She pulled at his arm.

He looked down at her. He was very tall. 'So that no man shall pull me by it.'

That was not why they laughed. Bera felt childish and excluded.

Voices grew louder and a crowd formed near the huge central fire. Hefnir caught hold of her and carried her under his arm.

'Put me down!' Bera hit his chest.

He laughed again, in high spirits. Perhaps he was already drunk. He used her to ram his way through to where a man was warming his hands.

His face, even half-turned, was clearly furrowed by a terrible scar.

Hefnir swung her down.

'My second is like my brother. He will protect you now, as he has me, for many years.' He took their hands and placed them together. 'Thorvald, meet my wife.'

Dismay was like a sword in the stomach. So Scarface was Thorvald, who was mentioned with respect. Bjorn's killer bowed low over her hand, keeping a tight hold so that she couldn't break free. She wanted to punch him so that he would jerk upright and be split open like Bjorn.

He raised his hideous face and scrutinised her. 'She's bloodless.'

'The sight of you would make anyone faint.'

'She's hungry. Like the rest of us.' He spoke thickly, through damaged lips.

Hefnir laughed and yelled, 'Let's eat!'

There were raucous cheers and wolfish folk jostled to get hunks of meat that were hacked from the beasts on the spit. Bera was breathless in the crush with its sudden tang of strange sweat. Needles pricked her cheeks and colours swirled. Hefnir swept her up in his arms again and got her away. He put her down at a long table where a small window let in sweeter sea air. At home she stood alone against Drorghers... yet here she was as weak as a baby.

'You nearly fainted.'

'I don't faint.'

'Look – Thorvald has some meat.'

'I'm not hungry.'

She was ravenous but would take nothing from that man, who offered her a wooden platter filled with juicy meat.

'We roasted this in your honour,' he said.

Bera could not tear her eyes away from the food. The smell was succulent. It was all she could do not to dribble.

'Thorvald's right,' said Hefnir. 'Folk are watching. So come on. Eat.'

He held up a slice of meat. Bera could resist no longer and she took it like a bear. It was delicious and she had another two slices in quick succession, sucking in the flavour of the meat juices. Hefnir patted her head and she regretted letting him see her hunger.

'I'm not your cur!'

A man was approaching. 'We need to speak, Thorvald, but I'll sort him out first.' Hefnir went to meet him.

'Aren't you going with your master like a good boy?' Bera spat.

'Don't act the mistress with me.' Thorvald sneered. 'He doesn't even know your name, does he?'

'Of course he does.'

'What he does know is what happened to that reckless boy. Exactly.'

Bera seethed. 'I'll make you pay the blood debt.'

'What was your name again?'

'Bera. A Valla, like my mother and her mother before her. So you had better look behind you, Thorvald. My revenge may come from the dead.'

He didn't flicker.

'My ancestors can strike you down, believe me.' The more she threatened, the weaker it sounded.

'I don't fear the dead,' he said. 'It's the living you have to worry about.'

'Do you not fear Drorghers?'

'Are they your boggelmen, to frighten children? Get that meat down you. It's better than your pickled Crapsby muck.'

She spat her mouthful onto the ground. It was taken at once by a scavenger dog.

'Wasteful,' he said. 'That's your first fresh meat for an age, isn't it?'

'It doesn't taste like pork,' said Bera.

'That's because it's horse.'

She refused to look shocked. 'I wait my time. You will pay the blood debt. My father may have taken money but I will have blood.'

'Your father! Don't you know that—'

Hefnir returned. 'Let's get the important bit over before they're too drunk.'

Bera wanted to know what Thorvald had to say about Ottar but the chance had slipped and she was damned if she would ask him.

Thorvald returned to the hearth and folk made a noisy circle about him. He tapped his sword point on the stones until there was quiet.

'You all know why we're here,' he said. 'Hefnir will take this girl, Ottar's daughter, as his wife. All kinsfolk should recognise his right. Many suffered in the latest skirmish, none more so than he, and it was settled that the loss of the first was not by his own hand. So, are we agreed?'

'Agreed,' came the ready response from folk wanting to get back to drinking.

'What did he mean?' Bera asked.

Hefnir kept his eyes on Thorvald, who went on, 'Let us now drink to their health and her fertility.'

The words were repeated and drinking horns emptied. The towering beams of the huge mead hall were a pressing weight. There was no escape. Seeing herself as an avenger was ridiculous. She was only a girl, brought in as a brood mare. In the yellow heart of the fire her skern's poor face twisted in twin despair and Bera's eyes burnt with tears.

'Her turn!' shouted some red-faced women.

The brood mare was expected to make her mark in Seabost. How could she do that when she saw nothing but Bjorn's guts on the sand and the man who had spilled them? Bera was out of her depth, with no idea what their customs were. They didn't seem to believe in anything they couldn't trade with. Failure would dishonour her, as well as Hefnir, who was clearly a leader. Sweat poured down her back and she could smell her own fear. She looked across at her skern in desperation. He tapped his neck. He meant the beads – but what about them?

Hefnir called out to her. 'Thorvald says you're a Valla. So make a prediction.'

There was excited murmuring. Bera fiddled with her necklace, which had never helped her predict anything. She tried to think of some likely future event but Seabost was a mystery to her. Her skern took pity.

Hold the black bead.

The crowd let a tall man through. He smiled at her and raised his ale. He was the first one to look kindly at her – and she could picture his face in every detail when she tried to see where he had gone.

She rolled the special bead; the only one her mother had picked out on her deathbed.

In desperation she began to tell Seabost about being six and losing a dear mother in the act of giving life to a boy, who had not thrived; about the earlier babies and how these deaths turned her kind father into a hard, ever-complaining master who would not let her show her feelings, ever.

Bera forgot she was amongst the enemy and spoke from the heart. Her simple truth touched everyone there who had faced such loss – and most had. She did not notice that she had won over the crowd, sentimental with drink, and thought instead about how her best friend Bjorn had become a foster-brother who needed her. Killed by her husband's second.

Sadness turned into fury. It felt good, as if she were already an avenging ancestor, so she did not fear death. For killing Thorvald would be at the cost of her own life, whether immediate or at Hefnir's hand. She moved through the hall, scanning blurred faces for her enemy.

There was a deeper darkness in the shadows that made her scalp prickle. It had the same menace as a Drorgher, though none could stand the mead hall's torches. It was the size of a trole and hooded. Then Thorvald appeared and started talking to it. They stood close, although no one was near them. Bera crept to where she ought to see inside the hood – but could not. This was some new evil Seabost drew to itself and she tried to prepare.

Hefnir slapped her on the backside, like a cow.

'Here's one of my tenant farmers, come for our wedding. I've trusted him to get you safely home.'

The stony-faced farmer had blood-lines crackling over his cheeks and nose. He offered Bera his arm but she ignored it.

'Are we wed, then?' she asked Hefnir.

'Did you miss it in your faint?'

Bera yearned for some sign of affection. 'Do you know my name?'

'There's years to learn it. Go home now.'

'It's Bera,' she said to his back.

Hefnir carried on in the direction of Thorvald and the hooded man. What was happening? All that remained of Bera was her threadbare pride, so she stalked out of the mead hall ahead of the farmer. Then she could not remember the way, which annoyed her. As did his scornful look when he overtook her.

'I don't need you,' she shouted. 'I'm used to going about on my own.'

'Why wouldn't you? There's only two hens and a goat at Crapsby.'

Bera hurried to catch him up, fuming. 'I keep Drorghers away. The walking dead.'

He showed no reaction.

'Perhaps you call them something else here,' she said.

'You superstitious peasants.'

'Then why do you have so many torches?'

'Light?' He looked at her as if she was simple.

Bera pulled her shoulders back. 'My father builds your best boats. He keeps two workers and a foster-child... who was killed in cold blood by a Seabost animal.'

'My, my.'

She felt for her knife, wanting to slice the smirk from his face. Then she came to her senses. It was Thorvald she should be killing. Things were different here in Seabost. Faces were harder, warier, more used to fighting. There would be no battle won yet, not by an inexperienced girl with a knife that had only gutted fish. She had to plan.

The man stopped. 'I wouldn't put on airs. The whole place knows that we're getting Ottar's boats at a price. Your father made Hefnir take you and all if he wanted them.' He walked on.

Bera reeled. So she hadn't been chosen; she hadn't even been bought. She was only some scrap added on to the deal, like stale fish. Now she was stripped of pride as well as everything else.

The full moon lit a white path ahead like a trail of gut. Whalebones loomed and soared above them. Every dead thing.

'Home.' The man gestured at Hefnir's longhouse. 'I'm going back. You get inside.'

He probably showed Hefnir's animals more respect.

Bera whistled over the ancestors as she groped for the inner door.

'Perfidy and violation...'

She clicked the heavy latch and rushed in, shutting out the threat, but their viciousness came hissing in the draught behind her.

'Perfidy...'

'Leave me alone!'

Rustling and skittering of large rats running for cover.

The fire was low and shadows flickered and danced on the walls. There was whispering from the far end of the longhouse and the darkness shifted. An old woman, bent like a weatherworn tree, hustled a white-haired child ahead of her. A dog followed, the only one to glance in her direction. They went off towards the back.

Sadness and loneliness were physical. Her rib cage was torn open as if her skern had just unclasped. Where was he? Even thralls had companionship. Bera felt vulnerable and made for her only lair: Hefnir's billet.

No thrall came to light her way and the billet was squid-ink black. Bera bashed her knee against the wedding chest and then felt her way like Blind Agnar to the sleeping platform, stubbing her toes when she got there. She burrowed into the rugs and furs and pulled them over her head. Perhaps her skern would never join her again in Seabost. Perhaps being married stopped all that. Or were her murderous thoughts stronger than her Valla powers?

She had done nothing but cry for years, or so it felt, and her eyes quickly became sore and swollen. She cried herself to sleep and woke with a start when Hefnir pulled the covers off her. He crashed down onto his knees and swore.

'Sh!' He put a finger to his lips.

His taper dripped fat onto her hand and she let it burn.

'Come, wife,' he said. Sickly mead breath. He tried to get up, chuckled, beckoned her and fell over.

It's all right. Get him on his feet.

Mad with relief at hearing her skern and practised from years of tending to her father in drink, Bera rescued the taper and tried to get Hefnir into bed. But he refused and began to tug her through the hall. Where to?

'Sh!' he said again, when a log fell on the fire.

They crossed to a sleeping platform farthest from the main door and paused at its hanging. A dark wooden chest and bench lost substance in the light of the driftwood fire whose flames flickered green and blue with salt.

'Mine,' said Hefnir. He put a hand on the chest.

Something nudged Bera's hand. It was the dog she had seen earlier. One friend.

'Rakki likes you.' Hefnir pulled aside the hanging.

The covers on the bed shifted and a child's face emerged. He had a shock of pale hair, like a pure light. It was the boy she had seen earlier.

'He's my dog,' he said, petulant.

Bera had an urge to shake him.

Hefnir smiled. 'Kiss your mother, Heggi. My son is your son, wife.'

'No!' They shouted together.

The boy disappeared under the covers.

'I wish it,' said Hefnir and took Bera's hand.

'Leave me alone!' She wrenched free and stamped back to the fire.

Behind her there were some stern words and crying, which stoked her own fury. When Hefnir came out she turned on him, a hurt child herself.

'Why pretend I have a choice? How would saying something out loud make any difference? You and Ottar have a bargain and I'm the add-on. What you Seabost men want you take with violence. That boy doesn't want it any more than I do but our Fate is sealed. I'm not swearing to anything.'

'Don't be frightened.'

'I am not frightened!'

Someone sniggered. 'She's scared all right.'

It was Scarface.

Bera's heart raced. 'I don't fear you.'

'Course you do.'

'Shut up, Thorvald,' said Hefnir and hiccupped.

'Why is he here?' Bera cried.

'I'm here because I'm more use to him than you'll ever be.'

'Thorvald, you ugly bastard, you're my second and that's all.' Hefnir hiccupped again. 'But my home is his home, wife.'

Thorvald kept his eyes on Bera. Having him live here would be a nightmare but would bring his death closer, so she would put up with it. And plan.

Hefnir was speaking to her. 'Heggi lost his mother only a short while ago and it is hard for him. You know how that is. I want you to be a new mother to him but it can wait. I can keep him out of your way, like I did today.'

Thorvald belched. 'Not that I'm meddling or anything but you've promised two fine redheads for that skinny bint from Crapsby there. If you get as far as the morning gift, that is. The Ser—'

'Careful, Thorvald. The mead's talking.' Hefnir's voice held a new threat.

'All right. I know we need boats but why is she involved?'

'She has Valla skills.'

'She has none.'

'Stop talking about me as if I were the house cow! Anyway, I don't have to answer to you, ever, the brave man who kills boys,' she spat.

'Poor little runt got more than he deserved. I didn't hear you warn him.'

Bera was dizzy with anger. She pulled out her knife and ran at him. Thorvald lazily held her off and chuckled while she lunged at him, her reach far too short.

'Stop it now, wife.' Hefnir grabbed her.

'Did you know he killed my friend? Am I part of the blood money you paid Ottar?'

'I know Thorvald got a narwhale horn that will keep us safe for a while. Won't it, Thorvald?'

'He's taken it, anyhow.' Thorvald shrugged. 'We'll see whose side he's on.'

Bera had no idea what they were talking about. 'Did Ottar take the tusk?'

'No. Someone who is none of your concern.'

She felt foolish standing there with both men ignoring the puny threat of her gutting knife, so she put it away.

'So am I part of the blood money?' She made her voice calm.

Hefnir assessed her. 'If you must know, weeks before your little hothead died, I had business with your father. Ottar wanted rid of you, that's all.'

So it was true. There could be no going home. Bera would have fallen to her knees except Thorvald was watching.

Hefnir pulled her close. 'Come on. Time we got down to business ourselves.'

Thorvald gave them a small salute and whistled his way off towards the men's quarters.

Don't worry, sweetheart. Revenge is a dish best eaten cold.

Her skern's riddle was no comfort. Her childhood was over.

Hefnir carried her back to his billet. 'You're like a bit of stockfish. Light but stiff.'

'I'm not used to being heaved about like a sack,' she snapped. His playfulness made her more tense, not less.

He put her down on the bed, nearly falling on top of her, and rolled aside to pull off his boots. 'Women like it a bit rough.'

Did they? His experience would make him choosy and Bera knew nothing. Nerves made her mouth too dry to respond. Would this hurt a lot?

'Thorvald's right! You are scared!'

'No, I'm not!'

Hefnir went out, taking the light with him. Had she failed already? Was he making a thrall do what his wife should? If she was a wife. There had been no proper vow-taking. But then he was back with a beaker. He drank some mead and kissed her, letting the strong, sweet liquid flow into her mouth. He made her drink and then kissed her again, mouth and breasts, and Bera was glad he was gentler. If only he would begin.

Bera knelt on the thick furs. Should she take off her own clothes? His? He wasn't doing much to help. Unused to mead, she fumbled with her new brooches and held the bundle of material near her eyes, trying to see the pin-catch.

Hefnir moved the taper closer and peered at her flushed face. 'Fancy that. This is your first time, isn't it?'

'That tallow stinks.'

He gave her a knowing look and snuffed the small flame with

thumb and finger. 'Suits me. You're more like a boy. Still, it's been a few weeks since...' He pulled down his trousers. The cloth brushed against her face.

'Should I...?'

He clamped his lips on hers. He was rough this time and Bera tasted the rust of blood. She pulled away, afraid again.

'I'll slow down,' he said, thickly, but couldn't.

Bera closed her eyes, desperate to have it over. Hefnir yanked her clothes up under her chin, which throttled her. Even in the dark, she hated being so shamed. He deftly nudged her legs apart with his knees and pushed. It was a shock and hurt with a particular strangeness. Hefnir began to thrust; his face a blank. There was no pleasure in it – she didn't think her body would thump about so much – but Bera was grateful that nature accommodated it, leaving her mind free. But not for long. Hefnir gave a slight sigh, fell off, smacked her nose with his arm and began to snore.

Bera wondered if he had been fully awake for any of it. She pulled down her clothes. She wanted to wash but had no idea where to go and no means of lighting the taper, even if she could find it. So she undressed down to her shift, pulled as many furs over her as she could reach and put up with the stickiness.

Was that all it was?

She was sore but also altered. As the indignity and disappointment waned, a dim pride warmed her. She hadn't wanted to grow up so fast but now Bera knew and was known; she was like every woman that had ever been born. There was unexpected comfort in being mortal and fully grown, smelling of the sea.

4

Bera could not get to sleep. Every time she dozed, Hefnir shifted and woke her again. No one had ever slept so close to her; perhaps her mother, but too long ago to remember. Time passed. There were sawing snores and the creaks and crackles of a longhouse she wasn't used to. Bera pulled a blanket up to her nose in an attempt to get warm. It didn't even smell like home. Her skern stroked the hair off her forehead and placed a sharp fingernail in the exact centre.

Watch and remember.

The vision was more real than the billet around her: a toddler with white-blond hair at the door of the longhouse peeping outside. She could taste his thoughts. He was excited but afraid. He fell back inside as a trole entered and towered over him, grinning with a toothless mouth.

Bera moaned, sharing the child's terror, and pushed away her skern's hand.

'No more!'

It's important. Watch and remember.

She let her skern continue.

The mood had changed. This was no trole but a human monster, hiding something behind his back: a wooden horse. He held it out to the child, who grinned and clapped his hands. It wobbled on its wheels when he sat on it and he fell over, laughing. The monster picked him up, with mottled black arms. Why did it not scare the child anymore? Then a surge of unreserved love when a woman came in and kissed them both. She was very beautiful. Her sky-blue cloak was held in place by two silver brooches.

'Was that Hefnir's son?'

The past, dearie. I can give it but never see it. But remember this in the future.

'I'll never sleep now!'

Bera tried to name the kind of love and failed; then wept for the lack of it in her own life.

Next morning Hefnir went out early, which suited Bera. She lay for a while, trying to recapture the dream the skern had shown her. Instead she became aware of wetness and wondered what was happening. Her shift was rusty. Blood. She rummaged in her wedding chest and found her monthly rags.

At first she feared he had damaged her but then she reckoned up the days and realised it was her normal courses slightly early. Not a mother after the first bout, luckily. Except she already was a mother of sorts and it made her angry. Was she to have no choice in life, ever? Folk said there were plants that Vallas used to keep themselves pure. Bera had taught herself how to make healing salves, so she determined to try out local plants and even if she fell with child, this would purge her of it. She would refuse to have anything to do with ... whatever Hefnir's son was called. Little swine. A worm of shame began in her stomach, as she was sure the child in the dream was him with his dead mother. Bera had never known a love like that so why should she pity him? He obviously hated her and she disliked their forced relationship as much as he did.

Jealousy will get you nowhere.

'I am not jealous.'

You should be kind to the motherless waif.

'Go away.'

You're afraid no one will ever love you like that.

She screwed her shift into a bundle and marched into the hall.

Thralls were busy. Bera asked a woman with a pail where she could wash her clothes. The woman frowned, took Bera's bloodstained shift and briskly gave it to another thrall. Then she led the way to the hot tub, every bone in her spine rebuking Bera for being a poor mistress.

She left before Bera could ask where the family latrine was, which she needed first. So she followed the stench.

It took her to a slurry pond beside a midden where some pigs were snuffling. It occurred to Bera that you could always smell other folk's heaps but never your own and she wondered if she would ever not notice this one.

A deep channel led up to a small rise between the longhouse and the home pasture, where she found the latrine. Bera reckoned it could hold ten at a sitting, to keep Hefnir safe from enemies. She wondered if torches would keep Drorghers away in dark winter days.

Inside, a few hens clucked in the dimness. It was a good roost. Bera sat on one of the long rails and her eyes adjusted. There were other folk in there, at the far end. The smallest had a shock of hair that was lit by a glimmer coming through a slat. Bera swore under her breath. The boy got up, hoisted his trousers and started towards her. The old woman with him tried to catch his arm but he ignored her.

He stopped some way away and gave her a level stare.

'Papa says I have to call you Mother from now on.' He looked as pleased at the idea as she was.

'I don't care if you do or if you don't.'

'Yes you do. You've wormed your way in.'

'I was snatched, you little runt. I'd rather die than be mother to you!'

'My real mother is dead and I hate you! I'll never call you Mother, ever, ever, ever!'

He stormed off, banging the door behind him, leaving Bera alone in a twilight full of hostile eyes. They built latrines big for group protection because a person alone in one was at their most defenceless. It gave her an idea. To be successful, though, first, she would need a better weapon – and to gain some standing in Seabost.

Respect in Seabost proved harder to win than at home. There, her father was the important figure thanks to his boat-building skills and her mother retained a high Valla reputation. Although Bera felt the weight of it, at least the inheritance gave her some standing. Here, as a new wife, and a second wife at that, Bera was like some small trinket Hefnir had slipped into a pocket.

It didn't help that no one properly feared the things they feared at home: Drorghers unheard of, troles and boggelmen things used to scare 'bairns' into better behaviour. Even skerns were only needed to get safely through to the Great Hall after death. So she couldn't protect them or impress with her bravery.

Plain healing was all she could do. Bera found some familiar plants, made salves and took them round to Hefnir's tenants, who couldn't refuse. Fate arranged a baby boy to be born and Bera eased the mother's pains with a brew. The boy thrived. The following week a child came to get Bera to help their mother. When they arrived at the hut, Bera was shocked to see so many scraps on the midden. Here, the rootling pigs grew fat on what kept folk from starving at home.

Inside, she could smell that the woman was not dying of hunger.

'We tried Dellingr,' her husband said, 'but he said she was beyond iron.'

'Your smith?' It put her in mind of her father's particular clenching of nails to save lives at sea. 'I can speed her passing, if you want.'

The man bit his knuckles and went outside.

Bera took the cooking pot from the fire and brewed a strong mash of sleeping herbs. Was it wrong to let the woman slip painlessly away? She could see the skern, drifting closer. It would be soon, whatever she did.

'Have some of this.' Bera held out a spoon.

'Pain,' she croaked. Her skern wreathed her head and smoothed her features.

'Your skern has come.'

'I feel him now.' She smiled and in that instant Bera saw the two become one.

There had been no need of her brew. She was careful to throw the mash onto the fire. It wouldn't do to kill anything.

The man was outside with a few neighbours, red-eyed but standing strong. Bera told him it had been a peaceful end and refused the coin he held in his big fist. But he explained it was his duty and opened his hand. No coin, but a shiny brown egg. Bera was moved and took it. It seemed a good custom.

She thanked him. 'I've heard about Dellingr before.'

'Our blacksmith? He's skilled in the old ways.'

Perhaps he would understand Valla ways. One person who might help.

A woman said, 'He does right by us. Don't charge if he can bundle the price up with Hefnir's sharpenings.'

A man nudged her.

'Only saying.'

'Where is the forge?' Bera asked.

The dead woman's husband looked worried. 'You'll not take it out on him, what that old biddy told you?'

The nudger did it harder. 'See? You should keep your mouth shut!'

Bera had to speak loudly. 'I'll thank him for his care.'

The husband agreed. 'He's been good since he were a lad.'

'His family all were,' said the biddy. 'All the men, leastways. Blacksmiths, handed down, father to son.'

Like mother to daughter. 'So he lives… ?'

'They've lived time out of mind up on the Rise, over by the crossroads.'

Bera was full of excitement. Meeting someone with some skill was good enough. But a kind blacksmith might have a knife she could buy.

A week or so passed before Bera's chance to visit Dellingr came. Every time she turned round, Thorvald was there. It maddened her. Then, one day, he and Hefnir were off on business. Bera quickly parcelled up some knives. A thrall tried to take them but she resisted and set off for the crossroads.

She had been told the forge was further on again, under the rune stone's protection and to keep the fire away from the other huts. It was a long walk from the jetties.

A dog appeared at her heels, snuffling at the parcel and grinning up at her.

'No food in here, Rakki,' she said. 'Is the brat with you?'

He was, but she refused to hurry and give him the impression she cared.

When they met, his words coiled up in frost-smoke. 'We're going puffin hunting.'

'It's the wrong time of year.'

'How would you know?' The boy held out his hand and Rakki went to him, gazing adoringly.

Bera felt a stab of jealousy. 'Dogs are supposed to be good judges of character.'

'Rakki is. He hates you. He was probably going to bite you.'

Bera marched off but he kept alongside. Why didn't he leave her alone?

'Where are you going?' he demanded.

'Wherever you're not.'

'Does my father know?'

'It's not his business.'

'He owns you.'

She swung round and slapped him on the cheek. It left red finger-marks and he was suddenly a young, motherless child again and Bera was ashamed.

'Heggi... I...'

He ran off, Rakki bounding beside him, barking. How dare he go before she could apologise? Good riddance. Let him fall off a cliff, as long as the dog was all right.

Bera felt shock at the creature she was becoming. Well, folk here were cruel. She blamed it all on Seabost. She started to pull off her blue cloak, then changed her mind. A little brutality would give her the courage to kill. She put on a grim face and made for a line of smoke rising straight up into the pale sky until it smudged and vanished. The forge.

A leather-aproned shape blocked the dark doorway.

'Never thought to see you up here,' said the smith. 'Is it urgent?' His voice was calm, low and husky with smoke. Bera wanted to get him outside and see what such a man would look like.

'It will wait till you're ready.'

He ducked under the lintel and came out to a nearby block of granite. It was the man who had smiled at her at the wedding feast.

Seeing him again, Bera understood her impatience to get to the forge. He placed the field tools he carried on a large stone, took one and placed it in a groove, ready to hone its edge.

Bera brushed the rime off a tree stump and sat. She watched him work, liking the dexterity of his black and scarred hands as he sharpened each tool. Strong, capable hands, the sort you could trust. The stone had a line of carved runes, blacksmith words, she supposed. She did not want to break Dellingr's intent silence and liked the fact he didn't worry at her like the folk at home. His untroubled strength made her long to tell him about her loneliness but she had no right to receive his comfort. He would also think it was madness, when she lived amongst so many. She found she wanted his good opinion, like a father. Not like Ottar, but a good father that was proud of her. Although he looked much younger than her father, or even Hefnir.

When he finished the job he turned. His eyes were keen as a sea eagle's, and they made her feel properly looked at for the first time ever. It wasn't entirely pleasant and she squirmed. Had he seen deep inside the desire for revenge? Would he understand a blood debt? Certainly – but he would also say it was a man's duty.

'Must be important, you coming.'

'What?'

Dellingr gestured at the bundle. Bera got up and gave it to him.

He took out a knife and rubbed his thumb over its blade. 'Won't take long. You want to wait inside?'

She shook her head. 'I'm warm enough.'

He began grinding.

While he worked, Bera struggled to find the right words.

In the end, she blurted it. 'Have you got a sword I could buy?'

He gave her another uncomfortable look. 'Did Hefnir not give you his father's sword at the marriage?'

'You were there. Did you see him do it?' Her nervousness made it sharper than she meant.

Dellingr rasped his face with his hand. There was a long crease in his cheek that would have been hidden by a full beard. It made him look strong.

'I suppose Heggi's got the one he gave... before.'

'Hefnir's first wife. What happened to her?' she asked.

A lad darted out of the forge and picked up the field tools. A bellows-boy. He might have been young but his thin face, dried out and blackened by heat, was old. Rough sacking made do as a tunic, torn and stippled with singe marks. He set off down the slope.

Dellingr called after him. 'Make sure he pays you today.'

'I heard you charge Hefnir.'

'This one takes advantage of that.'

'I wasn't complaining, anyway.'

He spoke slowly, weighing his words. 'I do have a sword but it was given to me by Hefnir in payment. It wouldn't be right to give it to any woman, let alone his wife. If you're saying he wants it for you...'

'No, he—'

No one must know she had a sword, so she wouldn't be suspected of killing Thorvald. Except Dellingr, of course. Could she trust him to say nothing? Not yet.

'Tell him to ask me himself.'

She smiled. 'You're right. I'll speak to Hefnir. Are they finished?'

Dellingr returned to the knives. He polished the blades, wrapped them into their cloth and handed the bundle to her. His eyes were the exact colour of the sea that morning.

'Sea-riders did it, on a raid. Right in front of Hefnir. He was overpowered. He told us they made him watch while they butchered his wife, then carted off her body.'

Bera gasped.

'I thought maybe you'd heard different,' he said. 'And now you've got Heggi—'

'No. Thank you.'

She shoved some coins into Dellingr's hands and set off blindly, making for the post marking the crossroads through a veil of hot blood and smoke. Then a face, Hefnir's, showing... rage? Or what? Her skern's visions unfolded like a dream, but this was sudden, like an animal's night-kill in a bolt of lightning. Although the half-vision puzzled her, Bera was glad that Dellingr might have brought it about.

Poor Heggi. She vowed to keep her temper, no matter how much the child provoked her. And perhaps grief could bind Hefnir and her together?

Before she reached the crossroads she heard hoof beats. It was Hefnir and Thorvald, coming from the direction of the forest. They were racing their horses, laughing and yelling. It shocked her that the man she pitied seemed unaffected by his loss. It must be Thorvald's fault. Bera directed a flash of anger to make him fall off his horse but nothing happened.

The men stopped smiling when they noticed her. Hefnir reined in his horse and trotted over. Bera remembered what she was carrying and threw down the incriminating bundle of knives as if it burned her.

'Have you come from the smithy, wife?'

'My name is Bera.'

Thorvald sniggered and wiped away the drool from his misshapen mouth.

Hefnir stroked his horse's mane. 'Why did you not send a thrall?'

'She's after our handsome Dellingr,' Thorvald said.

'You want the smith for yourself, then?' she jibed.

Thorvald was straight off his horse and had her by the throat. As fast as slicing a boy open. Bera couldn't breathe and made raspy, gurgling noises. Red specks danced in front of her eyes. She found her knife and jabbed it hard into his side. His jerkin was too thick, breaking her blade off well before it reached his flesh.

'Walrus hide.' Thorvald loosened his grip and she fell to her knees, spluttering, gasping for air.

Hefnir hauled her up and onto his horse, keeping a hand on her leg to keep her still.

'Your wife needs some manners, Hefnir. She shouldn't be disrespectful to Dellingr. And why was she there? She should be running your household.'

'I understand the trouble between you two,' Hefnir said. 'But I have more than paid the blood debt, Bera. I have ordered two boats from your father – and taken you as my wife. Remember that. Thorvald, take that bundle home.'

'I'm not part of any blood debt!' Bera kicked away Hefnir's hand.

He got up into the saddle, swung the horse round and headed up the slope, forcing Bera to cling on to him.

'Are we not going home?' she asked.

Hefnir could somehow render a question to nothing.

It was the first time Bera had ridden a horse and she tried to enjoy it. But the worry that there would be trouble when they reached the forge robbed her of any pleasure. They carried on, still climbing. Seabirds screamed and the air tasted saltier. Wind whipped her hair out of its braids and she shut her eyes, feeling the sway and dip of the motion as if she were sailing. She wished she could be alone on the horse, to understand its shifts in her bones and blood, as she did on a boat.

They stopped.

A rune stone thrust upwards at black clouds scudding in from the west, tall enough to shred them. It was set at the very top of the cliff that looked out over the Ice-Rimmed Sea, itself as grey as granite. A long shadow picked its way over wind-wizened scrub towards them, like the hand of Fate.

Hefnir dismounted and lifted her down. 'Light as a snowflake.'

'I was a stockfish the other day.'

'Well.' He kissed her. 'That was before I tasted you.'

He led her over to the stone. 'Can you read the runes?'

Bera left him and ran her fingers over the lines, following them round the broad base until she found her skern leaning against the seaward side. He was tapping the stone with a long fingernail.

'Where have you been?' she demanded.

And I'm pleased to see you, too.

'Anyway, I saw the past, thanks to the smith. You can't.'

I can show you it.

'Well, you didn't this time.'

He drew his nail down the stone until she winced at the sound and held up her hand as apology.

Look at this word. Study the runes and remember them.

There were three, reading ALU.

'Why remember them?'

I haven't the least idea. It was carved well before our time, dearie, so I can't tell you any more. You just said I don't do history.

'This is the future, so help.'

He pursed his lips to seem thoughtful.

Hefnir called from the other side. 'Are you ever coming back?'

'Quickly,' Bera hissed.

The skern frowned. *It's to do with spinning, I think.*

'Wool? You've come to tell me which runes to knit?'

Hefnir appeared. Her skern gave him a small wave, as you might to a child.

'What are you doing round here?' Hefnir marched over to her.

'Talking to my skern.'

'Where is it?' Hefnir looked the wrong way.

'These runes, look. ALU. It's important.'

'Ale.'

'No, he says—'

Hefnir stopped her with another kiss.

'Tell me why you brought me here,' Bera said.

He started burrowing under her skirts but it would be even worse to be taken here like a fishwife. Besides, she did not yet have the herbs to stop a baby coming.

'Let go, Hefnir.'

'Only if you do your duty afterwards.' He assumed consent. 'This is a touchstone, to make fast our bond. Come on, we join hands against it.'

It gave Bera an idea. 'You think us superstitious fools but our way is that you should present me with your father's sword.'

'The same with us, to give to our son... but that's not possible.'

'Tell me why!' She wanted to shatter his granite composure.

'You've spoiled my mood. I thought you'd like to feel more bonded. Most women do.'

'How many women have you taken as wife?'

Bera squared up to him as best she could. He reached over her head to take his horse's reins, led the horse round and swung himself up into the saddle.

'Are you coming or shall I leave you to walk home?'

'I hate you!'

She picked up a large stone and threw it at him. Temper spoiled her aim and it missed his head, smashing into a rocky outcrop beyond. The crack startled Hefnir's horse. It jittered and shied, threw its rider and cantered off down the hill.

Bera refused to feel guilty.

Hefnir got to his feet and brushed himself down. 'You could have killed me.'

They stared at each other.

Then Hefnir began a slow smile that made her glow; like a flame being lit. He tucked her under his arm and carried her down to his waiting horse. To her frustration, he threw her up into the saddle and they set off.

Her feelings were confused. Riling him about other women had started a flicker of jealousy and then, despite herself, desire. Was that love? Even when their bodies were joined, Hefnir's face was blank. Was he thinking about his first wife? Bera ought to pity her but couldn't. She wanted to matter to him and stared at his back, this stranger, her husband, willing him to speak, all the way home.

At the stable, a man came to take the reins and said something to Hefnir, who left the thrall to help Bera down. She jumped instead, even though it was a long way, and tried not to limp as she caught up with this supposed husband who was an unfeeling lump of... any horrible thing. She pounded his unflinching back with her small fist.

'I'm not staying here to be ignored. I'll take a boat and go home. I will!'

She froze. A strong, stocky figure came into view, pulling a heavy cart.

Her father.

Ottar had come by land, which had taken days. He had not come to take Bera home. The cart was piled with his boat tools, bedrolls, furs, cooking pots and ale barrels. A goat was tethered to it. In the middle of his belongings was a nest in which Sigrid lay, deathly still.

Bera was stricken. 'Red-spot?'

'She got worse on the way,' said Ottar. He leaned against the cart, pouring water over his face and throat. 'If she'd been this bad at home I might've got her on a boat.'

'Only if she was dead,' Bera said.

Hefnir grunted. 'Pity. Then we'd have another boat in exchange for your lodging.'

Bera studied Ottar's weathered face for any softness; to see if he was pleased to be back with his kin. There was only the same unrelenting control. She only felt sadness when she should have been furious with him for selling her.

'Why have you come, then?'

Ottar flicked a thumb at Sigrid. 'Look at her. I lost my workers to red-spot and all. Your old fool Blind Agnar's dead.'

'And his old dog?'

'Falki twisted its neck.'

Sadness upon sadness, stacked upon the loss of Bjorn. That day came clear to her mind; her skern saying there were conditions in taking a tusk and the narwhale's runes of death. She had misread it all then but was she still doing so? Sigrid was as green as seasickness and her eyes dark pits. Was she going to die? Bera held her necklace, tight.

Ottar spat. 'This 'un might live if Bera tends her.' He jabbed Hefnir's chest. 'Not like that pair of sickly redheads you gave me. There was no flesh on them.' He held up his little finger. 'Dropped dead soon as look at them.'

'Sigrid can't come into the longhouse,' Bera said.

Hefnir agreed. 'There is a sick house up by the smithy.' He his fingers for the thrall. 'This man will show you the way, Ottar.'

A vein swelled in Ottar's temple. 'My duty was bringing her. It's her turn now.' He cocked a thumb at Bera. 'I had the sickness ages since. Nothing'll kill me, I reckon. But I'm not doing woman's work.'

Bera pulled a blanket over Sigrid's shoulders. 'She feels the cold. I'll mash a healing brew and stay with her.' Even a sick Sigrid would be a comfort.

'No.' Hefnir moved her away from the cart. 'Make your potions, wife, but a thrall will take them and stay. Your place is at your own hearth.'

Ottar took off his cap and scratched his head. 'You two wed then?' He sounded surprised.

What had Ottar expected? That she would be Hefnir's slave? Or worse?

'My son needs a mother.'

She was furious. 'That was the deal, Father. Remember?'

'Aye, well, I'm glad you got on with it.'

Hefnir ordered some thralls to take Ottar's stuff off the cart and then set off with its sick passenger. Bera slipped the goat some bread as they left.

Hefnir led the way to the longhouse, his long strides leaving Bera and her father behind. Bera was too angry to speak.

Ottar finally broke the silence. 'Them two red-haired slave girls. Didn't last more'n two days before the sickness got 'em.'

'Am I supposed to feel sorry?'

'He tell you where they came from?'

She shook her head.

'Queer that. Hefnir goes and weds a scrawny brat like you cos sea-riders took the Seabost women. But I got them girls.'

'Well, they're dead now.'

Along with so many others. Bera began reckoning the losses back home.

'Hefnir mention a serpent thing at all?' Ottar asked.

Home, empty of folk. 'Who's left to burn the dead?'

'No one.' He dropped his voice. 'That's the other reason we came, to escape them Drorghers. That's all that's left now.'

Bera shivered. She had a vision of black, swollen corpses swarming through the deserted village. Would they stay there? Or would they seek out company? Perhaps rich Seabost was coming to their time of Drorghers. And through her fear came a rush of savage pride. If they came then perhaps Hefnir and his people would thank her for protecting them.

She spread her arms before the huge whalebone gates to the longhouse.

'Here's where we live.'

She enjoyed her father's look of awe and then the fact that he cringed as the ancestors pressed him when she deliberately delayed opening the inner door. They were hissing the usual words over and over.

He covered his ears. 'What they saying?'

She had no idea. 'That they hate you.'

That evening, Bera remembered her vow to be kinder to Heggi, so was furious when a bond formed in an instant between the boy and Ottar. Heggi laughed at his jokes and kept close to him all through the meal, like a clingworm. Hefnir and Thorvald were free with the ale but Ottar drank less than Bera expected. She was ignored by all of them and ate her food messily out of spite.

Afterwards, Ottar made a 'horse' with a few quick axe strokes. It was somehow manly and Heggi proudly rode it round the longhouse, with Rakki barking and thralls yelping as he charged at them. Hefnir wildly urged him on and the noise made Bera want to scream. Heggi finished by rearing up at his father, unsheathing an imaginary sword and plunging it into Hefnir's chest. His father promptly clutched his heart and fell to the floor, wailing. Heggi jumped onto his chest and tickled him.

Like she had done to Bjorn, that last morning.

Hefnir called for help. 'You're supposed to defend me, Thorvald!'

'So I will.'

He grabbed Heggi and bear hugged him till he screamed. Bera could stand it no longer and barged her way past them and out through the byre.

She may as well go up to the latrine. She felt excluded, unappreciated and unloved. Never had been loved.

Then the instinctive fear of being in the open kicked in. Were Drorghers really unknown in Seabost? Perhaps they were rich enough to always burn their dead. Or were they lying to hide their weakness or ignorance from her?

The full moonlight and line of fires kept her path free of them, but she sensed some movement in the shadows so she whistled a tune of protection as she climbed the slope, in case it wasn't a thrall. When she looked back, nothing stirred. And once inside, the purling of the hens in the quiet dark soothed her still more. Until she saw her skern, roosting amongst them.

'This is the place where Thorvald will suffer.'

You're thinking pinworms or skitters?

'I'm thinking death.'

Found the tusk, then?

'What has the tusk got—'

He whistled to ease her bladder but wouldn't speak again.

Things were calm when she returned. Bera got a thrall to place new branches on the fire and then she threw on some herbs to ward off sickness. For a while they all sat gazing at the flames through a scented haze and then Hefnir spoke.

'Do you have the sword safe, Heggi?'

'It's with all Mama's things.' The boy studied Bera with narrowed eyes. 'It's special. Mama gave it to me for when I have a son.'

Logs crackled.

A spasm twitched Bera's eyebrow. 'That's the custom.' She kept her voice reasonable, too proud to let her father know how much Heggi hated her. 'It was your father's and his father's before him. The sword belongs to you now. You keep it.'

Heggi did not wait to listen. He galloped off down the longhouse, leaving behind humiliation; as if he had slapped her, when she was making an effort to be fair. She pressed her brow to make the spasm stop.

'I'm an axe man, myself,' said Ottar.

Hefnir filled his horn with ale. 'But you want the proper bride day with a sword.'

Bera resented being left out again. 'You said that wasn't possible earlier.'

'Your father had not arrived then.'

Heggi galloped back to the hearth and pointed at Thorvald. 'Use his sword. His is special. Use that.'

Ripping upwards. Bera couldn't breathe. She wanted to take Thorvald's sword and drive it through his murdering ribs.

Ottar went and put his arm round the boy.

'See, his wouldn't work, lad. By right, Hefnir should dig up the sword from his forefathers' grave on his wedding night. He'd present it to his wife next day, to keep safe for their firstborn son.'

'I know. Papa did. That's why I've got it.'

'This being his second marriage, your Pa's got a problem.'

'I can bury your sword again,' said Hefnir.

Heggi wailed. 'It was Mama's sword and now it's mine. She's not going to have it. I hate her!'

'I don't want anything of hers,' Bera spat. She wrenched off her silver brooch, with the grooming kit that was touched by death, and threw them into the fire.

'I hate you!' Heggi cried.

He flung himself at her and they tussled. Bera's ring scratched his cheek and he bit her. Bera cuffed him. Hefnir strode across and pulled his son away like a burr from wool.

'You've made only enemies since you arrived. The bargain was all on your side, Ottar.'

Thorvald gave a long belch. 'Well, this enemy could do with more ale.'

'That's a lie!' shouted Bera. 'I could strike you all down! I am a Valla, like my mother!'

Ottar scraped the silver brooch away from the embers with a work-hardened hand. 'Stop your tantrums, girl, and get to bed. She wants taming, Hefnir.'

'I like a bint with spirit, don't I, Thorvald?'

All the men laughed.

Bera willed her skern to burn them to ash, knowing he couldn't, so she retreated, wishing she had anywhere to go but Hefnir's billet.

This is where trying to be kind got her. Bera lay in the dark, made crosser by the fact that no one followed her. Hefnir was saying something about debt. Then the high voice of an angry child, footsteps, a slap and cries of fear. A heavy door banged shut and it went quiet. Heggi must have been taken off somewhere. It didn't make her feel better. She would never sleep peacefully in this house as long as she lived. So she had better deal with Thorvald soon.

Her bride day arrived with a sea gale and driving rain. Bera was startled by a thrall with a bowl of buttermilk and a hunk of bread, well before the day meal. Hefnir's side of the bedroll was untouched. She snuggled back under the covers and listened to the hammering rain on the roof. It was so loud that she missed footsteps approaching.

It was Heggi, his face red and swollen.

Bera waited.

He kicked the spruce on the floor and then gazed up at the shutter, closed against the wind and rain. 'I have to say sorry,' he mumbled.

'Go on then.' Something in her did not want to make this easy.

'I just did.'

'What are you sorry for?'

He looked down at the floor, as if the answer was there. When he looked up, his eyes were cold. 'Nothing. I meant what I said and you know it.'

Bera sprang out of bed and swung him round to face her. 'Listen, you little scab. I don't want to be here. I'd leave in a heartbeat if I could but I'm stuck with it. Hate me all you like but don't you dare show me up in public again. Do you understand? I won't be your mother, it would make me sick. So we'll ignore each other. Now go away.'

She saw fresh tears on his face before he ran off and felt bad until she heard slow clapping behind her.

Her skern was sitting on her bed. *Priceless. You're so caring.*

'Leave me alone.'

I'm not so biddable as the youngster. Poor, motherless wee lamb.

'I'm motherless too.'

Quite. You of all people should understand how he feels. There he is, in his full grief, and yet you're nasty.

Bera threw the bowl of buttermilk at him. It trickled down the wall and soaked her blanket.

Dearie me. I came to warn you about something but it's gone right out of my head now, with all this unpleasantness.

Bera sat down next to him. She needed comfort and leaned her head against his chest. She fell onto her bed through nothingness and wept, alone.

The rain stopped before her visit to the bath hut. This time two women came with her: the silent one and an older thrall, who went off somewhere as soon as they got there. Bera soaked in the hot tub for a while, before being soaped and rubbed by the woman. It felt less strange.

'This is fine soap. Do you make it here?'

The woman's beautiful slanted eyes were expressionless.

It would be wrong to confide in a slave and lose authority but how Bera ached for a friend. It made her regret the times she had gone out fishing alone and not let Bjorn come with her. Wasted, like his life. But soon Thorvald would pay the blood debt; she was about to be presented with the sword to do it.

When she was ready, Bera was taken to a smaller hut. It was stiflingly hot inside. The older woman was in there, heating stones. She dipped a wooden ladle into a tub of water and sprinkled them with large drops. Steam rose and wrapped Bera in a blanket of damp heat. It was wonderful. The woman gestured at a long pine bench. Bera sat down and was given a bundle of thin birch twigs. Was she supposed to brush the floor? The thrall mimed switching herself, like a horse gets rid of flies. Bera tried it and found it made her sweat. She beat her feelings away. Guilt, fear, remorse, betrayal, all vanished in an ecstasy of scratching.

Afterwards, the woman led her to another wooden tub and she plunged into cold water. When her explosion of shivers relaxed, Bera saw that the rinse water had herbs and flowers strewn on the surface and there was a sweet scent of oils.

'For good night.' The older thrall winked.

The silent one mimed a swollen belly. Both women thought it was all mighty funny and Bera was reminded that she was merely a house cow, bought to breed. She couldn't run away. Her home village was teeming with Drorghers.

As she took her place at Hefnir's side, Bera was miserable. For a start, no villagers were there to witness it. Hefnir said it had all been settled the night she arrived, but was it true? Back home it was often the way that a man would sample his bride before the ceremony but this felt secret and wrong. She longed for Sigrid but she was surrounded by men she loathed and no kinswoman. Ottar ignored her and played with Heggi; Thorvald had a permanent smirk and kept making coarse jokes with Hefnir. She let herself imagine it was Dellingr beside her. The thought of him gave her strength.

A fine thing, thinking about the smith when you're stood next to your husband.

'It's his fault! He keeps joking with Bjorn's killer.'

Her skern settled round her neck with a shuddering sigh.

Bera concentrated on the fact that she would own a sword at the end of this sham.

It began as it did at home, with the man making a show of cleaning the sword. Hefnir then held the hilt towards her.

Bera lay a hand on it and lied. 'I take you as my husband,' she said, 'and swear that I shall give you children that shall be your own.'

Best not mention the poultice then.

'And I swear to protect and shelter you and all your kin,' Hefnir prompted.

Bera repeated his words then quickly took her hand off the sword.

'Wait,' Hefnir said. 'There's one more oath.'

'No, there isn't.'

'Swear that you will take Heggi as your own son. That he remains my firstborn and so shall take back the sword of my forefathers.'

That's a new one. What are you going to do now?

Bera's brain whirled.

'Get on with it,' said Ottar. 'My tongue's hanging out for a drink here. And if you're like your mother you'll only get daughters, or some misshapen brat—'

Hefnir insisted. 'It's an honest trade. I take you, your father and Sigrid under my protection. Remember, they're all dead in Crapsby.'

'Seabost has already sworn me as your wife, Hefnir, and I have done my duty for weeks. I need the sword for my own child.'

Heggi flung his carved horse to the floor. 'No! It's my sword! It's not fair! You promised, Papa. If I said sorry then I would have it back. She's not my mother and no one can make me.'

Hefnir gestured to Thorvald. 'Take him to his place.'

Thorvald lifted Heggi and the boy screamed frenziedly all the way through the byre.

'Give it back, girl,' said Ottar. 'It was never yours to keep.'

'All I ask is a small kindness, Bera,' said Hefnir. His voice was soft, like he might use on a spooked horse, and he looked baffled at why she would refuse; hurt, even.

She was young and lonely. Despite everything, Bera yearned for her new husband to smile at her and offer warmth and companionship. She was tired of being alone in warding off danger.

'Then I take Heggi as our firstborn son.'

And then Ottar shook Hefnir's hand.

Bera had sworn away any child's rights – and failed to keep the sword.

5

A few days later, Hefnir took Thorvald off trading to keep them apart. Sigrid was well enough to tell her so.

Bera was furious. 'My potions have kept you alive! The least you could do is show some gratitude and not gossip about me with whoever drops by the sick house.'

But Sigrid was too ill to argue.

Bera left her to doze. It was clear she needed to kill Thorvald before the poor woman came to join them in the longhouse and live beside her son's killer.

Hefnir stayed away, sending back furs and goods. After a while, Bera liked coping without being watched and the burden of taking revenge lifted. The thralls quickly became unthreatening tools, like boat parts. They did the heavy labour, leaving Bera free to tend the animals, which she loved. The livestock were good but dogs better, especially Rakki. His uncomplicated joy was so different from his boy's.

Heggi spent time at the boatyard with Ottar, who offered to teach him boat-building skills. One day, Bera took out a small workboat. She didn't tell her father that Hefnir had forbidden it. He was too busy fussing round the brat to notice, anyway.

Out on the water she felt closer to Bjorn and began their song.

> 'In the bones, in the bones,
> Feel the east wind in the rigging
> And the boat-song in your bones.'

Her throat closed over the last words. There was no Bjorn to sing the second verse. Tears burned her wind-chilled cheeks and she turned back. Thorvald had poisoned her sailing, as he had everything else.

Then one of the thralls got sick. It wasn't red-spot but still bad. Bera made a quick healing stick while she tried out brews of different local plants. A rat took one of the mashes and it never reached its nest; it died writhing with pain. Bera pitied it but noted what she had used. It might be useful to kill vermin.

Vermin like Thorvald.

'I'm busy healing, you might notice.'

He raised a finger. *Dishonour follows he who uses venom.*

'You just made that up!'

Your father's the one for sayings.

'Then how about "death cancels all debt"? That's one of his.'

Despite her skern, Bera concocted a useful remedy, which saved the thrall. She hoped it would impress Hefnir. And then she could not stop herself wondering if poisoning Thorvald would impress her father, who had loved Bjorn more than he loved her.

Sigrid finished her recovery in the longhouse. Sickness and bereavement had taken a heavy toll and she was different: listless and forlorn. She did not even seem grateful that Bera's potions had saved her. She sat at the loom but there was no happy chatter or sharing of confidences. Bera did not tell her who would be returning with Hefnir, under his protection and under the same roof. How could she load her with such knowledge? Bera wanted to protect her from more pain. It was her own fault so she would deal with Thorvald alone.

She devised a heavy hanging for the door and wove it with Sigrid. It made getting into the hall slower and panic-inducing but Bera had spoken words at the making of it so that it muffled the ancestors. It was also an extra barrier between her household and the malign forces that swept through the village in the darkness – whether folk believed it or not. Sigrid said it kept out the draught.

By chance, Bera found another role in Seabost. She came upon a fight to the death. They said it was their way to settle disputes. Bera persuaded them that an outsider and Valla had no favourites, so could judge fairly. They wanted to lose no more men, so let her try. It was the stealing of a midden pig, which she quickly resolved by saying the pig should be slaughtered and parcelled round all the neighbours. Bera was proud, until Sigrid said one day she might be as good a judge as her mother. Bera wanted her own special skill.

While Thorvald was out of the way, Bera tried other weapons she might use on him. She took a knot-spike from Ottar's workshop but he missed it at once since all his tools were either hanging in orderly rows or on his tool belt. She daren't risk taking it again. Everywhere she went in the boatyard, Heggi's eyes bored into her, as if he knew what she was about. So, in desperation, she decided to get her small knife fixed. It meant visiting Dellingr again. She did not scrutinise why the idea pleased her so much.

She went out so early that the low, bright sun made the frosted earth look bruised. A thin veil of mist trailed on the surface of the fjord. Boats swayed sluggishly against the wooden jetties, their sails hanging limp. Fishermen were getting ready to leave. The baker, who never went to bed, was turning out the first loaves and the smell of hot yeast made her stomach rumble.

At the crossroads, Bera took the path to the forge but then on impulse she made for the huge rune stone. It was steeper this way so she stopped to catch her breath before pressing on. Pain griped and she grasped the coarse tussock grass to help her. When she reached the level summit she stood panting. She straightened up and looked at the stone. Although the weather side was blasted by storm-force winds, the carvings facing her were etched with lichen. The earliest memory Bera had was of her mother showing her some runes. She wished she could picture the whole of her face.

'Are you there, Mama?' Her words were smoke in the still air.

Her skern was close, somewhere. A bad pain this time, like an iron claw rasping her stomach. She slid down against the rune stone and held tight to her necklace. Her skern was around her in an instant. Was she going to die like her mother? Was this how it felt?

It's only your courses.

'I know. But bad up here – and you're shrouding me.'

Remember that warning?

'No.'

You keep putting it out of my mind. Let's get warm. I can't think when I'm cold.

The two lay enfolded. The tightness comforted Bera. Was it why babies were swaddled when they parted from their skerns at birth? They must have shared a heartbeat in the womb but it was pointless to ask; her skern knew nothing of the past, just as she knew nothing of the future. Was this what death was like? Bera and her skern, together for eternity. Not having to face Thorvald. A languor soaked into her bones and she welcomed it. Falling asleep... not having to be afraid.

Not yet, sweetheart.

'I'm so lonely.'

Her skern's sad smile lingered and the ache of his unclasping was worse than ever. Bera stood up and stamped about, waving her arms to warm herself. The blood debt must be paid. Her duty was to see Dellingr to bring that closer.

The forge was empty. A bitter blow, and Bera was close to tears. The boy came round from the back and was startled, his eyes huge in his black face.

'Is Dellingr here?'

The boy shook his head violently and ran inside. She heard the bellows whumping. There was nothing for it but to go home. She dawdled to the crossroads but the smith did not appear.

Bera collected some loaves from the baker and her spirits lifted when he touched his forelock to her. Respect. She whistled on the way home. Dellingr was still in the world and there was time to prepare before Thorvald returned.

She turned into the last twitten and saw blood.

It did not shift her mood at first: it could have come from a chicken killed for the pot. She marvelled at the vivid red on the grey planks of the walkway until its saturation began to sear her brain. When she shut her eyes the splashes were still there, yellow against purple. The skern had forgotten his warning. Was it this?

Bera hurried on. The drips kept with her, punctuating her way. She began to panic. She slipped and tripped, terrified they were all dead. Sigrid! The shame of failing to protect them was too dreadful to think about.

Outside the door was a spray of scarlet, as if a vein had been opened right there.

She fumbled with the thick outer latch but then it was open and she burst in, tripping on the sill. Very bad luck. She stumbled through the dark passage and could not find the inner latch. The spirits screamed.

'Perfidy! Violation!'

The door crashed open. Two bodies lay sprawled across the hearth. One was Rakki, so the other must be Heggi. She had forgotten about him.

'Not him, Mama, please.'

Bera pictured blond hair matted with blood. She rushed over, dreading what she would find. The boy and his dog were sleeping, close as puppies.

Rakki opened one eye but did not stir.

'Good dog,' she whispered and stroked his head.

All was safe and calm. The blood must be a butchered animal. A thrall came in from her quarters. Bera was going to ask her but it was the mute bath hut woman. She hurried over with house shoes, put them down and Bera slipped off her boots and stepped into them. The woman helped her off with her cloak and Bera told her to mend the boots.

The woman's silence rattled her.

'Where is everyone?' Bera demanded.

The thrall lowered her head at her sharpness.

Bera found something to be cross about. 'The fire is low. Get a man to fetch the logs and bring fresh spruce.'

The woman bowed lower, so a wing of black hair hid her face entirely, then backed away.

She needed company. Was Sigrid outside? She was weak as a runt and certain to get sick again.

Heggi slept on, so Bera started clanging pans around the fire. At last his eyes unstuck; he buried his fingers in the thick fur around the dog's neck and kissed him.

Then he noticed Bera. 'I'm hungry.'

'When are you not? Leave that dog alone and come and have your day meal.'

'Is there any honey?'

'There's barley porridge.'

'Which needs honey.'

'Get up and get dressed quickly. And put your bedroll back where it belongs.'

'Papa sent some honeycomb from the Marsh Lands.'

'Then why ask?'

The boy sullenly pulled his thick woollen tunic over the clothes he had slept in.

'It's four more days till wash day,' she said. 'You'll smell even worse if you sleep in them.'

Heggi placed his shoulder against hers. 'I'm going to be much taller than you!'

'I'm not your mother.' She regretted saying it at once. 'I meant... It sounded like you might take after me.'

'It's easy to be taller than a dwarf.'

Rakki rushed over to the door of the store and snorted loudly at the gap at the foot. Then he began scratching furiously at the wood.

Heggi ran over to him. 'What is it, boy?'

The blood was no butchery.

'Get your dog away,' she said.

'No, I'll go in with him and see what it is.' Heggi's hand was on the latch.

'I'm telling you to stay here!'

Bera softly opened the door, peeped inside. The rusty smell of blood. It was dripping from the neck of a large reindeer that was hanging from a roof beam.

Something else, a slither of darkness, stirred.

She slammed the door shut, fast.

Heggi struggled to hold Rakki, who was stiff with rage, teeth bared and hackles bristling. His low continuous growl was more vibration than sound.

'What is it?' Heggi asked.

'Run to the boatyard,' said Bera. 'Tell Ottar to get back here quickly. But you stay there.'

'Why?'

'For once, just do as I say, will you!'

The boy glared at her, then dragged his rigid dog to the door. It slammed behind them, which brought a thrall running, his arms full of spruce.

'I have to deal with... something,' Bera said. 'Would you go and find Sigrid and get her back here as fast as possible?'

The man threw down the boughs and left.

Bera ran and took a knife from the pantry, longer than her gutting knife, though blunter. She slid it into her belt. The glimpse of the horror inside the store was enough to convince her she needed any weapon, as well as Valla words she wasn't sure of. She took some deep breaths and went in.

She faced a boggelman come to life, as tall as the beams. The saffron-yellow beard on his blue-black face shone like an inverted flame. He wore reindeer-skin trousers, above which his naked torso writhed with twisted snakes. Every small piece of visible skin, from stomach to neck and all along his arms, was alive with black-scaled vipers, including his face.

He stretched up his arms and swung from the crossbeams. Each armpit had a huge, slit snake eye that winked when he pulled himself up. It smelt like a snake pit, too. This was a performance. He opened his mouth to reveal four rows of teeth, then pushed a notched tongue between them and waggled it at her, fast. Bera gasped but then composed herself and fought to stop her knees trembling. It made him laugh. A lot.

'My father is at home,' she said. It was a child's lie.

'He is not. I see him go, early.' He had an accent she could not place and his forked tongue made him lisp. 'You go early, too.'

'Oh?'

'I see you at smithy. I wait for you.'

'Oh.' A muscle flickered above her mouth.

The man slapped the hanging carcass without taking his

unblinking, cold snake eyes off her. 'I bring you reindeer.'

'Thank you.' She tried to make it sound normal, as if politeness could make it so.

He grinned. She could see now that he had grooves cut across the teeth, stained green and black, making it look like four rows. He gave her the armpit flash again. It was revolting – and the fear of what may come was making it hard to breathe.

'You like my tattoos, yes? I know this. All women like.'

He turned his back, to show her the full effect. Bera went for her knife but he was taking no chances and quickly faced her again.

'What are tattoos? Do they hurt?' she asked, delaying.

'Hurt? Of course. We cut the skin, rub in ash from wood fire. Take many, many years to be full dragon-body. Only I, Serpent King, like such pain. Grow strong.'

He flexed his muscles and made the serpents dance. It was sickening.

'And your beard. It's as yellow as our colour-grasses.'

'Beech ash and goat fat.'

Bera was trying to keep him talking until Ottar might arrive but his smile was like a madman's. It was unnerving seeing him look at home here, relaxed. Her muscle twitch was so bad she wanted to hold it still with a hand but she feared to make a move. She made herself keep up the pretence that this was a formal call.

'The whole household will be back soon for the day meal. Why don't you come into the longhouse and eat with us? You must be cold, with your chest...'

'Reindeer is best meat. You must leave to hang here for seven nights. Or more. I can kill with one dagger. Look.'

He slipped the dagger from his belt, spun round and threw it at the door. It quivered slightly in a panel. His showing off was childish yet frightening.

'Why are you here?'

'At feast I first saw you.'

'What?'

He spat, a bubble of white froth in the dark blood. 'You were maid, virgin. I come to see you before marriage for special reason.'

There was a troubling memory from that night. A black hood...

'What reason?'

He tapped his nose. 'Is business with Hefnir.'

Business? Yet Hefnir had gone over to him and Thorvald.

He swung on the beams to land right in front of her.

'Now you are wife. You like it very much, I can smell.' He reeked of musk and moss and resin. His hand went straight where he wanted it and clutched her tight. 'I think you like me very much.'

Outrage scorched through her. How dare he dishonour her? She pulled out her knife but he was ready for her attack. He banged her hand down onto the bench, sending the knife flying, and leaned on it while he began to undo his belt. His breathing was heavy and her resistance was obviously arousing him, so Bera stopped struggling and tried to think.

Bjorn's advice: 'Let a man think he's winning then clutch and twist.'

Bjorn, thank you. She relaxed.

'Yes. We like this.' His voice was a low rumble.

Bera was close enough to see that his eyes were as black and empty as a Drorgher's. She kept her wits sharp. As soon as he was exposed she grabbed his high, tight balls and twisted.

It was an immediate success. He screamed and doubled up. There was a ringing crash and he slumped onto the floor, out cold. Behind him, Sigrid stood like a square block of granite. She kept the iron skillet raised to hit him again if he stirred.

'I was dealing with it,' Bera said.

'What did he do?'

'Nothing.'

Bera used his belt to tie his hands. She had time to do a proper boat knot.

Sigrid was staring at his back. 'What's all the black lines?'

'Tattoos. You make them with wood ash, he said.'

They looked at each other and started to giggle. Relief made Bera weep with laughter. It was to be over and forgotten, as quickly as possible, before she felt any shame. She found the pantry knife behind a churn.

He stirred. Bera sat on his back, pulled his braided hair and pressed the blade under his raised jaw as though he was a fish about to have its gills off.

'Don't like this so much, do you?' she said, close to his ear. 'Now listen. You have dishonoured my husband by insulting me. But I want no bloodshed. Whatever your business has been with Hefnir, it is at an end. Do you understand?'

He made a strangled noise that she took for assent.

'You clearly don't know that I am a Valla. I can snip the thread of your Fate as easily as slitting your throat. So be warned, trole-spit.'

'You're never going to let him go?' asked Sigrid.

'Watch him – and hit him with the skillet if he makes one false move.'

Sigrid stood at his head. Bera kept her knife at his throat as he got to his feet. He could not straighten up and swayed, looking blank.

'I never want to see your ugly face in Seabost again. There is nothing for you here except death. Now walk very slowly towards the door.'

It was all he could do. His thighs turned inwards as he clutched his groin with bound hands. Finally, he reached the door and gestured at it with his chin.

'Dagger,' he said.

'Forfeit.'

He stumbled outside.

The fresh air restored his voice. 'War band in mountains. I promise gold, owed by Hefnir. Blood money.'

Bera prodded him with her knife. 'I don't care what you think you're owed. Your dishonour has cost you your right to it.'

He gestured at Sigrid, who pulled his dagger out of the wood. 'Crazy woman nearly kill me!'

'But she didn't. There is no debt to pay. Go now and go quickly.'

'Need hands to ride.'

His horse was outside the byre with many furs strapped to it. When they reached it, Bera untied his hands and stepped quickly away. He clumsily swung himself onto its back and nearly fell off the other side. Sigrid sniggered. Bera glared at her. If he lost too much pride he would return and kill to restore it.

She took his dagger from Sigrid and slid it into her belt. At last she had a real weapon!

They made sure he kept heading towards the treeline and then kept a watch for his war band. The whole episode puzzled Bera. He could have killed Heggi before she got home. What was his business? Why had he brought the reindeer? He was wild and vile and yet these were not the actions of an enemy. Bera wanted certainty.

'I hope the wolves get him,' she said.

Sigrid threw a cloak round her. 'What will you tell Hefnir?'

'Nothing.'

'You must!'

'This is a dishonour, Sigrid. Hefnir might think I encouraged it. I don't want him to know I wasn't here, protecting his home. His son was in the next room, alone! Ottar's made him doubt I have any Valla skills and I should have done better. You're to say nothing about this, Sigrid, not to anyone, not ever.'

'You and your secrets. As bad as your mother.' Sigrid shivered. 'So why do you think he agreed to go?'

'His cock finally stopped making all the decisions.'

Sigrid laughed and went back inside as a flurry of may blossom fell. Bera let the pure white petals cleanse her. Then the welcome heat of her skern.

'Why did he come?' she asked.

Past.

'Is he a King?'

Of savages.

'Will he return?'

Oh, he won't be thinking clearly for days yet. They'll be halfway home by then so they won't turn back. Not that he's a genius at the best of times. Dead wood till the sap rises.

'Will he come when he does get his mind working?'

Revenge is a dish best eaten cold.

'You said that before and it wasn't very comforting then.'

I'm perished. Go on, in you go before you catch your death.

Bera stopped by the door. 'I've seen him before. But did I dream about him as well?'

Only you can say.

'I did. But I'm missing something... It's about Heggi. Did he kill Heggi's mother?'

Stop asking about the past, ducky. It's beginning to grate.

Heggi arrived soon afterwards. He blithely announced that Ottar was trying out a new sort of boat and would be along later.

'Did you say it was urgent?'

He shrugged.

'Did you speak to him at all?'

'He's on sea trials. I thought about waiting but I'm really hungry.' He gave a small gasp and looked over to the food store. 'I forgot. What was in there?'

'A reindeer. It's a gift.'

'Who from?'

Sigrid bustled over to him. 'It's all laid. The thralls are waiting at the table. Outdoor shoes off. Now.'

He scuffed at the pile of spruce as he went off to eat. There was a glorious smell of resin that cleansed the air.

'That's a fine dagger of that serpent creature,' Sigrid said. 'Why don't you give it to Heggi?'

'What did you say?'

'I asked if you were going to give his knife to Heggi.'

'No, the other bit. Hearing you say serpent was the way Ottar said it once, when you first arrived.' But what did he say exactly? Important sayings unravelled. If only she could clutch a thread and follow it.

Sigrid poked her. 'So will you give it to him?'

When the dagger was found in Thorvald's back it would be the Serpent who was suspected. Perfect. 'I'll keep it. A knife doesn't choose its master.'

'As Ottar would say. You can't let Hefnir see it.'

'Then how can I give it to Heggi? You can be so stupid, Sigrid!'

'I can.'

Sigrid pointlessly took some boughs from the pile and put them near the door. Her back had a hurt look. Bera sank down onto a platform and put her head in her hands. She didn't mean to be unkind but her tongue got the better of her too often.

Sigrid sat and put an arm around her, rocking her gently. 'Go on and cry. Stupid old Sigrid's here.'

The door burst open and Ottar swept in, bringing a north wind with him. The day was deteriorating. He punched the new hanging good-naturedly, stamped his feet and rubbed his hands.

Sigrid made herself scarce.

Ottar beamed. 'I did the sea trials myself and the boat's a success!'

Bera smoothed her garments, brushing away the dishonour. 'A new boat?'

Her father strode over and kissed her with icy lips and beard. It was a day for surprises. 'You didn't know, did you? She can be sailed short-handed but lose none of her speed. She sails in light airs, too. I designed her specially.'

What had made him kind again? Bera was too grateful to speak. Father and daughter shared a love of the sea and Ottar was giving her a way to get out there. Even Hefnir could not deny her the use of a father's gift. She could promise not to go fishing...

Ottar was bellowing. 'Heggi? Where is the boy? Get your arse over here, lad. I heard you were at the boatyard. Trying to find out what your surprise was, were you? After we've eaten we'll go down and I'll show you her proper.' He took Heggi's arm. 'She's a beauty, lad, and she's all yours.'

'I shall call her *Wave-Worm*.'

'You like horses. How about *Steed of the Sea*?'

Ottar didn't glance at her. She was such a speck he had no idea she might care.

'You bastard,' Bera said. 'I wish you'd died with the sickness.'

6

Bera had the weapon snug in her wedding chest, the plan formed and anger made her keen – but her target stayed away. She worried that her moment of jealousy when she wished Ottar dead might rebound on someone she cared for, like Sigrid, so she willed Thorvald to return to take Fate's weapon. There was no sign.

To spite everyone, she went out fishing a few times but no one cared. One day she mixed up a poultice for one of Hefnir's tenant farmers. It was a small gash from a farm tool but she took it herself. The farm was near the forge and when there was no glimpse of Dellingr, there was no hiding her disappointment. Visiting the forge would start tongues wagging so she had to rely on a chance meeting. Bera stayed a polite amount of time, then left, walking slowly. She longed to see the smith.

At home she shivered as she ran through the dark passage. The lurking ancestors were especially vicious.

'Perfidy and violation! Abomination!'

The new word sounded the worst. Bera nearly retreated but she would go to Hel before she lost face before the thralls.

'We'll have our meal now,' she said, steadily.

A man bowed his head and went off to the back.

'Come and help me,' Sigrid called. She was busy at the loom.

Bera had told her nothing about the ancestors; Sigrid had enough terrors of her own invention.

'I ought to check the pigs.'

Sigrid clucked. 'You and your animals.'

Bera took her place at Sigrid's right-hand side. They worked in silence until Sigrid changed wools.

'You care more for animals than you do people.'

Bera fiddled with some green wool.

Sigrid took it from her. 'Where is Heggi now?'

'Off with Rakki. Or at the boatyard. You know him.'

'He doesn't have many friends in the village.'

'He likes the dog. And Ottar.'

'Better for him to have friends his own age.'

Bera got back to weaving, crossly. Sigrid had a way of getting under her skin.

'I hope you're saying some words over this,' said Sigrid.

'Why?'

'It's a blanket for Asa's new baby.'

'Asa?'

'You know, Dellingr's wife. They fell in love as children.'

The pain stabbed like an unclasping. How stupid of her to think he was free.

It was usually soothing to have Sigrid beside her, working rhythmically. Today, it was agony. Trust Sigrid to find out Dellingr was married and then not tell her. No – the pain was jealousy, at the point when such feelings were hopeless.

'You look better, mind,' Sigrid said. 'Seemed heavy, last month. Lost a baby, maybe?'

This was the final insult. 'I hate everyone waiting for me to spawn! How can I possibly get a baby when Hefnir's away so long!'

'Heggi's cloak needs patching again,' Sigrid said in her 'patient' voice.

Bera wanted to slap her. 'I'll do it later!'

'I was only saying. No one expects you to do it.'

'Then why bring it up? So we know that good old Sigrid does all the chores as usual?'

'Look, you've pulled that thread too tight. Talk or work.'

'I can do both.'

You can't when you're in one of your moods.'

Bera marched off and sat on the raised hearth, glaring at the sullen flames.

Sigrid followed. 'You take too much on yourself, always have. I remember when you were little, you'd—'

Bera threw a log onto the fire.

'You'll use them all up at this rate.'

Bera shrugged. It would not be her job to cut more.

Sigrid studied her. 'You've changed,' she said.

'What do you mean?'

'You used to be kind.'

Bera searched for that old self in her friend's eyes. But it was Thorvald making her hard; and she could never tell Sigrid he killed her son.

Some thralls set the table and laid it with bread and ale.

Sigrid packed away a gaming board. 'Heggi won't miss his meal.'

They sat at the table but no one else came to join them. Perhaps the brat had drowned. She quickly crossed her fingers to stop Fate obliging. Sigrid slurped the hot stew and sucked the small rabbit bones. Bera wanted to hit her.

'He's been out of the house for ages and it'll be my fault if anything happens to him!'

Sigrid sighed. 'That's what I was saying.'

Bera's anger exploded. She picked up the stew dish and wanted to pour it over Sigrid's head but had just enough control to throw it to the ground instead. She strode through to the byre. A thrall coming in to milk the cows took one look at her and quickly went outside.

Bera leaned on the rail, fuming. Heggi always caused trouble. It wasn't fair that she should have to be in charge of such a wilful boy. As for Sigrid... Always pointing out what was wrong, never helping get it right. Bera tried a quiet scream but it didn't help. She couldn't even scream in her own home because there were thralls skulking all over it.

Anyway, she would hate to upset the animals.

A bird was delicately picking its way between the hooves and noses of the woolly cattle as they pushed into the hay and straw. Scavenging. Steam rose and Bera breathed in the familiar sweet yeastiness of sweat and dung. It calmed her. The nearest animal shook its head at her, rolling a sea anemone eye. It was Feima, the best natured, Heggi's pet cow. She blew softly and stamped. Bera offered her a handful of hay, which she took gently with a rasping tongue. It was endearing. Bera patted the animal's strong neck, liking the feel of the thick pelt and muscle. She much preferred the cow to Heggi, to be honest.

'You ought to milk those animals, not fuss at them,' said her father behind her.

She was cross again. 'Are you my skern suddenly? Creeping about like that.'

'I do not creep.'

'Why are you not at the boatyard?'

'Can't I eat?'

'If you turn up on time.'

They glared at each other.

'So are you Hefnir's spy? Making sure I'm doing my duty?'

Ottar rubbed the back of his neck. 'I came to ask how many barrels of mead are left.'

'I kept some back,' she said, 'but that's the finish until Hefnir brings more. But you're not here to supply the mead hall. You're checking up on me. The only time I have any peace is when I'm in a boat. Oh – I forgot, I don't have one, do I?'

He handed her the milking stool. 'They've seen the sails. Your husband's coming home. So now he can keep an eye on you.'

It explained her edginess. She liked the thought that her growing Valla skills sensed Thorvald's return. Now she had to carry out her plan. She took out the Serpent King's dagger. It felt cold in her hands and when she put her thumb to the blade it nicked her. A drop of blood bloomed but she did not suck it away – it felt like poison.

'Don't say a word about bad omens,' she said.

Serpent blood is serpent venom.

'You're as bad as the ancestors. What's venom?'

Poison. And those words they say at the threshold: remember them.

'I don't know what they mean!'

My point entirely.

Back inside, Sigrid pulled her shawl tighter and stalked off like an outraged hen when she saw her. Bera remembered her anger and vowed to suppress it. She regretted ever causing hurt and dealing with Thorvald was a way of making amends. If she did it quickly she might return to being kind. Until then, no one would suspect a killer if she faked kindness. She kept back a beaker of milk for Heggi, who liked to drink it fresh.

Bera made some soft cheese with the remainder. It was a pity that there wasn't enough salt left to make butter and she hoped they had some on board. She wondered what injuries they might have suffered. Maybe a sea-rider had killed Thorvald. No, that was cowardly. She had to do it herself or Bjorn wouldn't rest. Or was it that she wouldn't let Bjorn rest? Ottar was satisfied he had collected the blood debt. Was it her way of making her guilt less by forcing herself to kill?

'Ottar!' shouted Heggi from the byre. 'Papa's home! I've seen him!'

He dashed in with Rakki at his heels, both of them grinning. Until he saw Bera.

'Wipe your feet,' she said.

'Where's Ottar?'

Bera placed the milk out of danger. 'Counting barrels.'

'Rakki knew. He kept looking out to sea and then their sails came.'

'You missed your meal.'

Heggi slumped down onto a whalebone stool. 'It was important to properly greet our kin.'

Was he saying she didn't?

Bera mocked him with a bow. 'I present fresh milk for you, sir.'

'Is it Feima's?'

'Of course.'

'Is there any meat?'

'Have cheese till we see what your father has brought.'

The boy ate messily and Rakki waited under the table for scraps. Bera pretended not to notice and carried on with the cheesemaking.

She felt shy about Hefnir's return and she worried he would be a stranger. After all, she was changed. She wished he could stay in one place, doing a solid job for folk. For his family. Like Dellingr. She pushed the hurt of his marrying his sweetheart away. If only she and Bjorn had loved each other since childhood.

Bera shook her head. She never wanted Bjorn that way. The fact was that she was an outsider in a rushed marriage arranged for everyone's sake but her own. She got busy to stop fooling herself.

She put the utensils ready for the thralls and ordered fresh boughs and herbs to be strewn; sent someone to help Ottar cart the mead to the hall and make sure he didn't drink it; told Sigrid to kill enough chickens and to get the reindeer down to the mead hall, ready for the feast, and ignored her satisfied complaint about doing everything.

A thrall ran in to say the boat was alongside.

Bera was helped into her best clothes, the ones she wore on her bride day, because her fingers were clumsy with nerves. She couldn't remember what her husband even looked like.

Hefnir's face was cold and wet and he smelt different. His beard had grown and he was wearing a new cloak with an unfamiliar design on it. She felt embarrassed and awkward, almost like the first time. Perhaps he noticed, for he told Thorvald to leave them alone and take Heggi with him. Bera was grateful; she would deal with Thorvald later.

When Hefnir kissed her, he tasted foreign, too. They hardly spoke two words together. But he remembered the places she liked to be touched and her young body was easily reawakened and when they lay together afterwards it did not feel so strange.

Later, he helped her dress.

'I missed you, Bera.'

His simple words rang true and pleased her. Perhaps this was a new start for them both. Perhaps she could win him away from Thorvald.

'I was lonely.'

'Why? You have your kin and you're mistress of the house.'

She had shown him a weakness and he had not been tender. No one understood her. She snatched up her brooches.

'Here, let me.'

'I can manage.'

He brushed her hands away and pinned up her dress. She heard the scratch of hard skin against the cloth.

'When everything's off the boat, there are some presents for you. Some shearling boots, a new necklace.'

'I have my necklace.' She touched the beads and met her skern's hand. He held on, tight. Was it a warning?

Hefnir picked up his clothes. 'Well. I shall go to the bath hut and try to look like your husband again.'

'Shouldn't you have done that first?'

'Some things can't wait.' He bent to pick up his tunic.

There was a shiny pink scar on his shoulder.

'What's that?'

He put a finger to it. 'It's gone now.'

'I didn't see it before.'

He pulled on his tunic. 'It's new.'

'I'll make a healing salve for you.'

'A monk put on some herbs.'

Did he not trust her skill? 'And why would a monk do that for you?'

'Because Thorvald would have skewered him otherwise.'

Heggi was allowed to stay up when he declared he was a man now. The old woman who used to look after him was no longer seen and Sigrid let him do as he pleased. She had gone to her billet, leaving him dozing, sprawled like a young deer across his father's lap. Then he woke with new energy and racketed about the longhouse with Rakki yipping beside him. Bera's head ached with his desire to be noticed: a child again, when it suited.

Thorvald caught him. 'That's my ale you've spilled, Helhound.'

He held him upside down and Heggi squealed with delight. Getting what he wanted, as usual.

Bera caught hold of Rakki, wanting to stroke him, but he pulled away. 'Put Heggi down, Thorvald. He'll be sick.'

Thorvald pretended to stagger. 'He's grown.'

'Not too big to be carried by his papa.' Hefnir took the child off.

'Were there bears, Papa?'

'You're still going to bed.'

'Dragonboats? Did Thorvald kill any sea-riders?'

A mumbled reply.

Bera rebraided her hair and sensed Thorvald watching her.

He suddenly leaned across and seized her wrist. 'Have you told Sigrid?'

'And have her look at you every moment and be hurt?'

'Yet she carries the death of her son with strength.'

'Don't dare tell me about Sigrid! She'll be stronger once I've killed you.'

'Don't threaten me, dwarf-child.'

Bera spat at him. She burst out of the longhouse and kept running across the pasture until she reached the latrines. Luckily no one else was inside. She sat on the rail but there was not even a physical relief. She could have split him open there and then if only she had her dagger to hand.

Whistle and ride.

Her skern sat on the opposite rail, swinging his skinny legs.

'I came out here to be alone.'

No, you were running away.

'Go away!'

Let Fate arrange Thorvald's death. You have no sword skill and far too much anger to be a killer. And you're scared. So leave him alone, sweetheart. We're not ready to die yet.

'It's not dying I fear, I...'

Her skern whistled a reedy lament.

Of course she feared death and hated all endings, even saying goodbye. But there was no point staying alive if living meant this unending fear and guilt. She closed her eyes and silently vowed again to kill Thorvald – right here.

And here was a perfect place for Drorghers. On the way to the latrine she had been too angry to think of them. When she killed Thorvald she must make sure his skern joined him, otherwise his power as a Drorgher would be terrible. For now, her scalp prickling, she slowly checked every corner. It was clear, so she set off, but on the open stretch before the longhouse, she sensed movement at the edge of her sight. When she looked, there was nothing. Whenever she moved forward, it shadowed her; when she turned her head, nothing. She ran.

Hefnir was back, huddled with Thorvald. She sensed they wanted her to go to her billet. Bera listened for a moment but it was only a tedious listing of goods.

She interrupted. 'I hope you brought some salt.'

'It cost more again this time. I bought more honey. Whole skeps.'

'With the bees still in them?'

Hefnir laughed. 'Can you hear them buzzing? No, beekeepers soak the skeps to drown the bees.'

'I don't like to think of them all dead.'

Thorvald got up and stretched. 'He won't like it, Hefnir.'

'You and I get equal shares, Thorvald, but he gets the same as the crew.'

'He wants more and makes threats.'

'He's always making threats. We take all the risks. And he can't scare me with his serp—' Hefnir glanced at her.

'Who makes threats?' Bera asked, although she had guessed.

'A farmer.'

It was a lie. The listing was suddenly less tedious.

Bera tried not to look at Thorvald. She had not renewed the tapers and the firelight lit only the good side of his face but she stared at his scar as though at a spider. She longed to brag about the Serpent King's assault and have Thorvald begin to respect her – dwarf-child! – but then Hefnir might doubt her honour. Even if he blamed only the Serpent, he would have to fight him and his war band. And keeping Thorvald off guard was a good thing. She would have to gain respect another way.

'Folk use me to judge now. There were a couple of fights and I made the wrongdoers clean the stockfish racks.'

Thorvald guffawed. 'Scary!'

Hefnir kicked him good-naturedly. 'Has Heggi behaved?'

Pride made Bera want to hide their dislike. 'He feels the same way about animals as I do.'

'But?'

Her voice had given her away, as usual. 'He's always at the boatyard, or off on the boat Ottar built for him. He says he loves Feima but I'm the one who looks after her. All he does is drink her milk!'

She sounded as jealous as she felt. Luckily, Hefnir thought it was only about the cow, not boats. He mustn't know she had been out fishing.

'Good thing you like animals so much, then.'

Bera could not help yawning.

Hefnir came over and lifted her to her feet. 'Off to bed, shrimp. It will be a long day tomorrow, what with unloading all our goods and the feast.'

'Are you coming soon?'

'We have a lot to sort out before tomorrow,' Hefnir said.

He sat down near Thorvald and filled both their ale horns.

She was dismissed. Once she had got rid of Thorvald she would become Hefnir's loyal wife and trusted ally.

Hefnir kept Thorvald busy the next day. Bera got on with her own duties and made up some worming pills for the sheep.

Hefnir finally came home to escort them to the mead hall. He ordered a thrall to find Heggi and bring him at once. Bera asked him why it was so important but he did the blank thing. He was too good at making her feel stupid, or even invisible. Occasionally there was warmth, even humour. The trouble was, she never knew which Hefnir she would get.

At the hall they were met with a smell of roast meat that instantly made Bera's mouth spill. She hastily wiped her lips, hoping no one had noticed. The reindeer was on the largest spit, being slowly turned by sweaty youths with burning faces. Bera felt sick at the memory of the reindeer's slit throat and the steady drip of thickening blood. It was the fat that dripped onto the flames with a hiss. Its greasy smoke hung in the air instead of rising upwards into the darkness where freshly butchered meat was hanging. Various pots and cauldrons were slung over the fire on chains and curls of steam rose into the air, already heavy with sweat and mead. Firebrands flamed on the walls and the blaze of the great central hearth fire pushed the shadows into the farthest corners.

Red-faced men stood in groups, drinking. They smacked each other's backs, punched chests and shouted competitive stories of heroic raids. They ignored the children, who charged amongst them playing bully-bully, with all the village dogs barking and sparring as they ran.

Hefnir stood by the spit and showed no surprise at seeing reindeer roasting.

Thorvald came over to report. 'We're unloaded and most of it stowed. All the mead's over there now, with Ottar.'

'I'll make sure others have a chance to drink it,' Bera said. She wanted to ask Sigrid if she had told Hefnir about the reindeer.

When folk saw that Hefnir had arrived they broke into a song to welcome home a warrior. Bera liked it when children went swimming or flying round the hall like the creatures they praised. But three lines especially struck her:

> The lone eagle-screech
> Whets the heartstone on the iron anvil
> Of the whale roads, across the Ice-Rimmed Sea.

She loved the meaning and the shape of the words in her mind, like a wave rushing onto the shore, and looked for Dellingr to see if he was pleased to have a blacksmith's due. He was laughing with Thorvald and it enraged Bera to see it.

Thorvald toasted, 'To Hefnir!'

Bera's silent toast was to Thorvald: 'May you die tonight.' She crossed her fingers and then despised herself for cowardice.

Horns were upended to show they were empty and there were noisy demands for more. Bera hurried to the back of the hall, where she found a mountain of barrels. Hefnir had gone further than usual, though not as far as somewhere called the Black Sea. Folk talked about dried fruits and spices, which Bera had never tasted. One day, Hefnir would take her and be amazed at her boat skills and make all the blood debt struggle worthwhile. One day, with Thorvald dead, he would need her.

She filled two large jugs with mead and told Sigrid to go home for more and walked with her to the door.

'Before you go – who ordered the reindeer to be roasted?'

Sigrid winked at her. 'Don't worry, I didn't let on. I told Thorvald someone left it.'

'What did you tell him for?' Bera was scared of any advantage he might gain.

'He can get Hefnir to see sense if there's trouble. There won't be: he said one of the farmers must have left it as a tribute.'

Dellingr arrived and Sigrid greeted the woman behind him like a friend. Bera resented their easiness. Sigrid seized the baby, smothering it in kisses and making silly noises in its face. Then she passed it to Bera, who flung it back to its mother as if it was on fire.

Sigrid laughed. 'Don't mind her, Asa. Bera – this is Asa that I was telling you about. And her older daughter.'

Bera was conscious of Dellingr's nearness and her smile felt like a blade of ice.

Asa nodded briefly then swept in as if she were chief guest, followed by the girl, and settled in a prominent corner. Folk fussed over her, playing with the baby. Bera hated the woman's smugness and the way she took a breast out so everyone could marvel at how much milk she had. Well, so did house cows.

Sigrid patted her arm. 'Aren't they a fine little family? She's given him a boy and a girl now.'

'As opposed to me I suppose!'

Sigrid looked sad. 'No, Bera. As opposed to me.'

Bera went outside. She slapped her nasty cruel face and then went back in and forced herself to look happy and generous: playing the hostess, filling drinking horns and bowls and swapping banter all round the hall. Folk laughed at her quick wit and then she came back to Dellingr.

'You're as pale as a ghost owl,' he said.

He saw everything. She longed to tell him about the Serpent King, and be protected and loved. Be excused for becoming so hard. Instead, she made do with the comfort of his hand steadying hers as she poured his drink.

He beamed at her. 'I wish the same for you and Hefnir.'

'Same as what?'

'Our boy. I'm that proud.' He gazed across at his wife and child.

He hadn't seen at all. Bera wanted to slap him, to make him hurt as much as her. Well, perhaps she could make him as jealous. She went straight to Hefnir, determined to make him kiss her in public.

He raised a new chalice that glowed in the hall's gloom like a small sun. 'To the Abbot,' he said, with a meaning Bera tried to read.

'To the Abbot,' echoed Thorvald. 'And the rest of his hoard.'

His mouth looked particularly grotesque tonight. Perhaps the scar-heal was tightening, because more gum was showing: blood red against yellow teeth. Mead dribbled from the snagged lips and ran down his chin.

Most of this stuff is raided. Poor defenceless monks.

Her skern touched her brow and Bera had a vision of swords cleaving bald heads. Other men were making signs on their chests, like big hammer signs, before being stabbed. Screams. She felt sick at the splatter.

'What are monks?' she asked Hefnir.

He gestured to Thorvald. 'Heggi's here.'

'Then I'll start.' Thorvald set off for the hearth fire.

'Don't ignore me! My skern showed me violence and says they are defenceless. Is it true?'

'Go and stand with Thorvald.'

'Why?'

Hefnir raised the chalice to someone across the hall and went to join the group. He would never spoil his mood by answering an annoying question. Bera had no choice but to join Thorvald, where the fire began scorching her dress at the back. She stood as close to him as she could bear, to make him a fire screen. Heggi was on the other side, his face sullen under uncommonly tidy hair. He would not meet her eyes so she guessed he knew what was coming.

Thorvald rang his knife against a silver goblet until folk grew quiet and the children were still.

'It is time for the oath-taking,' he began. 'The boy has taken Bera as his mother.'

A lie. Heggi's face was proof of it: as strained and awful as hers.

'It is time for the oath of kinship, so that no man shall sever the link with a false word.' Thorvald turned to her. 'Bera, do you swear that Heggi will be your eldest child, no matter how many others shall come?'

The smiling faces around her started to frown as she hesitated.

'I have already sworn,' she said.

'Speak up,' yelled Ottar.

'Not that Heggi is your own firstborn son.' Thorvald would not let her cheat.

Heggi was biting his lip, trying desperately not to cry. Her heart softened a little. He wanted his own mother back but that was impossible. She knew how that felt. Perhaps they could try to help one another. She should make the first move and then Dellingr would see that she could be a kind mother, too. Besides, she would never have a baby of her own.

'I swear that Heggi is my own firstborn son.'

Thorvald put his huge hand on Heggi's head. 'And you, Heggi. Do you swear before all your kinsmen that Bera is your mother and you owe allegiance and payment of any blood debt to her and her alone?'

Heggi, stricken, choked and hiccupped his tears. Hefnir raised a hand to slap him.

Ottar caught his arm in a fist like a vice. 'We're kin, aren't we, lad?' He spoke gently to Heggi. 'You're a grandson to me, any rate.'

Bera's throat ached with sadness, for the long years since her father had spoken to her like that.

Hefnir wrenched his arm away from Ottar. 'Say it!'

It was soft as a sigh. 'I swear.'

Ottar swung him in the air. 'Good lad.'

Folk started to chatter, thinking the oath-taking was over.

Thorvald called them to order. 'So, I remind you of what you have heard, kinsmen of Seabost. Bera is Heggi's only mother. The woman who was lost has never been alive. Heggi is the firstborn son of Hefnir and his wife, Bera. Swear it!'

This time there was no quick acceptance. Dellingr seemed about to speak but Asa handed him the baby. There were murmurs. Bera saw why it troubled them so much: Heggi's mother had been declared a non-person. It was almost worse than being a Drorgher.

The tenant farmer with the blood-lined face stepped forward. 'What's it matter? The woman's dead, isn't she? Get on with it and we'll have a drink, boys! We swear... ' he prompted, folk cheered and then the serious drinking began.

Heggi swayed with shock. It was shattering. Bera felt bludgeoned, too, but it was Heggi that Ottar took away, without a kind word for his daughter. She strode over to where Hefnir was thanking his farmer. He looked at her with such softness and warmth that it stopped her tongue.

'I'm glad that's done,' he said. 'If any man talks about his birth mother now I can have him killed for oath-breaking.'

'Does it matter so much?'

'You are my wife, Bera. I want you to have all its rights.'

Then he was gone with the other men, leaving her wondering why she felt he had not told her the whole truth.

Time passed in a haze of heat and drink. Bera hated the atmosphere, fearing the ceremony might invoke the spirit of Heggi's mother, come to seek revenge. The oath was a lie. Everyone there knew she had lived – and Heggi was the proof. No one seemed to care. All about her, drink was loosening men's tongues and women's clothes. The thought of the Serpent made her feel shameful, filthy and sick. If only she had a real friend.

Sigrid might be some comfort.

Bera found her chivvying a pot girl. She pushed the girl away. 'Folk need to get some food inside them.'

Sigrid snorted. 'Go and sit down, Bera. You look awful.'

'That makes me feel so much better.'

'I'm only saying.' Sigrid clanged stewpots into a heap.

Heggi swaggered past with a group of older lads, making sure Bera saw him. They were comparing knives and he seemed quite recovered. Was he playing a part as much as she was playing the hostess? Her scalp was pricking.

'I'd better go and make sure he doesn't get into trouble.'

'Let the boy make some friends.'

There was a burst of raucous laughter.

Hefnir's crew were rowdy. 'Let's have a poem! Where's your wife, Hefnir? Bera! Bera! Bera! Bera!'

Thorvald came to fetch her. 'Time to pay for your supper. Tell of battles and blood-wounding.'

'I can't.'

Thorvald leaned close. 'You must praise the deeds of your husband and his men.'

'I wouldn't dare say what you do, Thorvald,' she said.

He shook her. 'Get over there and do your duty, like we all have to.'

'I'm going to do my duty all right, like Ottar should have. Watch your back.'

'If you could reach it.'

Heggi rushed to his father, who hugged him. Bera wanted to make Hefnir as proud of her, so she took her place at the hearth, fearing she could never be a poet like her mother. She held on to her beads, hoping her skern might help. She looked about for him. A yellow flame flickered in the shadows. A black face. But then Hefnir called for her to start.

And from a place deep inside her, the verse sprang.

> 'At the sound of the eagle-shriek the rowers made for shore,
> the sky like a wound-sea above them, and the cries of women
> echoed the eagle as they ran, fearing the skimming skull-cleave.

Some clutched brooches to their breasts,
with brimful arms of sea-bright gold.
Others held children, their precious store of future wealth,
while their men stood straight like reeds before an axe,
scythed by the stern onslaught of skilled sword-wielders.'

Bera could not go on. Those women and children were real to her. Mothers. There was a crushing weight of silence. She could only see a mass of odd shapes and colours in front of her, a sea of strangers, smelling hostile. Murmurs grew into threats. She was still clutching her beads and a droplet fell hot onto her hand. A tear.

Thorvald held high his ale horn. 'To all of us skilled sword-wielders!'

Everyone cheered and drank deeply. The moment passed.

Cooks shouted that the roasted meat was ready and the feasting began. Folk laughed wide with faces shiny with grease, celebrating the stores that would help see them through winter. Bera went round with ale and mead, checking the hall for a black-faced stranger. Would the Serpent King dare to come back?

Hefnir stopped her. 'That was a well-crafted poem but odd for the wife of a Northman.'

'I said you were skilled swordsmen.'

'You said nothing about our man who died.'

'I didn't know.'

'You had better go and thank Thorvald.'

'Why should I thank him? He should have told me one had been killed.'

'His toast saved you. There could have been a riot, they are in that mood.'

'He likely wants me dead.'

'Not while you are my wife. And Heggi's mother.'

A chill hung in the air. Bera could not read his expression, or even gauge how much he had drunk.

'Heggi doesn't care if I live or die.' The truth of it hurt.

'My son is your charge,' Hefnir said. 'Where is he now?'

Bera wafted a hand towards the spits. He and Rakki would be close to the food. 'So who died?'

It was Flat-Nose. He had taunted Bjorn into rushing at his killer, so it was fair. But Bera should have kept Bjorn safe and only killing Thorvald would seal that wound.

'Keep my son out of danger,' Hefnir warned and moved on.

Bera made for the roasting spit. Heggi was not there, blast him. Ottar was blustering with some of the seamen but the boy wasn't with him, either. Bera grew anxious. If any man had cared that she was not Heggi's natural mother, he had been reminded of it tonight. Then she saw Rakki. There was no sign of his boy but he was sure to be close, so Bera started after the dog.

Ottar barred her way.

He held up his ale and began a toast. 'Be your friend's true friend.'

Others joined in as they recognised it. 'Return gift for gift. Repay laughter with laughter.'

His mates roared and clapped backs as if this was the funniest thing they had ever heard.

'I say, repay laughter with laughter again...' He pushed his face into hers, '... but betrayal with treachery.'

Bera sidestepped him. Why question her loyalty?

'Don't you dare try and shame me in public!'

'Then mind you don't shame your husband.'

Bodies pressed. The scant air was stale with so many breaths and fires and the ringing uproar drained her will to argue. The hall suddenly reeked of approaching danger. Where was Heggi?

Bera pushed through the long jostle for food and saw a man in a black hood slip through the high doors. She was right! She followed him at once but when she got outside he was gone.

And she was alone.

Her scalp crackled with menace. They said there were no Drorghers in Seabost but she knew one was out there, hiding.

'Show yourself!'

Out of the shadows lumbered a recent corpse. It was not yet distended, though its features were blurred as if seen through frozen eyes. It came as far as the torch light and swayed, uncertain. Drorghers were unknown in Seabost. Was this the first of the red-spot corpses, following the trail to their kinsfolk's skerns? Or a sign of worsening evil here? Perhaps Hefnir did not have the grip of his folk that he claimed.

It's Flat-Nose. He's new to this so act fast before he gets the hang of it.

Bera wished she knew what had once been the creature's real name. Names were power.

I don't know it either, but get on with it!

'Stop distracting me!'

The Drorgher was gaining confidence as it began to sense its power, though it was wary of Bera. It cast about, looking for easier prey. In fact, she was fast losing control. She tried to fan her will-power into flame but being called a superstitious peasant in Seabost had made her lose confidence. Things were different here. How could she fight something no one else believed in? What weapons did she need?

The Drorgher gave a nasty smile when it smelt her panic. It sucked the air and will from Bera's lungs. An unnatural cold stilled her blood and dulled her brain.

A dog appeared. Rakki stood, hackles raised, too fearful to growl. Heggi would not be far away and Bera found the resolve to take on the Drorgher. She must protect the boy.

She pulled out her necklace and brandished the black bead. The creature moaned and stepped back, cringing.

'Yes. Feel that, Flat-Nose?' she cried. 'I am your deadly foe, a Valla. Beware of me, Drorgher.'

The Drorgher's dead black eyes were as pitiless as an ice shark's. You could drown in them.

There was a closer whistle. Heggi! The Drorgher's head swung, sniffing the air, questing for him.

Bera reacted the fastest. She lunged for the torch and held it high. The Drorgher's body was revealed as mottled blue and purple; its broad nose part of the blank smudge of its face.

'You must go and join the band of Drorghers and leave your old home. You belong here no longer.'

She pressed forwards, forcing it to move away from Rakki. Bera hoped it was away from Heggi, too. The Drorgher, confused, tottered backwards.

'Go to the forest! I am here to protect these folk and you need to fear me.'

Heggi called, 'Rakki! Here, boy!'

Bera's need to save Heggi became focused as a flame, which began deep in her womb and scorched upwards until it poured from her mouth in a blaze.

'Take your Drorgher envy away from my sight!'

It stumbled off towards the trees, defeated.

'Yes!' Bera shouted and punched the air for the joy of having total control. 'I was born for this, and let all Drorghers know it!'

Heggi finally turned up. 'You're frightening Rakki,' he said. He had missed it all.

The injustice and his piping voice enraged Bera and her blood was up. She growled and ran at him. He scampered off with his dog and they reached the doors together. Bera snatched at his tunic.

'I've just saved your scrawny neck, you ungrateful runt.'

'You're mad!'

The doors swung open and some men fell out, fighting. Hot air billowed with the swell of uproar. Heggi charged in. The brawlers were swinging punches and Bera had to duck and weave to avoid them. By the time she got inside the skirmish was fierce, with knives.

The women were spurring them on, bright-eyed and raucous. Heggi was already with his father, beyond them. Trust him to cause worry and then be snug. Bera snaked her way through the excited mob to reach them, her face hot and spittled from the barrage of insults spat at the fighters.

'Hefnir! Stop them!' she shouted.

Across the hall was a glimpse of a yellow beard.

The Serpent King is here, rabble-rousing. It will be carnage.

It was clear from Hefnir's expression that he took pleasure from the violence. Blood called to blood. Was the Serpent here to entice Hefnir – or here at his invitation? Either way he had defied her banishment. Humiliated her.

Time to go public, ducky.

Bera stood up on Hefnir's carved chair, unclasped her necklace and held it high. No one noticed.

The women got stuck in, followed by children, who began to throw pots and bowls at each other. Dogs snarled and bit. Bera caught a glimpse of Sigrid, behind Thorvald, who had his wide-bladed sword raised. She pictured it slicing Bjorn.

A scream came from her heart.

It was a scream that had built up from not telling Sigrid and leaving her son unavenged. It was a scream that the Serpent had ignored her order to stay away. It was a scream that she had just saved the brat from a foe these people did not even recognise.

Her fury pierced like an arrow through their bloodlust and the crowd stilled. They turned to look at her. There was a shout, then silence.

Bera felt changed. But what to say to them?

You've just defeated a Drorgher. Be tough.

Her head was ringing. 'There must be an end to fighting our own folk.'

They were all looking at her, expecting more.

'I judge disputes so no Seabost blood is spilt by Seabost. We should stand together against outsiders.'

'Like Crapsby?' said a deep and lisping voice.

'Yes, like Crapsby, too,' she agreed, to maintain the good humour.

Hefnir laughed. 'Well said, wife. Seabost against Crapsby.'

The drink that had made them hot for the fight made them quick to forget. All they wanted now was more of everything.

Hefnir swung Bera down from his chair and held her. His kiss was long and public and as it should be. She felt proud of her growing powers.

Then Heggi tugged her arm. 'Did you bring me any meat, Mama?' He spat the last word, like poison.

'You should be in bed.'

'For Rakki?' he coaxed.

Hefnir smiled at her. Back to the pretence of being honey-sweet, to shift suspicion, later.

'All right, Heggi, I'll go and fetch a few slices. You can eat them on the way home. Rakki too.'

Sigrid was stacking some empty stewpots. When she saw Bera she fanned her face with the bottom of her apron.

'I'm that tired. I've been on the go all day. I'll be off home soon.'

'Not alone, Sigrid. There was a Drorgher.'

'They don't get them here. Besides, I'll be safe enough with Thorvald.'

How could she think it? 'Give me some scrapings for the dog then we'll go together. You and I.'

Sigrid tutted but did it. 'I'll wait for you here, then, I suppose,' she said, moodily.

On the way back to Heggi, Bera wondered if she had missed an opportunity to kill Thorvald in the fight. It was chaotic but she would have been seen in the fray, or been injured herself. No, her own plan was better and would give her the chance to savour his fear before he died. And his skern would be present then. She dare not risk him becoming a mighty Drorgher.

Ottar pulled Bera into a corner. She could smell blood and drink heavy on his breath.

'I'm watching you, girlie,' he said.

'Take your hand off me, Father.'

He spat. 'Crapsby, eh? Betraying your home, now. Who'll you betray next?'

'Let go.'

'You Vallas think you know everything. Your mother thought she knew everything but she didn't. I know you, like I knew her. Your blood's hot. I been talking to someone here tonight.' He tapped his nose. 'I'm watching you.'

'The drink's made you stupid. Get back to the other sots and let me return to my husband.'

'Your husband!' He swooped, swayed and closed in. 'He only took you when he needed my boats. He didn't want you. I had to beg him.'

'You're a liar.'

Ottar belched. 'Ask him. Mind, he's as big a liar as you. Ask him about his real wife.'

'If Hefnir heard this he would have you killed.'

He wagged a finger at her. 'Just like your mother, looks, everything. You could get a child with another man, or a whole pack of 'em so you won't know whose bastard it is.'

Bera slapped him so hard that her hand stung. Ottar felt his cheek, laughed, and fell over. She stepped over him and walked away.

Bera and Sigrid took a torch up to the home latrine. There was no sign of the Drorgher. Inside, the hen stench made Bera's eyes water. Waiting in here would not be pleasant later.

'I'm not right, still,' said Sigrid. She was taking an age to lift her bundle of skirts and get down to business. 'I need a remedy.'

'You'll have to give me more of a clue than that,' said Bera.

'That's my affair.'

Bera finished and arranged her clothes. 'Then I'm no use to you.'

Sigrid hitched herself up on the rail and gave a sigh. 'That's better. Been bursting all night but I was that busy...'

'That's likely to be the problem.'

'No. It's … er … the other side.'

'Your bottom?'

'Sh!'

'There's no one to hear, Sigrid. Spit it out.'

The older woman jumped off the rail and bristled, like a hen shaking dusty feathers. 'Worse at night. Itching. Have to scratch.'

'Chicken mite.'

'Get on with you!'

'Pinworms, then.'

'I'm too old for them.'

'You probably caught them from Heggi. It would be like him to have them. I'll treat both of you.'

'You needn't sound so pleased about it. Come on, let's get out of here. I can hardly breathe.'

The men staggered to bed much later. Bera pretended to be asleep but Hefnir did not trouble to check and was soon snoring, flat on his back with an arm flung across her.

She carefully rolled away, took the Serpent King's dagger from underneath her bedroll, tiptoed away from the billet into the byre, then ran up to the latrines. Now all she had to do was wait.

The longer she waited, the more flaws she could see in her plan; it would help to be reassured. If only she had someone she could trust. Instead of which, her skern gleefully pinched her cheek.

He won't come out, you know. He's like a felled ox.

'Exactly. He's been drinking. So he'll visit the latrine.'

So he'll use the piss-pot like everyone else.

'I need him to be alone! During the day he's always got folk round him and so have I. This place is fit for danger.'

Which is precisely why he won't come alone, silly.

Her plan was useless. In a way she had known it all along but she had refused to see it. She pulled her shawl round her for some warmth and trudged home, miserable and ashamed.

Look out!

Her scalp crawled with the threat of evil and she could smell rot, centred on an old food store. It was not food that was turning her stomach, it was a Drorgher. Not Flat-Nose, who was a novice and had run away. This was a more assured malevolence.

'Why didn't you warn me?'

I just did.

Her skern flounced off to the byre, leaving Bera dithering. She would have to pass the store to get to the next torch. Fool! Coward! The touch of her black bead gave her clarity. She forced herself to go back to the latrine and fetch the torch from there. Holding it high, she raced all the way home, tore past the store and into the byre. She thrust the torch into its socket, banged the door behind her and leaned against it, panting, soaking up the byre's wholesomeness.

It was all too much. Why drive herself, anyway? Hefnir had paid the blood debt. She might not like it, especially the fact she was the add-on, but in a way that meant she was part of avenging Bjorn's death.

She slapped her cheeks. 'Cowardice.'

Some might say it's good sense at last. Now that Drorghers are come.

He was balancing on an upturned bucket.

'I have to kill Thorvald. Not doing it has made me weak.'

You make these rules for yourself.

It was the last act she could do for her best friend. It was only the means of doing it that was causing her to waver. If she was lucky, Thorvald would be too drunk to have a woman in his bed and too drunk to defend himself. It was a pity he would fail to acknowledge the blood debt but this way his death would be silent too. Bera took a straw and rested the dagger on it. It split in two.

She calmed her breathing, then softly passed through to Thorvald's billet. She paused by the curtain for only a moment and then slipped inside.

The air was sweet with meady sleep-breath and Bera gagged. One guttering taper peeled dark off dark until the sleeping form of Thorvald was apparent. He was alone. She had to kill him with one strike. The trouble was, she had no clue how to kill anyone, let alone silently. Earlier, when she had imagined it, she always had Thorvald at her mercy and after that it was a bit blank.

His breath was rattling and bubbling through his cloven mouth. She pushed away pity for his damaged face. Heart or throat? Surely the throat would be best as he was struggling to breathe anyway.

She wavered, faced with a living being. Killing someone in his sleep was monstrous. It went against everything brave and true; it abandoned duty, care and hospitality. This was her house now. There was something defenceless and childlike about him in his sleep; the way he had his covers up to his chin was strangely moving.

Bera batted the thoughts away again. He had killed Bjorn in an instant! To Hel with pity. She steeled herself for the kill, tiptoed towards his bed and raised her dagger. The point wobbled. She gripped it with both hands, trying to get it steady.

Thorvald was up, armed and had her by the hair.

'Did you think it would be that easy?' His spit wet her ear. 'I'd be dead a thousand times over by now.'

He dragged her across to the tapers and lit them. Bera was weak with shame. He twisted her wrist until it burned, making her drop the dagger, then heeled it to himself and picked it up, never loosening his grip.

'I'll have you one day, Thorvald.'

'Where did you get this?' His voice had a new edge.

She shrugged.

'Tell me.'

'I found it.'

'Liar.'

'I bought it from Dellingr.'

He wrenched her arm up behind her back.

'All right,' she gasped. 'That man. Covered in tattoos.'

He released her arm and held the taper up to her face. 'Little fool. Keep away from him, understand?'

'You needn't sound so worried. I dealt with him myself, with no one to help, so be sure that I can take you any time I like.' She longed to rub her sore arm.

'Get back to your husband's bed and be the wife you should be. He's had a poor bargain so far.'

'What will you tell him?'

'Nothing if you promise to behave.'

'I'm not a child!'

'Then stop acting like one. It's like playing bully-bully. But a man doesn't want to be watching his back the whole time. Agree to this truce or by Hel's teeth my patience will wear out and I'll make you suffer so much you'll beg me for death!'

'Give me back my dagger.'

'Do I look a fool? Agree to the truce.'

'No.'

'I don't want to kill you, Bera. But I swear I will if you come near me again.'

She had to get away. Was the promise so bad if it prevented her father and husband knowing she had tried to kill a man in his own bed? And worse: failed.

'All right! I will not seek revenge in this house.'

Now she would have to find another weapon and think of some way to kill him away from home. It would not be easy – because for a married woman, home was her whole world.

7

They woke late to a kindly sun. Bera dreaded meeting Thorvald but he and Hefnir had gone off early. She worried it was business with the Serpent King. Would Thorvald tell them how she used his dagger? To her surprise she thought he would stay quiet – but that meant she must keep her side of the bargain here at home.

She dutifully mixed up some bitter herbs for Heggi and Sigrid to take for pinworm and then took some food to a poor tenant. Folk were busy, grimly pretending their heads were not splitting. Many had black eyes or thick lips but no serious damage had been done and one woman thanked Bera for stopping the fight.

Bera was tempted to go on up to the forge but Ottar's warnings made her careful about her movements. She had enough to worry about without rumours spreading about unfaithfulness. Yet she came across Dellingr leaving the jetties. Her reward for all her acts of duty that morning, perhaps.

'Haven't seen you in an age,' she said, then bit her lip.

Today his eyes were the blue-grey of his cloak and his face was washed. He looked younger when he smiled.

'I meant, alone. I meant, the feast seems an age ago. Of course, it was only last night.' Her babble gave her away.

'Don't be sad, small one,' he said. 'You were brave to stop the fight.'

Bera liked to think of being wrapped under his heavy cloak and kept safe forever. In a fatherly way.

It was time to go. She didn't move. Only because she needed a weapon.

'That sword you told me about...'

'I'll have it ready for you as quick as I can.'

'What?'

'Hefnir saw me about it early this morning.'

Bera's bowels froze. 'Did you tell him I wanted it?'

'He wasn't in a mood for conversation. Never is.' The smith rubbed his chin.

'He must have said something?'

'Just that I was to put a smaller hilt on it ready for a woman's hand.'

It was what she wanted – but was Hefnir planning a trap?

The ancestors pounced on her return to the longhouse, blowing freezing poison on any frailty.

'Perfidy! Violation! Abomination! Maleficence!'

Words were power. She had heard the first two many times and tried to remember them.

'One day I'll return them threefold,' she hissed.

Hefnir was waiting for her. He took off her cloak, threw it for a thrall to take and then held her shoulders. It was all right – he was smiling.

'I've made a decision,' he said. 'You say you're lonely. So, wife, what do you say to coming north with me? I'll get walrus ivory and you get out to sea again. A good idea?'

It was a better idea than he knew. It would get Thorvald away from home to where she could kill him. She kissed Hefnir and managed to avoid mentioning the sword, or else he would know she had seen Dellingr.

During their meal Hefnir and Thorvald talked of nothing but the virtue of baleen strakes and ash masts. Afterwards, Sigrid did some mending, making use of the sunlight. While the men played dice, Heggi sat on a stool in front of Bera and she went through his hair with a lice comb.

'Ouch! You're pulling!'

Rakki made sure his boy was all right and settled down again. The only sound was the fire crackle and the squeak of Sigrid's stitching.

'When are you going to tell me where the reindeer came from?' asked Hefnir.

Sigrid glanced up at Bera.

'I said. Someone left it for you.' Bera's heart beat fast.

'Who?'

'I don't know.'

Heggi twisted round. 'Yes, you do. You sent me off to get Ottar.'

Bera's face burned. 'I mean, I don't know his name. He said you do business with him, Hefnir.'

'Did he have tattoos?' asked Thorvald innocently.

'I've seen you talking to him, Thorvald. You told Sigrid the reindeer was a tribute. So what dealings do you have with him?'

Thorvald looked at Hefnir, who shrugged.

It enraged Bera. 'For how long, Hefnir?'

He prodded the fire with one of the spit-skewers. 'Oh. Less than a year, I'd say.'

'So you both have business with him?'

'Look. When you start out you have to have high-quality goods to trade, to set up a demand. He has given us good walrus and white bear skins.'

'The Serpent King!' Thorvald said, in a boggelman voice.

Sigrid sniggered. Had she broken her promise and told him about the assault? Bera had a sudden urge to hurt her and tell her it was Thorvald who had killed her son but then Sigrid winked at her and carried on with her stitching. It was still their secret.

'He doesn't scare me,' said Heggi. 'He has a silly beard and a nice horse.'

Hefnir yanked the boy off his stool. 'I don't want you near him, do you understand?'

Heggi started to wail. 'I wasn't near him! I just saw him!'

'He said he won't be back,' Bera said, trying to tease out the truth.

'He talked of going to the Great City before,' said Thorvald.

'What's that?' Heggi forgot his tears. Did he feel anything deeply? Did she? It worried her that the skern helped her to look, not to feel.

Bera got Heggi back on the stool and began the vicious delousing again.

'The Great City is a long way away. It's made of gold, every building.'

'Ow! Bera! That hurt! Have you been there, Papa?'

'It's too far. We nearly got there one year but we trade for goods from the Great City.'

'Can you get those spices there?' Bera asked.

'That's not all,' Thorvald leered and disgusted Bera.

'That really hurt!' cried Heggi. He rubbed his head and went over to his father.

Hefnir let his son plait his hair while he talked. 'There are over a hundred towers full of soldiers to protect the gold. One side has the sea all round it, with a huge iron chain across the harbour, called the Golden Horn.'

'Do they blow it?' Heggi asked.

Hefnir laughed. 'We shall use this fine weather and hunt just for us.'

'When will we set off?' Thorvald asked.

'You're staying here.'

Bera needed to get him away from home. 'Surely Thorvald—'

'Stays here.'

She was furious. 'You two are joined at the hip! Why leave him behind?'

Thorvald chuckled, a wet sound. 'Didn't know you cared.'

Hefnir held up a hand. 'Heggi needs Thorvald's protection. Here.'

'I'm to come!' Heggi shouted. 'It's not fair. It's my boat, anyway. I want to hunt walrus. I'm better than her.'

'Enough!' Hefnir shook him.

'But I am better. So's Rakki!'

'Sigrid, give him some chores. And if you say another word, Heggi, you know where you'll go.'

The boy's lips turned white. Once again, Bera wondered where it was that Hefnir threatened to send him that had such a strong effect. Ottar's sharp clips were better than this terrorising. Sigrid's glance showed she shared Bera's sympathy but she led him out, the dog following. His sobs and her low voice grew more distant.

Something rustled in the strewn floor. Thorvald struck like an owl and silenced it.

Bera's thoughts teemed. She had lied about the Serpent, who had hidden himself at the feast. But if she started to tell Hefnir the truth the whole episode would come out and there would be bloodshed. So she began to see that Thorvald needed to stay behind and protect Heggi from him. Though that left Sigrid with him... but Thorvald would never own up to killing her son. He would protect the household, if only for Hefnir's sake. There would be another chance – where she wouldn't be the obvious suspect, as she would on the trip. And Bera longed to be away from stifling Seabost, wild and free, far from having to think like this.

'So that's settled,' said Hefnir. 'It will be a honeymoon, Bera, I promise you.'

Thorvald did not look happy about it – but that riven face was always hard to read.

They went about their own duties. Bera took some household silver coins, told Sigrid she was going to check the livestock, and set off for the forge.

Heggi was in the yard, leaning on a broom and sulking. He gave her a dark look and farted loudly as she passed.

'That'll be the pinworms,' Bera said breezily. 'I'll mix up more witchbane when I get back.'

'Cow.'

'I'll take that as a compliment, since you love Feima so much.'

Bera was nearly at the waymark when she heard a scatter of stones behind. She turned to find Sigrid puffing after her, wrapped in so many layers that she looked like a walrus. She waited for her to catch up. When she did, Sigrid tried to speak but was breathless. She bent over, put her hands roughly where her knees might be and gently steamed in the cold air.

'What is it?'

Sigrid wafted a mittened hand for more time.

'Come on, Sigrid, I haven't got all day. What's the rush?'

'Present. I made it.'

Bera supposed it was the blanket for Asa's baby but hid her jealousy. 'How did you know I was seeing Dellingr?'

'Obvious.'

'Is it?'

Sigrid looked at her.

Bera sighed. 'Oh, it doesn't matter. You'd better come with me.'

'As long as we walk slowly.'

Bera shifted from foot to foot while Sigrid and Dellingr discussed each hair on the baby's head, but when she finally saw the sword, it was worth the wait. It gleamed like white fire in the darkness of the forge.

'It's magnificent,' she said.

'It will be when I've finished.'

She handed over the coins, which shone in the smith's black hand.

Dellingr frowned. 'What's this for?'

'Is the sword called anything?'

'What, like Leg-Biter?' he teased. 'That's only for cowards.'

'I want you to mark some runes. It's not a name. It's ALU.'

He nodded. 'From the rune stone?'

And in that moment of connection it became clear to Bera that this was why she felt powerful here in the forge, near iron, with a man who respected runes.

'Do you know what it means?'

'Smiths sense the power. Best get to work and get this hilt changed first. Can I feel your grip?' Dellingr held his hand out flat.

Bera felt hot as she clasped it. He took a finger away until she was left holding only two, hard as iron. There was a moment when the known world tilted and Bera saw the promise of some other love.

He studied her hand. 'Tiny.'

'That's because she never does any work.'

She had forgotten Sigrid was there. At least their laughter gave Bera some excuse for being so flushed.

'And the goat milk?' he asked Sigrid.

'What goat milk?' Bera disliked Sigrid having a life outside the longhouse.

'It's for the bairn,' explained Dellingr. 'As well as the breast, Asa wants him to have goat milk. Our girl failed to thrive on cow's and she thinks the lad will be the same.'

'Heggi'll bring some milk,' Sigrid said.

Bera would not be outdone. 'Heggi will bring the goat!'

'I'll be shutting up shop soon as it gets dark.' Dellingr followed the two women outside.

'When should I come back?' Bera asked.

'Whenever you like.'

Ordinary life was restored – but Bera was sure Dellingr had felt their special connection, of ancient smithing and Valla powers.

Then Sigrid exclaimed, 'Nearly forgot!' and rummaged under her various cloaks and furs.

Trust Sigrid to bring a present for the wretched baby.

'If you wore less you'd shift quicker,' Bera snapped.

Sigrid's hand emerged, holding a piece of tooled leather. 'Made this,' she said and actually blushed. 'It's a sheath for your sword, Bera. To keep you safe.'

Bera kissed her, in shame and remorse. 'Let's go up to the rune stone.'

Bera stood the sheath against the seaward side of the rune stone. 'I'll think about what to say.'

'Have a bit of something first.' Sigrid sat down and burrowed under her layers again.

Bera took the weight of the furs, to help. 'You haven't got a stewpot in there, have you?'

Food and laughter; their way of making up. Sigrid pulled out a cloth that held a few hunks of smoked meat and a mangled piece of cheese. They chewed for a while and gazed out over the water, as still as stone today, as if still frozen. You could see beyond the Skerries, towards the Ice Rim. Bera wondered if Sigrid knew how close she was to where Bjorn met his death.

'Do you think I'm like my mother?' she asked.

'What way?'

'Babies. She only managed to have me and the last one killed her.'

'More than that killed her.'

'What do you mean?'

'Are you going to have that cheese?'

'It's too mashed.'

Sigrid gulped the cheese in one.

'What killed her, Sigrid?'

'Did you ever look about you back home, and wonder where all the girls were?'

'Not really.' But a tightness was inside Bera, something she had pushed away.

'Time was, there was enough food to go round. But we had a run of bad luck and things got scarce. Mouths to feed and that. Men had to choose.'

'What are you saying?'

'Open your eyes, Bera. It's nearly as bad here. You're so busy trying to be a Valla and pestering that skern that you don't see what's under your nose.'

'That's not fair!'

'Poor folk can't keep every baby. They make choices.'

'What did my father choose?' Bera knew the hardness in Ottar.

'Don't dare to let on I've told you.'

A squall hit and they gritted their teeth until it had passed.

'How many did he refuse to raise?'

'You don't need to worry about not being able to get pregnant,' Sigrid said. 'That wasn't her problem. And Hefnir's wealthy enough to raise girls. He's a good man, Bera. You want to be careful.'

'What do you mean?'

'Nothing. Only Ottar's been saying things.'

Bera took some ale. 'So how many did he refuse to raise?'

'Three girls. Then they had you. The last was a boy but his mouth was all wrong and he couldn't suckle.'

'So he put him out for the wolves. Why didn't he expose me?'

'He'd given up on having a son. Your mother told him you were special.'

'I am.'

'Every baby's special, Bera.'

They held hands. Bera had hoped that falling pregnant would be difficult. Now she would have to be sure to take her herbs on the hunting trip.

'Why does Ottar talk about unfaithfulness?'

Sigrid bundled herself upright. 'Come on. Do what you're going to do and let's get home.'

Bera took the sheath and pressed it against the runes spelling ALU. She felt a deep vibration running down her arm and the leather leapt like a fish in her hand. It would double the power of the sword once it was inside. If only Thorvald was coming hunting with them.

On the way home, a new thought struck her. 'So Hefnir only took me because they were short of young women in Seabost?'

Sigrid looked shifty. 'Sort of. The sea-riders carried what women they could off to the dragonboats, killing some in the process, like Hefnir's wife.'

'Who told you?'

'Asa.'

'What does she know? He still might have chosen me.'

'Ottar wanted you off his hands.'

'Why?'

'Oh – so you'd be fed and clothed by someone else.'

'And Hefnir needed boats.' It still hurt. 'Ottar says my mother was unfaithful. Is that true?'

'He should let sleeping dogs lie.'

'So it is true?'

Sigrid hid behind her hood. 'No.'

'No, it's a lie?'

'It's not exactly true. It's just...'

'What?'

'Don't judge Alfdis harshly, Bera. She was married so young and your father being what he is. And being a Valla makes you more... She could have had anyone.'

'And she wanted to?'

There was no reply.

'Sigrid? Did she?'

It came like a sigh. 'There was only one she loved.'

'Who was he?'

But Sigrid stomped off and Bera knew she would say no more. Were she and Ottar suggesting Valla power came with equal lust? As Bera's own skills were growing, were her appetites also? That rushing moment when she held Dellingr's fingers now made her feel ashamed. How far was she fooling herself?

She caught up with Sigrid. 'Did Asa tell you about the sword?'

'Course. Why else would I make the sheath?'

Bera dropped back, fuming. What had been something special between her and Dellingr now had Sigrid and his snotty wife trampling all over it.

The longhouse was silent through the threshold and empty when they went in.

It made Bera angrier still that Hefnir was not available to be shouted at.

'Where is everyone?' she shouted.

A thrall rushed in from the byre, wiping his hands on a rough piece of sacking.

'Where is my husband?'

He pointed behind him. 'All men went to latrine.'

'That's that then,' said Sigrid. 'We won't be seeing them once they get in there, talking.' She went over to the loom and did not ask Bera to join her.

That was all right; she needed to be on the water. She threw the tooled sheath onto the table. The gift was spoiled.

Ottar helped her push a boat down the slipway. Bera could hardly bear to look at him. All she could see were the cold blue bodies of dead babies. Silence suited her father, if he noticed it, but it oppressed her. He pushed her off and she took a few strokes of the oars, into deeper water. The sight of his back as he walked away enraged her.

'It's not my fault I'm not a boy!'

He stopped. Water dripped from the oars while she waited to see if he would turn. He carried on walking.

She used the rune stone to keep a straight course as she headed out across the mouth of the fjord. Her skern sat facing her, shivering.

Dangerous, boating in our beads.

She felt for her necklace in a sudden panic that it had dropped overboard, then got back on course.

'I wear them all the time.'

You don't feel the draught of my absence so much then, do you?

'No. But I also...'

... keep trying to summon me by touching them. Doesn't work, sweetie. Not me, not your ma.

Bera clenched her teeth and rowed on. The sun was low in the sky and the air had a chill. The slap of water against the hull grew louder and the call of seabirds more strident.

'I'm off soon on a hunting trip with Hefnir,' she said.

I know.

'I wanted Thorvald on the trip now I have the sword.'

I know.

'Stop saying you know! I know you know!'

Then ask me a question instead of stating the obvious.

'You never say anything useful. You just riddle and smirk or clear off at the first sign of trouble.'

I'm here now. And, if you don't mind me saying so, anger makes you splash the oars a lot and I'm cold and wet enough.

'Why do you turn up, then, if you don't like it?'

I don't 'turn up' as you put it so elegantly; I'm here all the time. We skerns are very misunderstood.

'It's sad that ordinary folk never see their skerns till they're about to die. Then they don't want to see them at all.'

They have each other before they're born.

'But that makes them sad the rest of their lives, even though they can't remember why.'

The skern embraced her like perfumed smoke. *Have a lovely trip.*

'Will I?'

There was no reply.

Bera's hands were sore. She shipped her oars and studied her palms. A couple of blisters were forming and she gave them a hard stare. How quickly her hands had become white and useless, like the bellies of dead fish. She blamed Hefnir.

'Let's get cracking,' she said.

She attached two lead weights to the length of strong line. Hefnir used them to measure goods for trading and she hoped he would not miss them. Bera pictured the waters of the fjord in layers of fish: the small ones at the top; then middlers, who came up to eat them; then bigger fish who ate them; then huge fish that ate them and so on. If she could get the line to sink low enough, she was certain she could catch something that would make Heggi jealous. Better than her, indeed!

She put her largest hook onto one end and tied ribbons of white cloth along the line to lure them. She threw it overboard and took a few turns round the biggest block Ottar had. Perhaps he wished he had exposed her when he fostered Bjorn. Now he had Heggi. She could drown for all he cared. Yet out here that didn't hurt so much: the music of the water running past the hull was the drumming of a mother's blood.

In no time at all the line twitched and Bera began to wind it in. She put the biggest of the catch safe in the fish keep, baited the line with another and threw it over.

A grey fin was slicing the water, surging towards the boat. Bera dashed to the oars and fumbled, trying to get one in. She managed it, pulled, and the boat did a circle. The creature lunged at the stern. It was an ugly Thorhammer shark.

It took the bait and dived. The line screamed through the block until it reached its end and the stern dipped towards the water. Bera slid, clutching the oar, and cracked her shins on the thwart. The boat was shipping water. She needed to free the line but the knife was clipped at the stern.

The boat bobbed upright, spun round and tilted sideways, plunging the rail underwater. Bera scrabbled for the high side. A bucket floated away with the smaller bait. There was one chance to cut free. In one swift action she lunged for the stern knife, banged it down hard and returned to the rail. She had only managed to fray it and the strands snapped one at a time.

'Mama, help me!' she cried.

The shark surfaced in frilled horror, its sickle-mouth gaping. Then the line broke and it flicked away, picking up the dead fish.

There was no time for relief. Ottar's boats were sturdy but it was too low in the water. Bera bailed for her life. Why had she believed she should be out on the water today? She was totally alone and very stupid. So much for her growing skills.

Her skern pointed. *Look!*

An arrowhead of troubled water coming in from the sea paths. It was the black and white death. Starkwhales. They never came as far as her home village but fishermen spoke of them in awe and Bera knew she needed help.

No sign of a boat.

The starkwhales spread out to form a hunting line that stretched across the fjord. Tall black fins dwarfed the lone grey shark fin. The whales sank down and surfaced as one, with loud hissing sighs, then dived again, closing their prey.

She had to get away from the kill, though it meant heading into the pack. Bera rammed the oars back in place, braced her feet and pulled hard, straining every muscle. Unfit as she now was, her stomach screamed as she desperately made for open water. When the vast black and white bodies streamed past, Bera's bravery was rewarded. Her small boat rocked in the wave surge but was not swamped.

The shark stood no chance. A gleaming starkwhale tossed it into the air; another lunged, snapped and fell back in a white mountain of water. Then a threshing, bright red boil.

The wind had got up without her noticing and a mackerel sky was darkening. She needed to get home.

Her father was waiting for her when she got back, which surprised her.

'Saw you out there,' he said. 'Boat tipping about. Trouble?'

She opened the keep and proudly showed him two grey fish, as thick as Ottar's thighs and longer.

'Bottom feeders,' he said. 'How'd you catch them with no net?'

'Help me with the boat.' She was not so quick to forgive him that she would share a sea adventure. Besides, it was her own precious meeting with the starkwhales, who had come to save her. Perhaps her mother had too, and he wouldn't like that.

They winched it up together, took out the fish and then upturned the vessel so that all the water drained out and would not freeze. Even a sliver of ice could unclench all the nails.

'I'll cook these later,' she said. 'You'll be there?'

Her father nodded. 'I'll get a lad to wheel them over. So how'd you catch 'em?'

'My secret Valla skill.'

'My arse.'

Ottar walked back through the boatyard with her. There was something on his mind, but he wasn't sharing it. He instructed his lads to get the boat off the slipway. Then, at the whalebone gates, he stopped.

'There was a boy,' he started, then looked off into the distance. 'After you. There was a boy but he... Has Sigrid never told you, or anyone?'

'I knew it was a boy that killed my mother.'

'Not as simple as that. Maybe it was a punishment, his jaw being cleft. Fine strapping lad he'd have made but a face like a monster.'

'You exposed him.'

Ottar looked at his hands. The palms were covered in fish blood. He rubbed them against his work smock.

'He couldn't feed, not with a mouth like that. It was a kindness, a quicker death overnight, in the cold. He would have fallen asleep, that's all. They say it's the gentlest death, like drowning in snow.'

Bera snapped. 'Gentle? With wolves? Bears? Drorghers!'

Ottar turned away abruptly but not before Bera saw the first tears she had ever seen him weep. She could not feel any pity.

Bera waved away a thrall and gutted and chopped the fish herself. The blisters on her hands were bleeding but it was good to do it again, even if it all took longer than it used to.

Heggi rushed in as she finished. She wanted to boast about the size of her catch but he had exciting news that he was bursting to tell.

'Guess what?'

'I don't know.'

'No, go on. Guess.'

Bera closed her eyes and saw a baby cow curled inside its gossamer sheath.

'Is it to do with Feima?'

'That's not fair, using Valla stuff.'

He kicked at the rushes on the floor. He was right to be cross, although Bera was pleased that her powers must be stronger – and that he recognised it. She rinsed her hands in a bucket of water, dried them on her apron and was kind.

'The cowman told me how potent this bull is, so I guessed.'

He perked up a bit. 'The cowman felt her and says he's sure she's got a calf ready to come, almost. He's the best cowman, too, so he ought to know.'

'Lucky girl.'

'Who's lucky?' Hefnir came in from the longhouse side, hiding something behind his back.

'My cow, Papa. She's about to calve.'

'I doubt it.' He put his arm round Bera. 'I have a surprise for you.'

'I completely forgot! Heggi, get one of the milking goats and take it up to Dellingr. Quickly – it's getting dark.'

The boy was glad to be off again. He whistled and Rakki followed him outside.

Hefnir removed his arm. 'Why are you giving Dellingr a goat?'

'They need goat milk for the baby.'

'And you give him a whole goat.'

'No.'

'Is it always going to be like this?'

'What?'

'Your lies. There's talk about you and the smith. Who should I believe?'

'Dellingr's like a father to me.'

'You already have a father. Who told me to watch you.' Hefnir turned over her hand and made a face. 'I told you I won't have you going out in the boat. And you stink of fish.'

She wanted to hurt him. 'And I know the surprise is a sword.'

His face closed. 'Then you can present it to yourself.' He went out without another word.

Spoiling his surprise only hurt herself.

That night they made plans for the journey and then Ottar went straight to the boat to supervise everything. Hefnir was as excited as a child and stomped about issuing instructions. Finally, Thorvald snapped and Bera got her agitated husband into the billet, where they lay together, pretending to sleep.

Next day, Hefnir told Bera to meet him at the jetty and left. Thorvald reamed out his ears with the end of his knife, looking as if he didn't care. Bera made sure all the herbs and potions were in the basket she had packed while Sigrid fussed. Then she was ready to leave.

'You'll not go off without saying goodbye to Heggi?'

It would be cruel.

When she woke him he was excited and then he remembered he was not going with them and sulked.

'I shan't eat while you're away and then I'll starve and then you'll be sorry.'

'Your father might be.'

His dog came and nestled against him, looking at Bera with accusing eyes.

She felt bad. 'And so would Rakki, and me. And what about poor Feima? She would think you didn't like her anymore, if you went off and left her behind, and there she is, going to give you a calf.'

Sigrid came in with a beaker of milk. 'Can't have rich milk going to waste.'

Heggi managed to drink it, for Feima's sake, not theirs, he said. Bera wanted to tip it over him, after she had made an effort.

They went back to the hall. The slant-eyed woman was trimming Thorvald's hair.

For all she detested him, Bera needed his strength. 'Take good care of Sigrid, won't you? And Heggi. Don't let him go and fall off a cliff looking for birds' eggs.'

'I've looked after him all his life.'

Sigrid pushed a shawl at her. 'Have you got your thick sea cloak? I don't like to think of you shrammed with the cold.'

'I have furs, Sigrid.'

A door banged. Heggi rushed at Bera, burying his face in a fierce hug that was almost violent. It startled her and she let go but then regretted it.

'Boykin,' she said.

She went out before she started to cry and did not look back.

As soon as they were clear of the headland the boat launched itself at the waves like an escaped beast. The wind was fair, thin clouds scudded across a blue sky and the waves sang, their ice chains a memory. Bera's blood thrilled to the song. Hefnir's most trusted boatmen raised the sail and he steered towards the tip of islands that made the sea-rim blue. She breathed deeply, filling her body with the spirit of the sea and touched the sword that hung from her belt in Sigrid's sheath. The connection with Dellingr through the runes on the blade made it special again. ALU made everything... more. That was all she knew; there would be time to understand properly. As soon as Thorvald was out of the way, life would be smooth.

After a few hours, Bera let herself look back. The coastline was a solid mass with tiny specks of whiteness like a snow flurry. It was the first time in her life that she could not see her home fjord. The boat movement was completely different too. There was a longer, rhythmic swell and a rushing hiss past the hull instead of the slap of a short chop. Sometimes, out fishing, it felt like being slopped in a bucket, whereas here there was a long send. She wondered what immensity swam beneath them but the boat was going so fast that she believed they could outstrip anything.

Bera went up to the bow where the water cleaved into two clean streams of white. She let the tang of the crisp, salt air wash away the smoke and darkness of Seabost, feeling like a child again with both her mother and skern close by.

After the exhilaration passed she went back to Hefnir, who refused to let her steer. Even that did not flatten her mood. The crew checked the boat, for this was the real sea trial. Bera wished her father was here to make any repairs, not trusting Hefnir's boatmender to be as good.

The passage washed her mind into serene emptiness. Hefnir finished his watch and came and sat with her. Bera gave him a cold meal then kissed him.

'Please let me steer for a while.'

'I suppose there's nothing to hit out here.' Hefnir reached for the ale.

Bera ignored the insult, longing to feel the quickness of the helm, as one with her body. The wind stayed fair, though decreasing all the time, and slowly the moon loomed pale and yellow on the rim of the sea. No one spoke much, lulled by the creak and sway.

When Hefnir steered again, he pointed at a small headland while there was still light enough to see.

'Seal Island,' he said.

The dying sun made the mountaintops flame. They lowered the sail and the men took up their oars, making a herringbone wake in the glassy water as it slipped behind them.

Night chill made Bera's scalp tingle. A spectral figure was standing on the beach. His silvery hair did not stir. Light was leaching by the moment and soon this halo was all they made for in the greying gloom.

The person stepped forward to hold the prow while the crew jumped over the side to pull the boat up onto the coarse shingle beach. He held out a hand to help Bera disembark. A real enough youth, except his luminous eyes were pale as moonstones. Eyes that knew death.

'Been waiting for boat.' His voice was rusty.

'Who were you waiting for?'

'You.'

The crew had the rollers ready to run the boat up the beach. Bera took her place at the rail and helped keep the boat moving. The boy stood at the tideline, to mark how high they should pull the boat.

She left the others and joined him. 'How long have you waited?'

Hefnir shouted, 'We'll sleep in the boat tonight, get going again early.' He was calling her away.

Bera touched the boy's arm. His bones were sharp as a bird's under the thin cloth and she hated the feeling.

'How did you know we were coming?'

He pointed to a rough hut on the top of the cliff. 'Seen you from up there, far off.'

Bera had not fulfilled some prophecy – it was only a boy using his sea eyes. Another disappointment.

Hefnir came to get her but the boy invited them up to the hut.

'Only you two. Men's too many.'

Hefnir and Bera grabbed bedrolls and scrambled after the agile youth, who knew every tussock and rock in the dusk. Bera often stubbed her toe and tripped. Judging from his cursing, so did Hefnir.

The moon was high when they reached the hut. Bera stopped to gaze at its yellow path across the sea, murmuring words of thanks for their safe passage.

The boy tugged at the weather-beaten door, cursing. 'Swollen.'

Hefnir wrenched it open and the boy went through to light a lamp. Bera smelt whale oil as she followed.

It was like stepping into a sailor's sea chest. The walls were covered in shelves, hanking with hooks and nets and weights and ropes; oars and sails and buckets and floats. Everything stowed, scrubbed clean and ready. Up in the roof was a small, pitch-bottomed boat, upside down on the beams. It was round, like a bowl.

'You don't go out in that, do you?' she asked.

The boy kept his back turned.

Hefnir was handling some of the boat tools. 'These feel good in your hands. Fit for work.'

'Father made them.' He had a fit of coughing.

There was no sign that he shared the hut.

Bera picked through bits of whittled flotsam on a bench: a driftwood stoat, an ice bear. A shard of sea-milled glass was like Agnar's eyes. And his dear old dog. A gutting knife, its handle smooth as butter. Walrus tusk.

'We've come to hunt walrus,' she said.

Hefnir quickly added, 'Or whatever's plentiful.'

The boy grinned. He had a small gap between his front teeth and Bera wondered how old he was. Not shaving yet, so Bjorn's age, maybe.

'No one here to stop you.' His tongue was loosening with use, though softer than a Northman.

'Can I smell a stew?' Bera asked. Her stomach roared.

'There's special bowl. For guest, if one came.' So he was lonely.

Bera went over to the small fire and stirred the stewpot. White gobbets of fish and a few green strands floated in oily liquid – but she could eat anything tonight.

Their host scrabbled under a wide shelf that ran round three sides of the hut, pushing aside rolled pieces of sailcloth and driftwood. Then with a cry of triumph he threw a stiff piece of fish skin out of the way and pulled out a cloth-wrapped parcel and brought it to the fire. The linen was grubby but it was finer than Bera's own underskirt. He folded back the cloth and there were four bowls.

One of them was a lustrous black.

He rubbed his elbow round it then held it out to her. 'For special guest.'

It throbbed in her hand, like a purring cat. It was so glossy that she could see the loom of her face in the base. Bera's heart jolted.

Hefnir seized it and gazed into it while he spoke. Could he also sense its power? 'I've seen this precious stone before, except it was a knife.' He frowned for an instant but could not tear his eyes from the bowl. 'How did this piece end up here? With a scrap like you?'

'Sailed many sea paths.'

'Let's eat first and talk later,' urged Bera. 'And that's mine.' She had to tug the bowl away from Hefnir.

The boy swilled some broth round two plain soapstone bowls to clean them. Bera stared down into her black one. Deep down.

She could scry! There were swirls of blue ice, with crimson fires curling on mountaintops beyond. Over the tallest peak there was a cone-shaped cloud of immense height and breadth at its uppermost, ash-white. It funnelled and twisted downwards, sharper, more like a pout at the base. It was the face of a trole, blowing on the mountaintop to keep it crusted with ice.

Then the boy ladled soup into it.

Bera gloried in the fact that she had seen it without her skern, whatever it meant. It did not stop her eating. After spooning out the fish pieces, Bera lifted the bowl and drank the rest. She wiped the grease from her chin with the hem of her smock while the boy refilled their bowls.

When they finished second helpings, Bera thanked him.

'What's your name?'

'Er... Egill.' He sounded unsure.

Bera's eyelids were drooping and she was fighting to stay awake.

Hefnir said, 'Go to bed, if you like.'

'I want to hear about the bowl.' Bera tried to scry again but the surface was too oily.

Egill took the bowls to stack on a bench near the door and blew out the lamp before returning to the fire. His beardless face had more colour.

'Heard of Iraland?' he asked.

Hefnir nodded. 'Rich pickings.' How different, harder, he sounded.

'Where's that?' Bera asked him.

Egill answered. 'Furthest west. Been there many times. Father traded for the black bowl with an old holy man, he said. Rich man, anyways.'

What was a holey man? 'From the Great City?' asked Bera, trying to give the impression that she knew about trade.

'Their precious goods are more home-grown,' said Hefnir, with a wink at Egill. 'I've traded for some in the Marsh Lands.'

The boy shivered. 'That bowl's like a giant eye from a starkwhale or a monster shark. A black and glistening eye, looking up from the deeps.'

'An eye not looking in but looking out,' said Bera.

Egill stared at her, sharing the fear.

Hefnir got up. The boat in the rafters grazed the top of his head as he went over to the bench. He picked up the black bowl, smoothed it against his cheek and sniffed it. 'Where did the holy man say it came from?'

Egill stared into the fire. 'Top edge of the Ice-Rimmed Sea.'

Something stirred deep inside Bera; some instinct that this land was important and that she had just glimpsed it.

'I stay south. Or east,' Hefnir said. 'It's a hard enough living at home.' He brought the bowl back to his seat. 'If there's any land up there, which I doubt.'

'But he said it came from this... topmost edge?' Bera insisted.

Hefnir flicked a finger against the rim to make it ring. Its blackness was reflected in his eyes. Bera pictured him killing the boy to possess it. She snatched the bowl and put it by her side, where he could not see it. He managed to smile but he did not fool her.

The land existed. 'Did you go there, Egill?' she asked.

'Fate took us. Nearly died getting away.' Egill rubbed his hands through his salt-bleached hair, making it stick up. 'Storm hit, coming back from Iraland. Raged for days, on and on, pushing us north. Lost a man overboard. Couldn't row against the wind or the waves. Then a huge cloud of smoke and a din like a trole smithy: whoosh of bellows, clang of hammer and anvil. Fiery lumps of rock fell and the sea boiled.' His eyes were reliving the horror.

Bera believed the black bowl was forged in such a flame. 'Don't go on,' she said but Hefnir put a finger to his lips.

'Whole land blazed. A ball of fire hit Father. C-caught light like a grease taper. P-p-pushed him overboard.' Egill made a sort of hammer sign. 'He screamed till he went down.'

Such a loss was beyond reckoning.

Hefnir's laugh broke the quiet. 'Sailor's tales. I'm telling you, that bowl's black gold and it came from the hot south, not the ice-rimmed north, even if such a place exists.'

Egill glared. 'That land took Father.'

Blue ice and crimson fire, heading for the sea. Over it all, a cloud Bera couldn't yet read. The vision was real and so was the land. Summoning her.

8

Bera slipped into sleep like a seal through ice. She briefly surfaced when Hefnir picked her up and wrapped her in a blanket. The boy was claiming he once lit a fire and cooked a stew on an island that turned out to be a whale's back. But she may have dreamed that.

Now she was wide awake on a hard floor. Her head hurt, she was curled like a fist between two large baskets and when she tried to stretch out her legs she hit something cold and solid. An anchor. There was a sharp pain where something in her pocket had dug into her flesh. She missed being up on a sleeping platform; here, her eyes looked straight along the sandy floorboards. She could see crumbs, small stones and mouse droppings edged silver by the thin light coming through the small window opposite. It was early.

There was hacking, a retching cough. Bera sat up and banged her head on the shelf above. She rolled out from her billet and rubbed it, then left Hefnir sleeping and went outside to see who it was.

Egill tipped a bucket of water over himself, turned to grab a drying cloth – and was a girl.

Bera gasped.

Egill looked anxious, then shrugged. 'Now you know.' She coughed again.

'I can help with that,' Bera said.

'Being a girl?'

'The cough. I have some salves aboard, to rub on your – er – chest.'

They giggled together, which sent Egill off into yet another fit. Bera rubbed her back and then bundled her into her few clothes.

'Don't tell him.' Egill cocked a thumb towards the hut. 'Promise.'

'What's your real name?'

'Doesn't matter. Took Father's after he died.'

'Others must know.'

'No one left here to tell.'

She was already Egill's friend. 'I promise. You can show us where the walrus are.'

Egill pointed at Bera's necklace. 'See that bead? The black one? It's made of the same stone as the precious bowl.'

The truth of it surged through her.

Hefnir came out, washed his face and agreed that Egill should come with them.

The black bead had never filled her with greed, like Hefnir with the bowl. The same ugliness had been on his face as in her glimpse of him with the monks, before Thorvald cleaved their bald heads.

The crew kicked sand over their fire, rolled the boat down to the water and launched her. Egill explained that they would enter a channel that should only be navigated at slack water. Bera glanced at the wake behind a withy mark.

'This isn't slack,' she said.

'Egill knows the safe sea paths.' Hefnir slapped Egill, who beamed.

Bera remembered stories about sailors arriving at the edge of the White Sea at the flood. Riptides squeezed through island gaps, sending boats plunging into the deep. Sigrid terrified Bjorn with tales of the monstrous Skraken rearing out of the abyss. A dank sea mist drained the crew's good spirits. They gave up trying to sail and rowed on.

She felt a weight on her chest. Her skern.

'Oh, no. Don't tell me there is a monstrous Skraken.'

He preened before his moment of revelation. *I've come to tell you about Egill. He's a girl.*

'I know.' A small triumph but it pleased her.

That won't be her only fraud. She claims more knowledge than she possesses and will lead you into danger. Like the Maelstrom. Watch!

Bera flew above a troubled sea. She swooped down towards swirls of dark, oily water, surrounded by ripples and eddies. Broad streaks of foam, stretching to the far shores, slowly began a creamy whorl that seeded a whirlpool, which grew in immensity until its vast waters sucked her in. She was caught in oozing blackness that swept into her mouth and choked her. A roar of sweltering water and the blood-pound of drowning filled her head. The vortex began to spin faster. A towering ridge of glittering black water teetered above her. There was no light or air. Below her waited the gaping maw that led to the limitless deeps and the creature that lived there. The Skraken.

She jerked awake, gasping.

Egill came and sat beside her. 'Bad dream?'

Bera's scalp was on fire. 'We must go back!'

'Too late.'

The boat began to move faster and the noise of troubled water hammered on the hull. A current surged through the channel, churning and twisting the boat. The crew quickly shipped their oars or the waters would snap them like bird bones. Egill strapped herself to the mast, wild-eyed and grinning. Bera stumbled to the stern, banging and bruising herself on every block and oar-end. The noise was a constant numbing roar.

'Turn back, Hefnir!'

'Egill is showing us the Maelstrom. It's exciting.'

'I've seen it. It's a terrible thing!'

Hefnir stared at her, looking for certainty.

'We must turn back. Please, Hefnir.'

Man would stand by man. It was his code. 'Valla nonsense. Strap yourself down and enjoy it.'

Egill shouted, 'There she is! She's pulling us eastwards all the time.'

'Look out!' yelled a crewman, as a huge pine trunk swept past them, missing the hull by an oar's-length.

Only a strong wind could wrest them out of the Maelstrom's grip. Bera got the men to raise the sail but it hung limp. In rising panic, they all stared at the Maelstrom, where the giant tree was spun like a splinter of driftwood, upended and then sucked down to the monster beneath. They would be next. Bera grasped her beads.

Hefnir touched her arm.

'I'm trying to think!' she cried.

'Help us, I beg you.' His face was suddenly vulnerable as a child's.

The palm of her hand was red from holding her beads so tightly. The B rune was imprinted there, a sign.

She took her sword from its sheath. 'ALU,' she said.

'ALU.' Hefnir nodded understanding.

They both held up their swords and the sun appeared, making the metal glint.

'ALU,' chanted the men. 'ALU.'

Egill joined them all. 'ALU.'

A small breeze made Bera's hair shift. She must whistle up what she had started. Bera blew a long, slow note towards the sail. Then, from astern, a woven greyness wrinkled the water.

'It's coming,' she said.

The wind arrived with a slap that made the sail crack and billow. They were off! Hefnir steered the planing boat to the island. They lowered the sail, rowed into the shallows, jumped ashore, rolled it up the beach and doubled over with exhaustion.

'Told you it was slack.' said Egill.

Bera ran at Egill and pushed her over. Her look of honest surprise made Bera laugh. Then they were all laughing, crying, shoving each other.

'Listen,' Bera said.

In the distance came the mellow, bugling call of hundreds of swans. From off the land came flock after flock, their golden wings translucent against the sun. They were whistling swans on their way to their breeding grounds in the farthest north. There were so many that it sounded like a terrible tearing of the sky. Bera felt the beat in her chest and her eyes streamed with tears. After an age, the sound grew less, until the few remaining birds were past.

Hefnir pulled her head round to his and kissed her hard and long.

'You did well,' he said, 'my little Valla.'

He respected her powers, at last.

Bera left the others tending to the boat and went to explore the island. Thousands of tiny pebbles and dead creatures, pounded and milled by the sea over eternities, pricked her feet. She pulled off her loose dress and raced her shadow on the white expanse, her hair flying and eyes streaming.

She stopped for a moment to see if Hefnir was following. He was at the shoreline, ripping off his clothes to be swifter in the chase. Bera felt fear and desire combine, quickening through her like the first lungful of sea air. She laughed and ran on; feet thrilling to the minute sharpness beneath them and every hair of her body taut with anticipation.

She shrieked as he grasped her from behind with boat-hardened hands. She turned, smiling, about to speak when Hefnir kissed her. Urgently. It had not been like this before. He knew her for her real self and respected her Valla power. And that burgeoning force brought an equal rush of desire. Her husband responded. They were sudden savages. His wind-chapped lips grazed her throat and he pulled her to him, their hearts pounding out of their chests. He carried her into the water like a new bride. A jolt of iciness made them scream together and laugh. And then the loving completion of flesh joining flesh took her breath away. An ordinary miracle of nature.

They unclenched and ran back up the beach, holding hands. Hefnir rubbed her briskly to get dry and they lay together, shivering. Bera wanted to stay in this moment. She walked her fingers down his chest to the darker hair below. Hefnir smiled. It was gentle this time, and longer, like the rock of her fishing boat when she lay on its sole.

Bera woke, frozen. Hefnir was gone, leaving her vulnerable and lonely. She collected her dress from where she had thrown it and instead of finding the others, she sat and sulked.

Her skern put icy fingers against her cheek. *Get a fire going, will you? You can use the thing in your pocket.*

Bera took out a smooth piece of glass, like dried flatfish skin.

It was the one she had absently picked up at Egill's, which had dug into her thigh overnight and hurt her. As lucky as Agnar, with his sea-milled eyes. She held it up to her own. The world turned glaucous and remote.

Her skern sighed. *You are such a baby sometimes. It's a wonder you haven't sucked it.*

She glared at him. 'My Valla instinct made me take it. What is it?'

He coughed behind his hand. *Clearly, it is a remnant of some wealthy object. A jug, or beaker perhaps. Fetch some driftwood.*

'This had better have a purpose.'

He buffed his fingernails.

Bera went up the beach, found three small branches and a piece of salt-bleached birch. She threw them down crossly.

He smiled. *Now. Hold the glass a small distance from the birch and you'll see a white light fall on the wood. It's a sunbeam to play with. Go on, try.*

Bera was fascinated. She found the exact distance to hold it so the white light made a thin brown line on the wood. When it became frail she moved the glass closer to make a strong, if wobbly, line. She laughed with delight and turned to speak but there was the unclasping ache in her ribs and Hefnir was there instead, with a pile of wood.

'You carry on playing and I'll set the fire,' he said.

'I'm not playing!'

Hefnir made a rough fire pit in a circle of stones, set struts of the driftwood in the centre and laid some twigs and driftwood against them, sloping away from the breeze. Then he sat down, took out his knife and cut a notch in the flattest piece of dry wood.

'Women. You always have to decorate things. You're not practical.' He carefully placed a thin piece of bark underneath, carved a shallow dip next to the notch and held a long thin branch against it, rolling the spindle fast between his flat hands.

Bera was not looking at what she was doing. There was a smell of burning where the glass had scorched the wood. It gave her an idea. She held the glass closer and saw a whisper of smoke.

'Hefnir, bring me some dry grass.'

'I'm busy.'

Bera marched across, put some of his grass on her burned wood and then held the glass close. A curl of smoke rose.

'Quick!'

Hefnir put some thin bark to it, which caught light. Bera carefully took the fireboard over to the pit and placed it under the stack. She blew softly on the tiny flames and then the wood caught and crackled, leaping into life.

They looked at each other.

'That's faster than a fire-steel,' Hefnir said. 'Where did you get it?'

'I found it in Egill's hut.' Perhaps she had got it away from Egill.

'It'll work even when it's wet.'

'Don't show it to Egill.'

Bera felt disloyal, but there was danger stirring deep in the glass and, even without her skern's warning, some instinct about Egill's eagerness for peril disturbed her.

After making love again, Bera let Hefnir roughly braid her hair.

'We should get back to the others.' He was withdrawing inside himself, like the Hefnir she was used to.

'Are you glad I came?'

His kiss was to avoid answering.

Bera ought to love him but how could she when he kept changing? Strange company he kept, too: the butcher Thorvald and the Serpent King. What was Hefnir's true nature?

'Who is that man? The one you do business with?'

'A trader.' He did not ask which man out of so many.

Hefnir drank, then passed her the ale flask.

Bera pushed it away. 'You treat me like a child. I'm supposed to be your equal partner.'

'What is this?'

'I know he's called the Serpent King!'

Her anger was being fed by fear. She picked up a fur and threw it at him, and then a blanket.

'Look at you standing there, smug. I hate you! I thought we were closer now but you're cold and not even there when I wake up!'

'Stop it, Bera. You always spoil it for yourself.'

Truth made it worse. She saw herself seizing a log from the fire and smacking him, hard. Perhaps he saw it in her face because he held her tight in a bear hug. When her breathing slowed he kissed her forehead tenderly.

She said, 'At least we can fight without everyone in Seabost hearing it.'

Hefnir laughed. 'I think they still might have heard you from here!'

She cuffed him without rancour and hugged him back.

'I don't know where to start,' he said, over the top of her head. 'You know nothing of the world, Bera. I know you think your father is hard, and Thorvald, but believe me, they are nothing compared to what's out there.'

'So what is this Serpent King?'

He moved away from her. 'It's better you don't know.'

'Why?'

He jabbed the embers with a stick.

'Does Thorvald know?'

He prodded the fire harder, so that some sparks flew.

'He does know, doesn't he? Why do you trust him more than me? You think because I'm young and a woman, that I couldn't...'

'I know you tried to kill him. That's why he's at home.'

Bera was livid. Thorvald must have told Hefnir she was in his billet. She was lucky all Hefnir had done was bring her hunting but couldn't stop herself.

'So this isn't my treat! You're keeping us apart!'

'Thorvald's important to me.'

'Give me one good reason.'

'Thorvald's the one who takes the tribute to... the king.'

Bera was spitting. 'He's not a real king! Why pay a tribute to a tattooed monster?'

'You see? I knew you would be angry.'

They glared at each other, their arms folded across their chests. Bera felt as if she had lost something, like when her skern left her.

'Anyway, Thorvald said the reindeer was a tribute to you!'

'I don't give anyone tributes.' Hefnir paused. 'I was using a word you'd understand. Look. We trade where we can and where we can't trade we take. Simple as that. Men die. It's the price we pay for our thralls and furs. But there are others who risk nothing. They are sea-riders, Bera, whose dragonboats lie in wait for our trading vessels to come home and then attack when we are already battle-weary. They take whatever they want.'

'But the Serpent lives in the mountains.'

'He's not one of them. He keeps the sea-riders off us. You've heard about the raid that took our young women and killed my wife? Well, he got them to leave Seabost. I owe him, Bera. It's simple: every season we pay him to let us get home with our goods. He either pays whoever it is that runs him, or he has to fight, so the price I pay is high.'

'I still don't understand why you deal with him.'

'The price of safety goes up all the time, Bera, and it's a price we must pay. With tusks.'

'You should have told me, Hefnir.' But he was telling her now. Was he starting to care?

'For so many years now I've only discussed business with—'

Bera kissed him before he could say the name, then lingered. There was one last question she wanted answered.

'I saw a vision of the Serpent King. He gave Heggi a wooden horse. A woman came …'

Hefnir pushed her away. 'Impossible! He is nothing! Do you understand? Not a king, nothing. He is a non-person, just like my dead wife. I don't ever want to hear you talk about him again.'

Hefnir threw together their belongings. Bera was even more confused and they returned to the others in silence, while the sea held a memory of light to show the way. It was the end of their honeymoon.

Later, Bera stared up at the stars, a buttermilk immensity, while Hefnir lay dozing beside her. His weight was keeping her warm but she gently wriggled away. The Serpent was still on her mind. She thought about the fire-blackened houses in Seabost. It was good that Hefnir had explained some of it to her but why would he not talk about her vision? And did Thorvald have a private deal with the Serpent? Two monsters together.

She rolled out, threw a fur round her, carried her sword and strode down to the sea. There was no fear of Drorghers in this barren land but there were other predators. The mysteries of being a married woman and a Valla weighed heavily.

'Mama. Please show me you're here.'

Valla power increased desire. Bera longed to be purified. Bathing in the moon's silver sea path would be numbingly cold and full of unseen jaws and coils. So she slipped off her fur, her skern sheathed her and they were soaked in moonlight.

Pebbles crunched. She grabbed the sword, twisting to see her foe.

It was Egill.

She lowered her weapon. 'What are you doing?'

'Lonely.'

'Me too.'

Egill put the fur round Bera's shoulders and they hugged to get warm. They sat together on one side of the fire; the sleeping men invisible on the other. There was a distant, lonely howl, then total silence.

In this secret darkness Bera spoke about all the losses in her life: about seeing her mother die; about Bjorn being like a brother and letting him die too. It brought her to the problem of Thorvald and she stopped.

Egill took her hand. 'Tell.'

She would never see Egill again once the hunt was over. Another loss, but for now it was a relief to talk to someone uninvolved.

'I'm going to make Thorvald pay the blood debt because paying Ottar for a boat is not enough.'

'He sounds like a Viking.'

'He's evil. He scares me.' Bera did not like admitting this.

'Bera, you see things so black and white. But things are shades of the same, even life and death. When you're born you're fit to die. Can't die if you've never lived. Only a heartbeat between the two.'

'I don't know what you mean.'

'Good, bad. Boy, girl. Right, wrong. What's the difference?'

Everything.

Bera let go of Egill's hand, went over to the driftwood heap and placed some on the glowing embers. They popped and crackled.

'As soon as we've got walrus we're going home. I think Hefnir needs to pay someone fast.' She dropped her voice even lower. 'He tried to force me, this snake he has to pay. He has black tattoos all over his body.'

Egill's eyes widened. 'Serpents?'

'You know him?'

'In Iraland.'

The Serpent King must infest the known world. 'I'm hoping he's killed Thorvald while we're away.'

'Seems you ought to scotch the snake, not Thorvald.'

'My skern's right. I'm no swordswoman.'

'Use other skills then.' Egill tapped her head.

'I don't have any. Except healing with plants.' A log cracked, making Bera jump. 'I did once, by mistake, mix poison...'

'Then use that.'

'No! It's dishonourable. There might be consequences. Although ...'

'What?'

'It might be different for a Valla.' She hoped it was.

'Revenge can destroy anyone, Bera.'

'Why do you care?'

Egill's gaze was like a finger, feeling the features. 'Friends?'

Bera made a Thor hammer sign. 'Friends.'

'Show mercy and be saved.' Egill did a big forehead to chest cross.

'What's mer-sea?'

Egill could not explain. 'Someone said. In Iraland.'

The men began to stir. Time to hunt.

They took knives and tackle from the boat, sharpened spears and axes. Bera went off behind a shrub. A white fox turned its pointed face to look at her before it trickled on between small mounds of snow, keeping low. It had a fine tail. She had not seen a live one before, though these days she wore the skins.

When she got back, Hefnir had a whale-hook ready, lashed to a long wooden stave with extra rope, which was coiled over his arm. The others mocked Egill's whittled staff but when she pointed with it to where they would find most walrus they followed.

Bera was happy. The rising sun striped the ground mauve and yellow and the frosty air twinkled like falling stars. Small creatures popped up and watched as they passed. High above them, birds with wide wings lazily circled and mewled. Bera's nostrils prickled and she sneezed, causing the men to make the hammer sign on their chests; except for Egill, who made her own version again.

The yowling, barking, mewling was deafening. Underneath was a deep roar, like an approaching gale. When they reached the next bay the smell hit. The shore was studded with seals of different size and colour; some of them with howling pups. They carefully picked a slippery way through the writhing mass. Pups squealed and mothers barked if a foot landed too close but mostly it was the chatter of seals going about their business.

The stench of fish and seal droppings made Bera's eyes stream. Egill nudged her, to show that all the others had covered their faces with neck-cloths. It helped.

At the far end, on a ledge that jutted into the sea, was a group of fifty or more walruses. They were dozing. Egill showed Bera the different tusk lengths of males and females. The creatures were ranged in colour, from almost pink to a soft brown. Their long whiskers twitched and occasionally a flipper would sleepily wave.

As they drew close, Hefnir gestured that they should get round behind the nearest group. Bera stayed at the rear as she was new to this, with Egill watching her back. Hefnir crawled towards the biggest male, keeping low. They followed him as closely as they could, to look like one animal to the sentinel walrus. Unlike the seals, this one was properly on guard, so whenever it showed any interest they would freeze until it settled once more. It was like the game of trole-stones they used to play as children. Bjorn used to beg her to stop. She pushed the memory away.

All went well until one of the men slipped. The sentinel let out a long warning wail and the massive creatures headed for the sea. They moved at a man's running speed, which surprised Bera, who thought they would lumber.

The hunters gave chase.

The prize bull had the longest tusks, which hampered him. Hefnir flung his spear just as the beast made it into the water and hit. The next man missed. The bull swam towards the rest of the pack, with the long staff sticking out of its back. Hefnir let the coils of rope unravel and the others grabbed the free end and took up their positions. Bera kept her mittens on, to stop rope burn. They all took the strain. At first the bull was too strong and they went skittering down onto the beach like children.

'Hold hard!' shouted Hefnir.

They dug in and slowly began to gain. The six of them heaved as one. There was gradual progress and then a rush and they got the beast quite close to shore. It maddened the watching walruses, who chanted a battle-cry: 'Uk-uk! Uk-uk!'

A female locked tusks with her mate, trying to drag him to deep water and safety, but he was tiring and she had to retreat. It was a signal to pull harder. The huge creature wallowed in the shallows, rolling in the undertow. With each wave surge they tried to get him further ashore; with each drag he was sucked out to sea. They were all tiring, too. Bera flung off her mittens, waited for the next wave to bring the bull closer, then grasped a flipper and heaved. She thought it would be slippery but the underside was rough and grazed her hands. Egill took the tail and others the tusks. This time, it did not go back out. Hefnir tied more ropes and they dragged the beast ashore.

Its skin was studded with fleshy nodules and folded in long wrinkles. There were old battle scars and a couple of new lesions, but the skin was so thick that no blood had yet reached the surface. The creature's sad, defeated face had whiskers that were more like thin fingers; now hardly stirring. Bera wanted to end its suffering. She unsheathed her sword and plunged it through its brown eye.

They sank onto the beach, exhausted.

Bera could not stop grinning. At last she had bravely killed something.

'That was the best thing I've ever done!'

'Only five more and we can go home,' Hefnir said.

She threw a mitten at him.

The exhilaration of courage didn't last past the first kill. Bera was ashamed of growing so cruel and said parting words rather than be in at any other death. It was enough that she knew she could do it when the time came to dispatch Thorvald. One practice kill was enough.

When at last they had their six walruses and Hefnir made ready to set off, a gale blew in with sharp hail. They laid the boat on its side and used the mainsail as a booth to sit it out. Their clothes dried on their backs while they ate and drank, especially the latter. It surprised Bera how much Egill put away, telling wild tales of whoring into the night until she fell into a stupor. Perhaps she had to be more of a boy – but was it to persuade others or herself?

No one slept as the storm raged. It let up just before dawn on the third day, so they righted the boat and rolled it down to the water, ready. Bera ran her hand along the side and saw that some boards had become unclenched with the flex of the hull.

Egill joined her. 'Done many boat repairs. Reckon on being the best.'

'Stay away from the mender,' Bera warned. 'He's proud, with a temper.'

Egill did not. Instead, she went straight to the boatmender and reasoned, with lots of pointing. The man could not speak because his mouth was full of nails. Egill gestured more wildly. The mender shoved. There was finger jabbing and then Egill threw a rabbit punch. Both Bera and Hefnir ran over and kept the two apart.

Hefnir laughed. 'I like your spirit. The mender's twice your size.'

'Only trying to help,' Egill said and shook the mender's hand.

All over. It was odd how quickly folk were inclined to forgive Egill. And when the heavy tusks broke the winch, the mender had to make running repairs and let Egill help.

Bera piled the discarded ballast stones into a rough marker and blessed all the creatures in this distant place so they would be plentiful. Then she asked for a safe passage back with no Maelstrom.

'We don't go till the last hour of the ebb,' she said to Hefnir, who did not argue.

Bera glowed. The honeymoon might be over but she was one of his advisors now.

The whole crew were grey with exhaustion. When it neared slack water they set off and the last of the tide spared them, taking the boat out safely through the channel and heading south. Bera liked short trips where you could let rip and feel the wind and spray in your face; or fishing, watching clouds roll past as you gazed up at a summer sky, not this long flog home.

'Need a bit more easting,' Egill said. 'Then you'll reach Seal Island, no time at all.'

Bera did not want Egill to go home. She kept away from her to avoid hurting more. A sea-chill crept into her bones, despite her heavily greased sea cloak. The wind stayed a steady north-easterly.

Then Egill rushed to the bow and pointed east. 'See those clouds? That's the Point. Home's not far off.'

Hefnir said nothing and when they saw Seal Island he did not change course to make for it.

Bera knew that look: he alone had made a decision and would discuss it with no one. But why was he bringing Egill, who gazed at her land with wet eyes, her head slowly turning as the day passed.

Bera pictured the little boat, high and dry in the rafters. 'Will you miss home?'

'Thought Hefnir would want that black bowl.'

'He easily forgets what's precious to him.' It was probably true.

Egill looked sideways at her. 'You liked it too. And kept it well away from him.'

'I scried in it. For the first time.'

'Heard tell of scrying.'

'I saw that land of fire. We could go there together.'

'Never! Never again, Bera, don't ever want to!'

Bera wondered why Egill never said 'I'. Perhaps she never had a 'you'. Freckles stood out on her ashen skin where blood coursed red and blue. Up close, her hair was like dull glass, made colourless by years underwater. She was a corpse whale: the opposite of a Drorgher. Black and white. Fearless and fearful.

Bera hugged Egill more tightly. The skern might be wrong about her. In any case, she could mend her troubled friend.

Much later, a line of deeper greyness on the sea-rim thickened and became the mountains that guarded the entrance to their fjord.

It was nearly dawn when they closed the land and too dark to see Hefnir's face until he kissed her.

'You're a jewel, Bera. Not many women are as fearless as you.'

'I'm full of fear.'

'But you ignore it, like a man.'

Is that what eventually made a man hard, like her father? Would driving herself beyond fear to kill Thorvald make her like Ottar? Worse?

'I want to be home.' Even Seabost. Bera longed to be back, boasting about her bravery to Dellingr, although it would also mean having to share Hefnir with Heggi and everyone else with a claim on him. The Serpent King. Thorvald.

'You got festivals, that sort of thing, at your place?' asked Egill.

'Midsummer, Yule,' Hefnir said. 'Why?'

'Sowun's good.'

'What's that?'

'Feast in Iraland. A good feast.' She nudged Hefnir. 'Plenty to drink and—'

'What's it for?' Bera interrupted, to stop Egill's pretend crudeness.

'End of harvest. Cattle come down off mountains. Start of winter.'

Hefnir said, 'It's hardly summer yet.'

Bera would make this festival hers. 'We need a new Seabost tradition! It can be a mix of this Sowun and Midsummer.'

Egill said, 'The doorway to the other world opens and dead souls revisit their homes. You'll see them again!'

Thorvald mustn't be one of them. If he wasn't dead already, Bera would have to wait until the feast was over.

9

The Serpent King had not attacked but the longhouse felt changed. Everyone in it looked different. Ottar was more muscular, Sigrid thinner and Heggi's legs were as long as a colt's. Bera had pictured the words of greeting and then the hugs, the smiles, but they were all tongue-tied. Perhaps she should be patient but that wasn't a skill she possessed. The biggest disappointment was Heggi. He was as surly with her as in the early days and he glowered at Egill. It was a relief when he set off, going hunting with some older boys.

Bera apologised to Egill. 'He should not be so rude.'

Ottar bristled. 'Be glad he's found some friends at last. I miss him at the boatyard, mind.'

'Egill's worked with boats and can even sail a round thing.'

'I'll give him work.' Ottar smacked Egill on the back. 'What's this round thing?'

'In Iraland, they tar skins stretched over a frame. A man with one oar...'

They went out talking boats. Ottar thought he had another lad to mould and it delighted Bera that he should be fooled. Hefnir followed them, leaving Bera alone with Sigrid.

'This is a fine welcome, Sigrid. You might try and look pleased to see me!'

Sigrid fussed about, pulling Bera's salt-stained garments from sacks. 'Look at the state of these. And you can't trust a thrall to do the job properly. I shall have to do it myself, as ever.' She gestured at the rips and marks. 'You go off and double my work. It's typical. You stay away twice as long as you said and then you expect songs of joy the moment you get back!'

'I don't!'

'You do.'

Bera pulled the clothes out of Sigrid's hands, threw them on the floor and kicked them towards the door. 'You don't have to do any of it!'

The women glared at each other. Then the corners of Sigrid's mouth twitched, trying not to smile. It looked funny and Bera roared with laughter. Sigrid joined in, opened her arms and Bera went to her, smuggling in as though she were a child again.

A couple of thralls took the clothes.

'I'll see to them, just leave them outside,' Sigrid called after them. It made her chest rumble.

Bera pulled away. 'Where's Thorvald?'

'How am I supposed to know?' Sigrid was sharp again.

'Did Thorvald... talk to you about anything? While we were away?'

'Did you think we'd sit in silence?'

Perhaps she resented being left alone with the monster but Hefnir came back in before Bera could find out.

'Where's Thorvald?'

'He had to meet someone,' said Sigrid.

'When did he go?'

'Early.' She went through to the pantry. 'I'd best get on.'

Bera was astounded. Why couldn't she have said so to her? Was Sigrid still seeing her as a child, not Hefnir's wife and in charge of the household?

Hefnir warmed his hands at the fire. 'I never used to feel the cold. Must be getting old.'

'Don't say that.'

'I will never be an old man, Bera.'

'Not the way you live your life, no.'

'To be old is a dishonour.'

Dishonourable to be old and blind like Agnar? Or to have scars only on the back like Hefnir? Men made up the rules of honour but one day she would know which were the right ones.

Hefnir sat near the fire. 'Your father and Egill have already started swapping stories.'

'My father only knows this fjord.'

'That didn't hinder him.' He looked round the longhouse. 'It always seems smaller to me, when I get home, than how I picture it.'

'Why did you not take Egill home?'

Hefnir turned away to pick up a gaming counter. He flicked it in the air, then pocketed it. 'So – a new feast! The folk at the jetty want something for fertility.'

'All men, were they?'

'Not all, no.' His voice softened. 'The village needs more babies, Bera. And so do we.' He held out his hand.

She ignored it. 'I'm going to the forge, with something for their baby. Shall I take the hunting weapons?'

'I don't want you going up there, Bera.'

She cracked a split log into two parts and threw them on the fire. 'Am I your captive now?'

In one strong move he had her across his knee and smacked her bottom, hard. Bera shouted in rage but he laughed and kissed her.

She was not a child anymore but played it. She let him think he had won but determined to see Dellingr. There was nothing to hide, so why shouldn't she? He was the only one who truly appreciated her skill. He understood her and knew about the old ways, which helped her scry and feel Valla power growing inside her. He made her more herself.

The smith rubbed his hands on a sooty piece of sacking and then used it to wipe the sweat off his brow. Both face and hands were left looking more grimed. This wasn't the face she had pictured in her time away and she was tongue-tied.

'I didn't know you were home,' he said. 'I've had my head in the furnace and banging away on these farm tools all morning. Asa says I'm deaf as a post already.'

'Are you so old?'

He grinned at her with clean, even teeth. 'Old enough to know when I'm being teased.'

Except she meant it. Her dismay continued.

'I've brought you this for the baby.' She pulled out the piece of walrus blubber on its stick.

Dellingr frowned. 'It'll get filthy here. Why not give it straight to Asa? She'll be that pleased. It'll keep little 'un quiet, that's for sure. He's on her breast every whip-stitch.'

His fond concern made her sick with jealousy. The soother was only an excuse to be here with him, not visiting his wife and the gaggle of womenfolk come to drool over the baby. Perhaps it showed on her face.

Dellingr said, 'I expect you're busy, just getting back and that. I'll get my blower to clean himself and take it over. Wrap it up in its cloth again and I'll fetch him.'

The boy came out to the pump, already stripped to the waist. He threw a bucket of water over his head, which streamed blackly over skin that was as white as a drowned man's. The second bucket revealed red spark-spots and scars where the fire had got the better of him. He stood, shivering, keeping his back turned to Bera. It pleased her that he showed no sign of being beaten. Not many masters failed to strike their boys. It was comforting to find her trust was well placed.

'Dry yourself on this,' said Dellingr.

He threw the lad a sack. The boy made a poor job of it and pulled on his scorched smock before he was dry. Bera held out the parcel and he grabbed it and made off.

They were alone.

Bera found a reason to stay. 'I wanted to thank you for your sword. It did well.'

'A fight, was it?'

'A fight against a walrus.'

At last she was able to brag; telling the story of the hunt, when she single-handedly brought down six monster walruses. She was beginning to feel close to him again when a slow handclap from behind made her falter. She spun round and there was Thorvald, smirking down at her from his horse.

Bera's horror at being overheard talking about slaughter by the man she intended to kill was doubled by his finding her at the forge.

Guilt turned to fury and she wished she had her sword with her while she was riled enough to use it away from home.

'How dare you follow me!'

'Don't flatter yourself. I've come to ask the smith to do his work.' He took out his own sword. 'Unlike some folk, who stop him.'

'It was a good tale,' said Dellingr. He took Thorvald's sword by the hilt. 'I'd best be getting on now, though.'

Thorvald pulled the horse round. 'Want a ride?'

Bera ignored him and started for the village.

'Too proud to sit behind me?'

'I suffer you at home, Thorvald. I like to breathe clean air when I'm outside.'

'Ever the madam.'

She left the men behind. Poor Dellingr, having to deal with someone like Thorvald. But had her temper made her miss an opportunity? Could she have pushed him off his horse? He was too skilled a rider. Now Thorvald would tell Hefnir that she was at the forge. Would he lock her up like Heggi? Where? Any confinement would send her mad. She had always believed it would bury her powers. Her mother had been confined, they said, and she died.

Thorvald was with Hefnir by the time Bera got back. She went into the byre and pretended to be busy. Hefnir did not come and scold her, so she decided Thorvald liked to wait for when any bad news about her might do most damage.

Rakki came home, in stages, with thirty-two puffins and when they ate some of them later Bera pronounced him the best dog ever. Heggi thawed enough to allow her to comb his caffled hair but he kept to the men's side when possible and followed them out to the latrine after they had eaten. Sigrid helped thralls clear the dishes and then stayed in the pantry. Bera had the impression she was avoiding her.

She put on her cloak and followed. 'I'm going to check the cattle.'

'They've managed without you all right.' Sigrid lowered a barrel into its pit.

'I want to see if Feima has calved.'

'Heggi would have told you, wouldn't he?'

Bera left Sigrid to her bad temper. It was unlike her to bear a grudge, if a grudge it was.

She quickly checked on dear, uncomplaining Feima then stayed outside. A few chickens squawked out of her way when she passed the slurry pond. A runnel brought the urine downhill into it and the warm air was thick with the stench. Bera hated being excluded now they were home. Eavesdropping was unthinkable – and yet she found herself standing by the runnel at the back of the latrine without planning to be there. She crept as close as she dared to one of the trapdoors, which was pegged open ready for thralls to collect the soil that dropped into the pail below. There was a precise smell, almost like seaweed, that she recognised as Heggi's. There was no taint of illness but Bera studied it for pinworms while she tried to hear who was speaking.

It was Thorvald. '... be enough.'

'You're certain?' Hefnir. Then mumbling.

Bera crouched down, leaning against one of the struts to get her ear close to the opening. Someone farted and she nearly fell over. It was comical – but dishonourable. Suppose one of the thralls found her? Or Rakki and Heggi? How could she face anyone again?

'I want no more to do with him.' Hefnir, loud. 'How many more times?'

'I need backup. He's still claiming blood money.'

'Tell him to go to Hel. I'll kill the bastard if I see his ugly face again, that's the only reason I'm not going.'

'He has rightful claims, Hefnir, as you well know.'

'I'll go with Thorvald.' Heggi!

'You will not,' said his father. 'No argument. Thorvald can go alone.'

'He will start something.' Thorvald.

There was a thump, as if Hefnir had slammed his fist into wood. Bera missed the start of his reply. '... if she ever was family!'

'So what is your answer?'

'Give him some – but less than he says they want. Four tusks.

Show them who's boss. How dare they say who they will and will not deal with? To Hel with them!'

A door crashed open. Bera leapt up, banged her head on a bucket and froze. Had they heard it? She stayed like a hare in a burning field until someone spoke again and then she ran for the shadows. They came out, talking.

Bera needed to hear the rest of it, so she tried to keep up with them yet stay hidden. The trouble was, she would be seen crossing the clear ground before the longhouse... but she would worry about that when they got there. She strained to hear what they were saying.

'I told Sigrid,' Thorvald said. 'So now she...' His voice faded into the distance.

Told Sigrid what? Was that why she was avoiding her? Bera waited until she thought they must be across the opening and then kept low and followed.

Hefnir was asking, '... and Heggi too?' Rage made his voice throb.

There was no reply, only the sound of footsteps treading onto stone.

Bera flew round to the main entrance and ran through the whispering passage, flung open the door, whipped off her cloak and sat at the loom, shaking.

There were voices in the byre. Sigrid came through from the pantry and raised her eyebrows when she saw Bera, who put a finger to her lips. Sigrid put a lit taper near the loom and sat next to her, which was unusually quick-witted.

When the men came through it looked normal but there was a new self-consciousness about Sigrid. The men smiled and joked and said nothing about tusks and blood money. They were all play-acting now. Bera did not know what was happening or who to trust anymore.

They sat up late, long after Heggi had reluctantly gone to bed. Bera wanted to find out why Hefnir had been so angry but she could not get him to their billet, nor could she will Thorvald into going to his. She couldn't ask Hefnir directly and be accused of eavesdropping. So the men talked about the hunting trip while Sigrid sewed and kept her head down. Their short honeymoon was entirely lost in Hefnir's version of the trip. Perhaps it only had ever been in her mind. But their coupling was special there and he could not destroy it. Or was he hiding his love from Thorvald? Was their bond more loyal than her marriage? All the more reason to kill him.

Thorvald's instinct to protect Hefnir shifted to Egill. 'Is this boy a fool or a traitor?'

'He brags, that's all,' said Bera, quick to protect her friend. 'He gets excited and then drunk.'

'He's a frail creature,' said Hefnir. 'Bera's the only one with any time for him.'

'Ah. Kind-hearted Bera,' said Thorvald. 'Killing with kindness. Ottar says—'

Sigrid squealed. 'Ow! This needle is so blunt I'm having to drag it through the cloth. It went right into my thumb. Oh, and now look – there's blood on it. I'll have to go and soak this in cold water. It's that new tunic you brought back from the Marsh Lands, Hefnir. It nearly fits Heggi now. I'm taking it in a bit for him.'

She blithered while she busied herself with gathering all her bits and going out with the tunic. Sigrid never squealed. Was she protecting Ottar? Or Bera? It couldn't be about Bjorn: she had never once mentioned her son. Bera would have to watch and wait to find out what had been happening while they were away – and if it all concerned the Serpent, as she believed it did.

Next day, Hefnir declared that he would announce the new feast at the mead hall, so Bera said she and Egill would plan what should happen. She collected Egill from the boatyard and took her to a small cove beside it. Huge rocks had tumbled into the sea so long ago that stunted trees grew in the crevices between them. It was very private and there was a large flat rock, perfect for sitting.

'I think Thorvald is plotting something with the Serpent King,' Bera said.

'To kill Hefnir?'

'Of course not. I have to deal with him soon but he's especially on guard. He even suspects you.'

'So use poison.'

The word made Bera recoil, although the idea kept tempting her. 'What if I use it and lose all my powers because I've abused them?'

'Fate made you mix those plants.'

And Fate had sent her a partner in Egill. 'I'll do it straight after the new festival, which will be at the next full moon.'

'Best for plant potency.'

'And he'll also be drunk. I want you with your wits about you.'

Egill looked sulky. 'Want some fun.'

'You can have fun but, listen, we need to purify them...' She outlined her plans, using fire to cleanse, as it did dead bodies.

Heggi returned from the bath hut as grubby as ever, so Bera marched him back and scrubbed him with a good deal of rigour. They arrived at the mead hall late and as soon as they got there he charged off, rubbed ash on his face and then joined his scruffier mates. She tried not to mind.

A group of women were standing around Ottar and Egill. Her father was at his lustful stage of drinking, when he would pucker his lips and lean towards any woman. Egill was bragging about Sowun, as though it was all her idea. The name had not been agreed, even. Bera went to find Sigrid before she lost her temper.

She was over by the food.

'You're here at last, then.' Sigrid kept working. 'Looks like we're stuck with this new feast of that Egill's.'

'It's my idea, mostly.'

Sigrid wound the large stewpot higher over the fire. 'You, him – either way means more work for us.'

'More for the thralls.'

'Let them poison us? Look at them. They understand every word. They only pretend to be stupid. I'm glad we never had any slaves at home. I wouldn't trust them as far as I could throw them.'

'Why don't they knife us in our beds, then? It's simpler.'

Sigrid made the hammer sign. 'Don't say that. I won't sleep a wink now.'

Bera went over to the ale barrels. 'Do you understand every word?' she asked the nearest thrall.

The woman smiled. It meant nothing; the household women were trained to smile when they provided any service. But if Sigrid believed the thralls were out to poison them, the finger of suspicion would point that way, which would work to Bera's advantage.

Heggi swaggered past with a loutish boy who reached down to Rakki. The dog cringed away.

Bera stopped Heggi. 'Has that boy ever been cruel to Rakki?'

'I'd knife him,' Heggi said.

He would, too, at once, with no dithering. Bera bent down to stroke Rakki, whose breath smelt suspiciously of cheese.

'Come on. Let's go and find your father.'

Hefnir was, of course, with Thorvald. 'Plenty of salt there,' he said.

Thorvald nodded. 'And wine.'

'What is wine?' asked Heggi.

'We make ale with grain and beer with apples,' his father explained. 'Other folk make wine with grapes, which are a sort of fruit, like fat cloudberries.'

'That sounds good,' said Bera. 'Why don't you bring some home?'

'It gets drunk too fast.'

'Gets us drunk too fast, you mean.' Thorvald laughed at his own joke.

'I can't wait for the new feast,' said Bera.

That night the moon was bright enough to cast shadows through the hall. Bera was still awake long after Hefnir had gone to sleep. The drink made Hefnir snore and she remembered the nights at her old home, listening to Ottar. She worried if she was about to break some rule of Valla healing. She had certainly promised not to attack Thorvald here. She let herself think about playing hide-and-seek and bears and trole-stones and bully-bully with Bjorn; so she nearly missed the quick movement of someone slipping out of the women's quarters. Probably one of the thralls going over to join her man in the male quarters. But the shadow passed the fire and Bera pitied her: whoever the woman was, she was heading for Thorvald's billet. Poison was definitely the only option, if the woman was to be a fixture there – though she would thank Bera for saving her, if she knew.

It rained continuously for the next week but work had to be done. Folk went about looking sour and smelling it, too, in their greased woollens. Bera hated the mud and creeping dampness. She sent a thrall to cut some fresh spruce and when he got back he said the men were up in the forest getting wood for the big fires as she had ordered but were doing nothing but complain. Folk's glumness gave her the name for the new feast: Brightening.

Later, she went out with some swill for the pigs. She liked to scratch their backs and think. Heggi was at the prize sow's sty.

'Why do we keep her in when the others roam?' he asked, by way of greeting.

'We need to watch what she's eating.' Bera put down the bucket. 'The others eat all sorts. They don't have the sense of chickens.'

Heggi wrinkled his face. 'Stuff on the midden heaps!'

The solid waste from the latrine went onto the midden, ready to be used on the fields.

'There's much more here than at home.'

'Than Crapsby?'

Bera let it go. The sow blinked her tiny eyes and sniffed the air. She trotted over to her, looking as if she was tiptoeing through the mud. It made Bera laugh.

Heggi came closer. 'You like animals a lot, don't you?'

Bera swung the bucket over the fence and poured its contents into the sow's long trough. The pig made small happy grunts as she ate.

'I don't want this old girl dying.'

'I don't want Feima to ever die.'

'She'll calve all right. You said he's the best cowman.'

They watched for a while.

'You know this feast thing...?' Heggi began.

The sow came over for a back scratch. Bera dug her nails into the coarse flesh, feeling the hairs like spines springing away. 'Spit it out, Heggi.'

'Well... you know Dellingr's daughter?' His face glowed hotly.

Bera hoped he would not notice that she was blushing too. 'Go on.'

'She's asked me to go with them that night. I don't know where, just with them.'

'Hefnir's said no, hasn't he?'

Heggi prodded the fence with a long stick. Just like his father.

'Heggi, I can't say yes if Hefnir has forbidden you.'

'It's not fair!'

He threw the stick in her direction and whistled for Rakki as he sped off. The dog left off ratting and raced after him.

He could have blinded her, the little swine.

The men returned from the forest a day or so later, dragging boughs behind them. Folk came out to watch and Egill was on hand to explain how to build the bonfires, as if they didn't know. Someone cuffed her and it began, again, to drizzle.

There was something so dismal about the scene, so unlike the idea she had planned, that Bera felt a weary dread.

My, we are glum.

Her skern was perched on top of a stack of branches. She hoped they would collapse and make him look foolish but he was as light as air.

'Will this rain never stop!'

Yes.

'It wasn't a question.'

It was an answer. What's more, I can tell you that the eve of Brightening will live up to its name and be fine and clear and as potent as you wish.

'I'm not worried about that.'

Yes, you are. And you are also correct in your... queasiness about the proceedings and their aftermath.

'What queasiness?'

Prevailing circumstances and all that.

'What does that mean? That I feel sick and the cause is something else?'

Only you could possibly say, dearie. You're as headstrong as ever if you ask me but then you seldom do these days.

'Is it any wonder when you're never here?'

He had gone, being a skern that could always give but not take criticism.

She did feel mizzy-mazey, as Sigrid would say. The word scared her suddenly. She hunted for red spots on her body but could find none.

The skern's weather prediction was accurate. By the time of Brightening the skies cleared and sunlight raised everyone's spirits for the eve. Bera chose to forget her worries, now the decision to poison Thorvald had been made. Let the consequences be dealt with later. She enjoyed helping Sigrid make plaited hats for the children, especially when Heggi brought more straw and stayed to watch, then made a clumsy attempt of his own.

'Where's Rakki?' she asked.

'Oh. He saw a rat when we came past the latrine and set off after it. He's the best ratter.'

'Not good enough,' Sigrid said. 'Those rats are bold. One stared at me all the time I was at the stool the other day. Little red beady eyes. Put me right off my stroke.'

Rakki chose that moment to return and stand by Sigrid, grinning, with no rat to show for his chase. They all laughed.

When the hats were ready, Sigrid took them round the village. Bera stayed with Heggi. He tied the rough hat he had made on Rakki, which set him capering about, furiously shaking his head.

'It would be good if Feima's calf is born at Brightening,' he said. 'I might go up and see.'

'Take that thing off Rakki. It's driving him mad.'

He called his dog and untied it.

'What is that hanging from your belt?'

He touched the twisted cloth. 'This? Um... a present for Feima and the calf.'

'What is it?'

'A piece of cheese,' he mumbled.

Bera laughed. 'You know cows only eat grass.'

'Well? We make cheese from their milk, don't we? Why shouldn't she try some? She might like it.'

'She might die laughing, more likely.'

He scowled and began to untie his belt.

'Oh, go on. Keep it. I dare say you and Rakki will eat it long before you reach the pasture.'

'So I can go?'

'Yes – and go with your friends later. I won't tell your father.'

Heggi rushed up, kissed her clumsily and dashed out with the dog at his heels. Bera wished he would stay like this. She could never be his mother but it was good to be agreeable – and she feared that Heggi grown would be as hard as the rest of Seabost. Bera set off in search of her own friend.

Egill was outside the village, demonstrating what should be cut or picked. She was certainly popular amongst the old and lame and ugly and shone like a silver taper.

'It's important things are right,' Egill said. 'In Iraland folk would come from all around to learn a natural kind of knowledge.'

Bera was not fond of her bragging mood but Egill sent the women off collecting and came over.

'Something to tell you,' she said. 'Slipped my mind till just now, with them.'

'You sound like my skern.'

Who appeared, hanging like a bat from a gnarled tree and trying to look hurt. Without success.

'It's about skerns and that.'

'So now you know all about skerns!'

Egill shrugged. 'Only saying normal folk can get help from the dead at Sowun.'

Bera felt a surge of hope. Her mother might advise her how to kill Thorvald without breaking Valla rules. 'Could we do it at Brightening?'

'Don't see why not.'

'How do you do it?'

'Gather rowan to shape into a circle that you look through.'

A liminal place, like a threshold. Could work. Ask about squid ink.

'Squid ink?'

There was something lost in Egill's eyes and Bera tried to imagine what she would be like if Hel had not taken her father.

She took her hand. 'I am your true friend, Egill. I worry about you.'

'Not used to folk. Help me, Bera.'

'Don't let my father give you so much ale.'

'Drink takes the pain away.'

Bera led her to the gnarled tree. 'Look. This is Hagthorn. It's a love potion if you soak the leaves and its berries heal a broken heart.' She pulled her skern's branch towards them.

'Mash some of it for me, then, Bera? Make me feel something.'

Folk took Sowun and made it Brightening. Men dressed as women and women as men and went in search of their favourites. The light night kindled a wild energy in the air. Bonfires and torches kept wild beasts away. Bera had shown folk how to shield and purify against other enemies and bowers were garlanded with rowan to keep out evil. Egill had also talked about making protections but when Bera glimpsed her she seemed set on mayhem.

She worried the Serpent King might get invited in. Folk in drink could be unpredictable. Bera tried to do some mending while she waited for Hefnir to come home but instead of coming up with a plan to thwart her enemy, she kept thinking about Dellingr chasing other women. Knowing him, he would save it all for Asa. It made her furious and she hurled the woollen hood away. Sigrid came in from the pantry and it flew past her like a ghost owl.

'So now it needs a wash as well as stitching.' Sigrid groaned as she bent to pick it up. 'I suppose I'll have to mend it later.'

Bera crossed the room at speed and snatched it from her. 'I'll do it.'

'You've ripped it now.'

'No, I haven't.'

'Yes, you have.'

'Where? Where is it ripped?'

Sigrid went to take it and Bera twisted away from her, holding it above her head. She ran. Suddenly they were chasing round and round the fire like a pair of children. Then a thrall came in and Bera stopped to straighten her dress and take charge again. Sigrid made faces at her behind the thrall's back and she fought hard not to giggle.

The man took an age replacing the billet hangings and Bera returned to her sewing while he worked. When the man had finished she put down her work.

'Shall we let our hair down?' she said.

Sigrid grinned. 'Like we're unmarried!'

Bera turned her back so that Sigrid could unbraid her hair. Sigrid ran her fingers through it to get rid of caffles and then combed it until Bera's whole body tingled with pleasure. Reluctantly, she allowed Sigrid to stop and do her own hair. They put garlands on each other and stood back to admire them.

'You should have looked like this on your bride day,' said Sigrid.

'And look at you. You're down to only fifty layers of clothes!'

Sigrid cuffed her.

'I mean it, Sigrid. There's a woman under there! Not an old one, either. You'll have no trouble finding someone to kiss you. Remember how it's done?'

Sigrid moved away and Bera was tearful with remorse. 'Oh, Sigrid, I'm sorry. Losing your husband and then Bjorn...' Bera wished she could tell her that she would make Thorvald die in agony for causing such hurt.

Sigrid's face was raw. 'Come on.'

'Where?'

'Out. Come on.'

Bera was caught in a few playful skirmishes but men were not too drunk to forget who she was. Then Sigrid vanished, leaving her feeling vulnerable on her own. If only she had Dellingr to protect her. She went looking for him and had not gone far when a pair of rough-skinned hands closed over her eyes, smelling of woodsmoke and mead.

'Hefnir!' she said, and was glad.

'How many times have you been kissed?' he asked, then did so himself.

'Too many times to reckon.'

'Have another, then.' This time he kissed her as if he meant it.

'Did you see Sigrid? I lost her.'

'I told her to keep Heggi at home,' he said.

'Oh, let the lad have a bit of fun.' She sounded like her father.

'So, is he at home?'

Bera crossed her fingers. 'He might be.'

'I heard there's a group of young fools going to sit up all night waiting for the dead to speak. I'm not having him mixed up in all that pigswill.'

'Pigswill like Valla skills?'

Hefnir's long kiss stopped her speaking. He announced he was off to find Thorvald.

'Egill says he's the Lord of Misrule or some such and has ordered me and Thorvald to drink as much mead as we can to bless the village.'

Egill must be trying to help by getting Thorvald drunk. Bera let Hefnir go. She was keen to start looking for the plants she needed but they had to be picked when the moon was at the very point of waning. Heggi would be staying close to Dellingr's daughter, so, until then, Bera could innocently see the smith and check on the boy, as she ought to. Folk were gathered at the fires, so she set off in the direction of the smoke.

The last few cows were being driven between the two fires, to cleanse them. There were shouts and screams from the watching crowd and terrified bellowing and grunting from the animals. Women wanting a husband stood at the biggest fire. They tucked in their garments while they waited their turn then screamed as they leapt the flames. One woman burned her foot and hopped about clutching it until she fell.

'You'll be married to Hel!' another woman shrieked and pushed her over. The others laughed so much that they collapsed on top of them.

When Bera reached Dellingr he told her he was waiting for his wife to jump.

'Have you seen Heggi?'

'He's with my girl and the rest of them. They watched the goats going through, then went off that way.' He pointed towards the racks.

'So why is Asa jumping the fire? She has you.'

He laughed. 'She reckons it'll give us the ten bairns she promised!'

That hurt.

Dellingr chuckled with pride and shared the joke with his neighbours. She waited to see if he would talk to her again but it was only to say he was off to get more mead. On the way he greeted a man who clapped him on his back. It was Thorvald! Was he watching her?

Bera slid away to look for Heggi. The earth-force rose up through the soles of her feet. The old ways would be visible if her mother was there to point them out: dragon paths coiling up into the mountains. She felt a sudden oddity of nature: a woman barren by choice; a mother only by an oath no one believed in. A motherless child herself.

Bera's solitary path brought her to the racks. Inside them, a circle of lit skulls surrounded a slight figure. There was a smell of roasting vegetables and Bera blinked. The skulls were wrinkled and shrunken turnips, cut into grotesque faces, with tapers inside.

Egill turned to look at her. Her eyes loomed in the darkness. Bera was suddenly afraid and wanted to leave.

Egill gestured around her. 'Been waiting. Made this for you.'

'What is it, Egill?'

'Special place to see the dead. Potent. In Iraland, it used to be a ring of skulls.'

Bera couldn't resist. She might see her mother. Or Bjorn, come to tell her how Thorvald was to be killed and then the act would not be hers alone. She sat cross-legged next to Egill, who gave her a rowan circlet. Bera's stomach was churning with excitement. She shut her eyes, making a wish, hardly daring to open them.

Then she did.

10

Her mother gazed back at her.

Eyes, deep and dark as scrying pools, under a sweep of eyebrow; a bruised smudge under the eye. Pain. This was already scored in Bera's mind – but behind it was a young face, a distant happiness.

At first Bera struggled to remember all the important questions she had never been able to ask but then it was enough to love and feel totally loved in return. Memories poured through her, long forgotten: making up silly songs, picking berries, milking a cow, tending a wound. Being kind. Infinite tenderness passed through a simple shape in the air. *'Feel no guilt.'* So when her skern settled at her back, she was whole. As it was in the beginning.

Time passed.

She was gently rocking.

Let her go now. Return to the living.

Bera heard it distantly, like a wave breaking on a shore. She would not part from her mother again, ever.

Bera. Let her go.

Anger scorched through her and her mother blurred and vanished. Bera threw herself to the ground, hit the earth with her fists and sobbed.

'No! I want her back!'

You sense her with you, don't you? When you're afraid? Well, so she is and so am I. Always here. When everything else is gone, there is Love.

'How would you know? I hate you!'

The skern said something that she couldn't hear above her wailing. She wanted to scream with the pain of it. 'Everything's always taken away from me! Anything I've ever loved.'

And then other arms had her and it was Egill, her friend, who was crying for her own loss. They shared the same pain and that was a comfort of sorts.

'Who was it, Bera? Who did you see?'

'Mama.'

Losing her mother a second time made her think of Heggi and how callously she had treated him – a boy who had seen his mother killed by sea-riders.

'I'll never be as good a mother. She was perfect.'

'No one is.'

Sigrid had said as much. But Valla blood ran in Bera's veins: the same power; the same passion. There was to be an end of guilt, so an end of blame.

'Did she warn you about using your skills?'

'She said not to be guilty about anything.'

'Did she mean killing?' Egill stared at the skull lanterns. 'Other ways to be strong, Bera. Have mercy.'

Something in Bera responded to the word, but it was not for her. The raw grief at losing her mother again reminded her of what Sigrid had lost. She owed it to her to go through with it. Then her father would be proud of her bravery.

Poisoning wasn't brave.

She pushed the thought away and got to her feet.

Egill stayed where she was. 'Shame your mother gave no knowledge.'

'I'm getting my baskets. I'll see you tomorrow.' How to explain what she did give? It was like being one person, like cleaving to her skern.

On the way home, Bera met a bedraggled group of youngsters carrying torches. Bringing up the rear was Heggi with his dog at his side. His hair was caffled with bits of leaf and twig, his clothes were filthy, as was his face, but he was lit up with pleasure.

Bera wanted to hug him; to make amends. 'Heggi, I'm so—'

'We stayed up all night!' His eyes were wide. 'It was the best thing. We dropped the rowan circlet in the pool and everyone thought it was lost but I dived in and found it. And then we had a meal and then we threw squid.'

'Squid?'

He looked at Dellingr's girl and giggled. 'Egill told us. You catch a squid and throw it over your shoulder and the ink squirt makes a rune of the person you most love.'

Bera did not need to ask whose rune Heggi had seen.

She yawned. 'Come on. We can get our heads down before work starts.'

They left the others and walked on.

Heggi paused when they reached the latrine. 'I suppose you'll tell Papa I was out all night?'

'He probably already knows.'

'But if he doesn't?'

Bera wanted to share her experience with him. 'I looked through a rowan circlet and saw my mother.' She expected him to be sad, envious, curious; anything they could talk about.

He laughed and the chance was gone. 'I forgot! Feima had her calf. I shall call her Dotta.'

'Very good. A daughter.' She felt sadder still.

After a latrine visit, Bera put Heggi to bed. Both of them crept, dreading waking Hefnir. Heggi snuggled against Rakki and fell asleep at once. All was quiet as she fetched her baskets from the pantry.

A woman's voice murmured, coming from the men's side. Bera was going to slip away but remembered she was mistress and decided to find out who it was and scold her. But that would be like snooping again. She shot out, grabbed a torch and made for the river before she was seen.

Moonlight bleached the landscape. The torch was to keep things away, not for light, in case the river was outside the protection. Bera searched for the plants she needed, hoping that the rain had brought them on. She came across some elf-nettle and picked a few stems, being careful not to get stung. Broadwort usually grew close by. At last she found some, picked off the few remaining leaves and laid them carefully in the basket, not to bruise them. Those were for healing. Seabost women used a mash of the similar lugwort. Judging by the fishermen's scars it did not work very well but if anyone looked in this basket, they would recognise the leaves as wholesome.

Now for the others, which were not.

Bera moved closer to the river. She held on to her mother's bead and asked her to help choose the most deadly. The odd chill of the glass was like ice-nip.

A twig snapped.

She waited for more noises but all was quiet. Surely it couldn't be a Drorgher, not here amongst the rowans. Ottar always said the monster that will kill you makes no noise and her scalp had no warning prickle. She walked on.

And yet she was afraid. The icy bead was some kind of warning and Bera felt stalked, as if a predator were herding her, closing for the kill. The river was loud, so she slanted sideways to get a line of old trees to muffle the noise. When the rustling came again, she heard it distinctly.

Bera put down the basket and turned to confront her fears.

A deer came out from between the rowan trees. It lowered its head to graze, scented Bera and flicked away with a crackle of undergrowth. Stillness. A ghost owl glided across the clearing, turning its head to scrutinise her. Its golden eyes were menacing but it was seeking smaller prey.

Nothing else moved.

Bera picked up her basket and passed through the glade. Here, the river was a surging melody, a clear song of water cascading out to sea to join the wild, deep music of the whale roads. How she yearned to have already dealt with Thorvald and be off on a boat, travelling with them.

She got on with hunting at the water's edge and found one shrivelled plant, the innocent-sounding milk mallow. She crouched down and picked it. A shudder of revulsion, not her own, made her retch. Was her mother warning her? The hairs on the back of her neck rose.

She sprang up, looking all round. 'Show yourself.' She wished her voice sounded stronger.

There was rustling behind her. A darker shadow moved under the trees and this time a man stepped out.

Her knees almost gave way with shock. It was the man these leaves were meant for.

'What are you doing here, Thorvald?'

'What do you think?'

'Following me.'

He stood, relaxed and balanced, in a sword-wielder's stance.

'A dog should follow its master. Go back to Hefnir,' she said.

'It's not safe to go walking alone in the dark.'

Bera took deeper breaths. 'Why are you here?'

'Have you nothing to fear from the Serpent King?'

'I don't know. Have I? He's your friend.'

She waited for the next thrust and parry.

'You can put your plant knife away,' he said. 'Much good it'd do against a sword.'

'So I should fear you, then? I've seen what you can do with it.'

'You can thank the Serpent for that and all.'

'You killed Bjorn, he didn't.'

Another pause. Bjorn's death was an unbridgeable chasm.

'Brightening, you called it,' he said.

'So?' She was trembling.

'Time to put grievances to rest.'

'By killing the offender?'

'By forgiving.'

Bera could never forgive him. 'Why were you hiding?'

'Why scare you if there's no need?'

'You don't scare me.'

'Don't I?' His jagged mouth yawned.

'Who sent you?'

It was the first time he had to think about his answer. 'Hefnir. He told me to keep you safe.'

'Then I shall carry on collecting what I need.'

Thorvald was right about the Serpent, so it was reassuring to have him there as long as he kept his distance. It gave her malicious pleasure to have him see the very plants that would kill him, as he was too stupid to know them. But when she reached for a bough of bogthorn and Thorvald helped her, she flinched with guilt and he quickly moved away. All the way home he kept his distance, watching her back. He was a solid presence and much as she disliked it, she began to see why Hefnir valued him as his second. If only he had not killed Bjorn.

'What did you mean about the Serpent killing Bjorn?' she asked. 'He wasn't there.'

'He doesn't have to be there to make things go bad.'

'Tell me.'

Thorvald looked at her, straight. 'You never believe anything I say.'

'Try me.' She put down her basket and folded her arms.

'Sea-riders came in a war fleet and torched some houses. The Serpent let them, to frighten us into paying him more to keep them away in future. Only they took more than he reckoned so he fought them and this time he's claiming blood money.'

'And Bjorn?'

'I was full of battle-madness. First in the Marsh Lands, then the raid. That boy shouldn't have charged me. Your hand moves faster than thought: it has to.'

She was shocked by the raw anguish on his ruined face. She turned away and left him, before pity could soften her.

Pity already had. Bera watched Thorvald safely into his billet, full of indecision. Would her planned poisoning be worse than his unthinking act? The blood debt had been accepted by Ottar, which weighed the scales down further on Thorvald's side. And yet... surely her mother and skern would have forbidden her if it was so wrong? Or was it, like everything else, a lesson she had to learn for herself? The feeling of revulsion remained but she decided it was sheer cowardice and got started.

She pounded the leaves in a bowl and stirred in honey, standing at the byre doorway so the moon's waning would make the brew more potent. There was a flicker as a figure ran past the outbuildings. Any thrall heading for the pastures would cross the clear ground up to the latrine. No one appeared.

When Bera finished, she went to one of the outhouses to hide the poisonous mash until mealtime. She was leaden with tiredness but this debt must be paid, soon now. Inside, there was a smell of old apples and something less wholesome. The most secret place would be further in, where a low door looked like an inner store.

She tried the handle.

Something dark reared up on the other side.

A Drorgher? This must be where she had sensed it before. Nothing would make her open that door onto pitch blackness. The ice-grip of her mother's bead had been a warning of this, and her revulsion. Thorvald had muddled it and exhausted her power to fight.

Some yearning seeped from the evil behind the door that was more than the need to steal a skern. Bera shoved the mash under some apple boxes and ran to her billet.

She undressed, slid into bed and cuddled up to Hefnir's warm, solid, human back. He grunted and flopped over, so that she was squashed under his heavy shoulder.

She pushed him, hard. 'Roll over, Hefnir, you're crushing me.'

'Mmm.' He was very sleepy.

She softly blew on his neck. 'Thanks for looking after me.'

'What?'

'Sending Thorvald to find me.'

'Didn't,' he said, and fell back on top of her again.

Bera woke to his heavy breathing, but beyond that, silence. Sunbeams sliced through shutters and dust motes danced. She quietly got dressed, whistling with relief that as soon as she got a dose of the mash in Thorvald's day meal it would be over. She guessed the thralls were busy in the fields. She left Hefnir to sleep it off and went into the empty hall.

A woman's soft voice was coming from Thorvald's billet. Did he give the thralls no peace? She made for the byre but heard the rattle of feet on the spruce behind her. Bera could be the confident mistress this time and have words with the thrall. She turned, and felt sick.

The woman was Sigrid.

The horror that Sigrid should have been forced – and by him!

For how long? Since the hunting trip? It was now obvious that Sigrid's odd behaviour was born of fear. Bera was aghast that her friend had not trusted her. Thorvald's fault. And to force her! He might be Hefnir's second but to Hel with the man! How dare he pretend, like last night, when all the time...

'Don't be angry,' said Sigrid.

'It's not you I'm angry with.'

'Still. Don't be angry. There's nothing to be done.'

Thorvald emerged, pulling on his tunic. His head appeared, revealing his disgusting puckered face. 'What's she angry about now?' he said.

'Leave this to me, Thorvald.' Sigrid was calm.

It confused Bera. 'I want to know what you did to her while we were away.'

'You've already decided. As usual.'

Sigrid caught his arm. 'She is mistress here, Thorvald. We should have told her.'

'Told me what?' Bera yelled in frustration.

'Can't a man sleep?' Hefnir strode into the hall, rubbing his eyes.

Bera was glad he would hear it fresh. 'Thorvald has forced himself on Sigrid and probably has been ever since we went off hunting.'

A look passed between the two men, shutting her out.

'It's not like that, Bera,' Sigrid said quietly. 'I know this makes no sense to you but this is my free choice.'

Bera was outraged. 'That can't be true.'

'Oh, let her believe what she likes,' said Thorvald, 'she always does.'

Bera met his glare.

Thorvald blinked first. 'Tell her, then.'

Sigrid smiled, suddenly young. 'Egill showed us handfasting, so now Thorvald and I are together for a year and a day.' And she kissed the monster.

Bera felt a sour burn in her throat. Egill too! There was no chance of honesty about anything ever again.

Hefnir punched Thorvald's arm, laughing. 'Never thought she'd make an honest man of you.'

Bera wanted to slap him. 'You knew, didn't you?'

'Of course,' said Hefnir. 'I've known from the start.'

Bera stomped out of the hall, slamming the door behind her. She stood in the dark corridor, seething. The ancestors hissed scathing shards into her ears.

'Violation! Abduction! Perfidy!'

This time she would find out what the ancient words meant. There was only one person in the world she could trust and that was Dellingr. And a smith would be able to tell her.

Dellingr was not in the forge. Perhaps he couldn't keep away from his brat. His blower was sweeping the floor, keeping his back turned. Bera moodily clomped outside, decided to slowly count to ten and got to four before walking as far as the crossroads to see if the smith was coming. Dark, empty ways.

Back at the forge the boy was returning from the midden. He looked startled to see her again.

'When will Dellingr return?'

The boy shrugged and blushed.

'Where did he go?'

The bucket he studied was more likely to answer.

'Are you to keep the fire hot?'

He dashed inside, his shyness painful. Bera kicked Dellingr's block of granite and hurt her foot. She ought to listen to Fate and leave at once. She had resisted temptation up to now but everyone in Hefnir's lying household had driven her to it. She hated waiting and yet here she was, waiting. This was dishonourable. If she left now, Hefnir would never know. She set off.

'Bera!'

The smith was some way off, wheeling an old barrow. Bera waited, telling herself it was necessary.

When Dellingr arrived, he was red-faced and sweaty. He let the barrow down with a thud and clatter. It was full of plain farm tools, not heroic weapons. No ancient magic, just honest friendliness. It was certainly for the best but Bera felt disappointed in him, almost cross. No spark. Perhaps between Hefnir and Dellingr was a type of man she could truly love. Who did not exist.

Dellingr picked up a billhook and threw it down in disgust. 'They're all blunt. A lad came up from the barns to say that Egill was sharpening their tools on a magical block of stone from Iraland.'

'That's Egill all over.'

'I thought he was your friend.' Dellingr lifted a large bucket of water and tipped it over his head. He flung his hair back and rainbows flew in an arc. Her hero again.

The blower appeared in the doorway.

Dellingr pointed to the barrow. 'More work.'

The boy scuttled over and wheeled it off into the dark.

'Poor creature, your bellows-boy,' said Bera. 'Is he an idiot?' She pulled a face like the silent boy, trying to make him laugh.

Then Dellingr understood. 'Ah. He can't speak. His father cut his tongue off.'

Shock and shame hissed through Bera's teeth.

'He used to beat the lad's mother when he'd had a skinful. One day the lad stood up for her and I got him away by giving him work.'

How unkind she could be, now she had learned Seabost ways. It made Bera respect Dellingr all the more. She wanted his good opinion yet behaved worse here than anywhere else. She liked his big hands and shoulders; his stillness around animals and children; his smell of hot metal and fresh sweat; the crinkling lines around keen grey eyes. He was smiling at her.

'Don't feel bad about the bellows-boy,' he said. 'Let me get him started. He's a good lad and he's learning.'

Dellingr went into the forge and she heard his low voice giving instructions. Bera knew she should go. Asking him what some words meant seemed futile now, even if she could recall them. She couldn't stop yawning.

Dellingr came out. 'That was a good feast you and Egill devised. Brightening.'

'I hardly slept at all,' she said, longing to tell him everything.

'Getting warm now. So I'm sharpening tools and it's good for the bairn, Asa says.'

Bera wished he would talk of anything other than his wife, the weather or his work. Her, for example.

She said, 'I used to think Egill was my friend.'

'He helps your father.'

'Not much help. There's lots of bragging. And drinking.'

'Boys will be boys.'

Bera itched to tell Dellingr that Egill was a girl.

'Egill betrayed me, making Sigrid do handfasting, like in Iraland. I'm sick of hearing about Iraland now.'

'Egill didn't make her do anything. He was showing a crowd of us how to handfast. They'd talked about marriage before.'

'Who?'

'Sigrid and Thorvald. He came to tell me the day you met him up here. Mind you, Sigrid had already told Asa but I didn't let on to him I knew.'

Bera shot to her feet. 'So I'm the only fool who didn't know! Well, thank you. How you must all be laughing at me!' She marched off.

Dellingr caught her arm. 'What's the problem? They're happy.'

'How could anyone be happy married to that monster?'

He gripped her more tightly. 'He got that scar in the service of your husband, Bera. He's an honourable man and—'

'You don't know him. That honourable man killed my best friend.'

She wrenched her arm free and stormed off on the warpath, looking for Egill.

Ottar banged the hull of an upturned boat. 'Well, I'm damned. There's a woman here the image of my daughter. Can't be her, though, she never comes this way these days.'

Bera refused to look at him.

'Still blaming me, are you?' he asked.

Egill crawled out from underneath the boat, groaning. 'Come to see me, I expect.' She rubbed her head. 'Was sleeping.'

'Sleeping it off, more like. No head for drink.' Ottar spoke with affection.

'You're never sober,' Bera snapped.

Egill took a few tottering steps and was sick.

Robbed of a good quarrel, Bera left the two of them. She found herself in the small cove that she had taken Egill to when they were friends. She clambered down towards the thumbnail of beach and was surprised to find Heggi there, skimming stones for his dog. At least the boy never hid his feelings. He was as obvious as Rakki, who was joyfully swimming after every splash.

Bera jumped down onto the shingle, making Heggi turn.

He made a face. 'Have you come to fetch me?'

'I'm escaping.'

'Me too. Rakki and I like it here.'

He carried on skimming but Bera could see that he wasn't choosing quite the right stones. 'Can I join in?'

He shrugged.

They each chose five pebbles. Rakki barked with excitement, splashing back and forth between them and the shallow wavelets. When they were poised at the water's edge, the dog swam out and turned in a small circle, waiting.

'Mind you don't hit Rakki,' Heggi said.

'Of course. One, two, three...'

They both skimmed. Their pebbles skipped either side of the dog, who went to grab one then changed course for the other. He grinned with pleasure, shipped water and coughed. Bera's went much further. She won the first four rounds.

Heggi got grumpier each time. 'Why are you so good?'

'You need the right shape, look.' She showed him a flat grey pebble.

'It's not just that.'

Bera demonstrated the flick of her throw. It bounced five times.

'Who taught you that?'

'A boy.'

She pictured Bjorn playing. Happy, innocent children on summer days that never grew dark.

Heggi found better stones and Bera let him beat her.

He pranced about, waving his arms, a child again. 'I won! I won!'

They went to sit on the flat rock and dangled their feet in the water. Rakki came over to them and shook. They scolded him and he lay down behind them, smelling strongly of wet dog. It was comforting.

'That boy,' Bera said. 'He died.'

'Now I know why you went sad, more than when you say about your mother.'

'Do I?'

Had she ever said anything meaningful to Heggi? He was studying her with blue eyes that were not like his father's. His mother's eyes, perhaps. Candid, trusting.

'He was called Bjorn,' she said.

'Sigrid's son?'

Another surprise. 'Has she told you about him?'

'Quite a lot. What he was like and about him being a fisherman like his father and...'

'And what?'

'Oh, about you being friends.'

'What were you really going to say?'

He stared out to sea. 'That folk all thought you would marry.'

Bera grunted. 'I never would have married Bjorn.'

'Sigrid said you couldn't.'

'Sigrid told you that? Why not?'

'I don't know. She got cross so I went off with Rakki.'

It must be true. Heggi was not a liar. In fact, he was unlike his father in many ways. Bera hoped he would never become a Seabost brute.

She brushed sand from his tunic. 'Did you go into the boatyard to see Ottar?'

'For a bit but it was boring. That weird boy came.'

'Egill?'

Heggi threw a stone. 'I don't like him.'

'Why not?'

He was weighing up his answer.

And then her skern was there, pointing back towards the boatyard. A line of black smoke was becoming a billow. It was the worst thing.

Bera jumped up, pulling Heggi. 'Fire!'

Ottar was shouting when they reached the boatyard. He ran towards the smoke, which was thickening all the time. Bera seized two buckets, gave them to Heggi, grabbed two more and charged down the slipway. They filled them with seawater and slopped back towards the fire. The flames were leaping and sparks flew towards the boats. Bera's eyes smarted. She emptied her buckets onto the nearest flames and scrambled away for more. Boatmen arrived with their own buckets and it looked like they were winning.

Then Ottar shouted, 'Pitch pails!'

If the pails of black tar caught the whole boatyard would go up. Bera ran to help. The pails were heavy and they struggled to haul them away. Ottar had the strength of ten and cleared several. His lads dashed up with more water again and again and gradually the flames were doused. They all took stock, hoping.

'That's you beaten, then, fire!' roared Egill, waving a small fist at the sky.

A flame snaked from a loose end of hawser along the ground to a heap of coiled ropes, tarred for use. They caught light. But, much worse, one of the workboats was smouldering.

'Look!' screamed Bera.

She left the lads to deal with the rope fire and ran to the jetty with Ottar. They grabbed a mainsail and threw it onto the flames. Egill arrived and leapt aboard, trampling the sail with bare feet, hopping like a scalded cat. Bera joined her, stamping, beating at any flames with a broom, while Ottar poured seawater over others. Sparks were in the air and stinging; blinding.

The fire had taken hold.

Bera pulled Egill away and they stumbled onto the jetty. Ottar took an axe to the mooring line and let the vessel float out, burning on the water. It was like an old-style funeral. It was the death of his boat and the end of any boat was a disastrous day.

'Won't spread now,' Egill said, before coughing and retching.

Ottar picked up a blackened rope, now only a stub of evil-smelling hide. 'Well, that's my best workboat gone and all our spares burned.' He turned on the men. 'So which of you scabs started it?'

They all looked at Egill. 'Bit of fine tracing, that's all.'

Bera held out an open hand. 'Give me the glass, Egill.'

She reeled away.

'Egill. Give it to me.'

Egill dipped into a pocket and pulled out a thick piece of glass, then slunk off and sat on a sawing block.

Ottar marched across and snatched it. 'What's this, then?'

'I have one, too,' Bera said. 'It makes the sun into a white-hot beam. Did you watch me, Egill? On the beach?' Bera wondered what else she might have seen.

'Little scab,' growled Ottar. 'You're not to be trusted.'

'Meant no harm,' Egill said in a small voice. 'Thought serpent coils on the prow would bring us luck.'

Ottar slammed her down, then picked her up with one hand. 'You leave the boats to me. Right?' There was real menace in the words.

Egill's tunic was rucked up and Bera was worried they would notice her slim waist. 'I'll deal with it, Father.'

Ottar dropped Egill, who pulled her tunic down and set off for her hut.

'What are you lot staring at? Get this cleaned up and back to work.' He glared at their backs. 'Lazy oafs. They're all wastrels in Seabost. Think they can buy more of anything, or steal, not make do and mend, like we did at home.'

Bera saw a reflection of her own homesickness on Ottar's face. 'There's no going home, Father. They're all dead, or worse.'

'There's never any going back for us folk. We can only go on.'

Seabost was destroying her. She needed to get in a boat again, where she could be herself. Out on the sea paths her head might clear enough to discover how devastating the loss of boats was – and how far she might have to go on, alone, in the future.

A workboat was drawn up on the slipway, though it was big for a single-handed sailor. Bera went to the stern and pulled. It was too heavy, so she went to the bow and pushed. Her cheeks ached with the strain but her feet kept skidding and the boat stayed where it was.

She wondered what to try next. The winch would pull but it couldn't push the boat into the water. She was damned if she'd ask Ottar to help, so she jumped when someone touched her.

'Sorry. So sorry.' Egill put her head on Bera's shoulder.

Bera was furious with her and pushed her away. 'You can't put it right, just like that! It won't work with me. Clear off, Egill, and stop ruining everything.'

'Trying to put it right, Bera. Know how much you love boats.'

She needed Egill to escape. 'Go round the other side, then, and help me lift the bow, to get her moving.'

Bera hunkered down to take the weight, then slowly straightened her legs and heaved at the same time. It was easier with two and she soon felt the boat lift in the water, like it was coming alive: the best feeling in the world.

They turned the bow seawards. Egill held on while Bera got aboard. She sat on the thwart, struggling with the cumbersome oars.

'Need two,' Egill said.

'I can manage!'

'Want to help.' She started to cry. 'Helping always goes bad.'

Hearing Egill say it softened Bera. 'Come on. Get in before anyone sees you crying like a girl.'

It felt good to be kind for a change, instead of angry. Egill had had no one for so long and was too eager to please now she did. Perhaps that was why she had helped Sigrid. There were times in Bera's own past when trying to help had turned bad. Perhaps she, like Egill, had wanted something to brag about, like the narwhale tusk. She was suddenly certain that had not yet fully played out, even if Thorvald died. Perhaps she should throw the poisoned mash away when she got back and use something more honourable.

They took an oar each and rowed strongly with the same rhythm. There was some wind out in the fjord but they were in the lee of the mountains and short cold gusts, which would flatten the boat if they raised the sail too soon, dropped down from them.

A gust fizzed past. It whipped Bera's hair out of its braiding and she tasted saltiness in her mouth: the taste of her element, the sea. She was a creature with brine for blood. For a moment she was part of the surge and suck of waves and their constant rattle against rock but then she was a sea bird. She swept up and soared, gliding over the creamy tops of ocean rollers, sleeping with wings outstretched and weathering the storms with lonely grace.

The sea lust was on her, reflected in Egill's glassy eyes.

It was time to raise the sail. Bera studied the neat coils of rope. Everything on board was tidy: Ottar would smack any boatboy who made a mungle of the lines. There were five of them, each coming from a point of the square sail.

'Is this one the haul-yard?' she asked.

Egill looked blank. She only knew rowing.

Bera hauled and, sure enough, the heavy yard twitched on the thwart. She waited till Egill got the bow into the wind and began to raise it. Years of weather proofing fat made the sail stiff and brown. As the rope passed through her hands, Bera noticed part of it was chafed.

'Look. Two strands are frayed right through. I hope the wind doesn't get up too much.'

'Will it break?'

'It might. And then the sail would drop and there's nothing to haul it up with again, unless I climb up the mast to reeve another line.'

Egill slapped an oar. 'Still got these.'

The wind was pushing the boat astern. Bera steered it round to fill the sail, which squared off, and she took the yard-lines to the best rail pins. It was a good breeze, brisk and steady. She was a sailor again, a woman in charge, with able crew.

They grinned at each other and Bera forgave Egill everything in the instant.

They headed out beyond the Skerries. Waves patted the hull like an old friend, some dolphins raced them and they were free. A small bird landed on the deck, looking startled. Perhaps it had only just fledged. Egill nursed it on the palm of her hand until it set off for the far shore. It fluttered, dipped and drowned. Bera glanced at Egill but she was looking ahead, so she kept the small death to herself. Was it an omen?

Bera meant to steer away from Bjorn's island but somehow Fate blew the boat ever closer to where her friend met his death. Even at the last, she thought she would skim past and go off and fish. She had fooled herself about her reason for coming out but now she gave in to it and dropped the sail, letting the boat drift in to nudge the shingle.

Egill made off a line at the bow, jumped over the side and knotted it round a large rock. She was standing on the killing beach, except she didn't know it. Bera was reluctant to join her, as if the island itself held the threat of sudden violence, and the bird's death was a warning. But Egill smiled and beckoned and she went ashore.

It was instantly warmer. Bera threw off her coarse smock and left her underskirt tucked up, liking the air on her bare legs. Egill took off her boy clothes and sat with her back to the rock.

'Can be anything we like here.' She yawned. 'So sleepy. Safe here with you.' She lay back and shut her eyes.

It was impossible for Bera to be anything she liked here. A memory from the narwhale day came, vivid:

> ... something coiling like smoke around its tusk.
> 'What have you seen?' Bjorn's face so white, blue veins at his temple.
> 'Staring at me like a boggelman! Let's take this tusk and...'

There was no hiding from it. She left Egill dozing to let what followed unreel, trying to breathe, as she came to the place.

She expected to see her young, stupid self waiting for her. There was only her skern.

There's no blood left.

She kept her eyes fixed on the sea-rim.

No need to brace. All the blood washed away many tides ago.

'I want to be alone here.'

No, you don't. You want to be alone with Bjorn.

Bera clutched her necklace, shut her eyes and willed her skern to leave. When she opened them he was still there, sitting on the sand and inspecting the underside of his foot.

I've come to tell you something important and this time I'm not going until I have.

'I want to ask you something first.'

He sighed but left his foot alone.

'Is Bjorn trapped here until I make Thorvald pay the blood debt?'

You've trapped him, sweetheart, in your own mind.

'Why did Sigrid say that I couldn't marry Bjorn?'

Too far in the past. Now – the important bit. My news.

He covered her eyes:

> ... the darkness was a sky split yellow with lightning. Thunderclouds stacked above the mountaintops and the sea was hammered lead. Seabost was sullenly remote and no folk could be seen but their boats lunged and surged at the jetties. A swollen river flowed through the fields and rolled on, flooding houses.

'We shall starve.'

Watch.

> A form loomed out of a frigid mist that made the fjord as milky as the dawn air. It was the shape of a fat teardrop, as dark and ribbed as the throat of a humpback whale. It was one of Ottar's boats, heading out to the sea path. A seabird cried and there was a crushing sense of grief.

She was kneeling on the sand, with the stab of loss in her ribs that was heartbreak.

Egill rushed to her. 'What is it? Bera? You've been crying out.'

'I saw terrible storms. Fog. We'll pay for this, come the change of season. All the rain will come at once and the river will flood.'

'Pay for what?'

'Everything I got wrong.'

'What shall we do?'

'Take to the longboats, Egill. It's all we can do. When it comes.'

There was no need to say Fall End was the wrong time of year to be setting out across the Ice-Rimmed Sea, with fewer boats, thanks to Egill. Bera would have to use all her Valla power to save them. First, she would have to persuade them she was right but feared they would never believe her with midsummer approaching. When the disaster struck, unprepared, there would be panic. She had to face the fact that she would need Thorvald's strength. She would deal with him when they were safe.

What Egill was thinking as they dressed she didn't know – and they got back aboard and rowed without speaking.

The wind was heading them, so they could not lay a course straight to Seabost under sail. Bera thought about the rope chafe in the haul-yard and listened out for warnings but all was well. The regular, rhythmic creaks of wood and rope; the tap-tap of the blocks and pins; the small snaps of the sail with every wind shift and the hiss of water past the hull were the song of her own life, like the surge and swell of blood.

She lifted her face to the hot sun in a clear sky and laughed.

'What's to laugh at?'

'Being alive!'

It was on a long tack away from Seabost when the line finally broke. There was no warning, just a bang as the yard came crashing down and the sail with it.

Bera cursed. 'Ottar will beat the lad for leaving a frayed rope rigged.'

They heaved the oars into place and took up the stroke. Bera's stomach muscles ached and her buttocks cramped. She was no longer fit. Egill was humming, damn her. The joy of sailing was gone and it was all Hefnir's fault for stopping her. He was trying to stop her being who she really was. Bera worked harder.

When they were nearing the boatyard, she was on her last reserves of energy and turned to check how much further they had to row.

A woman was on the slipway. Sigrid.

Bera wanted nothing to do with her. 'Did you tell Sigrid how to handfast?' she asked Egill, all her anger back.

'All the folk wanted to know.'

It was what Dellingr had said. This was all Sigrid's betrayal. The searing pain between Bera's shoulder blades made her more furious.

Sigrid did not wade to meet them with the winch hook. Her face was bloodless and drawn.

Bera spat. 'She's too scared to paddle.'

Sigrid shouted. 'Heggi's been poisoned.'

Terror coursed through Bera. Surely the mash for Thorvald was well enough hidden? She jumped out and left the boat to Egill.

The boatyard was acrid with wet smoke and no sign of her father.

'Ottar ran there, soon as I told him.' Sigrid puffed to keep up.

The lads were standing about, dazed from the fire.

'Help with the workboat,' Bera yelled as she passed, 'and get its ropes replaced!'

'What with? Most of them burned.'

That wasn't her problem. Heggi was. 'Tell me what happened.'

Sigrid panted. 'Hefnir angry – Heggi out all night – so apple boxes – and Thorvald...' She bent double. 'Got a stitch!'

Bera left her behind.

Had Thorvald found it and fed it to Heggi? No. He protected the child. Bera punched the side of her head. This was her fault alone.

The ancestors swooped with malevolent spite but there was deathly quiet inside the hall. Some thralls passed like shadows at the far end with buckets and bowls. There was a very bad smell that Bera feared was death.

Then the sound of terrible retching, like Heggi's ribcage coming up.

'Save him, Mama,' she prayed with her whole being, and ran.

Hefnir and Thorvald blocked the way to his billet. She panicked, thinking they would kill her, but she pushed her way through to see Heggi. Ottar was holding him over a bucket to be sick. Blood-flecked drool hung from his chin.

Ottar looked at her grimly. 'Where were you?'

Hefnir shook her. 'Some Valla you are! Do something!'

Bera pushed down her terror. Perhaps she could save Heggi and live.

'I need to know what he ate,' she said, 'and when.'

Heggi fell back, his eyes fluttering in a yellow face. Hefnir went to him and put a wet cloth on his brow. Thorvald gestured her out of the billet. He led her to the pantry, where Sigrid was sitting, rocking herself. Bera had never felt so bad in her whole life. Thorvald must know she was a murderer but surely he wouldn't kill her yet? She couldn't think straight.

'Heggi can't lie,' he began. 'Unlike you. Hefnir asked what he'd been doing at Brightening, so he told him straight about Dellingr's girl. Hefnir ordered him to fetch apple boxes and take them to be scrubbed as punishment.'

Sigrid interrupted. 'I told her. Heggi's scared stiff and refused to go.'

Thorvald nodded. 'So Hefnir told me to put him in the cell.'

'Cold store kind of a thing,' Sigrid said. 'It's what I'm saying. Terrifies Heggi.'

Bera knew. 'Where you've taken him before.'

'I never lock him in there. The old store's bad enough.'

The place of the Drorgher. Poor Heggi.

'The boy found one of your brews.' Thorvald's voice was stone.

Sigrid showed her the dish. 'I kept it. Look.'

She didn't have to look. Bera's guts twisted in torment. She would make any deal with Fate, with the ancestors, she would even let Thorvald live if Heggi would only survive. The ice-kiss of terror froze her lips.

Thorvald glared at her. 'What do we need? Come on. What plants?'

'I d-don't know! Sigrid, did my m-mother...'

Sigrid's eyes slid away. 'Her medicine wasn't like yours.'

'N-n-need...' She tried again. 'N-need to get it out of him.'

'Poor mite's throwing up all he can,' Sigrid said.

'S-Salt.' Bera staggered, like an old woman. 'I'll go and—'

'I saw you,' said Thorvald, anguished. 'I watched over you while you picked those plants.'

Sigrid bustled over to him. 'And I asked you to keep her safe. I told you, she'll have been dealing with the rats, won't you, Bera? Where it was hid and all. I moaned about the rats, didn't I? So it's all my fault. She was clearing the rats, ready for the summer stores coming.'

Sigrid was trying to save her by lying to her own husband. Thorvald's cold stare showed he suspected it. Bera was wracked with guilt for every cruel word and deed she had visited on her. Bera vowed to be as good and kind and forgiving as her mother had been – even to Thorvald. Then she might save Heggi. Perhaps a Valla had to be worthy of her power.

Her skern was doing nothing but complain.

This isn't at all my thing. I'm more the big picture, feast and famine, epics. I leave you with the domestic detail.

'Shut up and show me what I need.'

When are you going to warn folk about the flood?

'I'm trying to save Heggi's life.'

They're still planting crops up there.

Bera gave a low growl and he whistled across to a patch of bog plants she had never seen before.

Ooh, look! Cure-All. A rarity.

Bera gathered the brightest, wettest leaves. He pointed with a languid finger at another unknown plant.

That one, too. There are rules, you know.

'For healing?'

For getting the result you want. Something to do with intent.

Like some of his other statements, she already knew it, deep down. And ALU made intent stronger.

'Will he live?' She had to ask.

Her skern waggled his flat hands in a 'touch and go' gesture and vanished.

She had to want it for the best of reasons, not to save her own skin.

Hefnir came in and watched her pound the few plants with some honey.

'Heggi said it tasted sweet,' he said. 'At first. That's what attracted him.'

'To attract the rats,' Bera said quickly. 'I didn't think anyone would go in there.'

'If only I had sent a thrall instead.'

Bera hoped Hefnir meant a grown woman wouldn't eat it, not that she should die. But, then, she had meant it for Thorvald. Did that make her as bad as him?

His eyes were red and swollen and even his beard looked dismal. Bera touched his hand in pity and they took the potion through to the billet together. The bitter stench of bile made Bera gag. Sigrid and Thorvald stood near Rakki, who was lying in a tight ball. Ottar was on the bed, beside the still, small figure. Bera felt no jealousy. In fact, she was grateful, if Ottar's strength could only keep the boy alive.

He didn't take his eyes off Heggi. 'He's stopped being sick. It's too late.'

Bera crouched by them. 'Raise Heggi up a bit for me.'

She pushed a small spoonful of the mixture between the child's slack lips. He did not seem aware of anything, couldn't chew or swallow, so Bera held his nose and mouth until he did. He coughed but kept it down.

'More,' Hefnir urged.

Bera did the same thing three or four times. Then Heggi suddenly arched out of Ottar's arms, his eyes rolling back in his head. He thrashed in wild spasms, in what were surely his death throes. Rakki stood growling, hackles raised, as if a Drorgher had hold of his boy.

All they could do was watch in horror.

The seizure passed. Heggi fell back, a dead weight. Bera put her cheek near his mouth and could feel nothing.

'Come on, Heggi, breathe. Please, Boykin, come on now, be

strong and breathe for me.' She pushed the tousled hair off his forehead and kissed it. Cold as stone.

Ottar cursed softly and Rakki came to stand guard.

'Boykin.' Tears were drowning Bera, salt in her mouth, drips off her chin.

There was a rasping, shuddering breath and then Heggi coughed and was sick again. This time his eyes stayed open. He dug his fingers into Rakki's fur and burst into noisy tears. Bera hugged them both and then stood aside so that the others could get at him.

Afterwards, Hefnir and Thorvald left without a word to her.

Ottar cleaned up without complaint and took the bowl away while Bera made Heggi comfortable. Her care was real now, but was it too late? There remained a sense of some sorrow yet to come.

What would be the end of her attempts to poison Thorvald? And in the longhouse, too, so was she being punished for breaking the rules? A life for a life. She would give up killing Thorvald if it meant Heggi lived. For, against all reason, one truth was hammering her brain:

She loved this little stepson of hers.

11

That night Hefnir and Thorvald sat apart from everyone, drinking silently and determinedly. Bera wondered if Hefnir was working up the courage to kill her. Sigrid and Ottar stayed with Heggi. Whenever she checked on him no one looked up.

On one of her trips her skern settled on the big chest that stood on its own platform. Hadn't Hefnir said it was for important household chattels? As mistress she had all the keys. She found the right key, turned the lock and lifted the heavy lid. Inside was part of a whorled tusk.

I knew you'd be pleased. Gives some purpose to Seabost having it.

'I'll use it properly, too.'

Bera was confident that she could cure Heggi with it and give Bjorn's death some meaning.

Surely Hefnir would not kill her if she saved his son. She went through to the pantry and sent the thralls away. One of them was the slant-eyed woman from the bath hut. Bera realised she had been missing for a few days and wondered if Hefnir sent her off on other duties.

Alone in the shimmer of a short night, Bera stood at the threshold and held the tusk against her cheek. There was the faintest shiver, which she would have missed if she had not felt the living power of the whole tusk before.

She went back inside, fetched the sharpest skewer and carved: ALU.

A bold sun rose. Hefnir and Thorvald had drunk themselves into a stupor, slumped together near the fire, their limbs entwined like snakes. The sight made Bera sick. She was dog-tired when she slipped the special medicine stick under Heggi's pillow and nearly got in beside him. But she said a few words and then fell into her own bed. She would tell Hefnir about the coming flood when he was sober.

The men were gone by the time Bera got up. She checked on Heggi, who was pale but alive. The tusk was working. Normal life was going on outside with the bringing in of the first crops. Bera watched Hefnir and Thorvald supervising the sharing. It was meaningless. She should be there, warning them to store them high, keep them safe from flood. Instead, Thorvald's easy command put her in a despondent stupor.

Bera kept walking. Who was the monster: Thorvald or her? She had nearly murdered Heggi in her desire to kill the man everyone trusted. The man, she had to face it, that Sigrid loved. And yet... she had vowed to make him pay the blood debt. And now she had vowed to spare his life in return for Heggi's. Was that cowardice? Was the bargain with Fate useless because needing his strength made her reason selfish? Which rule could she break? How she longed to talk to someone she could trust.

And so Bera went to the boatyard to talk to the one person who shared her secret.

She collected up some coils of rope on her way to Egill's hut, where she sat alone, whittling. Bera cut off the burned pieces and then took the good lengths to splice alongside her friend, so she could pour out her worries and guilt without having to meet her eyes. As soon as she sat down, Egill asked her what she meant to do about Thorvald.

'I swore that if Heggi lived I would spare him.'

'But—'

'I've been thinking about it all morning.' Bera put down the ropes. 'It was my first vow, to Bjorn. Now I have to protect myself. Sigrid convinced everyone right from the start that it was rat bait, all except Thorvald. He knows it was meant for him.'

'How?'

'He saw me gather the plants and knows I want to kill him.'

'What's he doing about it?'

'He stores things up.'

Egill raised her eyebrows and got back to whittling.

'Go on, Egill. Say it.'

'Leave him alone. He loves Sigrid, Heggi is alive, so leave it to Fate.'

'He keeps glaring at me with that red droopy eye. He knows all right. I think he's waiting to see if Heggi dies before he tells Hefnir.'

'You daren't use poison again.'

'I'm worn out, Egill. I can't think straight. There's my skern's warning, too. I ought to tell folk but they'd either think I was mad or panic.'

'Don't drive yourself so hard. It's still summer, there's time. As for keeping Thorvald quiet, maybe hit him hard. If anything happened to Sigrid...'

'How can you suggest hurting Sigrid!' Egill might spout advice about mercy but then some inner demon would pop out of her mouth.

Ottar burst into the hut and pulled the stool from under Egill. 'Supposed to be sorry, says he'll help and then he clears off with you on a pleasure trip. Where'd you get to last night, eh?'

Egill hunkered down in a corner.

Ottar took the ropes from Bera. 'You used to splice better than this.'

'Haven't done much lately. You made sure Hefnir kept me away from boats.'

'How's Heggi?'

'Weak. Not dying. Wants to see you.'

'I'll get up there later. Best crack on now.'

'Wait!'

On impulse, Bera decided to tell her father about her vision of the flood. Her disgust with Egill brought an appreciation of Ottar's reliability in any trouble. So she described the coming ruin and watched his face age with every word.

'What does Hefnir say?'

'I'm telling you, not him. We need boats.'

Ottar slumped down onto Egill's stool. 'There won't be enough, even with their old fishing vessels.'

'You believe me then?'

Ottar narrowed his eyes. 'I know the weather as well as you. This heat will be paid for and storms sound about right.'

They each had their skills, after all. 'If folk find out they might kill to get onto a vessel. Father – how fast can you build more boats?'

'There's no long timber for it, not now. Sea-riders burned that and all.'

'We must give some hope!' Bera's mind raced. There should be a fair way of deciding who was to leave – but that was a problem for later. 'How about the workboat? Could you fit it out for a long passage, Father? No more frayed ropes.'

'That ruination of a boy, I beat him black and—'

'Can you do it?'

'I can do more than that. I'll make it bigger.'

Egill jumped up. 'In Iraland a boat could be bodged in—'

'There'll be no bodging in my yard. I can unclench the stern of a trade boat and open up the bow of the biggest workboat, double the keel and hog at the join. I'll have to double the gunnels and replank but...'

'How long?' Bera asked.

'You'll have a sea-going vessel near twice the size of the old one.'

'When?'

'Best start soonest. I'll tell the lads it's for Hefnir to go further. So mind you tell him.' He threw the ropes back at Bera. 'And get these spliced proper an' all.'

'Well, he believed about the flood,' Egill said, when Ottar had gone.

'He knows the power of nature. Hefnir does, too, but how does that help? This is your fault, Egill. What the sea-riders did in malice, you did with your clumsy helpfulness and we're one boat less.'

Egill looked serious. 'Must stop that flood in its tracks, then.'

Only Egill would think she could help by taking on nature herself.

Wash day was the first chance Bera had to speak to Hefnir alone. Before joining him at the bath hut, she went to check on Heggi, wanting some good news to report.

He was up, tottering towards Rakki.

'I feel hungry today,' he said, when he noticed her.

'That's a good sign.' Bera caught him as he fell. 'How about some of Feima's rich milk? Her calf's thriving. I saw her yesterday.'

'Dotta? I want to go.'

'When you're stronger.'

She got him back on his bed and took out the medicine stick. 'Look – it's getting darker as it makes you better.'

'It's not like your other ones.'

'It's narwhale tusk with very special runes on it, see? I carved them, to draw out mortal sickness.'

Bera thought again about how the tusk had come to Seabost. Was it supposed to save Heggi, or was this some sign from Bjorn? Some reminder of her vow to kill Thorvald?

'Bera, you're not listening! Rakki saved me. I liked that honey stuff. Rakki barked like mad and made me stop eating it.'

A dog's straightforward care. 'Thank you, Rakki. I'll fetch that milk and you can share it with him.'

'Can you leave your medicine stick?'

She slipped it back in place. 'Of course. You're not out of the wood yet.'

Heggi leaned forward and kissed her. 'Thanks, Bera.'

Her guts cramped with guilt.

Bera waited until Hefnir went into the hot room. Steam made it all the more secret. The usual thrall was tending the stones: the beautiful mute with slanted eyes.

'You were missing for a while.' Bera took a ladle of water from her. She smiled.

Hefnir hit his back with the switch. It was scored with thin red lines from the twigs as well as old scars.

'I saved Heggi,' Bera began. 'So you can see my Valla skills are more certain.'

'If you've something to say, say it.'

'Is it all right to speak in front of her?'

'She couldn't repeat it, anyway.'

Bera took her time. 'It's very bad, Hefnir, the worst it could possibly be. My skern showed me.'

He snorted. 'Your skern...'

'There will be violent thunderstorms and flooding. All our summer stores will be spoiled and we shall starve by the spring unless we leave.'

'Your skern told you this?'

'I saw it. It was like using the narwhale horn to heal Heggi – which I found in the first place!'

It was a clever thing to say and his expression changed.

She pressed on. 'Ottar believes me. He says the weather is odd. Have you ever known it as hot as this?'

'You don't know when this will happen.'

'My skern only warns me of close dangers.'

'If any of this is true...' Hefnir frowned until he found the flaw. 'We don't have enough boats.'

'Ottar has a plan for that. He's already started.'

Hefnir went out for a cold-water plunge. When he came back in he had the answer. 'Rain can't stop me trading for more stocks if the worst happens.'

'And leave us? Besides, what would you trade with? You're giving four tusks to the Serpent.'

'He's not getting any if we need them.'

'You told me this tax keeps us safe.'

'But if we're going anyway...'

'So we are, then?'

'Let me think, damn it.'

Bera went outside to drench.

After a while, Hefnir and the thrall followed her. 'How did you know I was giving him four tusks?'

Hot panic poured over her. How did she know? The memory of a smell hit her. The latrines. Dishonour. 'My skern told me.'

The woman switched Bera's back with twigs.

'The Serpent asked for six. I was going to send Thorvald with four but then all this Heggi business... and now you say we're leaving. I think he will have to do with that last bit of narwhale horn.'

'Heggi won't get better without it!' It wasn't the only reason. Bera's scalp crackled with the danger of giving him the tusk carved with ALU. 'Give him walrus. He's not a man to be denied!'

'How do you know?'

'I can see folk's deep desires. His all lead to trouble.'

So did the narwhale's tusk. It would be defiled by the Serpent – or was already, for no matter how well it healed, it also brought misery and death.

Bera muttered something about Heggi's next dose and left.

Hefnir wasn't listening.

Bera made the mistake of entering by the longhouse doors.

'Violation! Perfidy!' the ancestors snarled. *'Abomination! Abduction!'*

She turned on her heel and decided to tackle Sigrid, who was washing clothes at the river. She was telling the other women how put upon she was. Bera walked serenely over and helped fold the clothes to disprove it.

On the way back Sigrid pointed at a tree. 'An apple left on the tree means death.'

Bera quickly took the gnarled black apple and threw it away. They picked some berries, sat on the grass and feasted on them. Bera felt sad at the betrayal that existed between them. There was lack of honesty on both sides. Sigrid was the closest she had to a mother figure. A poor one, maybe, and now married to Thorvald, but Egill's suggestion she should injure her to get back at Thorvald was unthinkable. Besides, they were all facing calamity. She dreaded warning Sigrid about the flood, with her fear of drowning.

'Have you come unwell this month?' asked Sigrid, out of the blue.

'What?'

'Who washes the rags? I know the thralls should but I don't like them knowing... intimate things about us.'

'Do you still have your course each month?'

Sigrid smiled ruefully. 'Do you think I'm so old, Bera? Don't worry,

I'm barren. You'll have no competition. It was Thorvald's kindness and courtesy about it that made me decide on the handfasting.'

'I don't want to hear about it.'

'There's something to redeem everyone.'

'Why him, Sigrid?'

'There's a mate for the owl, my grandmother used to say.'

'He's more trole than owl.'

'It's what's inside that counts.'

Bera could not get past his ravaged face, even if he was not a killer.

'What happened at the handfasting?' she asked.

'Wondering if I can get out of it?'

'What did you have to do?'

'Come on, then.' Sigrid got to her feet and beckoned Bera up. 'You stand under a full moon, facing each other. You join right hands to join male souls and then left hands to join female souls. Like this.'

Bera flinched at Sigrid's touch. It made her Thorvald.

'Egill says the figure of eight means infinity.' Sigrid did not let go.

It was a kind of forgiveness.

'I have to tell you something,' said Bera.

Sigrid fell backwards onto the grass and did a whole big hammer sign, leaving her arms outstretched. Above them the sky gleamed, confounding the prediction.

'A flood! See, I always knew I'd drown, one way or another.'

'I saw my mother at Brightening,' Bera said. 'She looked right into me and said I was not to be guilty about a single thing.'

'So are you?'

Bera had felt guilty about her mother her whole life. For not saving her. For not being a proper Valla. For not being a good daughter. For so many failures. For feeling too much.

Nothing she could tell Sigrid.

'How soon will you all leave Seabost?'

'Before the storms.' Bera paused. 'What do you mean by "you all"? You're one of us.'

'I'm never going out to sea.'

'You won't be afraid, Sigrid, once you're out there. The air is different and so are all the colours and smells. Keen. There are whale spouts and the splash of diving birds and your hair stands on end with the whole... aliveness of it all!'

Sigrid sat up and brushed the grass from her shoulders. 'I'm not going.'

'You will die, Sigrid, if you stay here.'

'Then I'll have to die. I'm not setting foot on any boat.'

'You wretched, stubborn old fool!' Bera leapt up and walked away, to stop herself shaking Sigrid.

'I'm not, though.'

Bera came back and shook her. 'I don't care if I have to knock you senseless but you are coming with us and that's that!'

Sigrid pushed her away and stood. 'Stop bullying me.'

'Please, Sigrid!' Bera got down on her knees to beseech her.

Sigrid's mouth twitched. 'We'll see.'

'Don't you "we'll see" me. I know what "we'll see" means and you can forget it.'

'What about Thorvald?'

'Hefnir's telling him right now. You must make sure Thorvald knows it's a real threat. He won't believe me, he hates me.'

'No, you hate him.'

'And if he and Hefnir are behind me then I can get the right folk to come.'

Sigrid glared at her. 'So I'm to do my best to persuade my husband to leave me!'

'You're coming.'

'I can't.'

'You can.'

'You'll be glad I'm not going,' Sigrid said. 'There aren't enough boats for us all to make a sea passage.'

Despite sounding confident, Bera had no idea how to get Sigrid aboard. The two women went about their work and only met again when Hefnir and Thorvald returned to eat. They told them Ottar was staying at the boatyard, ready to work.

Nothing more was said while they ate a thick stew: Hefnir put up his screen of silence; Thorvald struggled to chew; and Sigrid kept her back turned to them all. Heggi was as white as an ice bear, so immediately afterwards Bera took him to bed.

'It's too early,' he moaned. 'I'm too hot.'

Bera pulled a hanging across his billet.

'It's still too light.'

'You need rest to keep getting well.'

'You just want to talk without me. I should be with my father, like Thorvald, like a partner.'

'He doesn't want partners.' Bera pulled a linen sheet over his shoulders and checked the medicine stick.

Raised voices carried and Heggi sat up. 'I need to get Rakki a bone.'

'Good try.' Bera laughed. 'The stick's here beside you. So lie down and go to sleep.'

He was right, of course. There were things to discuss that Hefnir did not want his son to hear. She went back to the fire where the others had begun without her.

Sigrid's face was red with indignation. 'You should let him choose for himself!'

Hefnir smirked. 'I always do.'

'Sit here with me, Sigrid,' Thorvald said quietly.

She did, and even smiled. Bera briefly wondered if he beat his wife into obedience but there was only love on Sigrid's face.

'Thorvald's chosen to come,' said Hefnir, 'but in any case, if you are too stubborn to come on the boat with us, why should he stay here to die?'

'I have a duty.' Thorvald put his arm round Sigrid. 'I am Hefnir's second.'

'You agree we have to leave?' Bera asked Hefnir. She was sure he did not believe in her gift of sight.

He got up. 'I've been thinking about it before this. Living here, we're cribbed by rock and ice. We should go south, to the Marsh Lands with their rich, fat holy men. Or try Iraland.' His voice caught, as it had when he spoke about the sharpest, blackest knife.

Bera sensed this was his true aim. 'Not Iraland!'

'Egill says it's even richer.'

'So now Egill's in charge!' Bera felt her throat burn with fury.

'It's my decision, Bera. I shall support you when you tell the village what you have seen. But where we go is up to me.'

Bera moved away in agitation. She rolled and rolled the black bead of her necklace, feeling its enduring heat, forged in Egill's land of fire. It came from the place she had scried in the black bowl that night on Seal Island, so that was where they must go. For her it was different. She would save folk by taking them there, not chasing some ultimate weapon. Hers was the purest reason. Wasn't it?

Bera could tell from Hefnir's breathing that he was pretending to sleep.

'Are you awake?' she whispered.

He huffed and bounced round onto his side to face her. 'I really want this to happen, Bera.'

'You're excited about people dying?'

'I want to lead folk to a better place. On some trading trips there have been times when it's been hard to come home.'

The truth stung.

Bera pressed on. 'I want Sigrid to come but what if she won't? She and Thorvald could go off overland and settle somewhere. Why must you part them?'

'She doesn't matter to him. This handfasting is an ugly bastard's ruse to get coupled. He's no fool. He wants to be with me.'

'I don't want him with us.'

'Why not?'

'The same as always.'

'Oh, Hel's teeth, Bera, not the Bjorn thing!' He rolled away from her.

It was always, and could only ever be, the Bjorn thing. One way or another.

Then he whispered in the dark. 'Why don't you tell Sigrid what he did? She'll be glad to be rid of him. I'll make sure Thorvald's ready to defend himself.'

'So he can kill Sigrid as well as her son?'

'Bera...'

'I've not seen Sigrid this happy, ever. The truth would kill her anyway. I can't do it to her.'

'Thorvald is mine. He's coming. It's up to you what you do about Sigrid.'

12

At the dangerous time, when a body can slip away, Bera checked on Heggi. She was alarmed at how waxen he looked. His breath was shallow. She kissed his forehead. It had no smell of fever and the medicine stick was darker. He sleepily turned to snuggle up with Rakki, so Bera left them, sure that the poison had all been drawn out and he only needed time to recover.

Ottar arrived for the day meal. He said he and Egill had talked about the flood and the shortage of boat space and they had formed a good plan that would keep folk safe.

'Hefnir came first thing and he agrees.'

'To what?'

'I'm not having you finding problems and claiming your skern forbids it,' he said. 'Now where's my porridge?'

Bera clicked her fingers and a man brought a bowl for them both. She seethed until he left.

'I left you to re-hog a boat. You agreed with me that we have to leave!'

Ottar tapped his nose. 'I'm not saying I don't agree with you.'

'But you'd rather plan with Egill?'

He carried on stolidly eating his meal.

Bera pushed her bowl away. If he believed Egill because she was a boy perhaps he needed his eyes opened. But then Egill arrived and announced that she had told folk to gather in the mead hall.

Bera lost her temper. 'It's Hefnir who calls meetings, not you two!'

'You mean, you want to call them,' Ottar said. He scraped his bowl, swilled some ale round his mouth and spat. 'Let's go.'

He put his arm round Egill's shoulders and they left for the mead hall. Bera searched for Sigrid, failed to find her and ran after them. Hefnir was waiting at the hearth and Bera couldn't get in front. Folk slapped Ottar on the back and ignored her. Then she saw that Dellingr was there and it was worse still: she wanted him to be proud of her, seeing her in command, solving problems. Not slinking behind like a midden dog.

Sigrid and Thorvald were already there, talking to Asa. It didn't help her mood.

Ottar's boatyard voice called them to order. Egill raised one leg onto a stool. It was a poor attempt to look masculine and looked more like a dog cocking its leg.

'What folk need is a project,' Ottar began. 'I know there's work on but it's long days and there's food in the store. Seems to me that there's good times coming for Seabost, a time of plenty, when we don't have to scrimp and save.'

It was the complete opposite! Bera glared at him. He said he still agreed with her. What was going on?

'Now Egill and me, we got a plan. That plan involves the whole village working together on the same scheme, like in the days when all Northmen stood shoulder to shoulder to put roofs over heads. Our plan starts up there, at the river.'

'The river,' Egill shouted and pointed the wrong way.

Folk laughed until Hefnir raised a hand. 'Listen up!' he said. 'There's work to be doing so let's hear the plan, vote on it and get on.'

Hefnir and her father must have hatched a plan to stop folk panicking, that was it. When Egill pointed a finger at the sky, trying to look important, her silliness finally managed to make Bera smile.

'This is a good plan,' Egill began. 'In Iraland it gave folk fresh water as well as a fish pool that made them easy to catch, even in winter.'

'They flying fish, Snowy?' shouted a man at the back.

Men laughed. Ottar clipped Egill round the head and she lowered her arm.

'All right then,' she said. 'It's a dam. It's what you do. You dam up the river to make a kind of lake thing.'

Bera was stunned. 'What if the river's a torrent after storms, what then?'

Ottar shrugged. 'Won't overflow. I'm the builder, see? So don't you worry about how it'll work. It'll work.'

Bera was horrified. He might believe her prediction, but he should be building boats, not wasting time with a hare-brained scheme.

'Good for farmers,' said Egill. 'Crops and that. Runnels bring the water straight down to where it's needed.'

'Then I'm for it,' said a farmer. 'I think it's a good idea.'

'We could wash the clothes in it,' said Sigrid, stupid as ever, and Asa agreed with her.

Bera was outraged and outnumbered. Worse still, Egill and her father thought they had solved the problem but dread was a stone in her stomach.

'We could go one better than that,' said Ottar. 'You could have a proper wash house down here and heat the water.'

Folk liked that.

Dellingr shouted above the excitement. 'Won't get to the forge, or the huts.'

'Fair enough, Dellingr, it won't. But that's no reason not to help other folk. Life's hard enough. And you'd like a bit o' fresh fish come winternights, wouldn't you?'

Bera so wanted it to work. The storms were coming – and if it stopped the flood they would never need to leave. But her scalp pricked. She wondered what Dellingr thought. Before she could reach him he collected his wife and daughter, took the baby from her and they set off. Sigrid went with them.

Feeling doubly betrayed, Bera insisted that Ottar and Egill should return to the longhouse. As she went out, Thorvald grabbed her.

'We need a boat!'

'Let go of me!' Bera was furious. 'Don't tell me my business. Get Sigrid aboard, that's all.'

She hurried after the others.

Once inside, Hefnir turned. 'I don't care about the dam, whether it works or not. We're leaving.'

Bera was bewildered. Had he lied to his people? 'You just backed this plan.'

'Egill told me it was to do with Iraland!'

'It was.' Egill's eyes were widely innocent.

Bera could use Hefnir's lust for Iraland but first she had to tackle her father. 'We need boats, not this mad idea.'

'The dam's a security,' said Ottar. 'Gives us time to leave properly, not with gales and drift ice threatening. That's what me and Egill planned. I could make more boats and all, not a bit of re-hogging.'

'There isn't enough timber,' said Hefnir. 'Though next spring I could— '

'Round boats are made of walrus skin,' Egill said. 'Thick as your hand, the hide, and when it's tarred...'

'I'm not putting to sea in a corpse,' said Hefnir.

'There isn't time!' Bera shouted. 'We have to go, gales or not. Or stay here and die!'

Ottar took some ale from a thrall. 'When you going to tell folk about the flood, then?'

Egill grinned. 'Won't be a flood, not with the dam.'

Hefnir ignored her. 'Tell them I need a bigger vessel for trading.'

Ottar rubbed his chin. 'Or do I stop re-hogging and just do the dam?'

Bera wanted to hit him. 'We should leave as soon as we can with the supplies we have. Or else we'll watch them float out to sea.'

They all looked at her.

'You're saying my dam won't work,' her father said quietly. 'That all my experience counts for nothing.'

'Your experience is in boatbuilding, not dams!'

'Exactly.' Hefnir prodded Ottar's chest. 'And I want to settle elsewhere before winter. So that's why you have to build a decent boat and build it fast.'

Ottar squared up to him. 'I'm telling you it can't be done.'

'Then we'll leave without you!'

Bera pushed her way between the two angry men. 'Stop it! I need time to think. I'll ask my skern about the boat.'

'As if he...' they both began.

Bera spoke over them. 'And about a fair way of choosing who goes.'

'What about the dam?' Egill wailed.

Bera was thinking aloud. 'I saw a trail of storms before Fall End. We might have time to wait till the boat's re-hogged.'

Ottar rubbed his hands together. 'Then I'll crack on with that right now – and you can look after the dam, Egill.'

Egill capered across to the table. 'Let's eat first, now everything's all right.'

Only all right for her. 'We've eaten, Egill. Let's talk while I get Heggi's medicine ready.'

Bera took Egill into the pantry. 'Egill – have you really seen this... thing?'

'Dam. Want to help you, Bera. And Ottar. Don't want to leave here.'

'But, Egill, we can be happy together in another place.'

'You keep touching that black bead.'

Bera took her hand away. She got a bowl and started mashing a few leaves.

This wasn't the moment to tell Egill she wanted to take them to the terrifying place that had burned her father alive. She gave her some pickles.

'Wouldn't you like to go back to Iraland?'

The slant-eyed thrall came in, fetched a pitcher and left.

'She's very beautiful,' said Egill. 'Eyes like almonds.'

'Are they something you have in Iraland?' Bera added honey to the mash.

Egill pointed at the bowl. 'That's not for...?'

'Never again.' Bera meant it.

'So what about Thorvald?'

Bera's feelings were chaotic. Thorvald was in favour of the new boat when he could have opposed her. She fought to keep pity out but the monster was gentle with Sigrid and his face caused him pain. Her duty was strong, though, and she could not bear to leave Sigrid behind. Perhaps he was waiting, too, to tell Hefnir about her trying to poison him once he and Sigrid were safe.

'I need him. Then I'll be ready for him in Iraland.'

Egill tapped her nose and went out, whistling. Was a lie so bad when it was used for good? Her skern was not there to answer. He had been absent a lot. Was it because she was hiding from herself so much of the time, knowing things were wrong? Bera was exhausted but she had to think straight and save all her folk.

Hefnir and Thorvald were together in the byre.

'Here's my idea,' Bera said. 'We'll ask who wants to explore new lands. That will explain the boat being re-hogged and we'll see who's adventurous enough to make the best settlers.'

Hefnir liked it. 'I could say I need more men to overwinter and try it out.'

'Some folk have to come,' Bera said airily. 'Like Dellingr.'

Hefnir's face darkened. 'Why him?'

'We must have a smith.'

'There are enough smiths in the Marsh Lands.'

Thorvald coughed. 'But not ones you can trust.'

Hefnir ran a hand over his beard. 'The tenant farmers will have to be told but I'll do it privately. Though I expect they will choose to stay.'

'If you start giving choices,' said Bera, 'it will be the end of secrecy.'

'Then no one is to tell Dellingr.'

'He'll keep his mouth shut,' Thorvald said. 'You can trust him.'

Bera was amazed that he should keep supporting the smith. Was he making Dellingr look good so that she was the guilty one?

'Enough, Thorvald,' said Hefnir. 'I can manage this.'

'With my help,' Bera said.

Bera was confused again; except for the need to see Dellingr. She would only ask him what he thought about the dam construction, though, and half obey Hefnir.

She told Dellingr everything.

Bera was sorry to watch his smile fade but the relief of telling him was huge. She hoped he might give another explanation of the skern's vision but he believed the flood was real.

'I could lose my whole family,' he said.

The catch in his voice made Bera jealous. She assured him that they needed a smith so he would not be left behind. 'And your family can come too,' she grudgingly added.

It only made him more anguished. 'I'm not taking any man's place on a boat.'

'You have to come.'

'No. It must be a fair choice.'

'What about Asa and the children?' She would use them, if he would only come.

'We'll go by honourable means, or how could I face folk?' He rubbed his strong, workman's hands. Honest hands.

He would not change his mind, so it was up to her to make sure he got onto a boat, as much as she admired his honour. And she was a Valla: she could nudge Fate a bit.

'I'll decide how we'll choose,' she said. 'Till then, please don't say a word, especially to Asa.'

His eyes were like the night sea. 'I won't say I like it. Asa and I have no secrets. But I won't tell her. I don't want her worrying herself sick and she would, for sure.'

He spat on his hand and they shook on it. Bera felt despicable. She had not been kind to Dellingr, disobeyed Hefnir and ignored her own sense of what was right for the sake of a momentary relief. What was worse, once again she was intending to cheat Fate. What might be the consequences? The ancestors would shriek when she got home. What were the words?

'Dellinger, can I ask you something? About the old tongue?'

He waited.

'Every time I pass the threshold the ancestors scream at me. Do you think it's a prediction?'

He rubbed his cheek. 'I think stone soaks up happening. My grandfather said it's a warning to the future.'

'There are some words they say all the time.'

'I don't know words of power. That's up to a Valla like you.'

Her champion! His belief made her strong enough to deal with the ancestors, whatever their words meant.

'I can only remember two: Perfidy! Violation!'

He spun away.

'What?'

'Don't come back up here alone.'

'Tell me!'

'The words. They mean Betrayal. And Rape.'

She ran. She ran for shame and ran as though Fate herself was at her heels. The ancestors could read her secret desires about Dellingr that she had hidden even from herself.

Bera was at the crossroads when Rakki rammed into the back of her knees, felling her. Heggi was behind. He fell down, panting, totally unable to speak. They lay for a while, exhausted, though Bera was also completely beyond words. The dog capered about, barking continuously. Bera got him sitting for an instant, though he did stop barking.

Then the fact Heggi was out of bed hit her. 'What are you doing here? And running! You'll get ill again!'

Heggi waved a hand for time. 'That... man.'

'Go on.'

'Man who...' Heggi started a fit of dry retching. He gingerly felt his belt-bag and pulled away a sticky hand. 'Gull eggs...'

'Never mind that. What man? Where?'

He gestured over at the top fields. 'Digging... thralls.'

'He's digging? Oh, come on, Heggi, talk sense.'

He let Rakki lick his hand. 'Where they're digging. Talking with a woman.'

'Which one?'

'A thrall. How would I know which one?'

'Try!'

Tears brimmed. 'Slanty eyes.'

Her! 'Is the man still here?'

He pointed at the far forest. 'Went off on that horse.'

'So why did you run?'

'It was weird.'

Bera looked at the sky for help.

Heggi kept his lips tight. 'Well, they spoke like this while he pretended to fix his saddle. It looked shifty.'

'Did you hear any of it?'

'No.'

Bera put the crushed eggs down for Rakki to clear up.

'Papa told me not to give a dog eggs or else it will eat them when it collects them.'

'Nonsense.' Bera put her lips to his brow. 'You're hot. I shouldn't have let you go out and get jitters.'

'I'm hungry.'

'Starve a fever.'

'Oh, Bera!'

She took pity on him. 'You can have something bland as long as you promise to rest afterwards.'

'What about that man!'

'Which man? You say it as if I should know!'

Heggi gave a deep, exasperated sigh. 'Because you do know. The one from before, with a nice horse. The one with black squirls, only this time he had his clothes on.'

Betrayal. Rape.

Bera went in through the byre. Sigrid was at the loom, making a piece to add to the mainsail to make it bigger, she announced as she helped Bera out of her boots.

'Thorvald has to take a tax to that monster tomorrow!'

'Heggi just saw him.'

'Not the Serpent King?'

'Talking to that slant-eyed thrall.'

'I told you not one of them's to be trusted.'

'Let's work. We'll need that sail soon if he's prowling.'

'He's up to no good, I'm telling you.'

'Sigrid, everyone knows he's up to no good. It's not some great insight of yours.'

'Thorvald shouldn't be going alone.'

They sat at the loom. Bera had heard enough at the latrine to know that Hefnir would not go with Thorvald, though she did not know why. Would the Serpent do her work for her? Then who would protect them all?

'That thrall.' Bera pulled her eyes. 'She does the hot room.'

Sigrid tapped her hand. 'Who's stopped working now?'

'Hefnir and I talked about the Serpent in there. Do you think she told him?'

'Sure as eggs are eggs. What did I tell you? We'll all be murdered in our beds.' Sigrid made a ferocious hammer sign. 'Thorvald's walking into a trap, Bera.'

But what trap? And what to do about it? Bera wondered who or what was doing the betraying that was soaked into the longhouse walls. She felt for Sigrid – but most of all, she felt very afraid.

As soon as he got home, Bera took Hefnir to the threshold of the byre and tried to get him to understand what she feared.

Though still light, colours were less intense. Day birds had not roosted but owls twitted and tweaked from beyond the hanking apple trees. It was the start of the season of confusion.

'I have no idea which woman you're talking about.' Hefnir started fiddling with one of the old harnesses hanging on the rail.

'I told you. She's the one in the bath hut.'

'Why would I notice a thrall?'

His denial, totally different from his son's, made Bera suspect he was hiding something. Did he use the woman, like his men sniggered in the mead hall?

'What did we talk about in the hot room?'

'I can't remember.'

Why was he lying? Surely he couldn't be saying things he wanted the thrall to report to the Serpent? Unthinkable.

'Then I'll remind you. Storms. Flood. Ruined food. A boat taking us away.'

He took the harness off its peg. 'All this should be inside, not left out here to rot.'

'Leave it alone, Hefnir. This is important.'

He threw it over the rail and rubbed his face with his hands. 'You worry too much.'

'Are you going with Thorvald tomorrow?' she asked.

'What do you care? You want him dead.'

It was no longer that simple. 'How do you know the goods have ever reached the Serpent? What if Thorvald's his partner?'

Hefnir's lips turned white. 'I trust Thorvald with my life.'

'We all make mistakes.'

Hefnir raised a hand to strike her. Bera flinched but stood her ground.

He turned and left her.

Hefnir had said the Serpent King could expect nothing after demanding even more. He had also said the woman couldn't talk but Heggi said she did. Bera trusted Heggi. So what did she say to the Serpent – and what was he capable of doing?

Hefnir relented. Thorvald was to take two walrus tusks and trade some salt. Bera hoped it was enough, as she stood beside Hefnir at dawn.

Thorvald was grimmer than usual that dawn, even as he held Sigrid in a quick embrace. He rode off, leading the packhorses, and she managed a small wave. But then she put her apron over her face and ran back inside.

'He'll demand more, won't he?' Bera said.

'He can rot in Hel. I've told Thorvald to make promises and by the time he realises no more is coming, we'll be long gone.'

'More lies.'

Hefnir studied the sky. 'No sign of rain, Bera.'

'That's not a lie. We'll have more rain than we want very soon.'

He shrugged. 'I'm going up to the dam. Once that's working we can get the water where it's needed.'

Being a Valla was truly lonely, especially without her skern. His absence made her uneasy and irritated. She should be at the loom but couldn't face Sigrid's fretting, so she decided to follow Hefnir up to the dam and have a word with Egill. Bera needed any kind of friend.

Two cabin-like structures were going up on either side of the river, using the skills folk had, which would then be joined. This was Ottar's plan. Her father's inventiveness impressed Bera, as did the strength and kinship of the workers that made teamwork natural. And yet their work was a waste of time. If only she could take all of them! She couldn't, so she must devise a fair way of choosing and until then boats had to be made seaworthy. Ottar was busy re-hogging and trying to manage this, too. These thoughts of him raised her spirits. It gave her hope. Then she saw the line of rowans had been cut down. Rowans, that protected from evil.

Egill, balanced on one of the crossbeams, was directing operations with wild sweeps of her arms. Bera wanted to stop it.

Egill jumped down when she saw her. 'It'll be finished in no time.'

'But still too late, Egill. The rains will come.'

'And the dam's to hold back the flood.'

'But what if there's too much water, like my vision?'

'See the two gates ready to go in the gap? Open them a bit and the river flows down slowly. Safer than before.'

'What if they won't open?'

'Rains all the time in Iraland but it wasn't a problem. It makes a lake behind the dam.'

Egill sprang onto the newly built platform; elfin as she was on the very first night they met. Bera had thought then that she was a boy of talent. So was she doubting Egill only because she was a girl? The dam did look sound enough, and if her father had planned it... Perhaps her warning had done its work.

And yet. Egill could never admit she was wrong. Well, nor could she.

The air was brooding. Change was coming, as any sailor would sense. Certainly Ottar would – and she hoped he was working through the light nights.

The sky was leaden when Bera next visited the boatyard. It was busy, with the reassuring sound of sawing, banging and hammering. Lads whistled as they rushed past with short planks and brushes.

Then she found Ottar in his hut, head in hands.

'Not like you, Father.'

'I'm never going to get this finished.' He looked at her with bloodshot eyes. 'Go on, say it.'

'What?'

'Told you so.'

She needed to see for herself. 'Shall I go alone?'

He pulled himself up with an effort, got his tool belt on and led her towards the slipway where the boat was up on blocks. He was right. It hardly looked any bigger.

'I'll finish off this bit,' Ottar said to his best lad. 'You go up to the shed and help the others.' He patted the hull like an old friend and Bera swallowed hard to hold back tears.

'We've had to make the best of short planks and worked through the night and all.' He spat on his hands. 'Still, there's no victory for a sleeping man.'

They walked round, admiring his work. Though small, this was a proper boat – and if a boat looked well she would sail well.

'You've kept her lines neat.' Bera's voice was thick.

'I'm a good builder and one of the lads is coming on.'

The smell of new-sawn wood brought back her early childhood, when Ottar was kind. Her father lovingly stroked the boards with his rough hands and whispered something she had long forgotten.

'Heart of oak for the gunnels; ash for the mast and oars. The mountain ash is the strongest and the whitest wood comes from the north face.'

'You said that for the first boat you ever made me.'

'You remember that?'

She did. And his look when she kissed the oar with her rune carved on it.

'Boats are always bigger inside than out.' Ottar had said that, too, and he knew it. He set up a work ladder. 'I haven't started work on the decks so be careful.'

Bera tucked her skirt through her legs into her belt.

'You used to scamper up ladders like a squirrel.'

'I liked being higher than everyone else.'

She did not go up like a squirrel but it was neatly done, despite her garments. She clambered over the rail and stood on the stern platform. It was a mess of unfinished sawing and Bera could not imagine how all the stores, animals and settlers could fit.

There was a low grumble, like a trole's stomach. The scudding sky was thickening and turning yellowish. Bera let herself down onto the ladder and joined Ottar below.

'Is this the storm that'll launch her?'

'I thought you believed in the dam?'

Ottar kicked some wood shavings. 'Egill finds mischief with nothing to do. And with my design it might do the trick.'

Bera was more anxious about the boat. 'You need to finish this soon.'

'Have you done the sail strip?'

'Nearly.'

'When will you tell folk? They need to get their heads straight.'

Bera drew him under the shelter of the hull. 'Hefnir's going to ask for settlers but there'll be too many.'

'Flood might drown 'em all.' He gave a wry laugh.

'Can you reckon how many folk could fit on our boats?'

'Why?'

'And make some wooden counters? I'll mark runes on the same number as can go and folk can draw them.'

He nodded. 'I get it. Looks fair. Could work.'

'The fishermen have their own boats.'

He snorted. 'Them boats'll sink soon as look at them.'

'Then fix them.'

They walked back up through the yard together.

'That's a good idea of yours,' said Ottar when they reached the gates. 'Counters of Fate.'

'I thought of it when I was talking to you.' Bera kissed her father's cheek.

He looked surprised.

She set off for home. After a while she turned, and he was still there, watching her go. Perhaps she was beginning to get her real father back.

She and Hefnir argued and carried on arguing in their billet. Unlike her father, he still believed the dam would give them time. When the last taper guttered he refused to hear any more and then fell asleep.

Thunder rolled overhead. Bera was hollowed out by worry. They were too slow and perhaps Fate would resent the drawing of lots. She tossed and turned and got the bedroll twisted round her so she had to get out and rearrange it. Then she stared at the hanging, which flickered with dry lightning. She longed for the comfort of her skern. There was an odd dragging sensation in the pit of her stomach, as if she were being eaten from the inside. Somehow it was linked with his absence, but she was too scared to look closer.

13

Midsummer came and went and still Thorvald did not return. Bera was anxious, rather than glad, for what might he be plotting with the Serpent King? Or, if he was dead, who would protect them? Sigrid was as jumpy and vicious as a scalded cat.

One night, when she was checking on Feima and her calf, Bera heard Thorvald return.

She put down her shovel, patted Dotta and went into the hall.

Thorvald wasn't even wounded. That secret part of her was glad he was here to look after Sigrid, who was happily bustling in from the pantry with some food. And then she was ashamed at how much she relied on his strength, as they all did.

Thorvald tore off a hunk of bread. 'He wasn't happy,' he said to Hefnir, 'but I told him the next tribute would hold what's promised and he calmed down.'

'So will he wait?' Bera walked over to them.

'He'll wait.' Hefnir's mouth twisted. 'He's all talk.'

Thorvald swallowed the bread whole. 'I said there'd be gold if he waits till after harvest but he wants it before.' He started on a big ham bone like a starving animal.

Sigrid gave him the whole platter. 'You'll all be gone by then.'

Thorvald pulled something from his teeth. 'Seems like the ground's parched to me, not flooded.'

Bera glared at him. 'So I'm lying?'

'Could be you're mistaken.'

'Could be we're mistaken about a lot of things. There we were, worrying about you and you come home without a scratch on you. What private deals have you struck with the Serpent?'

'Stop, Bera,' said Hefnir sharply.

Thorvald cheerfully waved the ham bone. 'Doesn't trouble me. Let her say what she likes. It's the same old story.'

Sigrid said, 'Well, I for one thank you, Hefnir, for not sending him off empty-handed.'

Hefnir raised his goblet. 'Let's drink to your success and the dam. We won't be forced to leave here now.'

'Do you understand nothing?' Bera kicked over a stool.

'I want to go so we will go. But it'll be in my time, not yours. It's why I'm helping build the dam,' said Hefnir.

'Then think on this. Flood or no flood, you'll be forced to leave here fast if you don't give the Serpent King exactly what Thorvald's just promised him. He'll be out for blood.'

Thunder rumbled and dry lightning shimmered nearly every night. Daylight shortened and work slowed but eventually the dam was finished. To Bera's dismay, Egill's boasts turned out to be true and the scheme began to improve everyone's life. Drinkable water (if rather muddy) came right down into the village and folk pictured a future full of ease. Why would they want to leave, now?

The final channel was dug at the back of the mead hall, so there was a celebration that evening. It was Bera's chance to end the secrecy and see if honesty would work. As soon as she saw Dellingr come into the hall with his daughter she took a jug of ale over to them. She wanted to show everyone she had no reason to avoid him.

'The dam's pleased everyone,' she said loudly.

He held out his drinking horn. 'Asa's over there with the baby.'

She would not be got rid of. A roistering mob of youths snatched up his daughter and rampaged off, Heggi amongst them.

'They're more unruly than I was at that age,' Bera said.

Dellingr smiled. 'You're still young. I think us lads were worse than them; fights and so on. Times change.'

'You sound like my father!' Bera regretted sounding familiar and babbled. 'Have you been thinking about what I told you? I mean, a fair way to choose and why.'

'No time like the present.'

'You mean it?'

'I don't like secrets and it's been hard keeping silent all this time, with Asa.'

'I'm sorry.'

He briefly touched her, like fire. 'You mustn't keep folk in the dark any longer.'

Bera wanted more from him. With his knowledge and strength, she could be a mighty Valla and have no need for Thorvald. Everything would be simple again. But Dellingr went straight to his wife and Bera's stomach twisted.

Bera told Hefnir to get folk gathered round. They probably thought she was going to bless the dam, which reminded her that she must.

Hefnir came back to stand beside her. 'Stick to our plan, Bera: ask who wants to settle in the Marsh Lands, all right?'

Between Ottar and Egill was her skern. At last! He saluted her, looking perky, which gave her confidence.

Thorvald bellowed for quiet.

Bera began. 'Imagine you have come home from a hunting trip. It has been a good trip, with a big haul of walrus.'

'Like Egill,' shouted someone, to cheers and laughter. They were sunny with success.

Bera hated to end it but she must. 'The weather is fair... it's midsummer ... but right then your skern warns you of a terrible danger. When you least expect it, would you believe him more – or less?'

She had the crowd's attention. Other folk drifted over. They were used to listening, even in drink.

Out poured the truth, unstoppably. 'I saw ruin with my own eyes. Our ancestors abandoned us and took the sun with them. The sky grew black as a raven's wing and lightning blasted the village. Downpours and deluge washed away everything. Folk were left to starve.'

Hefnir groaned.

Her skern tapped his head. She must think how to tell the truth and yet give hope.

'But then I saw a boat.'

Hefnir shouted. 'Our lifeblood is the sea. It brings us what we need to survive. Beyond these shores lie lands of plenty. A man can grab what he wants whenever he wants. You know where we traders have overwintered in the past and it's an easy life, a good life. Everything's gentler than it is here – especially the women, eh, boys?'

His men roared and raised their horns. They needed to leave soon, but in limited numbers, and not for the Marsh Lands. The black bead burned against her neck.

Hefnir was calling for volunteers. 'So step forward those who venture. We'll trade, raid and settle with the profits.'

'I've just broken my back on that dam,' said someone.

'Aye, what was the point of that?'

Hefnir raised his arms. 'It buys time for the daring and will feed the sluggards. So who's for it? Who wants to catch life by the throat?'

Asa marched to the front and beckoned to Dellingr. All the folk came forward apart from the farmers. There was bravado: some fishermen who were quick to start a fight and first to leave when a knife flashed. But there was excited good humour everywhere.

Then Ottar stumbled into the circle, held upright by Egill.

'We have finished... project,' slurred Ottar. 'My friend here, young Egill. Egill's project. To the dam!'

They drank the toast and Egill took a bow. Did her father think he was being helpful?

'Thank you, Father,' Bera began.

Ottar carried on. 'I want to say... this. Promised my daughter...' He waved his horn at her. 'Best one. She don't believe me but... promised her a bigger boat. But not big enough.'

She had to make them take the flood seriously. 'Listen, all of you. I want you to go home and ration what you have in store. Eat as little as possible and forage for wild food. There is plenty because of this fair summer. We must be ready when the rains come.'

A man said, 'She's always a barrel of laughs.'

Folk noisily set to drinking again.

Sigrid nudged her. 'You need to bend with the wind more.'

'I've learned to be plain, Sigrid, or else it all goes wrong. And I'm not bending if it means leaving you.'

Sigrid looked over at Thorvald. 'Then you'll do without me.' She made a hammer sign and left.

Hefnir barged through. 'So much for our plan. No thanks to you there wasn't panic.'

'I have no choice, Hefnir. I have to say truthfully what my skern has warned me.'

'We built the dam. We're in control, Bera. The world is ours for the taking. We're not superstitious Crapsby peasants but masters of our own Fate, with our own skills and labour.'

Bera shoved Hefnir, furious. 'There'll be some terrible revenge, speaking like that. We're in thrall to Fate and it will be deeper and darker now, thanks to you.'

'Don't dare to lay hands on me in public.'

Heggi ran up to her, holding his elbow. 'I fell and cut myself. It's quite bad.'

Bera gestured at the blood. 'You had better hope this is not the start of it.'

She took Heggi home, breaking off some hagthorn on the way. She sat him in the dairy, where it was cool and clean, got a thrall to fetch fresh water from the dam and studied the gash. It was deep enough to need clamping.

'I want you to be brave,' she said.

First she bathed the wound, then broke off three big thorns from the branch, pinched the sides of the wound together and pushed one of them through the middle. Tears poured down Heggi's face but he didn't make a sound, even when she set the other thorns each side. Perhaps he was becoming a better man than his father. Was he like his mother – or had Thorvald and Ottar influenced him? A strange thought that she pushed away.

She gently put some salve on, dressed it in strips of clean linen and kissed him. 'All done. It'll be better in the morning.'

'I know.'

She liked the way he trusted her to do good.

A night of dreams of drowning gave way to a day dark as night. Bera could taste the air, like in a sooty hall. She went to look for Heggi and a man pointed up to the home field where he and Sigrid had taken Feima and her calf. He did not know where the men were. Her head was thick, so she splashed her face in the cool running water in the channel outside. It only increased her irritation that the dam had its uses.

Everything was taking so long when they needed to set sail. Every passing day made her more afraid of the Serpent King, too. Man and nature oppressed her. She was beginning to worry that not killing Thorvald was causing all the bad luck. Perhaps she could wait until they were well out to sea and then push him overboard at night.

Her skern's face rippled.

Fooling yourself. Your body's weaker than your will.

'You're speaking to me again, are you?'

He gave her a stiff look.

'I thought there were rules.'

Listen, lovey, we both know you've always had to make them up.

'When I can't see him I forgive him for Sigrid's sake. Then that face of his makes me think of what he did.'

Then do something else. Sewing the sail, for example.

'Sigrid says that a Valla's skern disappears when she and a man have... and there's a baby inside her.'

Old fishwives' tales. You can't always see me and that's your own fault. Now, crack on.

Bera sat at the loom, weaving words of protection into the final piece of the sail-strip until the light was so dim she could see nothing. She felt pent up. Sweat trickled from underneath her breasts. It was too hot to work. The sky ripped overhead but there was no rain.

She went back to the byre doorway and stood under the overhang. The thunderclaps echoed and re-echoed and then a sizzling light stabbed the sea. Clouds squatted on the mountaintops, squeezing the hot air to a thin layer. She couldn't breathe. More spear lightning. Bera longed for a breeze but there was only suffocating thickness. She should dread rain but it would be more than a bodily release: it would prove her right.

Those who could were leaving the fields.

'Is Heggi coming?' she called out to a neighbour.

The woman shrugged and carried on.

His wound ought to be kept clean and dry. Bera waited anxiously, longing for some release. And then the loud pat of a fat raindrop. Another and another. The smell of dust made her sneeze. The lowering sky split and a curtain of water rippled the world. Its coolness made her want to rush out and be cleansed.

At last, two familiar figures were running towards her through the blur of rain.

They jumped over puddles and stomped into the byre, bringing a sweet smell with them. Bera kissed Heggi's chilled, wet face.

He shook his hair. 'Dotta's so funny in the rain. She licks it.'

'We're soaked to the skin.' Sigrid wrung out her top layer.

Bera said. 'Let's get you dry, Heggi, before you catch your death.'

They went through to the fire. Heggi stood steaming while Sigrid fetched a change of clothes. A woman brought a cloth and he reluctantly stripped off. Bera ignored his shy squirming and rubbed him down, deafened by rain hammering the roof. She made sure the thorns were still in place and put more salve on the raw wound. Sigrid returned and they got him changed. Bera held up his wet garments and wrinkled her nose.

'Have you been rolling about with the calf?'

'Not much,' Sigrid scoffed.

Bera was angry. 'I've never known a boy like you for hurting himself.'

'Feima and Dotta are coming on our boat, Father says. And Rakki, too.'

'Where is he?'

'Somewhere,' said Heggi vaguely.

'Go and get the bales ready.'

'That's a thrall's job.'

'I'm asking you.'

He scuffed off, making sure they knew what an indignity this was with every step.

The women went through to the pantry.

'Is this the storm?' asked Sigrid. She put Heggi's clothes over a flatbread pole and hoisted it.

On impulse Bera said, 'Let's be bad and have some ale. I know there's work to be done but there always is and it's never finished.'

Sigrid grinned and sat at the table. 'Just don't start on me about the sea passage.'

Bera took down a jug and tapped the barrel. She joined her friend, poured the ale into two beakers and they toasted each other.

Sigrid wiped the ale from her mouth. 'We'd best finish that sail when we've drunk this.'

'You ought to get into dry clothes first.' Bera gathered some crumbs from the table with the edge of her hand and threw them outside for the chickens.

'Have that ale.'

Bera took another sip. 'Ottar's making some counters so we can draw lots. I want you to pick one.'

'There you go!'

'Let Fate decide, Sigrid.'

'No. My doom is to drown. Or be eaten by some sea monster. I'm staying.'

Bera yearned to tell her about Thorvald and ruin him. But Sigrid's unguarded face, drinking her ale, was too innocent, too familiar.

She remembered. 'I haven't blessed the dam yet.'

'Best do it, then. If this rain stops. And I'd best get on.'

The rain slackened enough for Bera to go out. Egill was standing by a pool that was forming behind the dam.

'There'll be fish soon,' she said, pulling Bera to the edge. 'Look!'

There were yellow plants, submerged by the rising water, looking like they belonged in a world where things were bigger and brighter. The two watched for a while, marvelling at the familiar turned strange.

'Just like you,' Bera said. 'You dress like a boy in our world but underneath you're a natural girl.'

Egill carried on gazing.

'Aren't you?'

'Don't know what that means, natural,' Egill said. 'Been alone so long.'

'Has Ottar told you about drawing lots?'

Egill proudly prodded her chest. 'Used the burning-glass to mark the ones for going.'

'It's dangerous!' Bera wanted to clout her. 'I was going to do it.'

Egill blinked, then delved into a pocket and pulled out a counter. 'Special one for you. To make sure you go.' It had Bera's rune on it.

She was touched. 'That's kind, Egill. You keep it. I'll be going anyway, with Hefnir and our household and Ottar. If only Sigrid—' Bera jumped.

Her skern was underwater, waving at her with a stem of sneezewort. Or was he drowning? The surface shattered. The next storm had arrived in a cloudburst.

They ran their separate ways. Bera was drenched by the time she reached the byre. She still had not blessed the dam.

Storms rampaged over the following days and the dam held. Egill sauntered about the mead hall whenever folk gathered, declaring the genius of Iraland and accepting praise. Her friend's pride made Bera uneasy. Egill didn't even cross her fingers. Bera went to the boatyard and made the excuse of cutting Egill's hair to try and warn her privately.

'Boasting makes Fate punish us.'

Egill refused to listen. 'Fact is, the dam's saved us and you don't like that. You want to be the one to save folk, Bera, not anyone else.'

That hit home. Bera snipped savagely. 'I'm the only one who really can save them.'

'Ow! You haven't blessed the dam cos you want it to fail.'

'Bilge!'

'Not.'

'You said you feel safe with me.'

'Do.'

'Shut up, then.'

Egill did, but was nearly bald when Bera finished. She left her whittling furiously and went to find Ottar.

Bera insisted he should come with her to inspect the dam.

'Aye, there's too much swanking by half,' her father said. 'Fate's got a way of punishing folk for getting above themselves.'

'That's what I've been saying.'

'I'll tell Egill to help get spares on the boat. That'll shut him up. My work's about done, so we can go on up to the dam.'

The structure looked secure, even though the pool was swollen into a lake. Ottar pointed out the steep clay flood banks.

'Them's my own devising and the dam's solid enough. I'd best be getting back and check they're not skiving.' He shouted over his shoulder. 'You blessed it yet? Maybe we won't need to go after all.'

She was glad of his trust – but he was wrong.

Bera stepped up onto the dam's wooden structure and ran her hands along one of the supports. It was as well found as one of his vessels. She smiled when she saw the gates: one of Egill's better ideas. But the more she examined the way they were made, the more at odds they seemed. The woodcraft of Ottar's men was evident everywhere else but the two structures that braced the gates looked bodged and cumbersome. Her father was too far away now to ask.

Bera tried hard to bless it but doubt made it impossible. She needed reassurance from someone who understood shape, who might even say words in the old tongue and who was the only other person who questioned the dam.

Dellingr.

Her route took Bera a new way to the forge, past the poorest huts where the blower had had his tongue cut out by a drunken father. Some grimy youths, hunched on thin, bowed legs, watched her. Their eyes were huge in their hungry faces. They had likely eaten their meagre crops and couldn't trade. Even worse for the ones whose mothers drank the strong brew they made up here. These few huts were close to the sick house, where Sigrid had recovered, but furthest from the cleansing sea. Now they were the only ones to have no running water. The whole area was a latrine and the smell made Bera's stomach rise.

A stone hit the middle of her back. When she turned, no one had moved.

'My skern is at my side,' Bera warned.

'Oooooh!' said one in mock concern but they did not risk another throw.

The darkness of the forge blinded her. Bera closed her eyes for a moment and when she opened them Dellingr was right in front of her.

'I won't have time to do any new work. I've got the dam-building tools to sharpen or mend.'

'It's the dam I'm worried about.'

He turned away. 'Then speak to your husband.'

'Well, sorry to trouble you!'

He did not react to her tartness and began shovelling. His boy worked the bellows as if his life depended on it. Bera loved the smells of leather and sweat and hot metal and fire in here. Honest labour. But she left, vowing never to come back. They had agreed she wouldn't go up there alone so couldn't he see she needed him? To Hel with the pompous smith.

Long strides and temper got her to the crossroads quickly. She had not noticed that the same group of boys were there, waiting.

'Get back to your own side of the village,' she called out.

A hail of stones skittered around her feet. Then the biggest drew back his arm and threw a rock, making her duck.

It was too much.

Bera growled low in her throat, then charged at them, roaring with frustrated rage. It was a battle cry that would stop a Drorgher and the boys scattered. If anyone else noticed, they stayed indoors. It was satisfying for an instant. Then she thought about the flaw in the dam. If Dellingr would not help her, she must give Hefnir the chance to be the true partner she needed.

Hefnir was lit by a torch in the winter-dark day, waiting. Bera ran past the latrine and down to meet him at the byre.

She rested against the pig rail to catch her breath. 'I've been a fool.'

'True.'

'I'm sure the trouble's at the dam.'

'Oh, no. It's much closer to home.'

'What are you talking about?'

'You've dishonoured me. I've been hearing about what you get up to when I'm away trading, trying to put food on our table.'

'What?'

'Or any time my back's turned.'

'Did Thorvald—'

'I had to endure a visit from a gaggle of women, friends of Asa's, with tongues hanging out, telling me that you and Dellingr—'

'No! Hefnir, that's not—'

He slapped her hard across the face. The shock was worse than the pain. Her ears were ringing and she could taste blood.

'They're wrong! I was only asking Dellingr for help.'

He wasn't listening. He wasn't even present, behind his eyes. Perhaps he had been drinking.

'It's about the dam. Trust me.'

Hefnir seized her wrists and dragged her across the yard to the outhouse. He barged open the door and bundled her inside. There was an intense scent of over-ripe apples; ages of winter stores. Something darker. He unlocked the door in the far corner. Heggi's cell.

'No!' she screamed.

Hefnir's face was closed. He kicked the low door open and stood back. 'Get in there.'

'It's jealousy. Their boys threw stones and I threatened them. They don't like me being a Valla and they're trying to—'

Hefnir grabbed her, and thrust her into the small cell. She fell down a short distance and he slammed the door behind her. The lock clicked and Bera was alone in the dark. The smell of earth and decay. Below ground level, with a flood certain.

Still Bera tried to save the village. 'They don't want you listening to me! It was Egill's plan, those gates, wasn't it?'

The change of subject checked him. She sensed him thinking on the other side of the door.

Bera pressed her small advantage. 'Tell Ottar he must check them. Hefnir? Listen to me. The weakness is at the gates. Hefnir?' Three small circles of grey light gave her hope. 'Get Ottar!'

She groped and found some steps in the soil, leading up to the door. Before she could climb them the outer door closed and the circles vanished. The silence of the grave. Her mind cracked open and screamed danger. Confined.

There was a thickness to the dark. The hairs went up on the back of her neck. The Drorgher was crouched in a corner of the room like a black spider. This could only be a battle of wills now; she had no Valla power to draw on in here and no flame to frighten it away. No one believed her in Seabost. She had grown soft, unsure, and there was only unending darkness.

Death brushed her cheek like a cobweb.

The worst storm hit. Torrential rain came in waves and water levels were rising. Above the village the pool reached the outer clay boundary. Drumming rain brought big silver fish up from the deep. They swam in wide lazy circles, exploring the far reaches of their new kingdom. Beneath them, land plants swayed in the swell of water, trapped like flies in amber. The level had been rising as slowly as hair grows. Now it was nearing bursting point, going up a hand span in moments. The water picked and probed the banks for weakness, making the solid putty.

Bera sensed this but did not know if it was fact or fear. Her skern was wrapped about her but no comfort at all. She hid behind some empty boxes, held her beads and attempted some words of banishment. Hollow threats. This one was cunning and confident; something had invited it in. How long ago Bera did not know, but she dared not drowse. The Drorgher had roused to its prey, feeding off Bera's fear.

She kissed her black bead and there was a child's laughter; a wooden horse. Some connection with the dead thing with her. Then darkness pressed, squeezing out thought and memory.

14

The Drorgher began casting around, sniffing. Bera felt every shift in the air against her cheeks and was afraid. Then it came to her that something happening elsewhere was exciting the creature; drawing its attention. With that relief came the touch of her skern above her eyebrows and she arched towards escape, even while her body stayed locked inside the tiny cell. She saw...

... Thorvald waiting on the bank with two men. Pounding rain and strong gusts under a purple thundercloud lashed them, making their greased coats slick like sealskin.

'Where is Hefnir? Help me see!'

I'm doing my best.

Hefnir was up on the dam, looking at the gates. He struggled to keep his balance and kept pushing his drenched hair out of his eyes.

The water was near the top. Hefnir beckoned and Thorvald climbed onto the dam. He slipped and then moved cautiously, followed by the thralls, who wobbled wildly. When Thorvald reached him, Hefnir shouted in his ear and sent the thralls to check the braces on the other gate. Hefnir signalled that they should push – but the men carried straight on and back towards the village.

Thorvald followed but kept slipping.

Hefnir made for safety, sending pebbles slithering. The bund of earth and stones that joined the dam to the riverbank was beginning to slip. He scrabbled across the crumbling mound, making it more fragile, and jumped. He tumbled onto the grass and scrambled up to high ground.

Thorvald turned back. His feet went underwater but he kept on. Loud cracks and rumbles drummed above the storm. The whole structure was shifting. He made a rush, skated about, teetered and then leapt in a frantic twisting motion. He landed badly, halfway up the bank. He began sliding towards tar-black water. He punched his toes into the mud and clawed the sodden earth while reaching out with the other. Hefnir, white-faced, made no move.

'Hefnir! Help him!' Bera shouted. She saw a thorn tree and Thorvald made a last, desperate lunge for the tree and grasped it. He screamed in pain.

One edge of the bund tipped and water surged towards the gates. Egill's brackets snapped like kindling and something gave way inside Bera. A torrent barged through, gathering up willow, rowan and alder; bowling stones and boulders that crashed into fences; forging downwards until it caught up the two thralls and carried them off. The flood ripped through fields and smashed down crops; it snatched sheep, spilled and tumbled cattle.

Heading straight for the village.

Water poured into pantries and latrines; ale stores, byres and pigsties. It muddied the pure and impure and swept the filth into every crevice. An army of cats that normally went unnoticed massed the high places, looking with contempt at the dogs paddling beneath them. Rats sleekly swam for safety. Pigs squealed as they were lifted and deposited beneath rafters ringing with the terrified squawk of chickens. The swill and muck floated off amongst a bobbling wash of thimbles and cloth, beakers and bowls, milking stools and reels of twine.

She had been too bound up with avenging Bjorn the wrong way. Using poison had nearly killed Heggi and now folk would starve because she let others take charge. Even Egill! It was all too late. Icy water prickled Bera's feet and a rush of wild anger swept through her that Hefnir would lock her in here when she could have made amends.

A fury that was shared by the Drorgher. This creature, patient and cunning, hating Hefnir, was waiting for Bera to drown and become the blackest and most terrible threat with her Valla skills. Together, unstoppable.

That must not happen! Her skern was a fury at her neck.

Bera let the drilling force of her gaze turn on the Drorgher.

Its true shape finally appeared, shrinking back in the pure white intensity. Bera recognised who she had been and saw a dragonboat at sea; the abused woman seizing a black dagger and pressing it beneath her ear, making blood drip.

'Heggi!' the woman cried, before cutting through the cords to silence.

And Bera knew why the child had never been harmed in here and why the Drorgher had wanted to have a terrible revenge.

'Go now,' Bera said. 'I send you in peace to your long rest.' So, in pity, she used her force to blast her into eternity.

Bera pictured her entering the Great Hall; the huge doors swinging safely shut behind her. Gone.

Her skern was clinging to the top of her head with sharp nails. A present danger: the water was over her knees and rising.

Call him.

He meant Rakki. Bera turned her gaze inward and silently shouted for the dog. She knew the moment he leapt into the filthy water and urged him to find her.

The water was already up to her waist. The door was battered by tubs and crates as the water poured in any way it could. The earth steps would be mud. Bera cursed being short. Floating boxes barged into her and she held on to one, pushed it under water and stood on it. When she tried to do it with a second box she lost the first and had to wait to find another. She got her feet on the box and tried to keep her balance as the rising water lifted her.

Then, at last, a barking and distant voice.

'Come here, Rakki!' Heggi.

He would not come in here, the place he dreaded. The dog whined and scrabbled at the door, splashing.

The water was up to her chin, even with a box to stand on.

'Heggi!' Bera shouted. 'Heggi!'

Rakki barked dementedly. A loud thump.

'Bera?'

He had come! 'Get an axe!'

She was on tiptoes. She reached up to see if she could feel the ceiling and it was right above her head. He would have to get an axe from the byre and she would drown. She was afloat when she heard his shout.

'Stay back!'

The first blows were tame but then he thundered the axe into the door, which was thick and took a good hammering. Bera tried to keep her face up and tasted mud. Worse than drowning at sea. Then she was helpless; swept up and out like a wave crashing onto a beach.

She scrambled onto her hands and knees, blinking. 'What took you so long?'

Heggi declared his dog had a sixth sense and then burst into tears.

'He'll have some tasty meat – if there's anything left.' Around them, rubbish gently settled into sludge as the waters raced on towards the sea.

Heggi was grey. 'You look awful.'

'So do you!'

They laughed and Rakki licked her face clean.

'It was very brave to come for me,' said Bera. 'Please believe that I had no idea your father was locking you in this terrible place.'

'Thorvald lets me hide in the big store. But sometimes Papa locks me in that small one for my own good. Like when you first came.'

Bera shuddered. No wonder the child had hated her.

'I will never let you be shut in the dark again.' He must never know the monster was his own mother. 'But what was in there is now gone.'

He hugged her and she kissed the top of his head. They had both suffered so much.

Weighted with stuff, the waters slowed towards the fishermen's huts and left a heap of soiled belongings against their doors. The flood had no strength left to do more than lift their nets and it oozed through the boatyard where Ottar and Egill slept on, dead drunk. It let down the last remnants of its load and trickled towards the slipway, past pitch pails, brushes, blocks and tackle. Finally, exhausted, it slipped into the sea like an old woman welcoming her bed.

15

Sigrid was cleaning the pantry with some thralls. They were all as dirty and sodden as Bera, so she faced no questions. Then she remembered Heggi's wound. The linen bandage was soaked with floodwater. Heggi hitched it up and Bera smelt it.

'Oh, Heggi! It's gone bad. I must clean it.'

Sigrid gestured at the chaos around them. 'What with?'

'We'll find a way.'

One of the thorns had snapped but it had done its work and Bera gently pulled out the others. The sides stayed knitted. There was a jar of honey on the top shelf, so she spooned some on the scar.

Sigrid delved into an inside pocket and came out with the medicine stick. 'I rolled this up with his bedding.'

Bera tied the stick on top, ignoring his complaint that it hurt more.

'Be grateful to Sigrid.'

'All right,' he quavered. 'I'll be strong.'

Unlike his father. When they finally met over a scraped-together meal, Hefnir kept moaning about the unfairness of it all. The man who had locked her in! Bera despised his talent for blanking the disagreeable. He always talked big about leadership but his involved lying and whining, not being out there helping, like Sigrid – and Thorvald. Bera was finally witnessing the load that his second had to bear. Or, at least, admitting it; which made a difference to how she felt about Hefnir. Just let them get away safely and then she would settle all scores - in a new way. Till then, she didn't even respect Hefnir enough to argue. She could hardly bear to look at him.

The village was a brown slurry of ruined lives. At first folk were grateful that it was only the old and a few thralls that had died but as they began to reckon the other losses it dawned on them that this would become a slower kind of death. Some were at the longhouse asking for bowls of stew and other handouts, including clothes. It couldn't go on like this. Bera kept the confident strength that she had found in the darkness and called a meeting at the rune stone herself. It was the right place – and its distance from the village stench would be a blessing. She told Heggi to fetch Ottar and Egill and his father if he was with them.

They arrived without Hefnir and joined a silent, straggling line as they climbed. But as they left the wreckage behind them, spirits lifted and children started to play. This side of the village was untouched; at last some luck had come to the poorest. Bera paused at the crossroads and sent someone to the huts and forge to get them to the rune stone.

Bera went straight up to the stone, half expecting her skern to be waiting like before. He was not but she could cope alone. She briefly touched the runes but did not call on her mother for help. As soon as Dellingr arrived she spoke to her bedraggled folk.

'Together we are strong. So here's my plan. First, we must get clean. We must take soiled things down to the sea to scrub. Brine is good. Then we set them out for sunlight to purify. Our thralls will wash clothes and bedding, so take yours to the river and help if you can. I'll set some men to clean the bath hut so we can wash ourselves. Bring any odd bits of soap you can find. Don't put dirty fingers near your mouths and watch the children.' She turned to her father. 'Could your men build a field latrine? Everything spoiled or rotten can go in there, too, once it's dug.'

Ottar nodded. Egill drooped beside him, not meeting Bera's eyes. Was this guilt?

'You said about the children,' called out someone. 'How can we stop them playing in the filth?'

'They'll be too busy to play. The older ones can start by rounding up the animals and getting them back to fresh pasture. The younger ones can beat the wildlife out of houses.' It pleased

Bera that she sounded like her father at the start of a busy boatyard day.

Then Hefnir arrived and folk made way.

Bera was not going to let him take over. She explained what others were doing and asked him to head up a working party to collect heavy household goods and take them to the sea. She was in charge with a good plan and folk obeyed without question. Hefnir noted it, but she was careful to speak respectfully to him in front of them. He nodded as if it was his plan, although he darted a look at her that was all about revenge. He barged past Dellingr and blamed Heggi. Bera left the smith alone with his family.

After making sure everyone knew what they had to do, Bera went home to get the thralls busy. The mired hall was worse for coming back to it from the clean sea air. Her voice echoed in the empty room. Sigrid returned from organising the bath hut and told her several thralls had run away.

They got busy. Bera made a heap outside of anything damaged by the water; amongst them was Hefnir's favourite gaming board and a couple of Heggi's old toys. One of them was a small wooden horse.

Bera held it out and Sigrid took it. 'I've never seen this before.'

The Serpent, Heggi. 'Burn it all.' There was no time to fathom the connection.

They washed down the walls, floors and doors, shrieking every time a mouse or spider scuttled past, which was often. The children arrived, banging pots and pans together to rid the house of all creatures that had taken refuge there.

Bera had made sure they had something to take with them, if only hope. In a golden dusk she went round the village with spare food and explained that she had devised a fair draw. Some shrugged, or said things always got better again in Seabost. Others declared they would rather chance staying than face certain death on a risky sea passage. Bera persuaded them that whoever was chosen to be a settler should leave most of their belongings for those left behind. This made everyone feel generous and lifted spirits.

She told them all to gather in the scrubbed mead hall, as the only place fit and safe to sleep. Now was the time of reckoning, before they got to thinking.

There were still too many to get on the boats. Tiredness and tension took its toll. No children played chase. Pale faces followed her wherever she went, waiting for their Fate. Neighbour was pitched against neighbour and friends were wary.

Bera wanted Hefnir to stand beside her so they would appear united and strong and give confidence. She found him with Thorvald. It looked like Hefnir had been drinking all day while they had all worked hard, Thorvald especially.

She confronted Hefnir. 'More thralls have run off.'

'Plenty more over there.' Hefnir waved an arm vaguely westwards.

Thorvald leered. 'Iraland. Red-haired bints, like your father had. It's why he wants to go there in part.'

'Ottar?'

'Hefnir.'

Hefnir held out his gold chalice for more.

Bera ignored it. 'I want to start while folk are clear-headed. Ready, Hefnir?'

'You're best without him,' Thorvald said in her ear. 'I'll take care of him, as always.'

Thorvald had paid her another compliment of sorts. And he was sober. The stab of pleasure immediately made her ashamed.

Yet the glow of Thorvald's good opinion was in her voice as she stood alone in front of the Seabost folk like a shepherd before a herd of bewildered sheep. There was plenty of milling about and scratching of heads but no anger, even when Egill slunk into the back of the hall.

'We have tokens like this,' she began, holding up one of the counters. 'Some are blank but others, like this one, have a rune-mark on them.' She kept the token raised until the crowd was quiet. 'There are the same number of these as places on Hefnir's boats, marked ᚱ for the long journey. There are not enough places for everyone so this is a fair draw. There is one token for each free man if he wants it. They are all mixed in this leather pouch and each man will come and pick one out for his family. If you draw a blank you must either make provision here, use your own boat or move inland.'

Bears, wolves and troles lay inland. The Serpent King. Frightened voices echoed round the hall until Thorvald called for quiet. Dellingr came to stand next to him, then fixed his eyes on Bera.

'When you say there are tokens for us all, does that include you and your kin? Are you chancing with us?'

It was like slapping her face.

Bera's confidence leached away as guilt thickened her tongue. Hefnir was looking for courage at the bottom of his chalice. No help there. Ottar was at the back with Heggi and Egill. He raised a fist to brace her. And there was her skern, trying a similar move and looking ridiculous.

It made her smile and she calmly had her answer. 'The boats are Hefnir's. He risks his skin every season to keep them – and keeps this village too. Thorvald takes the same risks, as you told me yourself, Dellingr, so he has a place. Ottar built these boats, so he must go. And should we leave our son behind?'

Bera's challenge hung in the air.

Dellingr spoke so low that folk craned to hear him. 'But what about you, Bera? You'll draw with us, won't you?'

How could she? Yet it seemed to matter to him so much.

There was a roar and Hefnir charged forward, spit flying. 'Bera saw the danger. She got Ottar boatbuilding and you skivers to ration food. She must go and is going. She is my wife. My possession. I could sail out of here with boats laden with all my possessions. Instead of which, I'm offering places. Is it my fault there aren't more boats? Sea-riders came, remember? I lost much that day, but I've shared my gains over the years, haven't I?' He scowled round the hall. 'So who'll fight me for my place? Dellingr? You going to fight me?'

Thorvald was at Hefnir's side like a shadow, sword drawn.

Dellingr stared at Thorvald for a long moment, then turned away.

Bera started shaking the pouch. 'Who will be the first to draw?'

Folk hesitated.

'They won't come near him, Thorvald,' she hissed.

He took Hefnir's free arm and led him over to the barrels.

Bera shook the pouch again. 'Trust to Fate, who has already decided.'

'That's what we're afraid of,' said a fishwife.

'Go on, then, Dellingr,' said the baker. 'You go first.'

Bera's heart hammered.

Asa looked with meaning at the baby at her breast. Dellingr's jaw set firm and he stepped forward. Bera was no cheat but the marked token was still in her hand. Was Fate meaning her to let it slip as he drew? When Dellingr paused beside her she slid it down between two fingers.

'I'll let you draw,' he said. 'I want no man to think I've cheated.'

She was thrown. It shouldn't be this easy. She had his life between her fingers, like a thread, as a Valla would. 'No, Dellingr. You must draw.'

'Like you said, Fate's already decided.' He locked eyes with her.

Did he know? Dellingr was essential to settling successfully. And she wanted him to come. He must come.

Bera delved into the bag and gave him a token, face down. 'Only you must see the rune-mark.'

Dellingr closed his fist over it, without looking, and then went over and gave the token to Asa. She kissed it for luck and then slowly turned it over.

'We're going!' she shrieked.

Her daughter screamed and hugged her, Asa burst into happy tears and the baby wailed.

Dellingr looked back at Bera. His eyes made her feel unbearably sad.

Then folk clustered round her, keen to draw. Bera made sure there was enough to drink so no one noticed how few could leave. When it was over, Ottar and Egill came back to the longhouse in case there were reprisals.

After a rough meal, Ottar finished his ale, wiped his mouth and looked at Hefnir.

'What about Egill?'

'Other decent folk can't go.'

Hefnir had sobered now the difficult decisions were made. Bera caught a flicker of recognition in Thorvald's eye and felt disloyal.

'It's you that brought me here,' said Egill, matter-of-fact.

'That's true, Hefnir,' said Bera, 'and don't forget Egill can pilot.'

Hefnir snorted. 'I know the way backwards.'

'To Iraland?' Bera waited for him to deny it but his face was blank. 'Egill? He needs you, doesn't he?' It was suddenly clear to her. 'He took you from your island to get him there. He wasn't saving you, he was looking after himself.'

Egill smiled. Perhaps she knew she was safe.

'Ottar and I reckoned another two places on our boat,' Bera said, and looked pointedly at Sigrid.

They all looked.

Sigrid threw her apron over her head. 'Stop staring at me.'

Thorvald unveiled her and stroked her cheek. 'She has a mortal dread of the sea, as you all know. It might kill her to come on board. Someone else can go in my place. I'm stopping here with Sigrid.'

Hefnir gave a startled bark of laughter.

Bera was equally shocked. What was Thorvald's game? Was he trying to force Sigrid into going out of gratitude? A look passed between the couple that made Bera tearful with envy.

Hefnir gave a lazy, knowing smile. 'I see what you're doing, Thorvald.'

Thorvald kept his arm round Sigrid and led her gently to their billet.

Ottar stood up and stretched. 'You've been right all along, Bera. We need to get going soonest.'

Bera managed not to gloat. It was all too serious.

She took Heggi to his bed and helped him undress because his arm was sore.

'I'll look at it properly tomorrow. All right?'

Bera unwrapped the old dressing and gave it to a thrall to burn.

'You didn't say stepson,' he said.

'What?'

'At the choosing. You said "our son".' He curled up with Rakki.

'Was that all right?'

Heggi kept his head buried. Not avoiding the question, like his father, she now saw, but with shyness. She felt protective and kissed his hair. It smelt of oatmeal and honey.

Bera crossed the hall, yawning and longing for sleep. The others had gone to bed, apart from Thorvald, who was waiting for her.

'Sigrid insists you look at this.' He awkwardly held out his hand, palm upwards, where deep punctures and scratches had turned puffy.

Bera winced. 'What did that?'

'Thorns. At the dam.'

Of course. When Hefnir should have helped him.

'Come to the dairy.'

Bera tended him in silence. The act of care was awkward, probably for them both, as Thorvald kept his eyes fixed on what she was doing. Or did he think she would pack the wound with poison?

Afterwards, Bera went to her billet. She unpinned her brooches and laid down her keys on her marriage chest.

Hefnir had a fit of coughing. He got up, banged his chest and swigged some ale.

'Come here, wench, and give your master a kiss.' He grabbed her hips with both hands.

Bera was too tired to fight. Hefnir pulled off her dress and stood back. Her body became beautiful under his gaze and her breath caught, as it had on their honeymoon. Here was more proof of her Valla passion.

'I can be a brute,' he said, and kissed her. 'You did well tonight. I thought there would be a riot. I was proud of you.'

His pride in her increased desire. It was neither good nor bad; it simply was.

Afterwards they lay together, heads close. Bera's small feet stroked his shins. The thought came to her that desire could be his weakness, too, and she could use it to get at truth.

'What did you mean about Sigrid and Thorvald?' she asked. 'About what he's up to?'

'You never give up, do you, shrimp?' He sighed. 'You won't like it, but men would say anything to get under a woman's skirt.'

'Hefnir!'

'I'm serious. You watch. Come the day we leave he'll be the first one on the boat.'

'Are you the same?'

He studied every feature on her face, as though for the last time. It was an odd sensation and made Bera sick to her stomach.

'We're all the same when it comes to women, Bera. Don't believe any man if he seems kind.'

Was he warning her about himself?

The next day Hefnir gathered together the few remaining thralls and told them they would be free in a few days. One of them was the slant-eyed woman. Thorvald stood by in case there was trouble.

'You can try Crapsby, this side,' Hefnir said. 'They might have enough food.'

Bera shuddered, thinking of wind blowing through the empty ways, left to Drorghers. 'You must go further. We thank you for staying and will send you off with food.'

Hefnir clapped his hands. 'Heggi's small fishing boat could keep a man if he works hard and—'

'I claim that boat,' Thorvald said. 'I shall buy it from you. It will keep me and Sigrid this season.'

Hefnir snorted. 'You? A fisherman? That's funny.'

The slant-eyed thrall listened with the rest, her face closed. Hefnir was making no secret of their going. He must be sure that she was loyal to him. Or was he telling the Serpent King they would not pay for protection they no longer needed?

Thorvald asked to see the fishing boat.

Hefnir agreed, treating it like a shared joke. 'I'll bring Heggi to give some boating advice.'

Bera set the thralls to work and the woman was not among them. She told Hefnir.

'She's gone early, pleased to be free,' he said.

'Free to tell the Serpent. You seem unconcerned.' She had an idea. 'Are you hoping he'll come to Iraland and force Thorvald to come with us?'

Hefnir sighed. 'You always see things the way you want them to be.'

'No, Hefnir. It's usually the opposite.'

He left and Sigrid came in from the byre, her expression shifty.

'I went to see Asa,' she said breezily. 'I found some baby things of Heggi's that would do for theirs.'

'I wish you'd asked first.'

'You're too busy.' Sigrid went on into the pantry.

Bera was at her heels. 'Was Heggi up there?'

'Asa said he was off with the lads. Getting puffins for the poor folk or some such nonsense. That baby's the image of Asa.' Sigrid turned away.

'You love babies, don't you?' Bera said, all crossness gone.

She fought down the urge to tell her she had married the man who had killed her only child. It was a secret that must never be told. Bera could see the affection Sigrid had for Thorvald, much as she wished otherwise. And despite what Hefnir said, she believed Thorvald was staying with Sigrid. Otherwise why would he want a boat?

Sigrid rubbed her eyes on her apron. 'Anyway, your soft spot for Dellingr's done them some good. Even Asa admits it.'

'What soft spot?'

'It got them on a boat.'

'I drew the rune-mark by chance.'

'But you know what I'm talking about.'

Bera's face flared with the guilt of her original scheme. In the end, though, she had only willed it. Wasn't she a Valla?

Sigrid patted her arm. 'Folk know you'll need a smith.'

'I hate all this! What has Asa been saying?'

'Don't worry, she's grateful.'

'But I did nothing, I swear!' Bera marched over to the shelves and clattered some bowls and dishes onto the bench.

Her skern sat cross-legged at the end.

You have the gift of memory.

'Memory brings pain.'

Blind Agnar and his old dog came into her mind, Falki's wife. Poor Sigrid losing everyone she loved.

Pain's useful. It's how to be kind.

She went over and kissed her friend. 'How do you stay so strong?'

'Loss. It's loss that makes you strong. You'll see.'

16

The boat wasn't finished but Bera insisted they had to leave now. Folk needed no persuading that they must go before gale season began.

The night before they were due to set off, Bera returned to an empty hall. The thralls were gone and their quarters silent. A single stewpot was bubbling over the fire and there were no sweet-smelling boughs on the floor or hangings to brighten the walls. Only their bedrolls remained. Bera felt sad. This had become her home, eventually.

A groan came from Thorvald's billet. Inside, Bera found Sigrid sitting on the sleeping platform, head in hands.

'You can't stay in here,' Bera said. 'It's worse than the hall.'

Sigrid lowered her hands. 'I'm that mizzy-mazey.'

Bera felt her forehead. It couldn't be red-spot again. 'Have you been sick?'

'Twice. And I've got a splitting headache.'

'No fever, though. I know what this is...'

Sigrid shook her head. 'Leave me be.'

Bera sat beside her, thigh against thigh. 'Have I ever asked you for anything, Sigrid? Really asked, I mean.'

'Here we go.'

'You're sick because fear is forcing you to stay when your heart doesn't want to.'

'You sound like Thorvald.'

'Sigrid, I beg you. I implore you. Please come with me.'

Sigrid shot up. Her neck was cords of anger. 'It's not about begging, Bera! I'm the one who followed you here, much as Ottar tried to stop me, scared to death of what I'd say. Well. That's long ago.' She sat down again. 'Listen. You're my dear friend's daughter. I'd follow you beyond the known world – on land. I'm a stupid old fool and terrified.'

'So tell me about Ottar.'

Sigrid pulled a fur round her shoulders. 'We're going to have it out about Bjorn first.'

Bera's lips prickled as the blood left them. She struggled with what to say; what would do least damage. It was all too late. She should have told her at once. No. She should have killed Thorvald before Sigrid laid eyes on him.

Sigrid sighed. 'You did know that Bjorn loved you?'

So how could she not avenge his death? Bera lashed herself.

'You were sweet children, both of you. But then you grew up and Bjorn talked about wedding you. That was wrong, Bera, so Ottar did the deal with Hefnir. My poor Bjorn died, of course, but it was all arranged by then.'

'Stop.' Bera struggled to understand. 'Are you saying Ottar sold me so I wouldn't marry Bjorn?'

'He and I talked about what to do. Then Hefnir came wanting boats and it all fitted.'

Bera's throat ached when she thought of Bjorn's poor poem. 'Then Bjorn died.'

Sigrid clenched her jaw. 'I didn't want you leaving me with this secret between us.'

'What secret? I loved Bjorn like a brother. I'd never have married him.'

Sigrid held her face in both hands. 'We couldn't risk you lying together.'

'Why? He wasn't kin.'

'Oh, Bera. Ottar said he'd kill me if I ever told you.'

'But you need to.'

Sigrid whispered, 'Bjorn was your half blood brother.'

'Close kin?' Bera dreaded hearing more; perhaps she had known it already. 'So are you saying... Ottar was his real father?'

'He forced me, out of spite and jealousy.'

'What jealousy?'

Sigrid smiled, sadly. 'You keep trying to be like your mother, Bera. She was a Valla all right, but human, too. She took my husband.'

'Bjarni?'

Sigrid touched Bera's necklace. 'Bjarni gave her that bead with his rune on.'

The one Bjorn kept saying was his.

Never believe a man when he's being kind.

'Folk always said Bjorn was the image of his father but they didn't know that was Ottar.'

'You said you couldn't have children.'

'Nor could I with Bjarni. I had Ottar's son – his only son. I was even grateful, afterwards.'

Then, like good sail-trim, everything tracked clean: Ottar's raising Bjorn; his disrespect for Sigrid; his watchful guarding of a Valla's honour. Why Sigrid had kept quiet about wifely duties. Why no one talked about her mother. Jealousy.

'I didn't want you learning Valla stuff and getting like your mother.'

'You haven't told Asa all this?'

'Course not! I do feel better getting all this off my chest, mind. I should have told Bjorn and all, but Ottar plays everything close.'

Cramps clawed Bera's stomach, taking her breath away.

'Whatever is it?'

Bera feared blood with no idea why. An iron hook ripped her guts.

'Bad pain, Sigrid.'

'What pain? Your heart?'

'I don't know.' Not heart. Womb.

Thorvald's voice. 'We're starving. Is she ill?'

'She'll be all right. Go and fetch some water.'

'Need air.' Bera managed to walk through to the hall, leaning on Sigrid.

Hefnir was by the fire. 'My last night here ever,' he said, sounding pleased.

'Bera's ill.'

Thorvald came back with water. He moved a stool for her to sit and then put a beaker into her hands. Bera drank thirstily. Too late, she marvelled at taking something from Thorvald that might be poison. Or did the cramps mean she was poisoned already? She felt like she might die. The hall was spinning. Had Hefnir ordered Thorvald to poison her because she was in charge? Or was he jealous of Dellingr?

'Now.' Hefnir clapped his hands. 'Last chance, Sigrid. Stay or go?'

'Stay.'

'And I stay with her,' said Thorvald, calmly.

'You can stop this pretence now.'

'I stay with my wife.'

'Wife!' Hefnir pushed his face close to Thorvald's. 'You're coming with me.'

Thorvald stared him out.

Bera struggled to focus, to speak.

Hefnir approached Sigrid. 'His duty lies with me. Not with an old crone like you!'

She squared up to him. 'I want him here with me!'

'Then we'll have to make you not want him, won't we?'

'No. Stop it now, Hefnir.' Bera knocked over the stool.

Thorvald helped her back. 'Nothing you say will make a difference, Hefnir.'

Hefnir jabbed a finger in fury. 'Do you know who he is, Sigrid? Do you know who you married?'

'No, Hefnir. Enough.' Dots danced before Bera's eyes.

'Well, Thorvald, I won't shield a murderer any longer. That's what he is, Sigrid. This is the man who killed your son.'

Bera's sight narrowed to a point. Someone would end up dead. This was all her fault. It began that day on the beach. The hot iron smell of blood.

And then Sigrid's steady voice. 'I already know it all, Hefnir. I know how you pick fights and leave Thorvald to sort it out. I know what you made him do that day and I know...' Her voice finally cracked.

Thorvald ran to her. 'Dearest...'

Sigrid patted his hand. 'I'm all right. It doesn't mean I love Bjorn any the less.'

The known world was skewed, leaving Bera reeling. 'How long have you known?'

'Before the handfasting. We have no secrets.'

'How could you forgive him?'

'It's not about forgiving, Bera,' Sigrid said. 'It's about love. One day you'll understand.'

Hefnir roared. 'Mawkish crap! Would you really leave me, Thorvald? For that? For a fat, old, bandy-legged woman who's a scold and a gossip and—'

Thorvald punched him.

Hefnir put a hand to his mouth and was studying the bright blood from his split lip when the black tunnel closed.

Bera came round in her billet alone with Sigrid.

She put a hand on Bera's stomach. 'How far along are you?'

Not this, not now. Let Sigrid be wrong.

'I'm not...'

'You're not showing. Is it moving?'

Bera shook her head. 'I was using a potion, but I forgot in all the trouble. I don't want a baby! Don't hate me for saying it, Sigrid.'

'Lie back and rest. I wish we'd all kept our mouths shut.' She pulled some furs around Bera and stroked the hair off her forehead. 'I'm so stupid.'

'You're not. I'm glad I know everything.'

But a baby... Her skern had even hinted at it when she felt sick. She wanted them all to be wrong – or was Fate giving her the one reason to get Sigrid aboard?

'I'm afraid, Sigrid. What if the baby kills me, like my mother? I need you.'

'You do.' Sigrid looked her straight in the eye. 'I've been thinking, while you were in your faint. Someone needs to look after you and the babe.'

'You're coming with us!'

'I don't know how I'll manage, mind. I'll drown, for sure. And the thought of being eaten by monsters with teeth... the Skraken! Thorvald will have to club me to get me onto that vessel.'

'Believe me, Sigrid, I'd do it to get you aboard but Thorvald won't.'

'Won't do what?' It was Thorvald himself.

'Club Sigrid.'

Nor, of course, had he poisoned the water. Bera was recovered enough to go back to Hefnir, who was still staring into the fire.

'Sigrid's coming with us! So you can make it up with Thorvald because they are both coming.'

Hefnir gave no sign he had heard. But Thorvald swept up his wife and swung her like a child. His gashed face grinned. It was the ugliest sight Bera had ever seen but it touched her.

Thorvald carried his wife back to their billet.

'Tell him,' Sigrid called out, over his shoulder.

Bera was puzzled for a moment.

The baby.

Telling Hefnir would make it real for them both. His back was a wall. Would he be pleased? She refused to give him any joy. There was too much bitterness, too much falsehood and secrecy already, but some secrets must remain – because they were about to make passage to a shore Egill dreaded and they needed her boat-skills.

'There was no chance Thorvald was staying,' said Hefnir. 'That's why he punched me, because he knows he can't leave me. He loves me, Bera. He'll always choose me.'

How could he think this was true? Hefnir was so busy making up his version of Thorvald that he did not ask what Bera should tell him or why she had fainted.

Ottar and Egill arrived, playing bully-bully with Heggi like overgrown toddlers. The mood shifted to excitement then fear and back again. They ate the stew quickly and Sigrid went off to pack, as white and silent as a ghost owl. Heggi refused to get into his bedroll then fell asleep the minute he did. The others turned in soon after. The last thing Bera saw was a spurt of green flame from salty driftwood. It stirred some memory of the day her mother died. A smell of spruce, blood; a rat scuttling. Fear. She touched the bead with the B rune on it: not her rune, or Bjorn's. Given by Bjarni to her mother, pretending it was for Bera? A mother herself now, she fell into sleep praying the baby would not kill her.

And then it was morning and they were leaving Seabost for ever.

Their last few belongings went on barrows and the small procession set off. Bera stayed behind, needing to be in the house alone. Her last action was to place the household keys on the cold hearth. The ancestors were silent as she went through the passage. Even they had departed.

Before she entered the twitten, Bera made the mistake of looking back. The families with the stone-throwing boys were already moving in, their thin faces red and rapacious.

She caught up with the others, holding her head high and fighting back tears so she would not lower their spirits. The barrows rattled the wooden boards and Rakki barked all the way down onto Hefnir's jetty where the two boats were moored. Ottar was bustling about the deck of the bigger, re-hogged vessel, which would be theirs. A fog hung over the middle of the fjord, like a cloud come down to kiss the tide. On the other jetties, some fishing boats were packed with happy, boisterous families and all their hefty stuff. They were already too low in the water.

'Stupid oafs.' Ottar handed Bera aboard. 'I fixed the boats and they'll have 'em over before we make the Skerries.'

'You can't blame them.'

'They're up to the gunnels in junk.'

Hefnir was on his way to the animal pens. 'Keep your mouth shut, Ottar. It makes our leaving easier if they think they'll make it.'

Lying to his people again.

Adversity makes scoundrels of the scared.' Ottar muttered.

It was like a feast day, with laughter and drinking. Hefnir's tenant farmer appeared with Egill in tow, leading the animals down to the jetty. They were followed by a small procession so that by the time they reached the boat there was a racket of frightened beasts and raucous people. The livestock were loaded onto the boats and Heggi made certain that Feima and Dotta were on theirs. Bera joined them at the pen and marvelled at the calf's thick, sooty eyelashes and innocent eyes.

Egill promised to care for Dotta on the journey. 'In Iraland the fields are green as emeralds. There's so many cows that the sea's white with milk.'

'Egill!' Bera playfully cuffed her. 'We're not going to Iraland.'

'Hefnir says we are.'

'Let the wind decide.' Bera was a Valla who ruled the wind.

Heggi pulled Bera's sleeve. 'Have you named our boat?'

'It's only been re-hogged.'

His face fell. 'Ottar said you would.'

'All right. I will then.' Bera pulled out her necklace.

Egill studied the black bead. 'Obsidian.'

'That's a silly name for a boat,' declared Heggi, who went off in disgust.

Bera went up to the bow alone, thinking about the glossy black stone. Obsidian. Its purpose was too dark to name this boat of Ottar's with it. She thought of another and said a prayer for its safety. Once she would have kept her mother's naming of the boat. Now Bera felt she was as good a Valla and accepted what came with that position, which was to view honour differently. Sigrid must have seen Alfdis use some of her skills – what if her refusal to pass on any knowledge was really a fear of provoking infidelity in Bera?

Dellingr's voice was close but Bera kept her back turned. She would fight the passionate side of her nature as long as she could.

Ottar startled her. 'You naming her?'

'Raven.'

'Good one.'

'Is there any more work needs doing?'

'I can do it when we're underway. It's mostly strengthening the pens but they'll do for now.' He prodded her. 'I'll carve a fierce raven head when we get settled, once I've built the longhouse and that.'

The sail squeaked and rattled as it was raised.

Bera's scalp prickled. 'I wish we'd get going.'

'We've run out of ropes so I told them to use the mooring warp and make a slip of the haul-yard.'

'So you can stay on board to cast off. I wondered why the sail was going up.'

'Wind had better stay light till we're clear.'

They both checked the darkly striped sail. It was hanging limp, with the new patch glaringly clean against the weather-beaten original.

'Did you make sure it was all greased?' asked Ottar.

'Best I could.'

'Looks like we're about ready. Do you know where we're headed?'

'I have to get Hefnir to agree.'

'You will.' Ottar touched her lightly.

The other boat was ready, waiting for them to put out to sea. Its white-faced settlers were motionless, gazing at the edge of the known world.

'Father... before we go, I want to tell you...'

There was a loud curse. 'Got rope burn now!'

'Clumsy scab, I'll do it!' Ottar yelled and left.

Bera wanted to tell him she understood him better. That she had always valued him as a craftsman. That she felt safe in so well-found a vessel. Now that she had an unwanted new life inside her, she was grateful to him for raising her. She smiled fondly at his sturdiness and grace as he went amidships and was suddenly his little girl again.

She would tell him so, as soon as he had cast off.

Ottar let the haul-yard run past the block. The boat's nose scented the breeze and softly twitched towards the sea paths. They were off, with no skirmish or panic. Bera relaxed.

There was a blur of blond fur at the rails.

'Rakki! No!' Heggi shouted.

The dog set off up the jetty in full chase.

'Leave it!' shouted Hefnir, at the steer-board.

Bera tried to grab Heggi but he was off, charging after his dog. Her scalp flared like nettlerash.

'Good job I had hold of the rope,' said Ottar.

Bera turned on him. 'Why didn't you stop him?'

'I pulled the boat closer to the jetty so he didn't...'

She shouted to Hefnir. 'Send Thorvald after him.'

'You know that dog. As soon as the rat's lost or eaten, Heggi will be straight back.'

'Then I'll go.'

'Stay here, woman, and stop fretting.'

When she got to the rail Heggi was already running back with his dog. So why was her scalp on fire? Some horror was fast approaching. And then she saw the dust cloud rising behind her boy, coming down from the forest into the home field.

'War band!' Heggi screamed. 'On horses!'

The boat listed dangerously as the settlers crowded the side.

'Get back!' Hefnir began pulling them away from the rail.

Bera willed Heggi to hurry. He had to push through the crowd of dazed villagers loitering at the end of the jetty. A man made a step of his hands, Heggi clambered up and Thorvald swung him aboard. The man threw Rakki after him then ran to stand with his kin, the only villager who seemed to understand the danger.

Drumming hooves thundered into the village, as yet unseen.

'Slip the line, Ottar!' shouted Hefnir.

'Hel's teeth!' Ottar was tugging, cursing.

The jetty shuddered with the weight of horses and riders. They must have already mounted the far end of the wooden walkway, beyond the boatyard.

'Hurry, Father.'

'Man the oars!' yelled Hefnir. 'We need to get away fast.'

'The boat's not moving.' Bera looked for something to push off with.

Ottar shouted, 'The haul-yard's mungled.'

A knot was caught round the block on the jetty.

'Cut it!' said Egill.

Ottar refused. 'We'll have no sail power.'

He pulled the boat nearer the jetty with all the strength of his broad back, leapt ashore and started to pick at the knot with his spike. Bera was urging him to be quick, knowing no one could be faster. Ottar cursed, trying to drive the spike into the centre. It skidded and ripped his hand and the blood made the spike slip. He would not be beaten.

The horses appeared.

Six of them skidded to a halt at the end of the jetty. The Serpent King was leading, naked to the waist, the black shapes on his face and chest writhing. He swung his axe and chopped into a cowering huddle of terrified villagers. Someone screamed and fell. The others ran for their lives but were rounded up by other horsemen. One of them carelessly swiped his axe at the man who had helped Heggi aboard and laughed at the mutilation.

Ottar worked at the knot, sweating and cursing.

'Cut it!' yelled Bera.

'This is only for show,' said Hefnir. 'He's not going to harm us, only frighten us. He's come for money.'

'Wrong,' Bera spat. 'He's come for blood.'

'It's free!' Ottar threw the loose end aboard.

Many hands were held out to help him up. Ottar's fingertips brushed a crewman's but a gust caught the sail, taking the boat further from the jetty. He teetered for a moment and then regained his balance.

'You owe me!' bellowed the Serpent.

'Then come and get it,' said Hefnir.

Thorvald drew his sword and stood in front of him.

There was screaming at Ottar to jump.

Bera reached out for him. 'Papa!'

Ottar looked only at her as the boat moved further away.

'Swim, Ottar! We'll pick you up,' said someone.

'He can't swim,' said Egill, her voice as thin as a reed.

'Papa!' Bera screamed.

Ottar was lost. His square figure blurred and grew smaller.

'Papa,' she whispered.

The Serpent roared after them in fury. 'I'll come for you. I'll hunt you down and take my revenge. You've played me like a fool for years, brother, and owe me blood money too. Never dirty your own hands, do you? It's always that scar-faced son of a Helhound that does it for you, you cowardly, dishonourable, two-faced bastard.'

He swung his axe and Ottar's head came off as neatly as a child's toy.

17

Whenever Bera stood on a clifftop, the sea appeared to go on forever. From a small boat surrounded by a beaten-iron expanse, it seemed as if the entire known world was a dream. At the end of time it would be, for the ocean was spreading. The Skraken was always heaving and flexing at its monstrous boundaries. Beneath the Ice-Rimmed Sea it was especially active: it writhed over the abyssal plain, tearing open the wound on its belly. Its seeping black blood made the sea grow at the same rate as a human fingernail, until it would finally claim the land at the moment of drowning it. Sigrid's fears were not unfounded. The creatures swimming in this swollen realm were growing larger in size and numbers, so the boat sailed over the silver backs of teeming fish, facing the danger of being the prey of a sudden monster of the deep.

Bera didn't care. She was the walking dead.

The *Raven* wallowed in a sea fog that froze the bones. The other boat never entered it; Bera saw it scuttled at the jetty. The fishing boats were swamped. She felt nothing.

No one comforted her. Each family kept to its own small camp on deck, while Hefnir's crew worked round them. Egill stayed apart, keening, shamelessly behaving as though Ottar had been her own father. Sigrid was in a bad way with seasickness. Every time she leaned overboard, retching, Thorvald made sure she did not go over.

Heggi began asking Bera exactly what had happened to Ottar and why, and might he be alive, until she raged at him. He went off to Dellingr's camp looking baffled and hurt. When she went over to get him back Dellingr briefly smiled at her but Asa immediately made him tie her shawl tighter to keep their baby firmly inside. No matter; the smith was irrelevant now.

There was hardly room on deck. Ottar needed to strengthen the animal pens and make hull adjustments when the new boards swelled. Who knew what else was needed? He would never get to finish now, so this was how the *Raven* would stay, for however long it took. They were in an open boat and prey to the weather. They would have to endure every day that Heggi notched on the wooden passage-marker.

For the first time she cared nothing for being on a boat. Bera had no idea who or what she was anymore. She felt a blank. Ottar's death left her an orphan and her skern was too pale and silent. It was like being a child again, when he never spoke to her. Bera was a lonely figure in the midst of her folk and completely unable to advise them. She was the plaything of Fate, failing to save her father or even predict his death, and she blamed the baby for robbing her of both human and Valla strength.

The boat tracked steadily north-westwards in a stiffening breeze. Hefnir tried to edge further south but the wind kept heading them. Bera was aware of what he was doing. Hefnir was enthralled by Egill's Iraland and still thought it was his secret. He had looked into the heart of obsidian and wanted it to be a dagger: as dark and deep as the night sky in winter, with an edge that could kill. She was certain he had been visiting the boatyard to talk to Egill and make a passage plan for Iraland.

Let Egill also think they were heading there. Bera trusted that the boat was taking them towards her chosen destination and the wind stayed true. Egill was terrified of the place and they might indeed be passing through the gates of Hel but it was where the black stone was forged and she and Egill belonged there. The thought surprised her for a moment but quickly her mind returned to its obsessive replaying of the sequence leading up to Ottar's death. She believed that if she could only get the order right, she could change the ending. And, if she behaved well and kept everyone happy, perhaps her father would return and she could tell him she loved him.

This was madness and must stop.

The sound of laughing children intruded. They rampaged about the vessel, trailing fishing rods and pretending to fall overboard. Seething, she went below deck to check on the livestock. The raucous shouts and thundering feet must have upset them. Heggi was in the pen with two girls, one of them Dellingr's daughter. He had his arms round both of them and looked pleased with life. How dare he?

'Is Dotta safe? Your dear little calf.'

Heggi glowered. 'Go away, Bera.'

The girls smirked. Did he care so little for Ottar? Bera was tempted to explain how the world was a darker place than they could imagine. Dellingr's girl kissed him and provoked such an urge to shatter their happiness that Bera got herself away.

Back in their camp space, she took out the passage-marker and made a notch. Doing Heggi's duty made her more resentful, as she wanted it to. There was no one to be a wise, soothing friend. Sigrid was propped against the rail ready for her next bout, green-faced and sweaty, with Thorvald beside her as ever.

Hefnir called over to her, 'Will this damn wind ever set fair?'

There was, at least, her husband. Someone.

Bera went to him, rolling with the boat. 'It's strange and empty out here, with no sea birds and unknown clouds. I can't read it.'

'I've never seen waves like this, either, though I've never crossed deep ocean this far north with Fall coming. We should have hugged the coast.'

'Exactly as the Serpent would expect.'

A large roller creamed in. Hefnir swiftly adjusted the steering so that it safely hissed away beneath them.

'Don't want to meet a rogue wave broadside on,' he said.

Did he forget she'd ever sailed? She was seeking warmth and consolation. If they could not share grief they might at least have shared the names of waves for companionship. They never would.

There was only Heggi to bind them. 'Heggi has girls kissing him now.'

'He's a good-looking lad. Like his father.' Hefnir smiled and it was enough. Every passage needs a truce.

Bera returned to their billet. Seasoned sailors like Hefnir and Thorvald had their leather sea rolls with them, which kept their bedding dry during their off-watch. Bera had to endure a heap of damp blankets and furs. She found her workbox and took out her sewing kit. Clothing was more precious now that it was scarce. The trouble was, she had given away their old clothes to the poor folk before they left, so she had to improvise.

She hitched up her skirt and cut a small piece of the linen undergarment to patch Heggi's undervest, which he had torn when he jumped overboard. Bera flinched away from the memory and concentrated on her stitching. The regular prick and pull of the needle soothed her. She prided herself on her neatness, as if it could control life. Not that madness again.

'What are you doing?' Heggi flumped down beside her with his dog. 'I'm hungry.'

'Don't let Rakki trample on this vest.'

'Is that the one I ripped the bit off?' He pulled Rakki away. 'I'm sorry, Bera, don't cry.'

'I'm not.' She daren't, or she would never stop. 'It's this cold breeze.'

Bera stopped sewing, roughly pulled his head against her for a kiss then let him go. Heggi kept tight hold of his dog and groomed him. He was brewing about something. Bera wondered if he was thinking about the man who was like a grandfather to him.

'You know the crew?' he said, in the careless voice he used when he wanted something.

So that wasn't it at all. He probably wanted their ration. Bera waited, not making it easy.

'Well, can I help the bailer?'

'No.'

Heggi began playing with the thread and she tapped his hand away.

'Does he want your help?'

He pouted. 'Dotta is up to her knees in water and the pigs will be worse.'

Thorvald arrived with a smell of vomit. 'Sigrid's exhausted and I should do more to help the crew.'

'You're no sailor.'

'There's other work I could do.'

'So...?'

'Sigrid could come back here and use the bucket if she needs it, though she's eaten nothing.'

If Sigrid came, so would Thorvald. Close to, he made Bera's flesh creep. He was linked to the Serpent somehow. Why should they both live and Ottar die? Bera felt an urgent need to be savage.

'So can she?' he pressed.

She managed to think about Sigrid. 'This long, slow rolling is the worst. Sigrid doesn't move with the boat-song but fights it. If the wind gets up the boat will settle down and so will she.'

He grunted. 'Then she'll be terrified we'll capsize. I'll go and fetch her over. She needs a woman's touch.'

'Anyone's rather than yours,' Bera said.

His face hardened before he left and she felt a dart of shame for punishing his care for Sigrid.

Heggi leapt to his feet. 'So can I?'

'What?'

'Help the bailer. I'd be strong enough, wouldn't I?'

'Ask your father,' she said.

Heggi slouched across to the steer-board. and a moment later set off brightly towards the open hold. Of course Hefnir would have given him permission; boats leaked if they had enough flex to make quick passages and the bailer-boy was always tired. Ottar would... No, too painful. Bera bent her head and got on with her mending.

Thorvald carried Sigrid over and then returned with her bedding.

Bera wrinkled her nose. 'I hope the sea air will take the smell away.'

'That, or the driving rain,' said Thorvald. 'I reckon there's a storm building.'

She should have noticed. From the weather-side, there was a sooty smudge on the skyline that meant trouble.

Sigrid slumped onto her bedroll, her lips bloodless. 'Let me die,' she croaked.

They could all die.

Hefnir was steering out to sea – it was safer in unknown waters. Except that a bad storm was coming fast – and heavy weather in the middle of the deep ocean was beyond imagining.

Children were bound to their parents belt-to-belt. Asa's baby stayed tightly swaddled in her shawl. There was not enough rope to make lifelines, so Bera showed them what tackle was most securely fixed, so they could grip it on the high side of the boat. Then she checked that the on-deck stores were lashed down tight. They would survive extreme heel but not a roll. She prayed the animal pens were secure enough without Ottar's completion. The crew reefed the sail then tied themselves to their oars and bench. Although it was well within the boat's capacity at present, the sea was growing lumpier as the wind increased. Waves bumped the boat off course and Hefnir began a fight to keep them off the beam. Rain arrived in a drenching veil.

Sigrid was the only one to show no concern. She had passed into a realm like death and her eyes were glazed. Thorvald made a kind of hammock for her out of his sea roll and lashed her in as best he could.

'You'll look out for her, won't you?' he asked Bera.

'Of course I will,' she snapped.

There was so much to deal with already. Bera put her faith in Ottar's craft and heard his voice: *The mountain ash is the strongest and the whitest wood comes from the north face.* Bjorn used to say it with her. Her brother, quoting his father. Now they were both gone.

A woman prodded her. 'We need shelter. The children are soaked to the skin, like to die of it.'

'We daren't risk extra windage. When the gale has passed we'll rig up the spare sail. It will be worse before it gets better, so get back to your place and hang on for your life.'

The animals were bellowing; skidding about on their soiled bedding. Egill came up onto deck for fear of being trampled. There was no more to be done until the storm blew itself out.

'Poor Feima and Dotta,' said Heggi.

'Just as well you're tied to me,' said Bera. 'Or you'd be in there with them.'

'And Rakki's tied to me.'

The dog was the only creature smiling on the whole vessel.

A black fist hammered across the sky and punched the sails. The boat skewed and listed as the squall struck. Thunder crashed overhead and a heavy curtain of rain swept across the leaden sea. There was sharp hail scud, which icily drilled their heads until it eased. The gale strengthened throughout the afternoon and became full storm force by sunset. They had no choice but to run before it.

Bera heaved and clutched her way to the mast to help the crew take the sail off the yard. It bulged and billowed and struck her in the face, trying to escape like a live beast until it was bundled. They lashed the bare yardarm in place, to try and keep some steerage. All the gods of the air shrieked past, drilling their ears with screams of despair.

It was a howling night of total darkness. Wave-cloaked monsters swarmed invisibly towards their tiny vessel. At the last, there would be a crackle of white foam and the sea beasts could be seen for an instant, gnashing at the hull or sweeping them off course with glowing claws. The boat shivered with each assault.

There were no spare ropes to trail, so Hefnir got the crew to pour whale oil off the stern to flatten the sea. It did not stop the clattering and rattling of all their stores. Food would settle stomachs and cheer them but Bera gave up trying. She did manage to pass round some ale, which turned her mouth sour with worry.

The scant supply of whale oil ran out and the sea grew wilder still. Bera had to cling onto the rail. She was exhausted and fighting sleep and

... She was in her cradle. Her mother's hand, smelling of warm bread, gently rocking her; her soft voice singing a long-forgotten song:

> 'The raven made twelve pairs of rope from the twists and turns of its bowel;
> its claws were long and thin and sharp and made six pairs of trowel;

the beak was a black and shiny ship that cut the Ice-Rimmed Sea;
the feathers oars that tipped the waves as they flew across at speed;
its eyes—'

... And a smash of spray woke her to the battle against the sea. She loved this boat of Ottar's even more as it bravely took on all the forces of sea and air. She would look after the *Raven* until the end of its days and he would know.

The brief dawn was a thin, grey light, revealing a jumble of steeped seas. Dim shapes huddled around the deck. Icy rain returned shortly afterwards, driving in horizontally. Folk gritted their teeth harder.

It was a huge following sea. Hefnir got the men to rig a scrap of sailcloth behind the steer-board so that he could not see what towered over him and go off course in terror.

Bera yawned as seasickness threatened and kept her eyes on the skyline ahead whenever it was visible in the pitch and tilt. It was impossible to get used to this lurching motion. There was a sickening lift of the stern as the approaching wave started to pick them up, a short feeling of weightlessness, then a dizzying burst of speed as the wave rolled onwards; a sudden deafening shriek of the wind, followed by the sensation of slipping backwards, down into a breathless stall in the silent trough, waiting for the next mountainous surge.

Folk were used to a hard day's work but this clenching wait drained their strength. Grief was wearing Bera down and she began to fear that Hefnir's concentration must soon lapse. She offered to steer but in this ferocity he trusted no one but himself and would not move from the steer-board. Bera pitied the poor bailer-boy. He took every other turn, so did twice as much work as anyone else. Heggi said he counted two thousand shovelfuls in the last bailing.

Salt had worked its way into her nail beds and was lifting them. Her eyes stung with ice needles of rain and spray. Wool kept a body warm when it was wet but her thick cloak was now so sodden that she was beyond shivering. She reached the extremity of being cold, wet, mournful and afraid and a strange thing happened. It was a distinct feeling. The essential part of her that was Bera became something precious and tiny, locked deep within her core, so that her body was free to deal with any danger.

Bera studied the bleak faces around her impassively, even Heggi's. She was strong, fit, bright and able. Boats were her blood. She was a Valla – but even if those skills were gone she was also her father's daughter and she would survive. Ottar was present in the wood and iron of his boat and together they would help others survive. She looked for Egill, knowing her frailty, but she was as fleeting as a shadow.

Bera used her belt to tie Heggi to Dellingr. One she most trusted.

'Need food,' she shouted.

He nodded tightly.

She clawed her way to the barrels at the stern, making little rushes to find handholds between lurches. The last few steps in mid-air brought her crashing against the sternpost. She swung round and held on to the gunnel. The wind made it hard to breathe so she got her back to it and, with her other hand, picked at the knots that kept the lid tight. She couldn't feel her wrinkled fingers, which were white and clumsy. All the while she moved to the heaving of the boat, even though it meant a constant shifting back and fore and side to side. One check of the skyline to quell the nausea; one glance back down to work.

It was slow, determined progress but at last the lid came free. Bera wedged it between her knees and peered in. White, watery fluid slopped back and forth inside: sour whey, in which floated some new cheeses. They would quench the painful thirst, though they would be slippery to hold.

A large wave skewed the stern as it rose and she held on with both hands, legs braced between the barrel and the hull, feeling the sternpost bruising her backbone. It was hard to keep hold of the lid and deal with the cheeses. A crewman staggered across and locked her between his strong legs, so she could work.

Bera fished around in the freezing liquid for a ball of cheese. She gave it to the crewman, who passed it on with one hand. The next settler took the cheese and also passed it on so that small children could eat first. Bera kept them coming until everyone had something. There might only be a few mouthfuls but the mere fact of her managing it would lift morale.

Bera defied the storm and the wind dropped a notch. She sealed the lid and moved to the barrel of mead to give folk courage. The crewman slapped her back: man to man. Her own spirits lifted to be one of the crew.

The rolling of the boat changed: the waves became shorter and broke more frequently. It was like a giant version of chop-waves, the wind-against-tide effect on one of her fishing trips at home. She listened to the hissing and thud against the hull; the rattle of water right along the strakes; the creaks and groans of the blocks and thrumming of the rigging. Bera hauled her way to Hefnir. Ropes chafed her hands and every object on board shifted and cuffed her.

'They're shoaling! It may be getting shallower.'

'This bastard wind,' he roared. 'We're still too far north!'

'I believe we're meant to be on this course.'

'Did your skern say?' Hefnir sounded desperate. 'Any land would be good – but not yet.'

His eyes held the blankness of complete exhaustion. Then they widened to stare at something behind her head. There, off the wind, coming fast from a completely different direction from any other wave, was a single solid wall of green water. It had no spill of white foam at its peak and it swallowed the other waves as it headed for them with silent, malicious purpose.

The sky disappeared.

'Hang on for your lives!' screamed Hefnir. 'We're going over!'

Time slowed. Dellingr pulled Heggi close and got his family on the rail next to him; Thorvald had Sigrid braced against the hull. The bailer-boy stopped work and crouched down out of sight. Egill had vanished. Children's mouths were open in silent screams. Bera reached out for the rail.

It hit.

And noise returned in a constant, drumming roar of water and terrified cattle. Screams. The *Raven* tipped and began to slip away from the face of the monster, gunnels dipping as the boat heeled further and further. Hefnir was right; they were going to roll. Bera clung on with numb fingers. She stupidly looked down and saw open water beyond her feet. If she lost her grip, she would plunge straight into an icy sea. The pain in her arms and shoulders was unbearable. She dug her nails in until they bled.

The boat hung at an impossible angle for an age but then slid sideways and seemed to come up. But water engulfed them; not the crashing boil of spray but a constant clear sheet of water that kept pouring so that Bera felt she was already drowning. Only the mast stood clear of this green deluge. It was as though they had become the wave itself and up was down and air was water. Green became red, then black.

Her mother was close; she put a small, cold hand against Bera's cheek and the touch freed her. Her breath was leaving her like the tide, with the beads hanging between them like a cord.

No letting go! The beads made her a Valla – and she was her father's daughter too! She had brought her folk to this and must lead them to safety.

Bera chose life – and they were free.

The normal wave train heeled the boat so the deluge washed out as Ottar had designed; righting itself sufficiently for the crew to bail what was left in the bilges. Bera held her bead necklace tight and fervently thanked her father for his skill and all Vallas before her for theirs. Her own power had been forged anew. This time, she had chosen it. It didn't feel like some heavy cloak that she childishly struggled to wear.

And then it was time to look around her. They were safe for now; but at what cost?

Heggi was ashen: eyes wide, gnawing the back of his hand. Dellingr had his back to her. The small group around his family were still. Bera made her way over to them.

Asa's shawl was empty.

She stared at Dellingr aghast. He untied Heggi, passed the belt to Bera and went straight to his wife. Bera got Heggi away. He was dry-eyed but could not leave his hand alone. Behind them came a wail of despair. Asa pummelled her husband with her fists, cursing him; blaming him. It cut through Bera and must hurt Heggi.

She stroked the boy's hair. 'Not your fault, Boykin.'

He choked. 'If he hadn't had me tied...'

'The sea takes in an instant. Dellingr couldn't have saved the baby.'

'He could have jumped overboard.'

'Then Asa would have lost everything.'

Hefnir beckoned them to the helm.

'Their baby went over—' Bera began.

'Could have been all of us,' Hefnir said. 'Take the helm.'

Things were bad. He went to the crewmen, who were hanging over the side of the boat, trying to pick up what still floated. The settlers joined in and it listed further. Bera shouted at them to get across to the other side and steered a slow circle.

Heggi tugged at her. Two dark shapes were heading for the boat.

'Feima! Dotta! They must've gone overboard.'

Bera gripped his tunic. 'Their stalls have broken.'

Hefnir's farmer was desperately trying to secure the smaller animals below deck.

'They won't get a cow back aboard,' she said.

Heggi rounded on her. 'Don't say that! I'm going to help.'

'You will fetch a crewman. Now.'

He scampered.

When the man arrived she told him to steer and tied Heggi to him.

'Oh, no!' Heggi moaned. 'I thought we were both going!'

'Only Dellingr might have the strength.'

Heggi gave Bera a look of respect for facing that family.

Raw-faced women surrounded Asa. 'Haven't you done enough damage? You should look after your own kin,' said one of them.

'Get her away from me,' Asa screamed. 'We wouldn't be here, if you hadn't cheated...' She collapsed.

The circle of scowling women closed round her again.

Dellingr was unyielding. 'I shall never forgive myself.'

'And I am sorry for your loss. But we need you now. All of us.' Bera would not look away.

Dellingr shook his head but went to help. The poor creatures were wild-eyed, trying to get close to the boat. It was hard for the oarsmen to help without clubbing the calf with an oar.

'Come, Dotta, come!' Heggi sobbed. 'Swim!'

They used the free end of the haul-yard as a noose but it kept falling short. Dotta was tiring. Her small head kept ducking underwater and her mother bellowed forlornly by her side, only to swallow water and choke. It was hopeless.

But then a wave rolled the calf where they could grab her. Dellingr swung her on board. Dotta got up on wobbly legs, spluttered, coughed and was sick. The farmer bundled her into a pen.

'Raise the sail!' ordered Hefnir.

'No! What about Feima?' cried Heggi.

Hefnir ignored him.

Bera wanted to jump overboard and knew Heggi would have the same idea. She ran and clutched him, clinging on as he screamed at her. Heggi met her eyes and they understood each other. He stilled.

The crew got the sail back on the yard as quickly as they could but the boat was hardly moving. Feima kept swimming round the vessel, calling to her calf, and Dotta responded. It was an agony.

Finally, the sail filled.

'I'm pointing as far south as this wind allows,' Hefnir declared.

Any direction would leave poor Feima behind. The cow's despairing calls grew shorter and fainter and her calf's answering cries wrung Bera's heart.

Heggi wept noisily.

Hefnir looked up into the pitiless sky. 'Stop that. It's only a cow.'

'She's a mother,' Bera said and took Heggi's hand.

Her eyes were fixed on the boat's wake, where dear Feima was resolutely swimming after her calf. She was tiring but would carry on to her last breath to reach her. Bera continued to watch until she was a black speck on every wave crest and stared at the grey water long after she could be seen no more.

18

Time passed and the lumpen sea hugged the sullen memory of a storm. Clothes were wrung out and put back on and there was a strong smell of wet sheep around the boat. Folk were careful around each other; so careful that few spoke. They tiptoed on a ledge of grief and despair and watched for any loose ice.

When Hefnir spoke his voice cracked. 'Look! Is that a bank of cloud over there?'

Bera screwed up her eyes. 'It's a long way off.'

'But it could be land.'

She doubted it and was proved right later. The bank of cloud was an ice pack. They were heading over the Ice Rim.

Bera tried to raise their spirits by giving out extra rations and when at last a watery sun appeared and the waves flattened children ran wild with relief, though their mothers' eyes followed every move.

She took some food to Hefnir. 'Will you speak to them?'

'And say what?'

Bera could not stand this self-pitying moroseness and went to see if Sigrid still lived.

Her cheeks were hollow and she hardly breathed.

Thorvald was wracked. 'I've seen this before with a young lad on his first trip. Got seasick, gave up and died.'

'I'm not having it.' Bera slapped her friend's hand. 'Listen up, Sigrid. We are past the worst and land is in sight.'

It was a lie – but a skua flew by, skimming the waves. Sigrid would mistake its coarse mewling for a coast bird.

'Hear that? Now, buck up, Sigrid. I cannot do without you. Nor can Asa...' Better not mention the baby. 'I'm going to soak some flatbread in buttermilk. You will have some, Sigrid, if I have to cram it down your throat.'

'Very caring,' said Thorvald. 'That'll do the trick.'

Sigrid's eyelids flickered. Bera smiled, cracking her blistered lips.

Blood. The taste of fear.

Bera wanted to breathe clean air and scan to make land the truth before returning with Sigrid's food. When she saw Heggi with some children up on the bow platform she stopped to watch. The smallest child was trying, with difficulty, to hold himself steady and keep his father's big felt hat upside down on his head. It fell off to their amusement. She wondered why the child didn't just wear it properly.

'Try again,' said Heggi. 'Hold the bottom of it till I get there.'

'Don't want to.'

Dellingr's girl put the hat back on his head and held it there. Heggi had one hand holding invisible reins; holding himself proudly, as he had on the horse Ottar made for him. Bera was touched.

Then Heggi galloped towards the child, swung his arm and swiped at the hat, which fell onto the deck and rolled.

'Fall over then,' Heggi said.

The boy crumpled.

'No, not like that,' said Heggi. 'It was really slow, like this.' He toppled stiffly backwards.

Hot bile rose in Bera's throat. How dare he! She wanted to hurt Heggi as much as he had hurt her. She pictured herself screwing up his nasty little face like a rag.

The knowing eyes of one of the sows met hers.

Don't blame the boy.

Her skern was lounging against the pen, laughing at her.

You are funny – thinking the pig was talking.

'How can you? I'm distraught!'

So here I am, bringing light and joy into your drab world.

'Drab! I have suffered terrible losses.' Bera had a sudden thought. 'I'm not going to die, am I?'

Yes. We all are.

'I see you're quite your old self.'

I am. Which ought to tell you something.

Riddles. It was too much. She made a fist.

He drifted over like mist. *I'll tell you, then. Scry inside yourself.*

'No. I—'

Afraid?

Of course she was. She might have willed her baby dead.

Go on, have a peep.

There was a tiny union of opposites curled inside her, like two leaves within their liquid sac. Flesh and spirit, a child and her skern.

You have to keep going, for their sake.

'I haven't kept everyone safe.'

You weren't fully in control. Be brave enough to stand alone.

'Great comfort.' Although, in a way, it was. 'What else are you here for?'

The girl wants more. Well... that special bead on your necklace.

She touched it. 'The black one?'

It's made of obsidian, as is—

'Egill's black bowl.'

Which comes from Ice Island.

'Where?'

He smirked. *You don't know everything then. Did you see fire and ice? Yes, everyone does.*

'Not everyone can scry. And we're going to Ice Island.'

Obsidian is made there. It's why Egill is so terrified and she - Look out, Pretty Boy's coming.

He dissolved into Thorvald's grim face. 'Where's her bread, then?'

'What?'

'I think she might eat now.' He peered at her. 'Are you crying?'

'I can't.'

'Shall I fetch it?' Thorvald was suddenly mild.

'You don't know where it's stowed. I'll go now, but... Thorvald, I need to ask you something. Why would a child, a boy, why would Heggi pretend to be the Serpent King?'

Thorvald stiffened.

'I mean in play. Why would he get a boy to balance a hat on his head so he can chop it off?' Her throat closed on her last words.

Thorvald reached out towards her then let his hand drop. 'I swear to you the Serpent will pay the blood debt if our paths cross. And they will.'

'And Heggi?'

'There are times when you do something you regret forever but you can't take back the moment.'

He was talking about himself. 'Go on.'

'Heggi and Ottar were close, weren't they? Perhaps it's a child's way of making the nightmare pass.'

Bera found that astonishing. Heggi pretending to be the killer disturbed her more than she could explain.

'The Serpent King is evil.' She shook her head. 'And now... there's something worse.'

Thorvald studied the sky.

Bera pressed him. 'Did Hefnir plan to go to Iraland with Egill?'

'Yes.'

'Then that is where the Serpent will go. His spying thrall will have told him. So we stay here.'

Thorvald gestured at limitless water. 'Where?'

'It's called Ice Island.'

'Then don't tell Egill. Or Hefnir.'

Once she would have loathed the understanding of a killer. But she was increasingly glad to have this man's trust and began to see that things were never as simple as she had supposed.

Bera managed to get a few spoonfuls into Sigrid.

They rallied her enough to mutter darkly, 'If I can get through that storm I can get through anything,' before she sank back onto her bed and dozed.

Bera piled more furs over her, making sure her neck was covered. Sigrid hated draughts. When she looked up Thorvald was marching Heggi towards her. He stood the boy in front of her then backed right off.

Heggi was a child again, his face crumpled with tears, unable to get the words out for sobbing.

'I know, Boykin,' she said. 'I know.'

He rushed to her and at last they cried together, for as long as they both needed.

Afterwards he slept. Bera had time to let the vision of a very small Heggi and the Serpent play out. The wooden horse; the woman who came and hugged them. His mother, she knew.

But then it jumped forward to burning and anguish. Thorvald in the thick of it. Their longhouse, where sea-riders forced Heggi's mother, at her own hearth. A scene that the ancestral stones recorded.

Where was Hefnir?

Then the woman was on board the dragonboat and others abused her, singly, together, in every possible way and left her to slit her own skernless throat from ear to ear so that she became the ravaged Drorgher in the cellar.

One day she would tell Hefnir what had really happened and make him feel pity, too.

There was a perfect sunset. Bera thought of her mother, and being an orphan, and she kissed Heggi, who woke and they watched its progress together. Towards the end, heaped banks of clouds reached far up into the heavens, like the mauve mountains leading to the place where dead Vallas lived on. As one day she would.

Next day the waves were white with the splash of sea birds and spouting whales. Thorvald gave some cold porridge to Sigrid, who held his scarred hand as a child might, to guide the spoon.

Bera asked, 'How long has Hefnir known the Serpent King?'

Thorvald paused, carefully fed Sigrid, then wiped the corners of her mouth with his thumb.

'Come on, Thorvald, it's a simple enough question. How long?'

Sigrid nudged him. 'Tell her the truth.'

'Maybe ten, eleven years?'

Far longer than Hefnir had said. Why lie? What did it matter?

Thorvald spat overboard. 'Hefnir should never have trusted him.'

'Was he one of the sea-riders who forced Heggi's mother?'

Sigrid gasped, but then answered for Thorvald. 'He doesn't know, do you, Thorvald? He never caught up with their boat. It wasn't his fault, Bera, none of it.'

'Did Heggi see anything?'

Thorvald shook his head. 'The old woman had him safe, up with Asa.'

'So who was Hefnir protecting?' Bera didn't need to see their closed faces to know the answer. Himself.

'Where's Egill?' Sigrid asked.

'Best left alone.' Thorvald cocked his head towards the stern platform. 'Down under there.'

Bera went to the stores and took out some food. Ottar had cared for Egill and now she would take over the duty, however reluctantly. Egill brought out something in Bera she didn't care for. Poison. Pride. Had she ever been a friend or simply used Bera to get back to Iraland? In any case, she had backed Hefnir now.

Below decks it was dark as pitch and smelt of midden. Bera let her eyes adjust then crawled forward, peering across a space striped by ashy beams of light coming through gaps in the boards. The smell became yeastier and bundled in a corner was a small heap of sticks and rags.

It was Egill. She was in a tight ball, muttering shrill, guttural words, their sense lost in the cracking and creaking of the hull. How could she bear to be banged and bounced in the foul-smelling dimness with only animals for company?

'It's Bera. I've brought some cheese. Try and eat some.'

Egill stopped rocking.

'And flatbread, Egill, look.'

Egill's wild eyes gleamed and she held up a finger to listen. There was a high-pitched skitter, like the edge of thunder. *Crack!* It came again. *Crack!* Then the scuttling of a giant rat, from one end of the boat to the other.

'Ice,' said Egill, as though it was her lover's name. As if she were calling it.

Bera shuddered. 'Come up on deck with me. You're safer there.' But would others be? Egill had the smell of maelstrom madness on her.

There was shuffling behind Bera.

'Put down the food,' Thorvald said calmly. 'Then slowly get back here.'

Bera had to crawl backwards. Egill grinned like a starving wolf and Bera feared she would attack. After passing the animal pens, Thorvald lifted her up onto the deck and then swung himself up.

Rakki was waiting. He pushed his nose into her hands, trying to find some cheese. Bera stroked his head.

'Why do you keep looking after me?'

'Are you talking to me or the dog?' Thorvald gave his jagged smile.

'Does Hefnir know Egill's a girl?'

He looked across the deck at Sigrid. 'We all do.'

'Not my father. He wanted a son to mould.'

'Ottar knew. He was protecting her.'

'My father was a better man than he ever let me know.'

Thorvald's puckered scar was close. His eye looked sore where the lower lid dragged and his mouth was savagely pulled upwards. Bera wondered if she could ease it somehow.

'Did you get that protecting Hefnir?'

'It's my job.'

Thorvald's biggest scar was down his face, whereas Hefnir's scar was on his back. Someone once told her that Hefnir started battles that Thorvald had to finish. Bera was beginning to piece together a different picture of Hefnir and Thorvald; one where his second was more loyal than her husband deserved – and it didn't make her comfortable. Thorvald stood firm, while Hefnir ran.

The boat juddered.

Bera rushed to the rail to see a baby iceberg bump and twirl along the hull, grinding, crackling, then swirling away in their wake. The frigid sea glowed in the half-light. Bera strained to see what was ahead. Was her scalp prickling with the sudden intense cold or was it a warning? All was featureless, a scumble of sea and sky.

Then she saw a bobbled stretch of ice.

'Growlers coming!' she cried, all teeth.

'Drop the sail!'

The boat skin was beating like a drum. The crew got the stiff sail down and Bera clumsily lashed it with freezing fingers. She wiped the sail grease on her cloak and went to help others. The crew backed down to slow the boat then used their ice poles to push off from the nearest chunks. The settlers sat on each rail, using their feet.

They drifted, held in awe. The ice held its own luminosity in different shades of blue and green. The small bergs were mostly white, or a thin grey, with clouds of bubbles layered inside. Some had the colours and patterns of Bera's beads, with whorled runes. The ice groaned and sighed, or sometimes roared, as it sheered away. When the floes kissed the hull, there was a muttering and shivering. Whispers of peril. Bera worried about what she couldn't see below the surface.

The boat hit.

It stopped dead in the water, making the settlers stagger. Slowly, they slid sideways, to come up against another unseen chunk. The hull boomed. Then a berg reared up in jagged beauty and tipped the bow with a graunching and banging that sounded deadly.

This is bad, but ahead it is much, much worse.

Bera closed her eyes, willed it for herself, and dived into a numbing black chill, and embraced...

... Noise that surrounded her. Wails, groans, creaks and chittering; long, low moans and trilling chatter. The ocean teemed with hidden life. Like a seal, she swam sleekly through the pulsing darkness, past fish with huge torches for eyes and long, glowing spines and rods. She flicked through strangely curled and stretched transparencies that trailed twinkling lights. It grew lighter as a monstrous white mouth, serrated with small, sharp teeth, yawned before her. A long, mottled shape with a single tusk – a corpse whale! – charged up at her from below. She swerved away and met grasping tentacles but she jinked between the huge suckers before they could bind her.

Before her was always the promise of knowledge, even though it was to know her enemy. Ahead, there was a pure blue light, bluer than a sunlit cornflower, still shining through the gloom at depths that Bera couldn't fathom. She pierced veils of purple fish that scattered and reformed after she passed, drawn to the limitless blue like a moth to a flame. She slowed as she neared it and saw that it was not light but mass. Ice. A crystalline immensity, an uncut sapphire, that would coldly rip the heart out of their vessel.

Bera shot to reality, blinking in the stark light. Shocked and bloodless, she felt as though she had been gone for years.

'There are ice m-monsters ahead,' she stammered, her lips shrivelled and cracked.

'We're dealing with them,' said Hefnir.

'M-much bigger.'

'We're taking water!' yelled a crewman.

Folk grabbed bailing shovels and worked as quickly as they could but the level was rising all the time.

'Hefnir! Bear off,' Bera insisted. 'Our only chance.'

Speed could be fatal but Hefnir eventually nodded. 'Raise the sail!'

The men hoisted. Bera joined Heggi to help bail. There was a juddering, grinding, clattering, as they sped through the loose pack. It was worse for Bera, ankle-deep in freezing water, next to wooden boards that would crack open if the nails unclenched. She had to trust in her father's build – though nothing could withstand the monster she had seen.

'It's getting worse,' a man said. 'We must have sprung new leaks.'

Bera glared. 'Not in Ottar's boat.'

He kept his head down.

The wind was taking them south, away from the ice sheet but towards Iraland. Bera willed them westwards. It was a huge risk: the boat could be swamped before they reached Ice Island. They took turns to bail. Bera worked doggedly through all her shifts and did more than her share. She begged her mother to guide their little craft.

They managed to keep the water level steady but tiredness was slowing them and only land could save them. Repairs to the hull could not be done at sea. All the time Bera's scalp gave an insistent warning. In the ice-glow she got some simple food organised and made everyone eat to give them courage. She took some to Hefnir.

'I've no time for that.' He squinted to the west. 'What's your reckoning? Ice or land?'

The glittering might be an ice sheet but there were clouds above it in a particular pattern.

'It's land.'

Hefnir changed course. She did not need to tell him it was not Iraland.

All through the night they bailed. Bera suggested fixing the spare sail under the hull like another boat skin but they were short of ropes and it was hopeless. Morning confirmed it was land but the boat was heavy and wallowing. Would they reach it in time?

Starkwhales surged past in an arrowhead, leaving them rocking in their wake. Block whales came over in turn to inspect a chosen person then drift away, snorting and blowing with disappointment. Right whales loomed then dived, leaving behind the smell of a thousand fishy meals. An ice shark gave them a glassy stare, a grotesque pink worm hanging from its eyeball. Seals kept their distance until it had gone and then came to play around the sides of the boat, twitching long whiskers at the settlers. Dolphins swept under the bow and leapt or streaked alongside, grinning; giving them hope. So much life.

Sigrid groaned. 'So many horrors to eat you.'

Huge skuas soared over the boat on their way out to sea, as did other birds, unknown to Bera. Outlying islands were so steep that they were fit only for the thousands of birds that massed them. Beyond them were savage, white-topped ridges that glowered from the centre: Ice Island. She knew that in her bones.

Bera left Egill in her burrow, fearing what she might do if she saw it.

Hefnir was watching her. He must know that wherever they were they must land to make repairs. He would stay where she had brought them. This was her time and she felt her Valla powers increase with every breath of this different air.

Now they were so close to safety, the exhausted men had stopped bailing and water was pouring through every crack. Yet there was nowhere to get ashore: rocks would splinter the boat and they would be eaten before ever reaching land. The wind died and they rowed; desperately scanning for a river-mouth to enter. Everything at sea level was black, even the sand on the wide, shallow beach. Bera refused to despair and let her sea-going mind take the land's instruction.

'Put ashore,' she said.

Hefnir snorted. 'Are you mad?'

'It's wide and shallow.'

'But—'

'Here, Hefnir, before we sink.'

The land beckoned and Bera was at one with the injured boat, a dying narwhale coming to rest, as Hefnir let the boat ride in on a rolling wave. But this time landfall would restore life. All their lives, if they pulled together.

The crew leapt off to fix the land anchors as the boat was too full of water to pull up the beach.

Bera was all urgency. She jumped off and fell over, her legs were so weak, but kissed the sand in thanks for giving safe harbour. The black, gritty grains crunched between her teeth and made it real. Rakki landed next to her, followed by Heggi. The settlers wanted to be on dry land. They stumbled like drunkards to get higher up the beach, then toppled onto their backs, staring up at a strange sky.

Bodily needs soon became more pressing than their fear. A group of men went off behind a ridge of rocks and returned looking much relieved. Women and children followed, including Bera. It was a joy not to have to brace every muscle and cling on tight to a bucket.

Afterwards, Bera helped get the livestock off. At the sea's edge, she formally thanked Fate for their safe deliverance and glared defiantly inland. Jagged mountains couldn't frighten her, whatever they hid. Hadn't she faced down all the perils of the Ice-Rimmed Sea? She felt a surge of new life on a new shore and also inside her. The essential part of herself that she had packed away had made the baby strong, too.

Heggi ran along the strand, splashing and laughing, with Rakki prancing by his side. Hefnir was at the boat with his crew, starting repairs, back in charge. The settlers kept in their tight family groups, looking about them nervously. They kept close to the sea, as if some local band of troles might stride over the high ridge of black rocks that walled off the beach from whatever lay inland.

A river came down as far as the beach, fanning out in a myriad of streamlets that fingered their way to the sea. It was perfect for washing. Folk gradually began to chatter. Children chased and laughed, even Dellingr's girl. Bera thought back to her own childhood, when her mother died, and knew they would have no idea that what was lost could never be returned.

Bera avoided Asa. No mother could easily stop blaming someone for the death of her child, especially if guilt lay heavy on her own shoulders. Bera hoped the new land would gradually bring some sense of a fresh start, of possibility rather than only loss. It had worked its magic on her already.

The animals had forgotten their terror and begun to forage. Bera led Dotta to a large patch of grass beneath the black wall and the other beasts followed. She left them grazing.

There was no sign of Egill. Bera went to the boat and a crewman said she was still below deck, but even wilder.

'He's like some village cur, kicked and starved to madness.'

'I'll go below.'

'Watch it, he's nearly had my hand off.' He showed her the tooth marks.

Bera took some weak ale with her. The smell of filth and madness made her retch. She reminded herself that this was once her friend and managed to approach, matter-of-fact.

'Hear that banging, Egill? Ice unclenched a few boards and they are fixing them.'

A croak. 'Ottar?'

'The boatmender. You helped him once, remember?'

Egill whimpered, growled, keened. Bera coaxed her into drinking. She spoke directly about the passage, about Asa's baby; anything but where they were. It took time, an age, but finally Egill returned to a form of sanity.

'So lonely,' she managed.

'I know.'

They cried together for being orphans and said a prayer for poor Feima.

'That Heggi. He'll be a good stockman.' Egill drank to it.

'Hefnir wants him to be a trader.'

'Raider.'

'Heggi would never kill.' Bera's certainty was a comfort. 'But there's something about the Serpent King... Did Hefnir ever say anything?'

Egill tapped her forehead with her fingers. 'No one stronger than you.'

'When I was most afraid I found my Valla strength.'

'Folk trust you.'

'So come with me.'

Egill cringed away.

'Trust me, Egill. You've been through the same flame as me. We're forged by it. Like this bead!'

Egill reached towards the glossy black bead.

Bera seized the advantage. 'Let's get you washed and dressed so folk can see you're a woman.'

'Not one nor other. Shan't wear a dress.'

Bera lured her friend with the bead. At the freshwater stream she washed her. Egill's bones were sharp and frail like a bird's, but as the grime left her body, so she calmed. No one commented. Perhaps folk accepted her already – for whoever she was.

The women had got some food together that didn't need cooking. Children took it to a rough camp on the far side of the beach from Skits Mountain, as folk were calling the beach latrine. Sigrid managed to keep her meal down and declared it was the best commons she had ever tasted.

A quiet fell over them once they had eaten. Bera surveyed them all. They were her folk and she would make it right for them. Before that, she had to make them believe in this place as she did but she must also be truthful; she had found her true self on the passage across and would not be made into a puppet by the lies Hefnir told to control people. Even Egill would come to understand the land as Bera did. Until then, she would not name it.

It was time to seize the future.

She took Hefnir's beaker from him. 'Come on,' she said. 'We're going scouting.'

'Why hurry? There's no one to trade with. Nothing to trade. It's like a giant's hearth.' He lazily picked up a handful of black sand and let it slip through his fingers. It was like clinker, apart from the fact that it left his hand clean.

'So am I to go alone?'

Hefnir took back his beaker, downed his ale and got to his feet. 'Come, Thorvald, and you two. My wife wants to go raiding.'

The other crew laughed.

Bera strode ahead as best she could with sea legs and deep, dry sand to wade through. The men dawdled, chatting, as she clambered up higher ground to the wall of sharply pocked black rocks and rubble. She hurt her hand as she tried to scramble over to the other side, which made her scalp tingle. She found a gully that was exactly foot-width and it was easier. And then she stopped.

The landscape opened out before her. It was a vast open plain of vivid green pasture, rising to mossy foothills and mounds of ice-bound whiteness at great height beyond. There were rainbows over waterfalls; a fertile lushness that held the promise of grazing, crop-growing, survival. Better than that: thriving. She had trusted her instinct and now, after all they had been through, to find this! She turned to call the others but could not speak.

When they got there she opened her arms wide to present her gift.

'I brought us here, Hefnir. Not my skern, not my mother: me.'

'Then I'm sorry for you.'

Thorvald quickly said, 'A man could grow old here without shame.'

'There will be no old age for you and me,' Hefnir said.

Bera would not let him spoil it. 'The others must be shown this. It is our certain future.'

The settlers stood ranged along the ridge, looking with awe at a land that pushed back the bounds of their known world. They linked arms so the weakest could stand and then gazed some more, as if the sight could feed them.

Pale horses swept across the valley. Their manes and tails were silver and they looked like the wind.

'It's all the same but... more,' said Heggi, delighting Bera.

Thin wisps of cloud trailed the mountaintops. Above the tallest peak a high, wide cloud was forming. It funnelled and twisted downwards, pursing into a pout at the base.

'That's a special sign,' Bera said, having scried it in the black bowl. Then, Egill had swayed her into fearing it, now it was full of promise.

Hefnir blocked her view. 'There are no trees. What do we build with?'

'There's a strong spirit here, Hefnir. I can't yet reckon it exactly but it's a good place.'

'We'll stay close to the boat tonight and have a meeting.'

Bera was glad he would help choose where exactly to settle. Between them, she and Hefnir would reassure folk that this place held promise. It meant putting up with his weakness but so be it. The prickle in her scalp could only be about Thorvald. She wanted to leave the blood debt behind, on a crueller shore.

As they walked back she felt the first stirring from the child she carried. It made her real, this baby whose rights she had sworn away. Heggi was her firstborn; they had witnessed her oath. A son should lead but if Bera became a new kind of leader, her daughter could too.

Bera felt disloyal, so she inspected Heggi's wound. The sea air had crimped the edges and it looked like a sea slug crawling up his arm.

'This needs to dry out,' she said. 'Keep it clean. Don't let Rakki lick it.'

'Of course not.'

He had grown up on the passage, apparently, but into what? This sounded dismissive, like his father, and he was off as soon as he could.

The settlers worked as a team. Men unloaded some stores, ready for the feast, while the crew rigged up the spare sail between some rocks, forming a booth in the gully for shelter. Then they got back to repairs, letting Egill help.

Bera wanted a big fire, like the mead hall. Like home. Children gathered driftwood and dry brush. Some women made a hollow in the sand, while others collected large rocks, which they placed round it to make a wide hearth.

When the firestack was built, Bera called everyone over. She used her burning-glass to light it and this amazed them. Egill made no boasts about Iraland. Afterwards, she stayed close to Sigrid as she supervised the hot meal.

Bera would tell them about their new life when bellies were full. Till then, she took charge of drying their blankets. She found long pieces of wood, spat out by the restless sea that pounded this shore, which they used to fashion a drying rack. They set it up behind the fire, so it gave shelter from the wind that was blowing off the land.

Heggi was missing, as was Dellingr's girl. Growing up indeed – but they would soon be back when cooking smells reached them. Bera dribbled whenever she bent down. Hot food was enjoyed before it ever reached the mouth.

Sure enough, the pair returned in time for the first hot meal since Seabost. The feast was an end-of-passage mash-up stew but it tasted delicious.

'Can I have some more, Bera?' Heggi asked.

She filled his bowl. 'What were you doing earlier?'

'Rakki needed to catch some puffins.'

'Where are they then?'

He scruffled the dog's ears. 'He hasn't quite got his eye in here yet.'

But he blushed and looked across the fire to his love.

Later, Bera went inland to the river for fresh water. Heggi came with more containers, which pleased her. A group of swans glided off when they saw Rakki. He chased them and they lumbered into the air.

'Rakki likes it,' said Heggi. 'Is this the place where we'll settle?'

'Somewhere here. It'll be hard work but we're not cribbed by the lack of land like back home. There's pasture.'

'I wish...' His voice wobbled.

'Feima?'

He blinked away tears.

'We can't change the past, Heggi. We have to make the most of now, so that we have a future.'

She heard applause. Her skern. Was that why he would never discuss the past? He waved happily and capered along the riverbank.

Why did she still feel uneasy? Egill's terror that this was the gate of Hel must be as catching as red-spot. It was vital to keep her from knowing where they were as long as possible.

They emptied the brackish water from the containers, swilled them out and refilled them. They were ready to leave when Hefnir arrived with some leather flagons. He said nothing to Bera as he filled them, handed some of the full ones to Heggi and then led his son away. Perhaps Hefnir was also tainted with Egill's fear but daren't show it. Rakki sensed something because he came to Bera, pushing his head against her until she stroked him. The feel of the dog's rough fur comforted her but as soon as she picked up her flagons he scurried off after Heggi.

When she got back to the beach the sea was blood red. The strange funnelled cloud now covered the whole western sky and was aflame. The fire was dancing, sending golden runes up into the deepening sky with a message. This time she could read it.

Take charge, echoed her skern.

Bera called folk to the fire. 'Set up camp in the booth. Then we shall have a meeting about our new settlement.'

Dellingr held up a hand to stop anyone moving. 'Folk are dog-tired. Can't we talk tomorrow?'

Bera was furious. Did he think he was leading? 'We daren't stay on the beach longer than one night, so we need to plan whether to move inland or explore along the coast. We decide together, so we pull together to make it a success.'

The waves sucked and crackled on the shore.

'Or...' Hefnir opened his arms wide and smiled. 'You can show a deal more sense and come to a better land, with me.'

19

The rising moon squatted on the sea-rim, the colour of a great white bear. Its light made everything its own reverse. Bera looked across at her husband. His features were stark and the mouth she had once thought strong was merely stubborn. His hair hung in greasy, salt-crusted braids like hers, just as their clothes were oily and damp. She was bone-weary and wished they could sleep and wake refreshed, ready to work together. If only he would ever share his true thoughts with her.

'We should talk before the meeting starts,' she said.

'Why? The choice is the same for everyone, including you: come with me or stay here. Folk know who feeds them, so you'll come too when you're left with only the whey-faced Sigrid for company.'

'They don't need another hard sea voyage. Help me find the best place to settle here. You owe it to them, Hefnir.'

'I owe them nothing. I saved them, remember.'

'Wrong. But let's not argue. The boat is damaged. Stay safe here with us.'

'Safe? Here?' Hefnir snorted.

'The Serpent King waits for you in Iraland.'

'I've managed him for years.'

She waited for him to recall their last encounter with the Serpent but his face did not soften.

'No kind word, Hefnir? He killed my father and you have not spoken once about my loss. Do you see other folk's sorrow? Do you feel for Asa at all, whose baby was swept from her arms?'

'She was neglectful.'

'She blames me for hobbling Dellingr with Heggi.'

'Any decent mother would have jumped in after her child.'

Bera gave Hefnir a last chance to prove his worth. 'I am carrying your child.'

He looked away and spat. 'Probably Dellingr's.'

Once she might have cared enough to slap him. 'I pity you, Hefnir.'

He headed for the fire.

Bera had seen in his eyes that he didn't believe it was Dellingr's; he simply wanted an excuse to leave. If she had ever respected him, it was lost in that moment. Loss makes you strong.

Bera told the boys to build the fire up even higher, making a beacon. Weary folk shuffled into a wide arc, facing her. Hefnir stood in front of his crew. One of them was swaying, either the worse for drink or land-sickness. Children stood by their parents, wide-eyed, smelling fear just as Rakki did, staying pressed against Heggi, with Sigrid and Thorvald on the other side.

Moonlight was a silver sea path and the sand black gold by firelight. Could Hefnir not see the signs of richness here? There was movement where the waves licked white foam. It was her skern, paddling like a child, splashing. He saluted her cheerily and carried on.

Bera began. 'Hefnir demands we decide tonight: stay or go. First, I want to remind you all that we are here because I predicted famine in Seabost.'

'Which hasn't happened,' said Hefnir.

'Which may not now happen,' Bera agreed, keeping her voice level.

Hefnir prodded his chest. 'Only because folk who stayed behind can ration everything we couldn't take. And there aren't so many mouths now. Thanks to me.'

One of the men pointed homewards. 'What do you mean? Are you saying that Serpent King killed folk after...?' He faltered.

Bera broke in. 'Say it. After beheading my father. The Serpent's sworn enemy is Hefnir, not plain folk. Ottar was the scapegoat. Now he will travel to Iraland to fight Hefnir there.'

Hefnir jeered. 'Don't try to make folk fear the place. Why would he go there?'

'Because that's where you're going, with or without us. You made plans with Egill and shared them with your thrall: the Serpent's spy.'

Hefnir pointed at the moon and his head. Moonstruck.

'I've not lost my wits, Hefnir, but found them. It's true, Egill, isn't it?'

Egill looked everywhere but then nodded.

'You may have been using the spy to get news to the Serpent for years.'

Folk gasped. Bera kept her eyes on Thorvald, who didn't flicker.

She went on. 'I scried in Egill's bowl and saw this place. My skern says its name is Ice Island.'

'Your skern!' Hefnir sneered. 'I suppose it's standing next to you.'

'He's close.'

Hefnir put on a baby voice. 'It's an imaginary friend dreamt up by a lonely little girl. Whose father wanted a boy.'

Bera ignored him. 'You all believe in skerns. Twin spirits.'

Dellingr agreed. 'I forged entwined twins as iron brackets for every torch in the hall. Doubly safe.'

Bera wanted to frighten them. What they called superstition in Seabost was a reality – and she alone could protect them.

'Anyone not joined by his skern will become a Drorgher, and walk forever in search of company, preying on the living.'

There were no Drorghers on the beach but the folk who didn't believe in them made hammer signs and scanned the lengthening shadows all the same.

Bera took up her stance. 'I have beaten back Drorghers my whole life.'

Folk edged closer to her.

Hefnir forced a laugh. 'Superstitious crap. I say we are lucky to make it here alive.'

'Not luck. My Valla power and your boat-skill.'

He ignored her generosity. 'We'll die if we stay. This is where your famine will be.'

'So now you agree there will be a famine? So I can predict the future?'

'No! I—'

'You don't know your own folk, Hefnir. We're not afraid of hard work. The land looks rich.'

Hefnir picked up a handful of sand. 'Looks like Hel's arsehole if you ask me.' He looked cunning. 'In fact, we were told that's exactly what it is.'

'Who by?' Dellingr asked.

'Someone who came here by chance and had the sense to leave it.'

Bera held up her arms to stop the chatter. 'He's talking about Egill. The one who loves danger. But this isn't the land she described.'

Where was Egill? Perhaps she realised where she was, despite it being a kinder place than she feared.

'Besides, I use Valla skills to save us from her mischief.'

'What skills?' Hefnir scoffed. 'Ottar said you had none.'

'I was trying to learn my mother's instead of finding my own. You saw my success, Hefnir, and should trust me now.'

A bugling cry rose to a crescendo as eight swans came in from the sea, silver-winged and stately. The reminder softened Hefnir's face.

'Yes, Hefnir. Whistling swans.'

The small opening closed and he jabbed a finger at her. 'You did learn from your mother. Ottar said you make things up, just like her.'

'Ottar said I would be unfaithful but I have always been your good, true wife – and everyone knows it.'

It was a risk and Bera could smell unease. They all knew the rumours.

'It's the opposite.' Asa's voice was shrill. 'We've all seen you making cow-eyes at my man; going up to the forge every whip-stitch. You cheated to get Dellingr here and if you had only let us be... if you had only...' She fell to her knees on the black sand.

Her daughter knelt and hugged her. Accusation glittered in everyone's eyes, including Heggi's.

'Asa. I swear to you on all that is most precious to me; on my mother's necklace...'

Hefnir laughed. 'Very convincing, swearing on cheap beads, given by a betraying wife. Deny that!'

Bera felt panic flutter in her chest. 'Then I swear on... the head of my son Heggi that the draw was fair. Dellingr is no more than a trusted friend.'

'It's true,' Sigrid said.

Hefnir's voice was dark. 'You have sworn on my son's life and will forfeit your own if he suffers from your lies.'

Heggi roughly wiped the end of his nose with his sleeve but Bera couldn't comfort him. She was in a mortal battle with Hefnir for leadership. Why was it so important to go to Iraland? Was he a full partner of the Serpent King's?

'This is a distraction, Hefnir. I tell you all again, I am honest and I predict success in Ice Island.'

Hefnir pulled her round to face inland. His smell was sharp. 'Look. There's nothing out there. Nothing. There's no wood to build with. The place I am going to is a couple of days away. There is a city there called Dyflin with endless riches ready for the taking.'

'To be fair, we have not seen it,' said Thorvald.

Hefnir looked as though his dog had bitten him. 'Fair?'

Bera stepped away. 'What is a "city" but another of Egill's tales? Yes, that poor soul, mad with grief and loss. Greed makes Hefnir listen to her. Egill deserves our pity. She was completely wrong about this place and, frankly, I would not follow Egill into a pantry.'

Folk needed the relief of laughter and it was loud.

Hefnir shouted. 'I brought wealth to Seabost. You all did very well out of me.'

'That's the past, Hefnir. We're here to discuss our future.'

He went to stand with his crewmen. 'The discussion is over. Apart from these men, you are all free. Stay or go; the choice is yours.'

'Hefnir, folk are dropping. Let's begin again in the morning.'

'You know you'll be left here alone if they choose now.'

'I doubt it – but I'm only thinking of them.'

He skipped closer to the settlers and dropped his voice, so they had to strain to hear his silky words.

'It's easy,' he wheedled. 'Do you want to come with me and live or stay here and die?'

There was silence. Then a man said something to his neighbour, who punched him. There were more insults and shoving. All the pent-up emotion flared into a fistfight. Faces contorted into masks of rage. Women and children joined in, too.

Thorvald was at Hefnir's shoulder, sword ready. His wreck of a face was carved by moonlight, inscrutable as ever. Bera scanned the mob for Heggi and saw his dog first, standing rigid with hackles raised. He guarded the boy, who was sitting apart in a ball of fear. For a ghastly moment he looked like Egill.

The fight raged on.

Bera acted on the instinct of song. At first the ache of loss thinned her voice but she pressed on and then Sigrid joined in. When the second verse came the children's clear, high voices rang out:

> 'In the blood, in the blood,
> Feel the rumble and the tumble
> And the boat-song in your blood.'

Bjorn's verse. Bera was crying too much to sing well – but she had rekindled fellowship and brought folk to their senses. It was raw, full-chested singing that was truly a heart-song from all their childhoods, of innocence.

> 'In the heart, in the heart,
> Feel the pulsing of the whale-road
> And the boat-song in your heart.'

They made a hammer circle, arms outstretched to hold shoulders, forged into an unbroken link. They sang it again, louder, and their strong voices pushed back the creeping darkness and unknown terrors. They were telling the new land who they were and that they were not afraid.

The song conjured for Bera the first tiny boat Ottar made for her, with its particular melody and the boat-song of all his vessels. Longships were her lifeblood and she loved every plank and nail with a passion that might be her own Valla strength.

The song ended and Hefnir spoke before they could think. 'For the final time, I ask each man to choose: either to stay here with a rudderless girl or come with a battle-honed, storm-proved raider to unimagined riches!'

Folk looked down at the sand as if the answer was written there. A sudden wind flattened the fire and blew smoke out to sea. Some logs fell in with a crash and the flames crackled back into life.

Sigrid shook herself like a hen. 'Well, I'm staying. No one's getting me on a boat again, ever, but in any case I believe in Bera. This is the place.'

She left Thorvald and stomped across the sand to Bera, glaring at Hefnir as she passed.

Hefnir bowed. 'Thank you, Sigrid. Oh, but of course you never will get on a boat again. None of you will. Once my boat leaves, that's it. You'll have to stay here. There's no timber to build another and no Ottar to do it.'

He was attacking Bera. To never travel the sea paths again was to lose her being. Her whole body ached with loss. She could not let Hefnir take her father's one remaining boat. But how could she bear him to stay after this?

While she reeled, Dellingr stepped forward. If he chose to go with Hefnir they all would.

'Please. Wait!' Bera's voice cracked. The trail of unwitting harm she had done the smith's family counted against her and she desperately searched for the right words. But she was so, so tired.

'Bera, you don't need to try and persuade us,' Dellingr said. 'You don't have to argue against the glib stuff we know he can spout whenever he likes.'

He was telling her to give up. But then she properly heard what he had said and was glad.

'You lovesick fool,' sneered Hefnir.

Dellingr turned to the others. 'You all know what this is about. It's about what Bera has done in the past, as woman and Valla; her judgements and the warnings we took no heed of. She cured our sickness and kept the evil she calls Drorghers away. You saw how she worked like a thrall on the boat coming over. This is about who she is.' He moved closer to his family. 'Look at me, Asa. I never lie. There has been no dishonour between Bera and me.' He stretched out a hand.

Asa would not take it. 'Don't.'

'Come on. Trust me.'

She turned away, pulling her daughter closer to her.

Bera found a new kind of courage. There was a time to attack and a time to admit defeat.

She spoke quietly but forcefully. 'I am truly sorry, Asa. There was a time when I needed Dellingr's strength and that was what you saw. He's right: there was no dishonour, ever, but perhaps I took something from him that should have been yours alone. If you choose to go with Hefnir, I understand. I am strong now and your husband must not cause you to stay for my sake.'

Asa met her eyes. There was no warmth. 'We stay.'

She stiffly crossed to join Sigrid and Dellingr followed, though he did not acknowledge Bera. Another family came with them.

'Thank you,' said Bera. The time of guilt and fear, of wondering who she was, had ended and her folk saw that.

Hefnir seized a spar from the fire and made a furrow in the sand. 'Right. See this line, here? This is a serious choice. My side or hers. Come on. Where's your loyalty?'

Thorvald stepped over the furrow and joined Hefnir. Sigrid gave a low moan and seized Bera's hand. Her nails dug into the palm.

'Well, I'm glad you're showing sense,' Hefnir said.

Thorvald spoke slowly, holding his gashed lip taut, so that his words were clear. 'I have been your second for many years, Hefnir. I gained this ugly face in your service, protecting you when you were... busy. It was my own choice. I am a free man. So, as a free man, this is my choice. I did not cross the sand to join you. I came, in honour, to shake your hand in parting. I choose to stay here with my wife and my leader. I choose Bera.'

Bera was stunned. Thorvald chose her. She had always wanted his respect, she recognised. Joy throbbed in her hot hand, which Sigrid squeezed.

Hefnir put an arm round Thorvald.

'Don't leave me, Thorvald,' he wheedled. 'You don't mean it, do you? We're too close. You love me.'

'I served you too long, shutting my eyes to your weakness. For the money.'

Hefnir pushed him away.

'Well, I don't want you!' His spit flew. 'Stay with the old bitch, you coward. The whole scabrous lot of you are cowards! You dishonour your blood. Where's your ancestors' lust for sea and adventure? Why choose to stay here and do women's work?'

'Hardly cowardice to face the hardships you're predicting for us,' said Bera. 'Make your mind up, Hefnir.'

Heggi rushed forward, to stand between them.

'Stop it! Stop shouting! I thought we were coming here to be together! Don't go straight off again, Papa. You're always going off. I thought we were going to all live here like a proper family!'

'You'll have to come with me, son, if you want a proper family.' Hefnir held out a hand. 'It's you and me: father and son.'

Bera flashed. 'You asked me to be his mother.'

'Because you are not.'

'Folk swore that I am his mother. So did I.'

Their anger was like a wolf circling the beach, with Heggi at its centre. Hefnir slowly pointed at his crew, then his farmer, then the undecided and lastly the folk with Bera.

'Then you can all bear witness to this. Your real mother did not die, Heggi. The sea-riders took her. She might be in Iraland. Wouldn't you like to go and see her?'

'Not true!' Bera was in turmoil – what could she say that would not damage Heggi?

Thorvald got between them. 'If it's truth-time, Hefnir, I'll tell the whole of it. You let Heggi's mother be forced by the sea-riders at your own hearth and you did nothing except send me off in a chase-boat when it was too late. While you stood by it was the Serpent King who tried hardest to save her – and see where that ended. He's the living proof of your dishonour.'

Perfidy. Violation. Blood soaked into the longhouse walls. Bera dare not say Heggi's mother slit her own throat. He was already terrified.

Hefnir raised his sword. All the air seemed to vanish from the black well of the beach, where deep shadows stained the sand blacker. This was something about the Serpent, something bad. Bera tried to stop Hefnir but he shook her off and pointed the sword at Heggi.

'Then tell my son, Thorvald. Tell them all who I married. Tell them why the Serpent King tried to save her and whose black blood Heggi carries.'

Finally, Bera understood the final piece of the puzzle. The small boy playing with the Serpent. The lovely woman who kissed them, Heggi's mother, was his sister. No wonder her brother, the Serpent King, was out for blood. But it also meant his evil was in Heggi's nature.

'Stop this!' Bera pushed Hefnir's sword down. 'Heggi is your son. He is innocent. He needs no more pain.'

Hefnir crouched down to speak to him. 'You have stirrings in your blood, don't you, Heggi? Just like your family. You want to be a man like your father – and your uncle, the Serpent King.'

'No!' Heggi screamed.

He pushed past his father and ran full pelt with Rakki barking frenziedly beside him. They made for the line of rocks opposite.

If Bera went after him, she would lose the other settlers.

'Keep him safe, Thorvald,' she said. He was already on his way.

Bera swung at Hefnir. She punched him, hard, to wipe the smirk from his uncaring face. 'You bullying, selfish, dishonourable bastard. The Serpent said you were and he was right! We're better off without you.'

'It's like a flea bite, your hitting.' Though he rubbed his cheek.

Bera's anger was blazing ice, cold and pure. 'Well? You others. Make your mind up. Are you going with this... person, or staying with me?' She made the furrow clear again with the point of her foot. 'This side is a new beginning. There will be new laws of sharing and ownership. It's true that we cannot escape when things get difficult – like he has always done – so it means we have to make good where we are.'

The men looked at each other, then at their wives, then at the sky, clearly hoping Fate would decide for them. A few shuffled past

Hefnir, who snarled at them like a wolf, and they jumped the furrow to Bera's side. Others ran flat out.

All but the crew were now gathered behind Bera.

Hefnir laughed. 'Who needs cowards? The boat's about fixed, so we'll leave at first light. Any of you who want to join me can do so under cover of darkness and no more will be said about it. But a sluggish wolf gets no prey. I wait for no man.'

Bera knew the only defection he cared about was Thorvald's and the only man he would take back was his second. But Thorvald was gone.

Hefnir walked over to Dellingr. 'This is for you and your friend.' He spat in his face and then ran with his crew towards the boat.

Bera and Asa leapt to hold the smith back.

'He's not worth it,' said Asa.

Dellingr nodded and the women let him go.

'Which friend?' Bera asked.

'Thorvald. We've been close ever since boyhood.'

So that was why Thorvald was often at the forge – not to spy on her. Was Hefnir more jealous of Thorvald's friendship with Dellingr than hers?

'If you'd attacked Hefnir, Thorvald would have had to take revenge.'

'Is that why you stopped me?'

Perhaps. Bera needed to start being sure about her reasons.

'Hefnir's always been jealous of Dellingr,' Asa said. 'Long before you.' It wasn't meant to be kind.

'Well, now Hefnir's shown his true self to me,' Bera said. 'What has a bad beginning will have a bad ending.'

Her scalp was warning of trouble. She needed to find Heggi – and Egill.

First she went over to Sigrid. 'Set a watch over the livestock and take some stores from on board. They can have rations for the passage but get the rest off.'

'Just let him try and stop me.' Sigrid stamped off, then called back. 'You did well there. Your mother would be proud of you.'

Bera raised a hand in thanks – but that burden was gone.

That's the ticket.

'You're back, are you, now all the trouble's over?'

Oh, dearest one, you know it's far from over.

Her scalp was on fire.

'It's Heggi, isn't it?'

Yes.

She would kill with her bare hands whatever harmed her boy. Because he was her own, more than the baby inside her.

Where was he?

The *Raven* was afloat in the shallows and the crew holding the lines. It was the last time she would ever see it. But that wasn't causing this dread. Sigrid and the others were rolling some barrels towards the camp. The spare sail was gone and the moon was lighting the rocks where it had been.

Then, through a gap, Thorvald appeared. Alone! No – there was Heggi with Rakki behind. He lifted them down. The boy and his dog skipped off and Thorvald waved at her, to show they were all unharmed.

The dread remained. Think! Spare sail gone; crew with boat in shallows... Hefnir was putting out to sea at once. Where was he?

Heading at speed for Heggi.

Bera ran, though she could not reach Heggi before Hefnir grabbed him. But Thorvald could, if he knew what was happening behind his back.

'Thorvald!' she screamed and pointed. 'He's taking Heggi!'

He spun round.

Hefnir was advancing, his face grim. Thorvald lunged, swept Heggi up into his arms and ran. The dragging sand slowed everything. Both Thorvald and Bera moved as if through deep water but he had the boy's weight. Her son's mouth was a black O on his white face and silver light glinted off Hefnir's sword as he raised it.

'No!' Bera screamed.

Hefnir gave his friend no warning. The blade came crashing down onto Thorvald's shoulder, slicing into his neck. He pitched forward onto his knees, hurling Heggi towards her before he dropped. Bera seized her boy's hand and they stumbled back towards the others who were coming to help. Dellingr got there first. She put Heggi's hand in his. Asa and her daughter shielded Heggi from the sight of his protector lying on the sand; blood pooling round his head like pitch.

Hefnir was hers. Bera unsheathed her sword. She became aware of furious barking. Rakki would not let Hefnir pass. He ranged in front of him, snarling and snapping. But Hefnir didn't try. He had no second to fight for him. He looked dazed, perhaps with grief, if he could feel that deeply. In time, he would create another lie to live by, as he had about his first wife and the Serpent, but for now he could not move. He stood, head bowed, with his sword point in the sand.

Bera called Rakki off. He ran to Heggi.

'Hefnir.' Her voice was cold steel.

He looked up and tears glistened in the moonlight. Bera felt no pity. He had too much for himself. But she would not make him pay the blood debt. Things must be different here. She had said they had to make good, right from the start, even if it was to sacrifice the last boat she would ever sail. Her father's death had taught her that revenge was flawed. But she would speak the truth.

'You go and you go now,' she said, for him only. 'Thorvald died protecting your son and you killed him while he was unarmed and his back turned. You are a coward. You lie. You married me despite believing your wife lives to suffer the abuse of raiders. So you should know that she cut her own throat for the dishonour you did nothing to stop. She won't be waiting in Iraland, if you ever really thought she might. But you are in exile, Hefnir, and must never come back.'

He stood, undecided. 'I want my son.'

'And let you take him to the Serpent? I will never let Heggi learn from such an uncle. He is my son. I don't have to love him but I choose to. That's a stronger love than yours.'

Bera took up her stance; prepared to die to keep Heggi. The settlers closed in, strong at her back.

Perhaps Hefnir didn't care enough. Or Thorvald was right and he lacked all courage. Either way, instead of fighting for his son, he started to haggle.

'But it's dark! I can't set off in the dark.'

'That gave you no trouble when you schemed to leave at once. This is your last warning, Hefnir, or I shall collect the blood debt. Go. And you had better hope there are no hidden rocks because there will be no one to help you.'

'There is.' A slight figure emerged from the shadows.

'Egill?'

'Can't stay here, Bera. This place sent me mad and will again. My heart is in Iraland and Hefnir promised long ago to take me back.' Egill had found her voice in more ways than one.

Bera was sad to see Egill as she might have been. 'Then if you do belong in Iraland I hope you find peace. Beware of Hefnir. He cares for no one but himself. Keep your sword, Hefnir. Try to use it honourably and look after poor Egill, if you find the courage.'

Hefnir cleaned his sword in the sand, sheathed it and then slid away to the boat.

Egill wet her finger, drew a cross on Bera's forehead and then touched her lips to say no more.

She ran to the waiting boat. Hefnir scooped her up and scrambled in as the crew pushed off into deeper water. He took the helm and the others manned the oars. *Raven* dipped to meet the incoming swell and Bera felt the boat-song deep in her bones. The song was loss. Her father's craft had kept them safe through so much danger. Bera blessed the boat as it headed out to the sea path. There never would be another boat for her. No dip and dart or rolling swell.

The wind was blowing off the land. Bera watched until her patched sail was raised and then she could stand to watch no more.

Sigrid was kneeling by the body. She stroked his hair away from the gash and tenderly kissed Thorvald's scarred face. This was what love looked like.

'Sigrid. I am in true sorrow for your loss,' Bera said. And she was. She raised her voice to pay the tribute she had never given him in life. 'Thorvald was brave and strong to the last. I shall be forever grateful to our friend and protector. We shall burn him with all honours.'

There had been a rough kind of justice on the beach that night.

Bera watched over Sigrid and Thorvald as she had done over mother and son in another life. Her skern settled at her back, approving and silent. All the long night she tried to understand the twists and turns of Fate and how she might use the emotions that could overwhelm her to make her even stronger.

The first promise of dawn appeared in the eastern sky. Bera went up to the high ridge to watch the landscape slowly take shape in the gathering light. She imagined it in the future, full of their crops and livestock. She was born to lead, in her own way, and would. But that was all in the future and she must get the present right.

A dog's cold nose pushed into her hand and Bera smiled – for her boy would not be far behind and they would build this life together.

Acknowledgements

I'd like to thank all my supporters, some of whose names will not appear in the back of this book, and many of whom I met in Iceland: truly inspirational. Without Greg Mosse's teaching and Richard Wilde's support, it wouldn't have been written. I researched the Vikings for over four years but two other books stand out that readers may enjoy: *The Brendan Voyage* by Tim Severin, who recreates the sixth-century Voyage of St Brendan from Ireland to America and *Ocean Crossing Wayfarer: To Iceland and Norway in a 16ft Open Dinghy* by Frank & Margaret Dye. The title says it all.

Supporters

Unbound is a new kind of publishing house. Our books are funded directly by readers. This was a very popular idea during the late eighteenth and nineteenth centuries. Now we have revived it for the internet age. It allows authors to write the books they really want to write and readers to support the writing they would most like to see published.

The names listed below are of readers who have pledged their support and made this book happen. If you'd like to join them, visit: www.unbound.com.

Alison Ashdown
Isabel Ashdown
James Axtell
James Aylett
Juliana Babing
Jason Ballinger
Michael Banna
Jane Barker
Lily Barkes
Mike Barnett
Alix Beale
Caroline & Mike Beardall
Liesbeth Bennett
Fiona Beresford
Heather Birchenough
Tim Bouquet and Sarah Mansell
Dave Bowers
Rory Bremner
Dominic Carney
Anthony Carrick
Anthony Clark
Peter Clayton
Catherine Coe
Dom Conlon
Alan Copsey
Debbie and Phil Cornford
Lucy Crehan
Lesley Dampney
Margaret Dascalopoulos
Susan Davenport
Dorothea Davies
Gill Davies
Linda Davies
Michael Davies
Dana Dean
Julia Lee Dean
Charles Dedman
Annette DeVoil
Miranda Dickinson
John Doff
Kevin Doyle
Tom Edwards
Abla El-Sharnouby
Shannon Elliott
Nicola English
Jennifer Eremeeva
Kathryn Evans
Eva Falconer
Jack Fargerberg
David Fennell
Debbie Ford
Susan Fosbrook
Karen Galley
Antonia Galloway
Mark Gamble
Linda and Andrew Gebhart
Julie Gilmour
Carol Godsmark
Catherine Goldring
Sybil Grindrod
Tessa Beukelaar-van Gulik
Patti M Hall
Robert Hamlin
Jackie Hancock
Julie Hart
Andy Hawkins
Pamela Hawkins
Emma Hawksworth
Grace Hawksworth
Hope Hawksworth
Peter Hawksworth
Thea Hawksworth
Elizabeth Haynes
Ellie Hayward
Tim Hayward
Anita Heward
Ann Heward
Suzanne Hillen
John Hillier
L Hockley
Pamela Howard
Paul Howard
Philippa and Tony Hughes
Lizzie Hutchinson
Johari Ismail

Gigi Jefferson
Hannah Jenkins
Kirsty Jennings
Mike and Rosie Jennings
Samantha Jennings
Paul Jeorrett
Julie Iler Jones
Tiffin Jones
David Joyce
Eleanor Joyce
Liz Kent
Dan Kieran
Jonathan Kim
Simon King
Andy Knott
Harish Kohli
Lizzie Ladbrooke
Jon Lawson
Gerald Lenanton
Jean Levy
Kim Locke
K. M. Lockwoood
John & Christine Lomax
Peter Lovesey
Barbara MacWhirter
Ferran Mari
Sarah Martin
Gabrielle Maxwell
Joy May
Tim May
Tom May
Wendy May
Elizabeth McCann
Susan Henderson Miles
Karin Misak
Deborah Mitchelson
John Mitchinson
Iain Morrison
Leah Mottin
Tim Mudie
Rachel Munday
Maria Mutch
Carlo Navato
John New
Brian Newman-Holland
Ken Norman
Rodney O'Connor
Lucy Oliver
Michael Oliver
Stephen Pearce
Justin Pollard
Jenny Prager
Paul Pridmore
Alice Pullan
Saoirse Purkess
Ronald and Polly Rae
Hotel Rangá
Sara Read
Julia Rees
Eliza Reid
Paul Rigg
Katy Rishoff
Janet Ritchie
Orphee Ritchie
Paul & Cynthia Rivett
Peter Rossiter
Richard Sanderson
John Saulet
Joseph Saxon
Jenny Schwarz
Alethea Scott
Linda Sgoluppi
Stephen Sherlock
Andy Shewan
Paul Shove
Victoria Kate Simkin
Nicky Singer
Craig Smith
Danielle Smith
Eileen Smith
Harry & Mary Smith
Rob Smith
Susan Smith
Jane Sobanski
Heather Sorrell
Katherine Sprackling
Jason Stevens
Michael Strawson
Nicola Streeten
John Surace
Shelley Swan
David Swayne
Becky Swift
Stella-Maria Thomas
Lesley Thomson
Nick Tigg
Anita Tovell
Robin Townsend
Dina Turner
Eleanor Updale
Mark Vent
Robin Verschoren
Ben Wakefield
David Wakefield
John Wakefield
Katherine Wakefield
Niamh Wakefield
Steve Walford
Sue Wallman
Tanya Walters
Philip Ware
Shan Warnock-Smith
Helen Watson
Molly Watson
James Watts
Jane Weeks and Stephen Riley
Sophia Wickham
Andrew Wilde
Peter Wilde
Richard Wilde
Suzanne Wilkins
Griffin Scott Willett
Derek Wilson
Jacquie & John Wilson
Angela Wingfield
Michael Wooley
Michael Woolley
Glen Wright